THREADS OF THE MAIDEN'S MOON

The Witching Wood: Book 1

Myla Rose

Threads of the Maiden's Moon

Independently Published

ISBN: 979-8-9925516-0-0

Cover Design by GetCovers (www.getcovers.com)

For more information, visit www.MylaRoseWrites.com

For those who gather under the moonlight, whisper spells of resistance, love ferociously, and have dreams too wild to contain.
May you rise, unbreakable and unstoppable, no matter the odds.

TAINS
VESPERIAN MOUNTAINS
COMET'S
REST
CRAG
NS
MIDMIRE
CELESTARA
Rolling River
NRIDGE
STONEMERE
RUN
LLA
EST
COHAM
SOLEIRE
SPRINGS
LEISPORT
The Calanthan Sea

TRIGGER WARNINGS

Alcohol Consumption – sometimes in celebration, sometimes to forget

Anxiety – navigating stress, danger, and the occasional existential crisis

Villains Who Deserve It – Includes attempted sexual assault, sexual harassment and the swift, brutal justice that follows

Blood, Guts, & Gore – When swords clash and magic swirls, things get messy

Abortion – briefly mentioned as an area of alchemical and herbal expertise

Shredded Heartstrings – including disownment of a child, death, and grief that cuts deep

Family Drama – betrayal, lies, and the realization that found family might just be better

Blatant Feminism – strong female characters, zero tolerance for misogyny, and the patriarchy can get smashed

Colorful Language – for fucks sake, obviously

Fire & Burning – as in pyres, magic, campfires, and sexual tension

Open Door Sex Scenes – in toe curling detail

War Vibes – battles, bloodshed, and the fate of a kingdom at stake

PRONUNCIATION GUIDE

PEOPLE & NAMES

Nolei Venbella (NOH-lee Ven-BELL-ah)
Váliarë (VAH-lee-ah-ray)
Leo (LEE-oh) Eryn (EH-rin)
Cardin (CAR-din)
Sappha (SAF-uh)

Fenralei Alderynn (Fen-RAH-lee ALL-der-in)
Kathel (KATH-ell)
Aerony (AIR-uh-nee)
Onvyl (ON-vill)

Blesse (BLESS-eh)

Torin (TOR-in)
Leoric (LEE-oh-rick)
Graelis (GRAY-liss)
Camila (Cuh-MILL-uh)
Kellan (KELL-in)

Queen Ryellia Damay (Rye-ELL-ee-ah DUH-may)
King Nateo Alderynn (Nuh-TAY-oh ALL-der-in)

LOCATIONS

Lunaris (Loo-NAR-iss)
Eyloria (Ee-LORE-ee-ah)
Oriella Forest (Or-ee-EL-uh)
Lothariel (Low-THAR-ee-el)
Celestara (Sah-LESS-tar-uh)

THE DIVINE FEMININE

Calantha (Kuh-LAN-thuh)
Elowen (EL-oh-en)
Vespera (VES-pair-uh)

THE LESSER GODS

Thalor (THAY-lor)
Aurel (OR-ill)
Lysander (LYE-san-der)
Elendor (ELL-en-dor)
Seraphon (SAIR-uh-fon)

LOCATIONS

Lunaris (Loo-NAR-iss)
Eyloria (Ee-LORE-ee-ah)
Oriella Forest (Or-ee-EL-uh)
Lothariel (Low-THAR-ee-el)
Celestara (Sah-LESS-tar-uh)

LUNARIAN MOON CYCLE

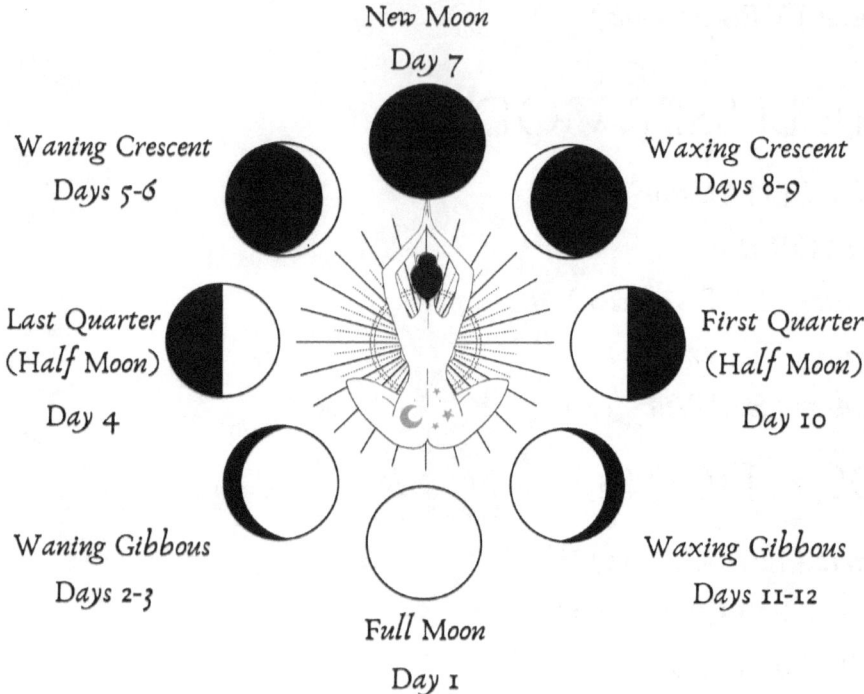

New Moon
Day 7

Waning Crescent
Days 5-6

Waxing Crescent
Days 8-9

Last Quarter
(Half Moon)
Day 4

First Quarter
(Half Moon)
Day 10

Waning Gibbous
Days 2-3

Waxing Gibbous
Days 11-12

Full Moon
Day 1

Meet The Divine Feminine

THE MAIDEN
Calantha

Symbolizes youth, pleasure, new beginnings, wildness, freedom, & innocence

THE MOTHER
Elowen

Symbolizes love, fertility, maturity, creativity, sexuality, abundance, and growth

THE CRONE
Vespera

Symbolizes time, wisdom, culmination, creativity, knowledge, independence, and courage

CHAPTER

ONE

A strange hum flickered through my veins as I held my breath. Foraging for herbs was frowned upon. Using them to brew healing elixirs? *Punishable by death.*

A twig crunched under the weight of my boot as I crouched behind a massive oak tree. Peeking around it, I caught sight of the crimson-clad soldiers who all swung their heads in my direction, scanning the trees. Even the surrounding plants seemed to hold their breath in solidarity. I stayed there long after the sound of hooves trotting through the mud had passed. Frozen, I watched the sun speckle over the leaves and moss until the sounds of birds and squirrels returned. Only then could I breathe normally again.

One would think after 13 years of watching The Dark Army patrol Eyloria, I would get used to their unsettling presence. Unfortunately, they were just as creepy now as they ever were.

I picked up my wicker basket, filled with fragrant chamomile and vibrant yellow calendula, and began the path back home. Burdock covered my woolen socks by the time I saw the rounded front door. I swept my long braids back over my shoulders and tucked a few sweat-dampened curls behind my pointed ears. My long dress was too heavy to be worn on such a hot day, but I didn't have many options to choose from. It was this or the faded gray pants that were hanging on the line after waiting far too long between washes.

Our cottage was quaint and cozy, nestled into the top of a large tree which had weeping purple flowers that flooded the branches. The thatched roof and chimney blended in almost seamlessly. The winding roots served as footholds that led up to the wooden door, which was nestled into the trunk of the massive tree.

Tiny golden lights flickered all around the cottage, from the million glow-wing bugs that danced in the moonlight. A balmy yellow light seeped from the windows, meaning that Gran was still awake and waiting for me. A smile washed over my face as I hurried up the worn path, eager to hear about her day.

As I creaked the heavy door open, the smell of herb-rich stew flooded my nostrils. I exhaled a breathy moan as my stomach did a little flip. Goddesses, that smelled incredible.

"You're home late," Gran said from near the hearth where she was stirring the stew. "Did you run into any trouble?"

"No," I replied quickly, stepping into the living room and unbuttoning my cloak. "Just came across some of The Dark Army in the woods. I lost track of time waiting for them to pass." I grabbed some twine and wound it around the bundles of herbs, hanging them upside down along a wooden shelf by the wall to dry.

"Their presence is becoming a more and more frequent occurrence. One that is not welcomed, at that," huffed Gran.

"Gran, please tell me you are more careful with your words when you are outside these walls than you are with me. Speaking such a thing is dangerous, especially if it falls upon the wrong ears." The last thing we needed was to draw the attention of The Dark Army, or worse, The Dark Enchantress who presided over them.

Queen Ryellia Damay, better known as The Dark Queen or The Dark Enchantress, was nothing if not filled with hate and thirsty for blood. She was said to sip the blood of her subjects from a golden chalice just for the fun of it. A fucking sadist, if you asked me. Not that I would ever dare speak such a thing out loud. I valued my life, after all.

A sly smile spread across her lips. "Always trying to keep the peace. That's my Nolei. Did you collect the herbs we discussed?"

I toed off my boots and lined them against the wall nearest the fire, then peeled off my socks and left them in balls near my boots. I'd have to de-burdock them later.

"Yes, I gathered everything we'll need to make the salve tomorrow. Hopefully, Mrs. Rivers will be feeling like herself again." I answered.

Gran ladled some stew into an earthen bowl and set it at the small wooden table for me. I practically floated toward the smell of it. I gulped down a spoonful and scalded my tongue. I forced myself to slow and allow it time to cool.

"I am surprised you are awake, Gran. With how early you rise, one would think you'd be sooner off to bed."

An old wooden rocking chair creaked as Gran sat back into it, pulling the burdock-ridden socks onto her lap and meticulously plucking them clean for me.

"I had to see you home safe, my dear. You know that."

3

"What the fuck was that for?" I shouted as I realized it was her who shoved me. I shoved her back.

A wild smile spread across her face. "For ignoring me, that's what."

Deep in my thoughts, I hadn't even realized she was talking to me. "And what was so important that you felt the need to give me an early morning bath in the fountain?"

"I was trying to tell you about my evening with Edmund."

"The farmer's son?" I asked quizzically.

"Yes, the farmer's son! Do you know another Edmund?" She replied, rolling her eyes.

"That would be a no," I mused, straightening out my tunic as the wiry, dull male came to mind. "And what is so pressing about this evening with Edmund?"

"He was boring, and he smelled like hay and horse pies." She said, crinkling her nose.

"Blechh," I faked a gag. "That is revolting."

"Good thing I figured out a way to ditch him before I began to smell the same." She sat straighter, wiggled her shoulders, and lifted her chin.

"And that was...?" I queried.

"I told him that I had my monthlies. Blurted it out, to be exact. In the middle of a sentence. While he was talking to me about the upcoming harvest." She boasted.

A smirk played on my lips as my eyes grew wide. "And how did he take that totally relevant news?"

"He just about choked on the piece of hay he was chewing like a cow chews its cud." Eryn looked up toward the sky, letting the sun wash over her face. "And then I blurted out 'Bye!' and took off. It was brilliant."

"Wow. Just Wow, Eryn. You really outdid yourself." I nodded as my smile grew.

Eryn could ditch a hundred fae males who she deemed 'boring' and still have three hundred more pining after her. She had something about her that was irresistible to the opposite sex. I, on the other hand, had mostly steered clear of males for the past several months. Except for an occasional romp in the hay, of course. It was important that *all* of a woman's needs were met, even the more...primal ones.

As for romantic dealings, I had more than enough of being lied to by arrogant males who couldn't keep their dicks out of the nearest willing participant's skirts. Calder had been the first and last male I had ever let trick me into thinking he actually cared about me. We had a lovely summer together, meeting in the evenings to watch the moon rise and exploring the lines of each other's bodies by the starlight. Until I found out months later that he was having the same romantic experiences with several other women in town. *Fuck him.*

"Anywho... I better be getting to the shop." Eryn's voice cut off my thoughts. "Apparently, one of the Crofton girls is getting married within a week and is in need of a dress. Unfortunately, I am the one who has to procure such a garment." Eryn hopped off the fountain and began making a show of walking painfully slow down across the courtyard to the shop with her shoulders drooping. I let out a loud laugh, forgetting we were in public.

I began sliding the leather strap of my bag back up my shoulder, realizing it had slipped after my near swim in the fountain when shouting broke out across the courtyard.

My head twisted sharply to my left in the direction of the screams as I shot to my feet. A member of The Dark Guard had a young boy by the wrist. He looked to be about eight years old and was clutching a dull gray, wide-eyed fish.

"Where do you think you're going with that?" The guard growled, showing his yellow teeth.

"I'm sorry!" The boy yelped.

"Sorry ain't goin' to help you now, boy." He tugged the boy closer, almost knocking him to his knees. The soldier was dressed in all red, a deep crimson on thick fabric that stood out starkly against everyone else's earth-toned, thread-bare clothing. He was tall but thin, with a scraggly, dark beard.

"I was just tryin' to bring home some food for my family. I have two younger brothers who need to eat!" he pleaded with wide eyes.

"Well, now you're going to have two hungry brothers and one less hand." He threatened with an eerie smile full of hate as he lifted a knife to the boy's wrist.

A fluttering feeling in my chest started up. A feeling urging me to stop standing there and do something.

But what could I do? I definitely couldn't fight the man. The power in my chest ramped up, taking my heart rate with it. Forcing me to act. I bent down and grabbed the first thing I saw, a rock the size of a walnut. I hurled it at the guard's head as hard as I could.

It missed.

Great job, Nolei.

Luckily, the guard turned his head in the opposite direction, searching for the source of the sound after it crashed into the side of a wooden cart. The boy looked at me, though.

Goddesses, I wished Eryn was here. She would know what to do.

My chest felt hot, and it was starting to feel like the fish in the boy's hand was alive and well, but located inside my rib cage. A scorching sensation started in my chest and rippled down my arms, causing my hands to shake.

The wind in the courtyard started picking up, but it didn't seem like anyone noticed but me.

I bent down to grab another piece of rock that had crumbled from the stone of the fountain. My eyes focused on the rubble surrounding my boots; the rocks seemed like they were bouncing up and down off of the earth. Supposing that my adrenaline was causing me to see things, I searched for another rock and found one about the size of an apple. When I reached my hand toward it, it appeared to have shot from the ground into my palm. As if I had summoned it to myself. I'm going to have to process that later.

I whispered a silent prayer to The Mother Goddess, Elowen, hoping she would see fit to protect this young boy. Then I chucked the rock at the guard's head with as much force as I could muster.

This time it connected, causing a cracking sound that I could practically feel crawling down my spine. The guard released the boy's wrist as he doubled over, bellowing and clutching his now bloodied head. The boy froze briefly, stunned.

"Run!" I yelled to the boy. Yelled to myself.

He looked up at me and then sprinted down an alley behind where the first rock had landed. I turned on my heel and started running, too.

Looking over my shoulder, I saw the wounded guard glancing up at me and two other guards surrounding him, bending down to see if he was okay. "Get her!" he yelled at them. They stared dumbly at him for a moment and then began after me.

Fuck. I said to myself, as I wished I had any sort of athletic ability or stamina to speak of. I picked up my pace, sprinting north toward the edge of town. I did my best to avoid running into the few people lining the dusty streets. Buildings blurred in my peripheral view. I could hear my heart hammering in my ears. My breath began to burn in my throat.

As I neared the edge of the city, the tree line became visible. My eyes flicked from left to right, trying to decide which way to go. Where was I leading them? To my house, apparently. I needed a better plan than that one.

I took a sharp left turn, dodging into a side street and ducking under the clotheslines that stretched between the buildings. Panting, I kept running. The sound of heavy boot steps pounded behind me, sounding like they were slowing in search of which direction I had gone.

"This way!" I heard a guard shout as he thundered down the side street in my direction, tearing the linens down as he went.

"Come on, Nolei." I urged myself out loud, the muscles in my legs starting to heat and cramp. My breaths were quick and too shallow, doing little to fuel me. Just as I was nearing another crossroads in the streets, an arm reached out from an open doorway, wrapped around my waist, and pulled me inside.

CHAPTER

TWO

My body slammed against something firm. The hand around my waist tightened, and another sealed over my mouth, silencing my shriek of surprise. It was a male's body, a male who was much taller than me.

My adrenaline was fire in my veins. Full-body fear ruled me and I acted on pure, unfettered instinct. I slammed my head back, hoping to connect with his face. All I ended up doing was connecting with his hard, muscled chest, knocking a grunt out of him. He now held me even tighter to himself and whispered into my ear, "I'm not going to hurt you. You're safe with me." His breath danced along my ear and down my neck, causing shivers to roll down my spine. He smelled like pine trees and campfire.

I wriggled and thrashed the best I could, hardly moving him at all. I tried screaming, but he kept his hand firmly pressed against my mouth. My breaths were coming too quickly now.

Everything was happening too quickly. First the guard, then running for my life, and now this. "Breathe, Nolei. Breathe through your nose. You are safe with me. I won't hurt you, but you need to stay quiet." He purred into my ear.

I tried to will myself to slow my breathing, but couldn't. Either this hulking fae male was going to kill me, and I'd be too dead to care, or he was telling the truth. I was kind of running out of options here.

"Breathe with me," he commanded. "In." His chest rose slightly against my back as he took a long, slow inhale. "Hold." He said calmly. "Out." I felt his warm breath wind down my neck again as he let out a slow, audible exhale. "Again," He said, repeating the sequence over and over until my breath matched his and my body relaxed.

He lessened the pressure of the hand covering my mouth. "I'm going to let you go. You need to stay here and stay quiet. If you run back out there or scream, they'll find you and they'll kill you. Do you understand me?"

I nodded shakily and hoped I could remain standing once he let go. His hands slipped away from me and he took a step back, the warm press of him behind me disappearing. I whirled to face him.

He had a black cloak on, the large hood pulled up over his head. Given that he was at least a head taller than me, I could look easily at his face under the hood. The first thing I noticed were his mesmerizing beautiful brown eyes, set below dark brows and long lashes. They were captivating.

My gaze then took in his other features. As far as I could tell, he had dark brown hair, cropped close along the side of his head, and slightly longer on top. He had just a hint of facial hair, enough to draw attention to his well-defined jaw. His cloak cascaded over his large shoulders and hid what looked to be several swords and weapons that were tied closely to his body with leather straps that crossed over his chest and hips.

Did I hit my own head with a rock? How was it possible for a male to be this beautiful? This beautiful and looking directly at me? I stared at him dumbly, my feet heavy where I stood.

I felt this odd pulling sensation in my chest now, almost like something was tugging me closer to him, but I was not moving. His chestnut eyes were searching mine. I willed my mind to work and my tongue to move. But I was only met with silence.

He pressed a long finger to his lips, reminding me to stay quiet, as he silently side-stepped around me and peered into the street, looking both ways carefully before ducking back inside. "It's clear now," he declared, turning toward me.

Speak, Nolei. Remember words? Remember how to use them? I chided myself. I took a sharp inhale and then blurted out, "How do you know my name?"

"What?" He asked, seemingly not understanding my jumbled outburst.

"You said my name. How do you know my name?" I asked, speaking more clearly now and raising my chin defiantly.

"I heard you say it when you were running. You said 'Come on, Nolei' and I assumed you were talking to yourself since you were alone." He replied, one side of his lips kicking up. "Unless there is someone else here with us I am unaware of...?" he turned from side to side with open palms, gesturing to the space around us.

My eyes narrowed on him. "Very funny," I replied, crossing my arms.

"I don't know what you did to piss them off, but you need to get out of here before they come back." He instructed, changing the subject. "Come with me." He said softly, reaching his hand out toward me for me to grab onto.

My eyes locked with his, searching them. *You are safe with me.* His words repeated in my head. I was already this deep into shit. I might as well

15

commit. I tentatively reached out and grabbed his hand, feeling a spark of energy shoot up my arm with the touch. I tried to ignore the brief surge between us.

He silently closed the distance between us and then led me up a narrow staircase that was apparently right behind me. I had been so preoccupied with looking at him, I hadn't even thought to observe my surroundings. My survival instincts were seriously lacking. My heart rate sped up and my stomach tightened at the realization. I repeated his words to myself again. *You are safe with me.* I took another steadying breath.

He led me down an uneven hall with several sets of closed doors along both sides and then down another set of stairs that led out the opposite side of the building. He again checked to make sure it was clear outside before allowing me any further.

Releasing the grasp on my hand, he unfastened his cloak. "Take this," he said, draping it over my shoulders and tugging the hood up. It was far too big on me and smelled... like fresh pine and wood smoke. His muscled arms and shoulders strained against the fabric of his dark gray tunic, accented by the straps of leather holding his small armament to his chest and back. "Go left out of this door, cross the main street there, and then take another left on the first side street. Follow that path straight north. It will take you to the edge of the city," he advised, tugging the hood up over my head.

Looking up at him, my heart still beating wildly, I stuttered, "Th... thank you."

He flashed me a full smile that reached those deep brown eyes as he looked down at me. "No need to thank me, Nolei. Just get home safely." With that, he slid past me and back up the stairs behind me, disappearing.

I stood there in the dim entryway, blinking slowly. What had just happened? Before I could hone in on what exactly I was feeling, I forced my feet to move and resurfaced back in the street.

I followed his directions exactly to navigate out of Eyloria and into the north woods. I sprinted from the edge of the city into the wooded area and avoided the footpath I typically took. I ran as quickly as I could once I hit the woods and didn't stop. I had to get back home and tell Gran everything. As my breath started to burn my lungs and my legs saddled me with a near-constant ache, I slowed to a brisk walk.

My thoughts whirred as I tried to comprehend everything that had just happened. First, my mind flashed to the young boy who tried to get away with one single fish to feed his family. He was far too young to be worried about such things, especially the burden of feeding the mouths of his siblings. That the people of Eyloria were so strapped for coin that children had to resort to stealing just to fill their empty bellies made my blood boil. Meanwhile, the soldiers' bellies are full of ale and pockets are brimming with gold for The Dark Enchantress.

Secondly, I threw a fucking rock at a soldier. And *hit him*. In the skull. Where did that even come from? It is an absolute miracle that I managed to aim well enough to make contact but also... where did I get the bravery for that kind of act of heroism? Not to mention the stupidity. I attacked a soldier. I might as well have attacked Queen Damay herself. I was so dead.

Next, I tried to wrap my mind around how I summoned that rock toward my hand. Was I seeing things or did that actually just happen? Was it tied to that bizarre hum I've been feeling in my chest and arms? I needed to ask Gran if she had ever heard of such a thing. If anyone would know, it would be her.

Lastly, who was that male who literally rescued me from a handful of angry soldiers? How did he just appear out of nowhere at the perfect time? Why did he save me? Why did he care enough to do so? Oh Goddesses, I didn't even think to ask him his name. What kind of person doesn't even ask the name of her rescuer?

My mind racing, I slowed to a stop. I sank to the ground against the nearest tree and buried my face in my hands. I tried to slow my breathing. Slow my mind. His words came back to me. *Breathe. Inhale. Hold. Exhale.* I willed my body to follow the instructions.

I felt the wind flow rhythmically against the edges of my face, gently swishing my hair back and forth as if it were trying to soothe me with its lullaby. I closed my eyes and tuned into the surrounding sounds. I heard two birds chirping to each other a few trees away. Some squirrels chattered to my left. I heard the creek trickling softly in the distance. Whenever my mind started going faster than I could handle and pulled my heart along with it, connecting to my senses and nature always calmed me.

I had to talk to Eryn. She would know what to say. What to do. I got up, dusted off my pants, and started back toward the city.

I would see Gran after. She was probably back from morning rounds by now and working on restocking our store of elixirs after my foraging yesterday.

CHAPTER

THREE

With my new-to-me cloak pulled up to hide my features, I snuck back into the city and took side streets until I found Eryn's mother's shop. To avoid being spotted by anyone, I approached the rear of the narrow building until I could see the window to the room where I knew Eryn was likely working on a garment. I bent down, grabbed a pebble, and threw it at the window. No answer. I grabbed another and threw it a little harder this time. Goddesses, what was with me and throwing rocks today?

Eryn looked down at me from the window. I looked around quickly before briefly pulling down my hood to reveal my face and giving her a wide-eyed look that said 'Get your ass down here right now, it's an emergency.' She turned away from the window and was in the back alley with me within seconds.

"Nolei? What's going on?"

"I need you to get out of work right now. I don't care what you tell your mom, but I need to talk to you... somewhere else." I whispered, glancing back and forth and scanning the alley.

"Are you okay? What happened?" She questioned, grabbing my arm.

"Yes, I'm fine. Can you meet me at The Bay of The Tides? Something happened." Realizing I was scaring her, I met her gaze and held it. "I'm fine. Please, just meet me."

"Okay. Give me 15 minutes." She rushed forward and hugged me close, causing me to stiffen momentarily before relaxing into her embrace. She then scurried back inside and shut the door behind her.

I found myself at the western bay where the waters of The Sleeping Tides met the sandy beaches on the Western border of Eyloria. The rhythmic sound of the waves slowly crashing and then receding acted like a balm to my nerves. The smooth stones and fragments of shells crunched below my boots as I paced.

"Okay. Start talking." A strong, feminine voice demanded as I looked up to see Eryn strolling down a dune toward the beach. She climbed up and sat on the large boulder we had spent many hours upon, either lying under the sun or gazing up at the moon. She opened up a mauve scrap of linen and revealed two large muffins, both still steamy and warm.

"I stopped for reinforcements." She smirked, placing a muffin in my hand as I sat down next to her. The coolness of the stone pressed through the fabric of my pants.

"Where did you get these from? From Collyn?" I asked, referencing the baker's son who we had both had our own little rendezvous with a few summers ago, both ultimately deciding that he was better friend material than anything more. He was fun, though, and had a way of making us laugh that had us both coming back for more, more times than was probably smart. That ended two summers ago, though.

"Of course. You know his sweets heal the soul," she cooed, taking a bite of her muffin. "Like I said, start talking."

An exasperated exhale left me, followed by a frenzied stream of word vomit. "I attacked a soldier from The Dark Army and then ran for my life. This massive male wearing all black saved me and gave me his cloak to escape in. I also think I might have some type of weird magical powers developing. Now The Dark Army is looking for me and I need you to tell me what to do." Realizing I hadn't stopped to breathe during that little summary, I took a brisk inhale.

Wide-eyed, Eryn looked at me with a perfectly arched brow. "Excuse me. What?"

I flopped onto my back on the rock, staring up at the sun, which was now directly overhead. "Right after you left the courtyard, I saw a soldier threatening a little boy who had stolen something. He said he was going to cut the boy's hand off. I felt this feeling in my whole body that was urging me to do something. I kind of...summoned a rock into my hand and threw it at the soldier's head."

"You threw a rock at a guard's head?! And actually hit him?" She exclaimed, obviously shocked.

"Yes, I actually hit him. With a rock. He started bleeding and everything."

"That is surprising on so many levels, Nolei."

"I'm aware." I deadpanned, continuing. "Then I tried to run away, and they were chasing me. I didn't know where to go. I just kept running as quickly as I could and then suddenly some male grabbed me and pulled me into the entryway of one of the buildings off of a side street."

"A male grabbed you? That is so creepy!" She replied.

"Surprisingly, it wasn't. I was terrified at first, obviously, but he was more of a tall, dark, and exquisitely handsome male than a creepy one." I reflected, continuing to stare up at the sky. "He was so muscular, had all these swords strapped to him, and smelled so good."

She lay on her back beside me, turning onto her left and propping her head up on her palm with her elbow on the rock. "Go on... you have my undivided attention."

Eryn loved to hear about any interaction I had with the male species. She always found it riveting, no matter how benign.

I shoved her playfully. "This is serious, Eryn! He made sure the soldiers were gone, gave me his cloak so I could stay hidden, and told me how to escape out of the city."

"And what was this heroic, thoughtful male's name?" She prodded.

Heat rushed to my cheeks as I remembered how I didn't even ask him. Wondering what was wrong with me, I cringed. "I didn't ask him."

"A total stranger rescued you... a deliciously handsome one at that... and you didn't have the decency to ask him his name? Magnolia Venbella!" She scolded, sitting back upright and leaning over the top of me.

My cringe deepened I pressed my hands over my face. "I know, I know." I let out a sigh.

"Wait. Did you say you summoned a rock to your hand? As in ... pulled it toward yourself without touching it?" Her confused stare replaced the view of the vibrant blue sky.

"Yeah. I've been feeling.... Weird lately." What I'd been feeling was hard to put into words. It was almost like the wind and rocks responded to me. I was seriously going to have to ask Gran if she had ever heard of such a thing.

Her voice startled me from my thoughts. "You're going to have to expound on that."

"It's like ..." the words fizzled out on my tongue. I could hardly comprehend it, let alone put words to it. "...like when I'm feeling angry, or scared, or anxious ... sometimes the things around me react to those feelings."

"What things react?" She asked, puzzled.

"So far I've noticed the wind calm or stir in response to me, and earlier today, that rock. But I've never noticed it with anything else before." I pushed myself up to sit, letting my gaze rest on the turquoise water along the horizon. "I've always felt comforted by being in nature, but this is something different entirely."

"We have to ask your Gran about this. If anyone would know about it, it would be her." Eryn declared. Love for her flooded through me. It was as if she could read my mind sometimes.

"I'm going to talk to her about it as soon as I get home." I bit down on my lower lip and exhaled slowly through my nose, trying to release the tension in my shoulders.

"I'm scared, Eryn. How am I supposed to go back into the city again without being identified and punished? If they were going to cut that boy's hand off for stealing one dead fish, what would they do to me for hurting a member of The Dark Army?" I shuddered and closed my eyes, trying to focus on my breath and keep my heart rate from racing as quickly as my thoughts.

Eryn's hand ran back and forth along my upper back, helping to calm me. "We're going to figure this out, Nolei. I'm sure this will blow over. They probably didn't even see who you were." She reassured.

"Thanks, Eryn," I whispered, knowing damn well that they absolutely saw me. I sighed again, pulling my hands down my face.

"I have to run back to the shop. I told my mother I had to run a quick errand to get more leather cording and she'll be wondering where I am. We'll figure this out together, Nolei. We always do." She gave me a quick hug and then slid off the boulder, heading back up the dune toward the city.

Standing, I pulled the hood of the cloak back up over my head. As I inhaled deeply, the scent of him flooded my senses. It was oddly comforting and... familiar. His words came back to me. *You're always safe with me.*

CHAPTER

FOUR

I nstead of going back through Eyloria, I skirted around the west side of the city along the beach and then headed north toward the cottage. I cut through the dense trees until I hit the worn path that led home.

Hoof prints marked the path, having stirred the dust. Remembering Gran had taken the Camila this morning and hoping that was all they were from, I continued.

Even though Eryn didn't have any true advice on how to navigate the soldiers or what to think of the whole rock-summoning thing, I felt lighter after speaking to her. It was as if these burdens were no longer just mine to shoulder alone.

I was eager to hear Gran's thoughts on what I'd been experiencing. The depth of her knowledge of the arcane was unparalleled, a mastery of the otherworldly and mystical forces that shaped the world. Even as a young girl, I remember her pulling one of the large tomes she kept on the shelves, dusting it off, and opening it onto our wooden dining table. She thumbed the pages in search of the specific instructions she sought. The pages were ancient-looking, and the letters were written in inky calligraphy. Drawings were dispersed throughout the book, adding to the intrigue. Depictions of rare ingredients, creatures only heard of in lore, and exotic herbs filled the pages.

She taught me all that I knew of such things. Although my official training was in healing and using my knowledge of botany to assist with healing, my schooling went much deeper than that.

Gran was sure to include me when others would come in search of potions to aid in other matters. Like young women who were late for their monthlies but not yet ready to mother a child. Or when an infliction of the heart was too painful to bear any longer.

There was much more that could be altered with the use of the forbidden magic than could be done with basic mending and herbs. But it was just that: forbidden. If word got out that we were meddling in such mystical acts, we would be taken by The Dark Army and killed, as per The Dark Enchantress' orders. She did not tolerate the use of magic, nor did she tolerate those who practiced it.

My breath caught in my throat as the cottage came into view. Several black horses stood outside my home, wearing crimson caparisons marked with the insignia of The Dark Queen's royal crest. A black crown encircled with thorns and coated in jewels.

Adrenaline coursed through my veins like fire as my eyes landed on the front door. It was ajar.

I shot behind the nearest tree, peeking out from behind it. They were looking for me. My mind raced as I tried to think through how they would have known to look here. Then my stomach sank.

Gran. Goddesses, I hope she wasn't home. I knew she was, though. She should be, at least. I prayed to the Goddess Vespera, The Crone, who symbolized wisdom, culmination, and courage. I held my breath as I slowly circled the cottage, trying to see far enough behind it to see if Camila was in the meadow behind the cottage.

No. A guttural pain shot through me as I laid eyes on the beautiful white mare. That meant Gran was inside. Inside with those ruthless, hateful soldiers.

Without warning, that feeling inside my chest flared to life, urging me to act again. It was as if it was this... this energy inside of me demanded that I do *something*. But what?

What could I do against — I counted the horses — against five armed soldiers. Armed soldiers who were filled with contempt and served The Dark Enchantress. Who smiled in response to unnecessary death.

Without thinking about it further, my feet began moving forward, fueled by that strange feeling inside of me.

I climbed up to the nearest window and peeked in, not revealing my face beneath the hood of my new cloak. My eyebrows knitted together as I tried to process what I was seeing.

A tall, black-haired soldier with deeply colored skin was standing in the kitchen area, looking through one of the ancient tomes. He was reading the page headings aloud to his comrades with a sinister smile and laughing as if they were some kind of joke. *Fuck.*

A second with broad shoulders and sandy blonde hair was walking along the shelving that lined the walls, knocking all the wares onto the floor. Various glass jars filled with foraged ingredients, dried herbs, and powders all toppled onto the floor, crashing onto the wooden boards. His wicked smile and proud strut made my stomach turn.

A third soldier was standing in front of the hearth, a stack of books cradled in his arm as he casually tossed one at a time into the flames.

No, I whispered to myself again. Those books were priceless. One of a kind. Handed down through women from generation to generation. They were irreplaceable.

I covered my mouth with my hand, willing myself to stay silent as I searched the room for my Gran.

There, in a wooden chair at the far side of the cottage. Her frail figure was tense as she sat with her wrists bound behind her. A scrap of cloth was bound around her face, covering her mouth. Terror filled her eyes. A large, red-bearded male stood behind her, holding a fistful of her wispy gray hair. He forced her head up and made her watch as the other males destroyed all that we treasured.

The soldier from the courtyard was at the center of the chaos. "Ay, Dokine," the black-haired male who was reading shouted to the male who seemed to be the highest ranking. The cut on the side of his head had stopped bleeding, but dried blood matted his hair. He stood with his chin up, hands on his hips, and a wide smile fixed on his face. As if this was some great accomplishment. As though this was the best entertainment he could wish for himself.

Bile stung my throat as I took in the scene. I had to get to Gran.

My pulse was ramping up again. Maybe I could lure them out with a distraction? No, that wouldn't work. They probably wouldn't even hear any sort of distraction I could muster from out here with all that was going on inside the cottage, anyway. I could run back into town and find Eryn and her brothers. Maybe even Collyn. They might know how to help.

I shook my head. I didn't have that kind of time to spare and I sure as The Cinder Wastes didn't have any to drag either of them into this. I turned away from the window, facing out into the woods. Breathing slowly, I tried to slow my thoughts and come up with some type of plan.

I could try to fight them? I considered that option. Then, the voice of reason told me all the reasons that idea was the worst one yet. Like how I didn't know how to fight, did not have a weapon, and would not last three minutes attempting such a thing.

I let out a frustrated huff. Why did I have to be so fucking useless in the physical strength department?

What if I turned myself in? My life would likely be forfeited, but at least Gran would be saved. Or hopefully she would be, anyway.

I could offer to trade myself for her. I would gladly give up myself to save her. She was everything to me.

She raised me. My earliest memories were of her. Everything I've learned and who I've become, it was all thanks to her patient lessons, wisdom, and kindness. Her ferocity and belief in the innate strength that all women carry.

That is what I'd have to do.

I just prayed to The Maiden, The Mother, and The Crone that they would let her go. Hopefully, The Divine Feminine will bless me today.

I had little choice. I had to do something.

Standing outside the front door, I took a deep inhale, followed by a slow exhale. I raised my chin and let determination wash over me.

My hands drew the hood of my cloak down. The energy that flared to life within me lit anew as I slammed open the front door, causing it to smash against the wall. Five heads swiveled in my direction, staring at me. My Gran turned her head slightly to the left, motion limited by the male's fist still wrapped in her hair. Her eyebrows furrowed as she gave me a desperate look, shaking her head in a silent plea.

"What do we have here?" Cooed the head soldier who I had injured, his savage smile widening. Dokine, was it?

"Came to join the party, did we?"

"You came in search of me. You found me. So let her go," I nodded my chin in Gran's direction, trying to let courage steel my features and to keep my fear locked up tight.

"Ah, we came in search of you. But we found so much more than just you. A wicked old sorceress, elbow deep in witchcraft. Surrounded by more than enough evidence to justify her death." Dokine motioned to the books and supplies thrown about and then spat on the floor in disgust.

I swallowed thickly as I glanced around the room, my heart hammering out of my chest now. I had to think quickly. Had to save her.

"These are my belongings and mine alone. She is innocent here. Let her go and you can have me." I tried again.

He let out an amused laugh. "Why settle for one when I can have both?" The other males laughed in response.

Gran squirmed in the chair. The male with the red beard behind her tugged tightly on her hair, stilling her.

Shit. This was not how I had wanted this to go.

Glancing around the room for a weapon of some sort, I found none aside from the broken shards of glass littering the ground. If I tried to get to a piece, they'd surely catch me before I was even close.

"How did you find me?" I tried to buy myself time by getting them to talk. My mind racing for a solution.

His eyes narrowed on me. "It's none of your business, but since you'll be dead shortly anyway, it won't hurt to shed some light on how we came to find this cess-hole."

Hatred burned through me. Maybe it was contagious. Not only were they mistreating Gran, but they had destroyed our belongings, belongings that we used to aid the people of this city. And now he was insulting our home.

"Do enlighten me," I sneered.

He pulled out a chair at the wooden table, sat down, and crossed one foot casually over a knee. As if he lived here and what was happening was a mere chat over tea. Disgust roiled through me.

"Well, after you managed to outrun my men..." he shot a glare at the males standing near the hearth, who quickly dropped their eyes to their boots. "... a mistake that will not go unpunished, might I add." His gaze drifted back to me.

"We circled back to the courtyard and scoped out the morning's crowd. Many more people had drifted in by then, you see. Ready to go about their day's business."

Working tirelessly only to be forced to shovel their coins into this man's pocket. I thought to myself. I didn't say it out loud, though, which was by the grace of the Goddesses.

"We asked a few people if they knew of you. Just a group of friendly males from The Dark Army, looking to reward a local girl for her assistance." His hand began stroking his grimy beard.

"I'm no girl," I practically snarled at him.

Amused that he had gleaned such a response from me, he continued. "Didn't take much to convince that male at the bread stand to help us find the brown-haired girl about this height...." He motioned above him with an outstretched arm, indicating how tall I was. "...who often hung around the fountain in the mornings."

Aldall. He was around the same age as Eryn and I, and often ran the bread cart in the courtyard while his family remained in the shop, baking and preparing more loaves. Although he wasn't a close friend, we knew each other. He was kindhearted and quiet. Harmless. And he would never give me away out of malice.

"He was happy to tell us who you are and where you live, Magnolia. He wanted you to get the reward you deserved for aiding a soldier who had turned their ankle awry on the road into town, after all." A smug look washed over his features.

This extra time I was buying myself by listening to this Dokine ramble on was not helping me figure out a plan here.

My gaze slipped to Gran and found her eyes boring into mine. It was like she was trying to tell me something with that look of steely determination, but I wasn't quite picking up on it. My brows knitted as I tried to discern the meaning behind her look. She almost seemed like she was urging me on. Encouraging me to keep going. To keep being brave.

I remembered the words of the male who saved me again. Breathe. Inhale. Hold. Exhale. I took a slow breath and exhaled the tension out of my shoulders, squaring up to the lead soldier with renewed resolve.

"Ah, well. I'm ready for this reward you speak of." I directed a pretty smile at him.

He stared at me for a moment. The blonde-haired male spoke up with a smile. "Maybe we should have some fun with her before we kill her, boss."

"As exciting as this all is, I'm growing bored. It's time for you to release her and take me in her stead." I tried a third time, mustering every bit of nonchalance I could and willing my pulse to slow. I could always figure out how to escape them later on.

I quickly looked at Gran again, her eyes still set on me... pleading with me to do... something. But what? Her eyes shot to the broken jars scattering across the floor and back to me, eyes widening briefly.

That feeling in my chest ignited again in response, beckoning me again. I closed my eyes briefly, trying to focus inward on what it was trying to tell me. My eyes flashed open, realization hitting hard.

The head soldier's face grew ruddy. "Last I checked, I was the one giving commands around here." He moved to stand, his hand going to the hilt of his sword. The other males mirrored his actions.

"Even though we're in a den of witches, I'm still in charge. You'd do right to remember that." His foul upper lip curled upward.

A wicked smile hit my lips as I stared directly at him. *Into him.* "Well, you're right about one thing. You are in the witch's den."

CHAPTER

FIVE

I lunged for the pile of broken vessels, dipping one palm into a mound of bright red powder. *Rose Bloom*. Foraged from the crimson roses that grow near the Pinebarrow mountains, and ground into a fine powder with mortar and pestle.

I was quick on my feet. The males were stunned and slow to respond.

My other hand scooped into a pile of iridescent, golden sand, collected under the light of a Gilded Moon. *Moonlit Gold*. The guard closest to me, his shaggy brown hair making him appear young, tried to grab hold of me, but I ducked below his outstretched arms.

"Get her!" Shouted Dokine.

The males all darted toward me, but I sidestepped the first to reach me. I then crouched down quickly below the second male, causing them to collide. They both stumbled.

I shot back up to my feet.

The innate fire boiled inside of me and ran down my arms, fueling the energy tingling at my hands. The tree that melded with the cottage began trembling.

Gran's eyes were bright with pride. With excitement. But her captor gripped her tightly. My heart raced and my chest urged me on.

Clasping my hands together, I joined the floral powder with the golden sand. I rubbed my palms together and then brought my fingers to my face, pressing my three middle fingers below each eye. I smiled boldly at the lead soldier again.

I dragged the powerful mixture down the skin of my face and left behind a thick trail of deeply hued powder. Words poured from me in a rich voice laced with intensity. Not knowing what I was about to say, I tuned into the burning heat that bubbled up my chest as it collided with the energy of the mighty tree we were standing within.

"*Viss detyne*" The wooden floor boards shook violently. The soldiers froze mid-stride. From my words or from fear, I did not know.

"*Armae Relinkai,*" I continued, the branches of the tree whipping wildly outside the cottage windows.

"*Fu-ghei Nostrai Daa!*" I demanded in a guttural growl. My hands pressing out and away from me. From them, a burst of energy rippled through the air. The males fell onto the ground with their arms covering their heads. Their forgotten swords clanked as they hit the floor.

Hold power. Release the weapons. Grant us escape. An archaic spell, spoken in Ancient Lunarian, that, when combined with the right carrier powder, could cause enough chaos to buy us the time needed to escape.

Shock rippled through me. I have never cast such a spell before. Nor had I any type of powers that could cause trees to tremble or males to fall in trepidation.

My heart was.... Beating steadily. It pumped at a normal pace, unwavering and sure. That was ... *odd*.

The soldiers' scrambling to their knees and grabbing their swords cut my thoughts short. I had to get Gran and me out of here while I had the chance.

I raced to her side, pulling the gag free from her mouth first. She let out a ragged exhale — "*Váliarë*". *Moon-blessed*.

Pride emanated from her. A flood of relief washed through me at the sound of her voice.

I darted behind her chair, trying to free her from the ropes tightly binding her wrists. Scanning my immediate surroundings, I found nothing to slice through the rope with. *Fuck*.

The red-haired male who had been holding Gran and was closest to us had risen to one knee. Still unsteady from the blast, he swayed slightly.

I lurched for the nearest broken glass jar. The cloth that had been used to gag Gran would work as an extra layer of protection. Quickly wrapping the fabric around my hand, I reached for a broken jar.

I stretched my arm out toward the man, steadying myself with half-bent knees and leveling my newfound weapon at him. I was ready to fight for our lives.

He let out a shout as he charged me, all 6-plus feet of him. Luckily, he hadn't grabbed his sword yet. That meant that I had a weapon, and he did not. What I could do with that knowledge was still a mystery to me, as I had *no fucking clue* how to fight.

"Nolei!" Gran shouted. I inhaled quickly, trying to tune into what that energy in my chest was trying to lead me to do.

He ran at me and I crouched down slightly, slamming my broken jar right into his gut as I bore the brunt of his weight with my shoulder. *Goddesses, forgive me. As a matter of fact, I better beg for Seraphon's forgiveness, too.* I thought to myself, referencing the lesser God of Compassion who was known for his gentleness and empathy toward others.

The male had a hold of me but let out an ear-rupturing howl as the pain sliced through him. I let go of the jar.

Quickly releasing me, he grabbed for his stomach, which was now spilling blood down the front of his uniform. A dark complement to the deadly crimson fabric.

One of the males had made it to his feet but was whispering a feverish prayer under his breath as he slunk along the edge of the cottage, trying to make his way to the door. He kept his wide eyes glued to me as he inched his way toward the exit.

"You fucking coward," the dark-skinned male bit out in his direction, bending down to put pressure on the red-haired man's gushing wound.

"I have had enough of this," Dokine announced from behind me.

I turned to see him stalking toward me with fury etched into his features. *Uh oh.* My left hand cradled my right shoulder, which was pulsing with a molten pain from taking the massive weight of Gran's captor.

"As have I." I spat back, trying to muster any confidence I could find.

"I changed my mind. You need to leave *now.* Without either of us. My generous offer to trade myself for her has expired." I declared with false bravado while I looked around the room, trying to figure out what the fuck I was supposed to do next.

"You will all rot in The Cinder Wastes for this!" Gran cursed, referencing the scorched, desolate realm where the tortured souls of those deserving of such a fate spent eternity after passing on.

"How about I kill you both, burn this shit hole to the ground, and get home in time for supper?" He taunted, continuing to walk toward me, his long sword drawn.

The tree our cottage was nestled into felt like it *shuddered* in response to his statement. I felt its energy pulsing toward me. *Into* me. Begging me to retaliate.

My mind still raced, but my body felt steady and in control. It felt powerful and wild. Tuning into what I was feeling, I tried to silence my thoughts and just act.

I bent down and grabbed the closest fallen sword to me. Never having held one in my life, I tried to adjust to the weight of it in my hand.

"Clueless girls should not play with weapons they do not know how to wield." The captain stopped a few steps from me, sword raised at the ready.

"Ignorant males should not try to attack a woman who has already bested them once today." I shot back with a savage smile.

Deciding my best course of action was to use the element of surprise, I thrusted my sword straight at him. He side-stepped, raising his eyebrows in response. My feet pushed me forward, causing him to take a few steps back. I jabbed at him again, giving him little time to recover.

He responded, swinging downward toward my right arm. I jumped to the side. *Gods, this sword was heavy.* Trying a backhand swipe, I swung the blade upward from my left side, toward his exposed middle. Catching him by surprise, I managed to cut into his lower abdomen. I sent a quick prayer of thanks up to Thalor, the God of Valor, for guiding me in what was the very first fight of my life.

Dokine's crimson tunic fell open, revealing an angry slice to his stomach, which immediately started welling with blood. Jolting back, he hissed, "As I said, I've had *enough* of this."

I stepped back a few steps, creating space between us. His lips curled over his teeth as he stepped toward me, footsteps loud and intimidating. His eyes lit up as a smile brushed over his face. My brows furrowed in confusion.

I backed right into something firm. *Fuck.* A sudden force pinned my arms to my sides and ripped my sword out of my grasp. *No, no, no.* I bucked my head back, trying to connect with his face as I had tried and failed to do with the male who had rescued me earlier. This time, it worked.

The male behind me grunted and then sputtered, "Fucking Bitch."

I tried turning my head slightly and glimpsed the blonde-haired soldier behind me. His grip on me only tightened. He was holding me tightly to him, one hand wrapped around my waist, binding my arms down, and his right hand clasped tightly onto my chin. He forced my head toward the right, holding me firmly and exposing my neck. I fruitlessly thrashed against him as fury burned through me.

"I was going to make this easy on you two. Just bring you to the courtyard, let you remain chained for a few days to the posts in the square as an example for all to see, and then burn you alive as you ought to be." His smug smirk returned.

This was exactly the fate I had expected from him, knowing how much The Dark Army loved making examples of people and using every excuse possible to show off their sadistic love for violence. All in the name of the Dark Queen.

It wasn't always like this. The fae that populated Lunaris used to use the magic of our ancestors in peace and without fear of retribution. The fae used the magic for good, to aid others, and to better our lands.

Criminals received fair trials and were sentenced to rehabilitation and community work, not dealt a bloody death in a public setting. That all went away when The Dark Enchantress, Queen Ryellia Damay, usurped the crown and led a legacy of violence and death.

Hatred stoked the fire in my veins at the thought of her cruelty.

He gritted his teeth, wincing. "But since you've gravely injured one of my soldiers and somehow sliced through me, I'm going to carve you up and make you *beg* for death." His wicked smile was a hateful promise.

"I should have thrown that rock harder this morning." I spat, bucking in my captor's grip. "Or stuck around to finish the job with a larger one."

Dokine ignored me. "But first, I'm going to make you watch me kill *her*." He nodded his head in Gran's direction, not breaking eye contact with me.

"No!" My foot stomped on the soldier's boot and my head flung backwards again. He just grunted once more and held firm.

"Stop fighting me, you little wench, or I'll snap your neck before Sir Dokine has his chance with you," His voice was a gravelly whisper in my ear.

I wriggled and screamed. Pleaded. Tried violently to get free. To stop this.

Dokine swung toward Gran. She was fiddling with the ropes binding her wrists, but sitting straight with her head held high. Her eyes opened wide and became iridescent. An ethereal bright blue that reminded me of Moonlit Bay in the early morning, when the fog was still lifting.

She spoke slowly and clearly, commanding the attention of all in the room: "*Peer into the verdant eye, where the shadows of yesterday whisper their truths.*"

My breath caught in my throat. *What*? I did not know what that meant or why she had chosen now to say it.

Before I could scream in protest, Dokine ended my confusion by closing his hand around her chin, staring directly into her bright eyes, and burying his sword deep into her chest. Right through the wooden chair behind her.

CHAPTER

SIX

I felt my heart lurch and then drop in my chest. "No!" Disbelief rocked through me. I screamed as my pulse boiled back up into my ears and everything around me seemed to turn to slow motion.

"Gran! No!" I shrieked. Pleaded. I couldn't believe this was happening. Not Gran. She was my everything. Day after day was spent teaching me everything from how to advocate for myself to how to heal a common burn. She cared for me and helped me grow. Taught me to be brave and always listen to the world around me. *This couldn't be happening.*

The soldier behind me gripped me roughly.

Dokine dropped his grip on her chin and yanked his sword free. "That was enough of that mindless chatter," he stated cooly.

Shock washed over me, burning and potent.

Her bright blue eyes remained open as her head fell, her chin dropping to her chest. Blood flowed freely from her wound and her mouth, trickling over her lap and pooling at the legs of the chair.

A ragged sob left me. Gran was gone. Her body was limp. Her blood was spilling onto the floor of our own home.

Dokine moved towards me, his sword still dripping blood as he walked. Everything seemed to go still. Agony poured through me and left a white-hot hole in its wake. My chest felt empty, as if I was the one who had been stabbed.

I couldn't go on without Gran. I didn't know what to do. She was my only family. She was all I had left.

I inhaled sharply as my head tipped up toward the ceiling. As I felt myself *change* from the inside out. Broken and raw. *Feral.*

The windows of the cottage cracked, and the wind whipped in through them, lifting my hair and cloak. The tree surrounding the cottage trembled, knocking more of our belongings off the wall.

The male behind me released his hold on me. The soldier I had wounded and the male who was holding pressure to his abdomen both shouted, covering their heads. Dokine stood to face me, blood-drenched sword at the ready.

I leaned into the chaos, letting the power of the wind and the ancient tree feed into my rage. Arms now free, I lifted them with open palms. The wind began circling inside the cottage, creating a twister of debris that wound around us.

Dokine covered his mouth and nose with his elbow in an attempt to filter the air he breathed.

My eyes locked with his. I raised my hands even higher and then clenched my fists tightly in the air. Tree branches sprouted from the walls and roots from the floor. They grew rapidly from every direction, coiling around the soldiers like angry serpents.

A root shot up from beneath the captain, wrapped around his body, and lifted him into the air. Panic and terror replaced his smug features as he frantically grasped at the roots tightly spinning around his neck.

No thoughts filled my mind. I only felt blinding, searing rage. It pulsed through me with every beat of my heart. Coursed through every part of me. I *became* rage. Welcomed it. Allowed the charred taste of revenge on my tongue to be all the sustenance I needed.

I kept my hands raised and fists clenched until roots and branches covered every soldier. Until they snuffed out their last breaths. Or screams, rather.

When they had thoroughly paid for what they had done to my innocent, selfless grandmother. For what Dokine had wanted to do to that boy in the square. Only then did I let go.

My palms fell open at my sides. The branches and roots gave a final squeeze before all of them, and the males they held, disappeared completely. Their bodies gone. Every single one of them.

They would rot in The Cinder Wastes, indeed.

All that was left behind was our disheveled cottage and a faint glimmer of dust floating down in the late afternoon beams of sun that shone through the windows. All that remained was our destroyed home, my shattered heart, and Gran's lifeless body.

I don't know how long I sat on the hard floor beside Gran, holding her. Time seemed to stand still. I hovered there, in an empty daze, with nothing to accompany me but the surreal beat of my heart sounding in my ears.

I had sliced through the ropes that bound her hands, hands that had healed countless others. They had cooked meals, braided my hair, and tended to our wild garden.

I slid her onto her back on the floor, closing her eyes and straightening her muted gray skirt.

I moved so that her head rested on my lap as I leaned against the wall.

My body felt empty and cold. All the energy that flowed into and out of me vanished with the wild branches and heartless members of The Dark Army.

No matter how many times it played over in my head, I still couldn't believe any of it. From what happened in the courtyard this morning to the bloodshed that had befallen our home. None of it felt real. An icy numbness held me, keeping the events separate from myself.

No tears fell as I sat there, watching the afternoon light fade into the moody purples and grays of dusk. My breaths were slow and distant. My mouth was too dry. My mind was an endless loop, replaying the events through to the end and then restarting again. My mind didn't ask questions or "what ifs", just cycled through the interactions as if I were watching them from a distance. Watching them happen to someone else. They played on repeat in my mind, and I had zero control over the whirling flashbacks.

As the last of the day's light slipped through the shattered windows, I heard the crunch of twigs outside the door. It was probably the soldier who had snuck toward the exit and escaped. He likely had returned with a small company of males ready to burn me at the stake for the atrocities I've committed.

I tried to will myself to care.

A familiar voice lured me out of my shock-driven stupor. "Nolei?"

I took a breath that I actually felt move through my body. *Eryn*.

"Nolei, are you in there?" Her voice prodded cautiously.

She pushed the ajar door open further and took in the cottage's state. Smashed jars, strewn powders, and liquids. The table was broken in several places, chairs were scattered, and there were piles of blood and gore.

"For fuck's sake, Nolei. What in the Goddess' names happened in here?!"

I tilted my head back against the cool, hard wall as I raised my eyes in her direction. My face and body otherwise stayed frozen in place. Limp. Numb.

Her eyes shot to my lap and then she saw Gran. She gasped, rushing to my side.

"No. No. No. No," she murmured, kneeling next to me with her hands covering her mouth. "Gran! Oh Gods, Nolei, what happened?!" She turned to face me more directly, grasping my face between her hands now.

I met her gaze, staring into her cool blue eyes, and felt my eyes well with tears.

Gran was all I had. My parents had passed from poisoning of the blood when I was a babe. They were both victims of a bear attack outside our cottage one morning. Their wounds festered, and they could not beat the fever that overtook them. Gran had raised me my entire life. She was the only family I had ever known.

I went from hiding behind her apron during her visits around the city to aid the ill, to working alongside her as her apprentice. She taught me everything I knew.

She was full of compassion, kindness, and a spark that kept her fighting for what she believed was right — even if it put her at risk.

Eryn pulled me into her chest, stroking my hair. My emotions poured out of me suddenly and all at once. The all-encompassing rage had dissipated, and the fog of shock lifted. I felt layer after layer of painful emotion bubble to the surface. Heartbreak. Disbelief. Guilt. Confusion. Bone-deep grief. The feelings crested, wave after wave, spilling out in broken sobs and endless tears. Until I had no tears left to shed and a fractured shell of a person was all that remained of me.

What would I do without her? Who would I become? The questions came to the surface now. I was lost without my Gran. This was our home. Our apothecary. The people of Eyloria relied on her, on *us*, to keep them well and heal their ailments. To be *with* them during some of life's hardest times.

I couldn't just replace her. There was so much I did not yet know. So much left to learn.

After my sobs had turned to a silent whimper, I finally answered Eryn. "She's gone, Eryn. She's gone, and it's all because of me."

"Shhh" she cooed. Running her hand along my hair, holding me to her. Holding space for me to share this, however slowly I needed to. "Tell me everything," she whispered into the crown of my head. "I've got you."

I did just that. I told her everything that had happened from the moment I had left her side earlier. Every painful detail. Even the unfathomable parts where I somehow killed multiple fae males with some type of nature-driven magic that I had never even heard of before, let alone knew I possessed.

She listened quietly, stroking my hair and holding me steady. If the words I spoke shocked her, she didn't show it.

I reeled, trying to wrap my head around the truth that Gran was gone. Everything happened so fast. *Too* fast. I didn't even get to share my suspicions with her about how nature seemed to respond to me somehow.

For fuck's sake, look what I had done. It more than just "responded" to me. I felt like I had pulled all the energy from the air and the ancient tree we called home to myself and turned it into a weapon.

Gran had borne witness to all of that and didn't look one bit surprised. She seemed ... proud. As if she *knew* I could do that. Whatever *that* was.

This was all my fault. If I hadn't attacked that soldier in the first place, none of this would have happened. That boy would spend the rest of his life with only one hand and his family would likely suffer further as a result, but at least Gran would still be here.

How many other families would suffer from her loss? She was our healer. Our matron. She helped people conceive children and eased the passing of the oldest among us. She ensured families had ample supplies of salve to ward off fever after flesh wounds, and ointments to ease aching joints and muscles.

But what was it she had said? My mind flicked back to her very last words to me. *Peer into the verdant eye, where the shadows of yesterday whisper their truths.*

What did that even mean? I ran them over in my head. Turned them over on my lips. Whispered them to myself.

Eryn's hand stilled on my hair. "What did you say?"

"That was the last thing she had said to me. Right before he killed her. Her eyes got bright blue, and she said '*Peer into the verdant eye, where the shadows of yesterday whisper their truths.*'" I lifted my head from her chest and looked at her.

"It was like she had to tell me that before she passed on. Had to make sure I knew that."

Her brows furrowed. "But what does it *mean*?"

"I have no idea. It's almost like a riddle or something. She never spoke like that." I closed my eyes, trying to focus. "Maybe she was trying to tell me something that she needed me to know but couldn't say in front of the soldiers."

My mind kept playing over the words as I stared down at Gran's body. I felt some relief knowing that she had passed into The Garden Sanctum. The realm where those who deserved a blissful afterlife would live in eternal tranquility. It was said that there was an expansive garden filled with beautiful greenery that glowed with twilight, the moon and stars constantly casting their radiance on the land. Its vastness was said to be incomprehensible, as was its beauty.

As I stared down at her now lifeless body, my heart still feeling like a brick in my chest, it hit me. Look into *the verdant eye.* I gasped. *Her necklace.*

She always wore this golden necklace, the pendant shaped like an all-seeing eye. The iris was fastened out of emerald, and the shades of green created a depth to the eye that deepened its beauty. Fixed onto a dainty gold chain, the eye rested safely at the center of her chest in every memory I had of her.

She once told me it symbolized the omniscience of The Divine Feminine. The combined wisdom of the Goddesses Calantha, Elowen, and Vespera. The Maiden, The Mother, and The Crone. To wear it is to carry their blessing and wisdom.

There were five lesser Gods we valued, too. They all existed to serve and worship The Divine Feminine, though. Thalor: The God of Valor, Aurel: The God of Wit, Lysander: The God of Romance, Elendor: The God of Loyalty, and Seraphon: The God of Compassion. All crafted by The Divine Feminine themselves as representations of the desirable traits in a male. Their sole purpose is to uplift, respect and support women in all their power and complexity. To exalt the females who lead with wisdom, embody strength, and carry the future of the realm in their hands. As it should be.

Each lesser God oversaw their specific area of expertise, but it was the three Goddesses, The Divine Feminine, who were almighty. They were responsible for the birth of the stars. The rise of the moon. For the natural order of things, from new beginnings and growth to the absolute culmination of a life well lived.

"What is it?" Eryn asked, drawing me from my thoughts.

I eased Gran's head off of my lap and got to my knees, bending over her. Grasping the gold chain, my fingers eased it out from under the neckline of her blouse. I gently removed it so I could get a closer look.

Peer into the verdant eye.

I did just that. Gazing into it, I half expected a magical doorway to another realm to open or something after what had happened earlier today. But *nothing* happened.

"This necklace. It's a green eye. Maybe what she was saying had something to do with this." I kept my gaze locked onto it, tracing the grooves that made up the shape and lines of it.

Eryn's head tilted as she stared at it. "Does it open?"

My fingers explored the edges of it, searching for a clasp or latch. *Nothing.* "Not that I can tell."

"Give it here." Eryn reached for it.

I reluctantly placed it in her palm. "*Peer into the verdant eye,*" she mused, turning it over in her hand. "This has to be it. I mean, what else could it be?"

I kicked my head back and stared up at the tall ceilings that had exposed branches weaving through them. "Ugh. I have no idea. I wish she could have said something a little less cryptic." Frustration coursed through me.

" Especially if she had any hopes of *us* figuring it out." Eryn teased.

"She was always optimistic about our abilities to have ... common sense." I glanced toward her, smiling gently.

"And to choose to listen to said common sense when it did appear." She bumped her shoulder against mine playfully. She turned more fully to me then, placing the necklace over my head so it now rested on *my* chest.

"Nolei. I can't even begin to comprehend everything that has happened to you today and what it all must feel like. All I know is that you are *so brave.* Nobody else would have stood up for that child at the risk of their own life. Nobody else would have taken on soldiers of The Dark Army, whether or not they were saving a loved one." She tucked a stray strand of hair behind my ear.

"Not only that, but you somehow managed to fight them and win — even though the Goddesses only know how clueless you are when it comes to any type of physical feat." She gave me a reassuring smile.

"I don't know what the next steps are going to be, but I do know that I will be here for you no matter what they are. We will figure it out. *Together*"

Her promise settled into me. I exhaled and some of the tension left my shoulders. Goddesses, I was exhausted. *What was I going to do now?* All I could do was hope she was right, that we would figure it out. *Together.*

CHAPTER

SEVEN

E ryn had managed to convince me to stay the night at her house with her. Even though I'd rather be in my bed, I knew I couldn't stay alone in that cottage. Not after everything that had just happened. Not with Gran's blood staining the floor. Not with the blood of those males staining my ... *hands*? My *soul*?

We lifted Gran's body onto her bed and rested her head on the pillow, arranging her hair around her shoulders. Her hand-sewn quilt rested over her. I placed her hands, one over the other, on top of the quilt, and kissed her forehead goodbye.

Camila, understandably spooked, paced restlessly behind the cottage, but didn't stray far. I brought my nose to hers and whispered to her, "*Placydel, mo carissyme.*" Reassuring her in some of the few words of Ancient Lunarian I knew. Just as Gran had taught me to do when settling a horse. *Gently, my dear one.*

After she had calmed, Eryn and I saddled her and began the journey to the Eastern edge of Eyloria. Her home was nestled near the base of the closest of the Pinebarrow mountains. The light from the moonrise guided our path, although we both knew it by heart.

Eryn's family had always been the closest I had to family outside of Gran. Her parents were always warm and welcoming, and more than happy to share the food on their table with me. Her brothers, Cade and Malv, were like brothers to me. They had joined us on many adventures over the years and kept their mouths shut about the escapades we had gone on alone.

Like when Eryn and I etched tattoos into each other's skin with night-black ink and the tip of a fine, sharpened blade. We both wore the inked phases of the moon beneath our breasts proudly, albeit secretly.

Or like the time... Or several times... when we would steal off to spend an evening under the stars with their male companions. Some of those particular romps required bribery on our part to win her brothers' silence.

I doubted I could ever rest peacefully again. But before we could try, we had to care for Gran's body. If Eryn and I had the strength to prepare her body for her final voyage alone, we would have. But for this task, we needed her brothers.

Eryn had ventured inside to fill them in, leaving out details of how exactly I had managed to *take care of* the soldiers. Meanwhile, I paced restlessly outside. Before long, they followed her outside silently. Their faces remained solemn as they both hugged me close to them.

A few hours later, we had positioned Gran on a wooden raft. Her frail body was now adorned with fragrant blooms and lush greenery. Wax candles surrounded her, outlining her shape. I anointed her forehead with fragrant juniper oil, tracing the eye of The Divine Feminine just above her brow.

We set her adrift into Moonlit Bay at an area where we knew the current would be strong enough to carry her out into The Sea of Elowen. Into the arms of its namesake, The Mother Goddess. The flickering glow washed over her as the tides reclaimed her body, and I returned to the land, knowing her soul already resided peacefully in The Garden Sanctum.

The soft sound of Eryn's breathing was a rhythmic enough lullaby, her bed a soft enough place to rest. But despite my best efforts, I didn't come close to achieving the solace from my thoughts that sleep would provide. I stared up at the dark ceiling, the moonlit shadows providing a slight distraction.

What will I do now? I thought of trying to take over Gran's work with the people of Eyloria. There was more than enough work to keep me busy tending to everyone's ailments and needs. To keep my mind busy. But I would be a sorry replacement for Gran.

She was so knowledgeable and the cornerstone of our community to many. Despite the hours and years I had spent by her side, my knowledge was only a drop in the kettle compared to hers. Not only would I let the people down if I tried to replace her, but doing such work would be too painful. Every day would be spent yearning for her company and expertise, replaying her death in my mind, despite my best efforts to black it out. I would be constantly trying to live up to her memory and would fall bitterly short of it every time.

What was I thinking? I wouldn't even be able to show my face in Eyloria again. One soldier had escaped.

My mind replayed the events of the day yet again. The young-looking male slipping silently toward the door and the dark-skinned one calling him a "*fucking coward.*"

He had made it out. I had *terrified* him. Enough to leave his duties behind in favor of his life.

But would he tell the other members of The Dark Army about me? He could give a clear description of me. Could tell of all the atrocities I had committed against The Dark Enchantress by harming them, especially my use of magic. If that was what that even *was*. If I was caught, I would surely face the pyre.

I shuttered, squeezing my eyes shut. *I had to get out of here.*

I couldn't let anyone learn of my powers. It didn't matter that I had no clue what the fuck that power was or how I did it. What mattered was that I *had* done it.

I prayed to The Divine Feminine that nobody else in the square had seen me summon that rock earlier.

Having had enough of this internal banter, I rose silently from Eryn's bed and slipped outside.

Resuming my pacing under the stars, I tried to come up with a plan.

Where would I go? The question plagued me, my thoughts rippling like water after being struck by a stone. I can't stay here in hiding forever. I had to move on. Find some place to start new. Some place where I could get these *powers* under control before I hurt someone...else.

The clouds cleared, and the full Weaver's moon shone brightly, catching my attention. It reminded me of my Gran. She had spent many evenings by the hearth teaching me all she knew about each of the different full moons and how to celebrate them properly. The Weaver's Moon represented destiny, fate, and the threads of life coming together. She would often braid my hair on the nights under this moon as a ritual to honor it.

A painful crack returned to my chest. How could I think about myself when all my heart could think about was *her*? What I had cost her.

Peer into the verdant eye, where the shadows of yesterday whisper their truths.

I grabbed the necklace with both hands, examining it under the moonlight. *To wear it is to carry their blessing and wisdom.* It was even more magnificent in the moonlight, the greens almost twinkling with an iridescent quality similar to starlight. As I studied it, a silver glow formed around the perimeter, as if it was being lit from within. I inhaled sharply, looking closer. I pried at it gently. It opened.

My breath hitched. Of course, Gran would have enchanted it to require moonlight. That was so typical of Gran. Why I hadn't considered that earlier was beyond me. If anything, it was yet another testament to how she had truly overestimated my ability to solve such a riddle.

Inside of it lay a scrap of parchment, coiled tightly onto itself. I unfurled it and it lifted out of my hands, growing in size and floating above my palms. The moonlight seemed to cause some type of response, causing the text to brighten to a white vivid enough to read even on the darkest of nights. Captivated, I frantically read the flowy script.

Past secrets lie in veiled depths,
Seek where moonlit shadows dance,
In the grove where twilight steps,
And whispers weave their cryptic trance.

In shadowed woods where Wolfsbane blooms,
And ancient trees hold silent sway,
A mirror pond reflects the truth,
guiding you on your way.

Your mother's voice, a siren's song,
Her magic dark and great.
Your father, nature's gentle grace,
A secret love they keep.
In mirror's depths, the truth you face,
Of bloodlines dark and deep.

Follow rivers' twining path,
Through shadowed glens, unseen.
There, the truth of blood and wrath,
Awaits in forest green.

I fell to my knees. I couldn't take my eyes off the Scroll. They flicked back and forth, memorizing every word, starting over again as soon as I reached the bottom.

I could hear my pulse in my ears again. A pounding drum, the backdrop to my frantic thoughts. What the actual *fuck*?

Reeling, I tried to wrap my mind around everything. This spoke of my mother and father. Not the mother and father that I always thought had passed away when I was a babe. Not the parents who I knew to be commoners who were kind and worked hard to keep food on the table. Who died tragically after being attacked by a bear near our cottage, resulting in my Gran raising me for my entire life. But parents I knew nothing about. My *real* parents.

She had been hiding all of this from me? Every single day she had acted as if nothing was amiss, meanwhile she carried the weight of *this* around her neck quite literally. Did she *write* this? Enchant it so that it would open for me at the right moment?

Anger flashed like breeze-lifted embers through my body. She had been lying to me my whole fucking life. The only person I could call family had been keeping secrets from me. Hiding my own past from me. A past I deserved to know the truth about.

How did she know something like this would happen? So many questions raced relentlessly through my head. I tried to steady my breathing. Focusing on the surrounding sensations, I tried to ground myself.

I felt the sharp pressure of small stones beneath my knees. The gentle whirring of the wind along my hair coaxed me to calm as it did earlier in the woods. I smelled the woody smoke from the hearth in Eryn's house and the dampness of the ground. Coming back into my body, I tried to urge my thoughts to slow. To stop bombarding me and to come only one at a time.

Exhaling slowly, I tried to regain control of myself. She had to know that I would develop these powers if she knew all of *this* about my parents.

About *who* or *what* they were. *I had to find out more.* I had to figure out who they were and what was happening to me.

But where do I go?

I re-read the Scroll about thirty more times, trying to picture the locations it hinted at.

"*Seek where moonlit shadows dance, In the grove where twilight steps...* I had no fucking clue.

"*... In shadowed woods where Wolfsbane blooms, And ancient trees hold silent sway, A mirror pond reflects the truth, guiding you on your way....*" My brows furrowed even more deeply.

"*... Follow rivers' twining path, Through shadowed glens, unseen. There, the truth of blood and wrath, Awaits in forest green....*"

I ran the clues through my mind again, more slowly this time. The river part seemed like the best place to start. I knew nothing of shadowed glens or groves, but I knew that the Sanguine River bordered the southwestern edge of Eyloria. I would start there.

I gently grasped the edges of the parchment and rolled up the Scroll. A bright white light sparked from it as it shrank and coiled back onto itself, landing in my open hand.

That was... *interesting.* I placed it back inside the pendant and slipped it back under my shirt, easing the emerald eye between my breasts.

After returning inside, the warmth of Eryn's back against mine paired with the weight of the quilt overtop of me lulled me to sleep for a handful of hours. I wouldn't call it restful, but it was sleep. Sleep I desperately needed because I was leaving with the rise of the sun.

CHAPTER

EIGHT

I silently laced up my boots and slinked back outside while the shadows of night mingled with the gray hues of morning. Fetching Camila from the barn, I led her to the worn path as we navigated back through the woods toward the cottage. I tried to soak in every detail of this journey, knowing it would be the last time I'd make the trek from Eryn's place to mine.

After arriving, I sat on the thatched roof of the cottage I called home, even though it no longer felt like such. Not anymore.

The first rays of balmy sunlight leaked between the forest leaves and left a speckled design along the moss-covered boulders and twig-strewn ground. I quietly got to my feet and crawled back down the side of what *used* to be our home. My feet remembered exactly where branches rested and notches in the wood left footholds.

I walked around the tree, passing by herb-filled garden beds and pots brimming with various mushrooms. I cracked the rounded wooden door open and slipped inside, taking the narrow ladder up the base of the tree to the main room.

My cloak fell from my hands onto the back of a wooden chair. I glanced over at the other chair sitting at the opposite end of the table. *Empty.*

A shuddered breath left me as I felt my gut twist with pain and then fill with coldness.

I padded over to the large basin of cool water that sat on the small table next to the bed and splashed it onto my face. The chill sent a bolt of awareness through me, bringing my attention back to the here and now. I exhaled raggedly, scrubbing at my face. My long brown hair fell over my shoulder, the ends accidentally dipping into the water. I tried to untangle the mass of waves with my fingers and began forming the tiny plaits that traced from my temple to behind my pointed ears, where they fell down the length of my hair along my back. Three on the right side today. I clasped a silver cuff onto a thin braid from a ceramic bowl of trinkets. My favorite one, imprinted with the face of a wolf on it.

I looked down at her necklace again, the one she had worn every day for as long as I could remember. Seeing it brought me right back to hours spent side by side, watching her work the yarn and hook or grind the mortal and pestle.

Another icy pang shot through my chest. I polished the necklace on my muted green tunic and slid it back into my top. *To wear it is to carry their blessing and wisdom.* That is all I would take of her. No woolen blankets or hand-written tomes. No other mementos. I had to travel light.

Plus, I already had all that she had gifted me with ... I just carried it inside of me instead. Hours of endless lessons, intricate knowledge of herbs and plants, how to get quiet so that I could hear the world around me, how to sense what is ailing someone, and how to soothe it with my touch.

My gaze lifted to the shelving that lined the cottage, that had once been brimming with rarities and ingredients. Now mostly bare, with scattered glass and debris covering the floor.

I toed some shards of glass to the side that had settled next to my bed. Kneeling, I pulled out the wooden crate that held the few outfits that I owned. All in dingy earth tones, well-worn and threadbare. I gathered two tunics, a pair of woolen socks, and my leather bodice. Slipping the bodice on over my tunic, I cinched it tightly over my chest.

Considering what else one may need on such a journey, I glanced around the disheveled cottage. I grabbed a water skin, some dried fruits and salted meats, and my new oversized cloak. I shoved my supplies into a leather bag I could fasten to the saddle. Feeling as ready as I'd ever be, I made my way to Camila.

With my back to the cottage, I readied myself to mount the white mare.

A familiar voice broke through the early morning silence.

"Nolei!" Eryn shouted. "What in the Goddesses' name do you think you are doing?"

I shut my eyes, cringing. I slowly turned to face her. I had hoped I could have left without having to do any goodbyes or listen to her try to persuade me not to go.

"I have to leave, Eryn. I can't stay here."

She dismounted her horse and started toward me, her annoyance palpable. "I knew you'd try to pull something like this the second I woke up to find you gone. You better not be attempting to leave without me. After everything we've been through, you are just hopping on your horse and trying to disappear?"

"You have a life here, Eryn. A family. I wouldn't ask you to leave that." The reminder that she had what I did not stung like a fresh cut.

"You're daft if you think I'd rather stay here than join you in ...." She hesitated.

"What is it you are doing? Where are you even going?" She stopped a few feet from me, hands on her hips.

I exhaled a laugh at her blind loyalty.

"I haven't figured that out yet exactly..." I looked at my feet. The less she knew about it, the better. I didn't want her to feel obliged to join me and throw her life away just because of the shit-tastic hand I'd been dealt. I didn't want her to be in harm's way just because I had to be. She meant too much to me to be involved in this mess.

"So you were just going to ride into the woods until you... What? Walked into the Pinebarrow mountains? Then what?"

I sighed. "I was going to follow the river."

She raised her eyebrows at me. "...to where exactly?"

"I don't know yet" I balled my hands into fists at my side, realizing I wasn't making any ground on pitching this independent journey of mine.

"To wherever I am supposed to go to find out what I need to know," I spat. Realizing how stupid that sounded the moment it left my mouth, I snapped my mouth shut.

She stared at me with an almost bored look. "Are you done yet?"

"Done what?" My eyebrows pinched together.

"Done acting all tough and secretive? Just tell me what the *fuck* is going on, Nolei. I don't care if you don't know where you are going or what you are doing, but I *do* care that you are trying to go alone. No part of this friendship..." She motioned back and forth between us. "...Involves being alone. *Ever*."

Her blue eyes were icy with frustration. "After all the shit we've been through. With all the sneaking out and bad decisions, do you think you can just walk away on your own? I can't believe you'd even think that, Nolei! I am your best friend. *Unconditionally.* Nothing can come between us. And you're mad if you think I'll let some Dark Army creeps be the thing to separate us!"

I let out a frustrated little huff at her rant. Then my shoulders softened, and I exhaled slowly. *Why was I trying to do this all alone?*

I hadn't even told her about The Scroll yet. There was no way I could navigate a fresh start on my own. I would be clueless. I had never been outside of Eyloria and didn't know the first thing about traveling. Not to mention the danger of traveling by myself as a woman, especially when the realm was crawling with the corrupt soldiers of The Dark Army.

We had always been side by side, no matter how good, bad, or stupid the adventure was. This should be no different.

"Fine. You can come. But don't complain about having to sleep on the ground or not being able to have a bath!" I spat at her, trying to act like I had some semblance of the upper hand here.

She flashed her radiant smile at me, one that reached her blue eyes and lit up her face. "Gods, I thought you'd never ask. Of course, I will go with you!" She clenched her hands together at her heart.

I rolled my eyes.

She glanced around me toward Camila. "Where is all your stuff?"

I looked over my shoulder at the white horse. "What stuff?"

"All the stuff you are planning to take with you on this grand adventure of yours." She side-stepped me, placing a hand on Camila's neck as she nudged at the leather bag.

"In my bag, obviously. We have to pack light, Eryn." My chin rose defiantly.

She opened it gingerly, pawing around inside.

"Surely you can't mean this bag that has only two tunics and a pair of socks in it." She glanced at me with a blonde raised eyebrow.

"It has more than that in it! I packed some food and—"

"You won't make it to Pinebarrow pass with these supplies, Nolei!" She cut me off.

"What were you planning to sleep on?"

I raised my arms out to my sides, causing the oversized cloak that smelled of crackling campfire and pine to hang from my arms. "My cloak."

"Ah." She nodded, her fingers going to her chin. "And what weapons did you bring to defend yourself against all manner of evil creatures and villainous strangers you may encounter?"

My mouth snapped shut. *Shit.* I hadn't even thought about that.

"And what do you plan to eat after you have finished off this portion of dried meats before moonrise today?" She continued. "And how will you warm yourself when following the river inevitably leads you north, where the climate is much cooler and snow falls from the sky like sifted flour?"

Irritation rising, I let out another growl of frustration and looked up at the sky. The sun was fully out now, nudging the forest awake.

"I get it! I didn't pack enough and have no clue what I'm doing." I glared at her. "Point taken."

She smiled back at me, clearly proud of herself.

"And what do *you* suggest we pack, oh wise and knowledgeable one?" I replied.

It was her turn to roll her eyes. "You go back inside and gather some blankets, whatever other food you can scrounge up, a small cooking pot, and any healing supplies you can fit into your bags." My eyebrows rose.

"Well, that was oddly specific." I crossed my arms over my chest. "And exactly how long have you been contemplating this last-minute journey, Eryn?"

She strode back to her mare, Lady Lace. "Just get those things and any trinkets that may be of value. We may need to trade some things for coin."

She said with a smirk. "I'm running back home to grab the rest of what we'll need. I'll be back as soon as I can."

"Yes, master." I teased, walking slowly back toward the cottage.

"Oh, and Nolei --" she turned Lace toward the trail but still faced me.

I looked toward her.

"If you try to leave without me before I get back, I will hunt you down and I will *hurt* you." She promised, smiling at me.

I let out a short laugh. Gods, after yesterday, I didn't think I'd ever laugh again.

"Noted."

CHAPTER

NINE

I had gathered the supplies that Eryn had listed, rolling up the blankets into bed rolls and fastening them to Camila. By the time she had returned, I was finishing packing the last of the items.

Eryn trotted up to us on her bay mare, Lady Lace. She climbed off her horse and immediately handed me something wrapped in plain brown cloth. I reached out both of my hands to grab it, looking up at her. "What is this?"

"Your new weapon." She beamed down at me.

My eyes widened, unfolding the cloth to reveal a beautiful silver short-sword. Swirls and leaves marked the hilt, winding up to a moon-crested pommel. It was fucking glorious.

"And where did you find this on such short notice?" I held onto the grip and turned the sword over in my hand. "It's beautiful."

"Aren't they?" She was holding a nearly identical one. Eryn reached over and handed me a dagger that was much smaller, but just as intricately designed. I accepted it with wide eyes.

"I stole them from Cade and Malv." She replied cooly.

My jaw dropped. "Well, we better get the fuck out of here before they realize it, then."

She laughed and handed me a leather scabbard for my hip and a leather strap to attach the dagger to my thigh. I looked to see how she had fastened hers and did the same.

"Exactly my thoughts."

I turned and mounted Camila as she climbed back onto Lady Lace. "Did you tell your family?"

Her smile faded. "I left them a note."

I was silent for a moment.

Unlike Eryn, I *had* to leave. The Dark Army would look for me. There were far too many painful memories here to spend another night in the cottage. Not to mention my need to learn more about these developing powers of mine. I couldn't keep hiding them forever. And what of my parents? If they were still alive, I had to find them. I had to find out what Gran knew, but couldn't tell me. Or *wouldn't* tell me.

But Eryn, everything she knew and loved, was *here*. She had a family that cared deeply for her. Even though she hated working as a seamstress, she was talented at it and had plenty of work to stay busy. She was giving up everything to come with me. Giving it up for me.

"Thank you." I met her stare..

"For the sword? Of course, its --"

"No. For coming with me. I know you are giving up everything to do so, and I appreciate it. I don't know what I did to deserve a friend like you, Eryn, but I'm so grateful to have you."

Her bowed lips curved up into a soft smile. "*Am-cytiah Sympeil-tur-na*," she replied in Ancient Lunarian. *Eternal friendship.*

We were a sight to behold. Both dressed in our pants and cloaks. From a distance, we looked like any other fae travelers. As someone approached, though, they'd see our wild, long hair adorned with braids. Our array of leather straps secured our weapons, complementing our favored corset vests fiercely. We were feminine strength embodied.

We were no ordinary travelers, that was for damn sure. My lips kicked up into a smile as we rode side by side.

We skirted along the outside edge of Eyloria, passing through the woods on the Eastern border of the city and traveling south toward the Sanguine River. Needing to make a stop for the rest of our provisions before heading out, Eryn rode back into the city center while I waited on the outskirts with my hood up. The last thing we needed was for me to be recognized by The Dark Army before we even left Eyloria. My stomach flopped restlessly as I waited for her to return, eager to be out of this city.

Eryn returned within a half hour with a few fresh loaves of bread, an array of cheeses, some dried oats, and a bottle of wine.

"Focusing on the necessities here, aren't we?" I eyed the wine.

She gave me a sideways glance paired with a smirk as she tucked her haul into a saddlebag. "Figured we'd need to celebrate this next chapter and what better way than splitting a bottle of Eyloria's best-mulled wine?"

I snorted. "More like Eyloria's *cheapest* mulled wine."

"Hasn't stopped you from enjoying it before, Nolei."

She had a point there.

We made it out of the city and to the bridge that crossed the Sanguine River. A crossing that signified our official leaving behind of everything and everyone we knew.

We had traveled out of Eyloria's domain and were now entering uncharted territory, as far as Eryn and I were concerned. We had studied maps of the continent in our school classes before we began our apprenticeships, and knew the large cities and natural landmarks of Lunaris. But knowing these things on a surface level and navigating through them on horseback were two vastly different things.

Was that going to stop us? *Absolutely not.* Would it slow us down? *Probably.*

After crossing the bridge, we traveled north along the river, keeping it in sight as we meandered through meadows and lightly wooded areas.

"So, now that I have demonstrated my allegiance to you by following you blindly out of the only home we have ever known and into this," Eryn gestured to the lightly wooded area we were now traveling through. "Do you care to fill me in on what we are doing and where we are going?"

I worked on a swallow, trying to wrap my mind around how to tell her about The Scroll. There was no point in trying to hide anything from her any longer. She was pretty much thigh-deep in shit right beside me by this point.

"Remember how Gran had said that thing about the Verdant Eye?" Speaking Gran's name aloud caused my chest to sting, despite any frustration I held from her lies.

"That cryptic message that you thought was about her necklace? Obviously."

"Yeah, that one. Well, turns out it *was* about her necklace," I started, keeping my gaze on the road ahead. "Last night I couldn't sleep, so I went outside to get some fresh air. When the moonlight hit the necklace, it activated it somehow, opening it."

"Really?" She looked at me with wide, blue eyes. "And what was inside of it?"

"This little parchment scroll was inside. When I unrolled it, the strangest thing happened. It started to glow and float out of my hands. The paper grew until it was the size of a regular page and the moonlight illuminated all the text." Thinking back to it, a sense of wonder and awe flowed through me at the experience. I had never seen anything like that in my life.

She pulled Lace to a stop and looked right at me. "Are you dicking me around?" She deadpanned.

I kept Camila moving forward and huffed out a laugh. "Do you think I could make this shit up, Eryn?"

She started back forward, pulling Lady Lace up beside me again.

"Knowing you, probably."

"Well, I didn't. This is a true story from my real life."

She nodded, impressed. "And what did this magical growing scroll say exactly?"

"It had a lot to say, actually." Taking a deep breath, I remembered the lines of script that left me feeling hollow and confused. "I read it so many times that I memorized it. You want to hear?"

"Nah, sounds boring." She stated blandly and looked forward again.

Catching on to her sarcasm, I went with it. "Mighty boring. Well, let us keep riding then." I went silent.

She turned and glared at me. "You better start telling me *right the fuck now*, Nolei."

I laughed and raised my hands in mock surrender. Clearing my throat, I recounted every single word.

I glanced at her when I had finished, trying to catch her reaction. Eryn's jaw was hanging open like a fish.

"Wow." She shook her head. "First of all, you have the mind of a book-keeper, and the fact that you even memorized that already is disturbing."

I smiled proudly, her cursory response helping to ease the tension that lined my entire body. "Secondly, what in the actual *fuck*?"

"That's exactly what I said." I nodded.

"But your parents passed when you were a babe. That doesn't make sense."

I stared down the path, admiring the variety of trees and shrubs that surrounded us. I couldn't quite believe that we were outside of Eyloria and exploring areas of the realm we never thought we'd see.

"I know.." I sighed. "But Gran must have known all of this the entire time... my entire *life*, and kept it a secret from me."

"But why?" Her brows pinched together as she looked over at me.

"You are asking brilliant questions that I do not know the answers to, Eryn."

She was silent for a few minutes. The scent of mossy earth and pine enveloped me as I tried to focus on the woods around us in an attempt to quiet my restless mind.

"Okay, so — your mystical parents' identities have remained hidden for over 25 years," she summarized.

I nodded.

"And there is a possibility that these new powers you are developing are linked to that?"

"They have to be. It can't be a coincidence that I am noticing these abilities that I have never heard of or seen before, right as I discover my parents are possibly still alive and may have powers of their own." I shook my head in disbelief. "It has to be connected."

"Wow. How are you processing all of this, Nolei? I mean... this is a fucking *lot* to sort through. We're not talking about reflecting on a romp in the hay with a muscular male. We're talking about coming to terms with a *secret heritage*." She emphasized the last two words.

"Yes, I'm aware," I stated blandly. "I'm fine." I lied.

"Let's try that again." She glared at me. "This time you tell me the truth because I'm your best friend and I can tell when you are lying." She spoke louder this time, exaggerating the words.

"Nolei, how are you doing processing all of this?" She extended her tan arm out in my direction. "Now you reply."

I glared right back at her, adjusting my seat on the horse. "I am *not* processing this." My voice became louder, too. "Yesterday, I attacked a guard. A mysterious, handsome fae male in the shadows briefly captured and then released me. I battled several soldiers in my home, and somehow managed to kill all of them, *and* I witnessed the murder of the only family member I ever knew."

The reality of these truths hit me like a boulder to the head. I exhaled raggedly and took a slow inhale before continuing.

"Then I learned my parents are not actually who I thought they were and may still be alive. It's *a lot* to fucking process, Eryn."

She nodded and sighed. "Good job, Nolei. It's not easy to admit that you're not fine." She shrugged. "At least you are on the same page with reality now, though." She teased, lightening the mood.

Goddesses, I loved her. This is exactly why I needed her. To call me on my bullshit and keep me moving forward.

"So we're looking for this lake? Some lake that is supposed to help us learn more about everything?"

"It's a pond, but yes. I guess so. I've been running it over in my mind so many times, trying to figure out where to go. We're going to start by following the river and see where it takes us. But, yes, we are looking for some *'mirror pond'* in a forest." *Which should only take us about 15 years to find.*

We traveled quietly for the rest of the day, leading the horses along the lightly worn path that snaked beside the river.

My lower back and hips were screaming at me for riding such a distance on horseback. I'm sure Eryn felt the same, but she didn't make a peep about it, keeping her oath not to complain.

I couldn't help but notice this sensation of feeling *called* somehow, though. As if something was pulling me forward, drawing me towards it. Even though I had no idea where we were going, I knew we were on the right path. The tug in my chest kept reeling me forward, reassuring me of our path and reminding me to keep trusting that tug. Even if the sensation left me feeling a little wary beneath it all.

Although we rode in silence, my mind continued to prattle on. I had to find this mirror lake, to see what truths it beheld. If I could somehow find it and learn about who my mother and father were, maybe I could find *them.*

The thought of actually being able to spend time with my parents was unnatural to me. I felt a slight wiggle of hope flicker in my chest, but quickly tamped it down.

If I could meet my parents, maybe I could learn more about these powers that I'm feeling. About who I *am.* Or where I came from, at least.

My mind flicked back to Gran and those malicious soldiers. Grief flooded my veins again as I then thought of the boy in the square who almost lost his hand just for trying to feed his starving family. His family would not be starving if The Dark Army didn't squeeze every coin out of the people of Lunaris to fuel Queen Damay's treasure trove.

My grief was quickly replaced with anger, which left me feeling too hot and too tense. I had to stop them from hurting more people. More *innocent* people.

Hopefully, word hadn't spread among The Dark Army too quickly. Although I was sure before long they would all be looking for the brown-haired "girl" who used some type of magic to kill several soldiers. Soon, they'd all be looking for *me*.

CHAPTER

TEN

We rode on until dusk and then set up camp for the night. We trekked a short way into the woods from the river's edge until we found a space where the trees were more spread out.

I knotted a rope around one tree, then handed the other end to Eryn. She fastened it to another trunk nearby. We draped a heavy canvas that Eryn had packed over the string, securing the sides to the ground to create a makeshift shelter. We unpacked our bedrolls and laid them beneath the canopy on the moss-covered ground. Stepping back, we admired our work.

Feeling pretty damn proud of ourselves, we began searching for kindling and firewood. We lit a small fire using the techniques Cade and Malv taught us growing up. Sitting on some fallen logs we had dragged next to the fire, we had a supper of salted meats and bread.

Resting my hands on the log at my sides, I looked up at the sky. The Weaver's Moon was still almost full, casting a bright light along the wispy clouds that floated before it.

Eryn was intently poking a stick into the fire, rearranging the twigs and ashes.

Today had been exactly what I'd needed after last night's events. It had helped to lessen the burning grief in my chest. To quiet the vacant hollowness. We'd been together, present, and taking in all the beauty of the countryside of Lunaris. Traveling land I never thought I'd get a chance to explore.

A surge of recklessness whipped through me. Without warning, I cupped my hands around my mouth, tilted my head back and let out a wild howl. Mimicking what was said to be the call of the legendary *Úlfraedors*. The name was Ancient Lunarian for *Shadow-Wolf*, referencing the giant wolf-like creatures that were only spoken of in whispers around fires or in ale-fueled stories within dank taverns.

Eryn launched across the fire circle toward me, clasping her hands around my mouth, silencing me. Her response time was impressive.

"Are you trying to get us *killed*, Nolei?!" She squeezed her hand tighter over my mouth.

"We are two women alone in the woods. The last thing we need is to draw the attention of a patrolling unit of soldiers or whatever *else* is lurking in these trees." She glanced sideways into the shadows of the forest.

My eyes wide, I let out a muffled giggle. "I mean, this blazing campfire is pretty subtle."

She released me and gave me a shove. "Well, I'm glad you find this funny."

I caught myself before I fell backward off the log. "What? I'm just celebrating the first night of our maiden voyage."

Standing up, I walked over to her saddlebag and rummaged around until I found what I was looking for. Popping the cork off the wine, I took several large gulps from the bottle.

Handing it to her, I wiped my mouth with the back of my hand. Smiling, she lifted the bottle in a silent salute before taking several chugs of her own.

Crouching over my bag, I searched until my hand wrapped around a small glass vial tightly wrapped in cloth. Hiding it behind my back, I re-approached Eryn.

"Now what are you up to?" She took another swallow, handing the bottle back to me.

"You aren't the only one who thought to bring supplies to commemorate this adventure." I chirped. I pulled the vial out from behind my back, revealing the small jar of dark ink.

Her eyebrows raised, the fire casting flickering shadows across her face. Her smile was just as mischievous as my own.

"Figured we could add a little flair to our bodies, this time in a more obvious location than the phases of the moon resting beneath our breasts." The bitterness of my next swig of wine burned down my throat, but quickly warmed my senses and fanned my sense of adventure.

She coughed out a laugh. Taking the bottle back from me, she took another long pull before placing the bottle by her boots. "And on what part of my body would you like to commemorate this adventure?" She queried playfully.

I stood back, placing my hand on my chin as I pretended to observe her like a merchant observing fine silks. "Our arms, obviously." I declared.

She glanced down at her arms and then back at me. "And what do you plan to ink on my arm?"

That I hadn't yet figured out. "Something to show others not to mess with us. That we're not some 'girls' to be taken advantage of. Something to show our strength and ferocity." I said, determination bubbling up. I never wanted to be thought of as some helpless *girl*. Ever. Again.

She nodded several times, thinking it over. "Well, since you're out here howling like an Úlfraedor, why not do that?"

I sat down across from her, beginning to heat the metal needle of my makeshift tattooing tool in the fire to purify it.

Eryn continued. "They are notorious for their pure strength and raw power. Having such a reminder inked onto us will hopefully help us harness their ferocity and demand the respect that the *Úlfraedor* do."

I stared at her blankly for several moments, long enough to cause her to fidget under my stare. I broke the silence. "Clever. I fucking love it."

We spent the next few hours etching ancient wolves onto each other's arms, a symbol of our strength and bravery. A call for the wisdom and fierceness of the Úlfraedor. A reminder of our capabilities. The wolves' faces were snarling and wild, their bodies muscular. We showed them shattering chains woven around our arms, symbolizing our breaking free from anything that dared restrain us. Botanical vines, flowers, ethereal stars, and swirls intertwined the chains.

The cheap wine dulled the pain and quieted any inhibitions. Eryn's steadfast presence softened the sharp misery of continuing to live a life without Gran. Exhausted, we fell asleep quickly and slept soundly.

The next day's travel went by quickly and without incident. We packed up camp efficiently and rode for most of the day. The landscape was breathtaking and filled with flora I'd never seen before. The towering trees were made up of rich, brown trunks so large I couldn't fit my arms around them if I tried. I could only imagine how old these trees must be.

Some flowers we came across I had recognized for their healing properties, foraging what I could carry in my saddlebag. The babble of the river provided a soothing backdrop as we traveled.

We continued northeast along the river over the next few days. Setting up camp was becoming second nature already and Eryn and I were getting quicker with our fire building as well. Thankfully, we had encountered no wildlife aside from the small rodents and birds that scurried and fluttered about.

The time passed easily, and focusing on our present surroundings was a welcome reprieve from what happened in my mind when I started thinking about the past. My thoughts continued to wander there, pulling me back into those chaotic moments in flashes.

The rocks vibrated and lifted to my hands in the courtyard before I assaulted Dokine, that brutal head guard. That mysterious, tall male who rescued me at just the right moment and helped me escape. Returning home to find Gran had been bound and gagged by The Dark Army. The bloodshed that ensued.

I shuddered and inhaled quickly, trying to come back to the present moment. A cold sweat covered my neck and temples, and my heartbeat raced. I urged my pulse to slow by taking several long, slow breaths, repeating the words of the male from the alleyway. *Breathe. Inhale. Hold. Exhale.*

I glanced at Eryn to see if she had noticed my panic. She was riding slightly ahead of me and whistling idly. Good.

We set up camp near where the mouth of the Sanguine River twisted northward into the base of the Pinebarrow Mountains. If our memory served us correctly, a small village should be nearby. Nestled at the base of the mountains, between the Sanguine River to the west and the Rolling River to the east. From camp, we expected the village to be about half a day's ride.

Eryn and I had debated what the next best move would be. We needed to gather more provisions and food, not quite ready to try our hand at hunting. Despite the oversized hooded cloak, I still felt uneasy about walking freely in a nearby village. The fear that The Dark Army would search for me was constantly nagging at me. I just *knew* that word had spread of how I had killed several soldiers, with forbidden magic nonetheless. I couldn't risk it.

We needed food. There was no arguing about that. After much debate and several curse words, I had gotten my way and convinced Eryn to venture into the village in search of more food while I remained behind in the woods. I would forage for edible plants and herbs while she was bartering in the village. She had no qualms about having to do the trading, but was hesitant to leave me behind alone.

The next morning, we packed our supplies and rode as far east as we could before the river began to twist northward, and it was there that we went our separate ways. We had made a plan to meet back here, between the river and the edge of the woods bordering the village of Ashenridge, by nightfall. Eryn squeezed me, looked over me with wary eyes, then mounted Lady Lace and trotted down the path toward town.

CHAPTER

ELEVEN

I left Camila to graze in the grasses at the edge of the forest. My bags and most of my belongings sat at the base of a tree near her, giving her a break from carrying them all.

I made my way into the woods to the south with a cloth bag on one shoulder for any foraged goods I may find, and my sword on my hip. I was getting used to the weight of it there. Hopefully, soon I could learn how to use it to protect myself.

The trees nestled in more closely and the greenery was lush. Vines trailed up branches. Mushrooms and moss covered half-decomposed logs.

I exhaled slowly, feeling the tension lift from my shoulders. Being surrounded by nature always had a way of calming me. It had unfailingly felt safe and had a sense of rightness to me. I smiled, soaking up how alive the forest was around me. How it emanated a sense of primordial wisdom and balance. Its trees and flora are the perfect example of the balance of life and death. The forest knew how to create, heal, and renew itself, weaving together the cycles of growth and change. The harmony that came from being surrounded by such inherent serenity was almost intoxicating.

I wandered into the woods for quite a way until the sun was high in the sky. I had come across several bushes of sun-ripened berries, which I had painstakingly picked at the expense of my thorn-pricked, purple-stained fingers.

I had also found some herbs useful for alchemy and potion-making — a talent I inherited from Gran, and one that could help us barter for supplies. The red-purple flowers of Dittany of Crete were easy to spot if one knew what to look for. The plant could be used in healing tonics and for potions of the heart. The white flowers of bloodroot appeared innocent enough, but the knobby root revealed a blood-like sap when cracked open. The sap could be used for salves in traditional healing arts, for protection and connection to ancestral bloodlines in the more forbidden arts. Henbane's delicate flowers starkly contrasted with its deadly effects when ingested, leading to its frequent use in potions and spells.

My bag was full of berries, stone fruits, herbs, and several varieties of mushrooms by late afternoon. I had turned back northward. At least I thought I had from what I could tell from the sun's position in the sky a few hours ago, but still had a way to travel before I reached the edge of the forest.

The crunching of my footsteps over fallen twigs and leaves provided a steady tempo for my churning mess of thoughts. My breath, a barely audible cadence.

I couldn't hide away in the woods forever. Couldn't avoid showing my face for fear of being discovered. The whole point of me leaving Eyloria was to have a fresh start where I didn't have to conceal who I was or what I could do.

Well, I'd have to hide my abilities regardless of where we went. If anyone caught word of me using magic, they would be obligated to report me to The Dark Army or risk the wrath of The Dark Enchantress, Queen Damay. And her wrath was *deadly*. Deadly enough that she single-handedly overthrew the entire royal Graelis family when she stole the crown thirteen years ago.

That was one point in my leaving, anyway. I also had to figure out this obscure message Gran had left me with. Why couldn't The Scroll have contained something a little more concrete? I huffed a laugh out loud to myself. I managed to interpret her bizarre last words only to be rewarded with a far longer and far more convoluted missive.

My surge of annoyance with her quickly fizzled out as a pang of grief flooded through me. Tears began flowing silently down my cheeks again. I sighed.

Maybe The Divine Feminine would pity me and help to guide me to this *mirror pond* of secrets that The Scroll mentioned. I would find this pond, learn who my parents are, find them, and—. A ragged breath left me.

Just the thought of being in the presence of my parents felt foreign to me. I had always thought them to be dead. To have died when I was an infant. Now to think that they were alive and I could meet them. Spend *time* with them. *Learn* from them. It was more than I had been able to process yet.

Goddesses, maybe *they* would know how I had somehow controlled the natural world around me. The wind and the rocks and the trees. I'd never heard of this type of magic before, but it had happened far too many times now to just be a coincidence. Maybe my parents knew why it was happening to me or how to control it. How to use it to my advantage.

As I remembered how the use of *any* magic was forbidden, a tense anger boiled up inside of me again. Even the use of healing magic was punishable by death. Why would anyone want to forbid others from healing other people?

It had been this way ever since The Dark Enchantress, Queen Ryellia Damay, had taken over the crown and began to rule over Lunaris. I felt my jaw tighten as I continued walking. She preferred to oppress the people and make their lives miserable instead of caring for them. Instead of ensuring Lunaris was a safe and desirable place to live.

And yet *she* could use magic freely. I had heard whispers she preferred to revel in dark magic. That did not surprise me one bit. Meanwhile, they could kill the rest of us for using even the slightest alchemy to help each other. I huffed, shaking my head to myself.

Now her cronies were crawling all over the realm. One could hardly go a few hours without seeing soldiers from The Dark Army. Couldn't collect their weekly earnings without having to shell it over to them in the name of The Dark Queen. They were just as bad as she was. Threatening to hurt children and steal from innocent people. Running rampant and acting without honor.

No sooner had this thought passed through my mind than I heard the voices of males echoing through the woods nearby. My breath caught and fear sliced through me.

What the fuck was I doing *alone* in the woods? *It's a little too late for that thought, Nolei.* I chided myself.

I slipped against a towering tree and tried to discern where they were coming from. They were coming from my right. Slowly, I peeked out from behind the tree, clutching the bark tightly.

Three males were on foot about 30 yards away from me, all dressed in the crimson hue of The Dark Army. My stomach felt like it sank right into my boots. They were heading directly toward me. *Fuck.*

I glanced around, as if scanning my surroundings would save me. I could make a run for it. But I likely would not make it very far before they caught me. Not to mention I wouldn't have any buildings to dash in to hide from them as I did the last time I tried that tactic. And running would make me arguably more suspicious when caught. Potential plans raced through my head.

I could hide, but there was no way they wouldn't see me. I was directly in front of where they were walking. They would be more likely to brush into me by accident than they were to not notice me.

What if I just kept walking like I never saw them? When they stopped me, I could just tell them I was gathering food.

I had to decide quickly, as they were getting closer. I took in a quick inhale, looked internally for some sense of bravery, and began walking north again. Chin up, one hand resting on my bag at my shoulder and the other swinging freely, I strode through the woods and hoped they wouldn't think twice about me. I forced myself to appear *normal...* whatever that meant.

"Look what we have here." I heard one male say. They all chucked together in a sick way that made my stomach churn.

"Halt." One of them demanded.

I stopped, turning towards them with a hand to my chest, pretending they had caught me off guard. "Oh," I stared at them, doe-eyed. "You startled me."

They smiled at each other, seemingly proud of themselves for stumbling upon me. Goddesses, I hope they let me continue without any issues. The *last* place I wanted to be was in the woods alone with these males and their questionable intentions.

"What is a pretty girl like you doing way out here in the woods all by herself?" The tallest of them asked. Here we go with the *girl* thing again. I tucked a brown wave of hair behind my sharply pointed ear.

"I was just gathering some berries." I motioned to my bag. "It's the perfect time of year to do so. They are wonderfully ripe." I continued with a saccharine smile, trying to be convincing.

The better question was, what the fuck were *they* doing out here?

"Is that so? I love berries." The heftier soldier said, licking his lips in a way that made me fight back a cringe. I gave him a bland smile.

"Why don't you share some with us, miss?" The oldest one said, reaching out as if to grab my bag.

"Plenty are lining the bushes south of here." I began backing away from them slowly, realizing quickly that was not the answer they expected of me. They were about to become a lot more disappointed in me than that if they thought I was letting them get within arm's reach of me.

"Ahh, but we'd like to sample *your* berries." The paunchy one said. "Somethin' tells me they are just as sweet as those breasts of yours."

Nausea roiled through me as fear pricked at the back of my neck. Hopefully, Thalor, The God of Valor, known for his strength and desire to protect, would drop out of the sky and save me from these vile males.

I had to get out of here. *Now.*

"Easy now, Jermaine." The older guard smiled at me. "Ignore him, miss. He doesn't know how to speak to *a lady*."

"I have to be going. My family will look for me shortly. They'll come in search of me if I don't appear back home soon." I lied, continuing to back up.

"Just let us have a look at what's in yer bag and we'll be lettin' you on your way." The tall one coaxed, extending his hand out to me.

"Yes, sir," I said as I tossed the bag across the distance and into his hands. I'd rather lose everything in it than let them get their slimy hands on me. He caught it, not expecting me to have thrown it in the first place.

They began pawing through my bag. The large one tossed a few berries into his mouth and looked in my direction, his gaze crawling all over me. "Mmmm, sweet as I imagine you are. Just like I thought they would be." The other males laughed with him.

"See, berries, like I had said." I turned slightly, readying myself to escape. "I'll be on my way now. My brothers will look for me."

"Now wait a minute." The older male started, "What do we have *here*?" He was pulling my herbs and foraged ingredients out of the bag, tossing them onto the ground. "What is a little wench like you doing with these things? They don't look like berries to me."

I swallowed, taking another step behind me. I backed right into a large tree. My voice cracked as I spoke, panic surging recklessly through me now as they began closing in towards me. "I'm a healer. I'm just collecting some things to be used in salves and such."

"Ain't no way you're healin' anyone with this Henbane, are ya, miss?" The tall one leaned forward, close enough that I could see his crooked yellow teeth.

"And this bright red thing? That sure as The Cinder Wastes ain't berries and it definitely don't look like somethin' you heal someone with."

He was speaking of the Bloodroot. I had no idea how they could recognize what herbs may or may not be used for healing but I didn't have time to figure it out.

"Somethin' is tellin' me you are doin' somethin' you shouldn't be with these plants." The large one, Jermaine, said.

My rapid heartbeat was a steady drum in my ears now.

This plan was obviously not working. There were three of them and only one of me. My mind raced, trying to come up with a way out of this and away from these repulsive males.

"Aye, and word comes from Eyloria that there's a maiden runnin' about who knows how to use magic and ain't afraid to do so." The older soldier said. "Even killed a couple of soldiers out that way, from what I hear." He positioned himself so he was directly in front of me.

I couldn't let fear be a weakness here. I refused to allow it to be. One thing was becoming clear: I had to fight if I wanted to survive. I had to kill if I wanted to live.

I looked up at him, my doe-eyed look fading from innocent to deadly.

My voice was calm and calculating now. "I hear she isn't afraid to kill a few more."

CHAPTER

TWELVE

Following my instincts, I kneed the older soldier between the legs as hard as I could. "Fucking Gods," he groaned, collapsing to the ground and curling into a ball with his hands between his thighs. The other two soldiers stood on either side of him, momentarily stunned by my little outburst.

A moment which I used to my advantage. I withdrew my sword from my left hip, not forgetting for one second that I had no fucking clue what to do with it. I jabbed at the male on my right with a shout, causing him to jump backward.

"You're a feisty little one, aren't ya?" Jermaine cooed, withdrawing his blade.

I swung at him, his block reverberating down my arm.

This was going nowhere fast. I had to hurt them enough to get out of here. I glanced down at the soldier, who was cradling himself on the ground. I had to take care of him while he was down. If he stood again, my odds of walking away from this would be even worse.

Keeping my sword at the ready, I stomped on his ribs as hard as I could. A crunch sounded below my boot. He let out a cry of pain and a wheezy cough. I cringed. I'd have to process *that* later.

The tall guard had a look of horror on his face at what had befallen his friend. Wasting no time, I shot forward at him. He blocked me, but my attack took him by surprise. We volleyed back and forth, me barely dodging his much more skilled strikes, and him trying to keep up with my relative speed.

The older guard tried to join in, leaving me outnumbered yet again. But a quick kick to his chest had him windmilling his arms as he staggered backward. The hefty soldier, Jermaine, reached out to help his comrade before he fell.

I saw my opening. Spinning between them, I held my sword in both hands and thrust it into Jermaine's middle. It took every ounce of strength I had to do so, but I fucking did it. He looked down at his stomach where my sword was jutting out of him, wrapped his hands around the blade in a sorry attempt to remove it, and then looked back at me wide-eyed.

I released my grip on the sword. *Holy Shit.* My hands were shaking. I could not believe I had just done that.

He stumbled backward, blood pouring out of the sides of his mouth and down his stomach. *Goddesses, forgive me.*

Turning back toward the last soldier standing, I came face to face with him, swinging his sword at me. I ducked, causing his blade to hit the tree I was standing next to. His sword stuck in the trunk while I reached for the dagger.

Still having no idea what to do with a dagger, I tried to listen to my intuition. I held tightly to the handle as he turned from the tree toward me, pulling his sword free. Swinging my blade down, I tried to slam my dagger into his shoulder. He caught my wrist, spinning me so my back was against his chest. He wrapped his other arm tightly around my waist.

This was it. This is how I die. I tried to fight free with everything I had left in me. I bucked and strained against his hold. He didn't budge.

His foul breath wrapped around me as he whispered into my ear, "Maybe I'll get a taste of you after all." A chill of disgust rippled through me.

Panicked, I reared my head back, connecting with his face. He howled, loosening his grip on me but still holding me tight enough that I couldn't break free. Terror rose even further in my chest, threatening to suffocate me.

I felt the wind whipping up around us, the energy of the forest stirring. Answering my call. A call I hadn't even realized I was invoking.

Just then, an arrow whizzed through the air directly at my face. I screamed, ducking my head as far as I could within his grasp.

A fleshy sound came from behind me and my captor's arms went limp. I whirled, seeing an arrow protruding from the head of the soldier, pinning him to the tree where his sword had first landed.

My breaths came out raggedly as I spun back around to look for the source of the arrow. An impressively tall male clad in all black strode casually out from between the nearby trees.

It was him.

CHAPTER

THIRTEEN

The male who had saved me was *here*. In the middle of the woods. Thinking this must be some panic-induced hallucination, I squeezed my eyes shut. Blinking them open, I stared at him as he prowled towards me.

Goddesses, he was even more striking than I remembered. My heart pounded so loudly I could hear every beat in my ears. My breaths came too quickly. They were too shallow.

He was unnaturally tall, easily a head or more taller than I was. His face was all sharp lines. His jaw was strong, with a hint of stubble. He was wearing all black, just as before. His muscled chest and shoulders were impressively wide, strapped with various swords and daggers. And his eyes. Gods, his eyes were so dark they were almost black. His hair was the same, shaved close to his head in a fade that ended in tousled dark waves at the top. Messy, but like it was meant to be that way.

Realizing my jaw had fallen open, I forced it shut. My tongue was too damn dry.

He passed the moaning male who I had stomped on. He shifted his bow to his left hand, and without breaking eye contact with me, he withdrew his sword and plunged it into the man's chest. I flinched. But a shiver of something else ran down my spine.

He flashed a white smile at me. This male came out of nowhere, witnessed this chaotic scene unfolding, joined in, and now is smiling about it?

Who was this male and how the fuck did he get here? What was wrong with him? And more importantly, what was wrong with *me*?

He was a stranger and might be after the same thing that those soldiers were. I should get out of here. Should run for my life. But I couldn't force myself to move.

"Do you always get yourself into trouble, or is this another special occasion?" He knelt and wiped the blood from his sword onto the fallen man's crimson cloak.

He recognized me.

I had to slow my breathing. Had to get myself under control. My heart was beating too quickly, the panic in my blood still too present. I wiped my forehead with the back of my hand, clearing the sweat-soaked brown curls away. I took a slow, deep inhale.

Remembering that he had just shot an arrow directly at my head, anger started to replace the panic. I lifted my eyes and met his stare. His eyes reminded me of molten chocolate.

"I wasn't getting into trouble," I growled. "I was doing just fine before you got here."

"Didn't look like it." He replied cooly as the left side of his mouth kicked up into a delicious smirk. He straightened back up to standing.

"You looked like a damsel in distress, If I've ever seen one. I've heard a lot about them before, in fairy tales and such. But never met one until now."

His smirk turned into an outright smile as he prowled toward me with his hand outstretched.

My gaze slid from his hand up his arm. His very toned, extremely muscular arm. Tattoos etched his skin, spiraling upward until they vanished beneath his cuffed sleeve.

I snapped my mouth shut again as my eyes darted back up to his face. The pounding in my ears was lessening, but my whole body still felt hot and tense.

"What... What did you say?" I asked, realizing that he had said something else.

"I said, the name is Leo." His hand was still outstretched toward me. "What are you doing all the way out here, *my sweet damsel?*"

He now stood just in front of me. Goddesses, he was *massive*. I should run.

I straightened, but my breath did not slow. It seemed somehow more shallow and insufficient than it was a few moments ago.

He was... Gods, he was beautiful. The way his near black, sweaty curls lay disheveled on his forehead and contrasted with the closely cropped sides showed off all the masculine features of his face.

My ears must have started working again, because I began to process what he had just said. *Damsel? I am no damsel.* I fixed a glare on him and pursed my lips.

"I am no damsel, and especially not 'your' damsel," I spat. I reached quickly for the dagger in my boot and lifted it defensively. "Stay back," I demanded.

His eyebrows shot up; Hands raising in surrender. "Feisty, are we? And after I rescued you and all?"

"You did *not* rescue me. Like I said, I was doing just fine."

He gave the male behind me a pointed look. The male who was now pinned to a tree by an arrow through his head and was also very, *very* dead.

"I think we're going to have to agree to disagree on that one." He said with another smirk, ignoring the fact that I had a blade extended toward him.

I eyed him wearily and dropped my arm. I huffed out a grunt of frustration and shoved past him, not stopping to shake his hand or curtsy at him or whatever it was he expected of me.

I stomped up to Jermaine, put my boot on his chest, and yanked my sword out before re-sheathing it at my hip.

Turning around, I drew up short as I realized my face was just a few inches from his chest. *Leo.* I turned his name over in my mind, repeating it to myself.

How did he get so close to me so quickly? I didn't even hear him walking up behind me. I looked up and up and right into his stunning, dark brown eyes. My breath caught in my chest.

"Let's try this again." His voice was smooth as smoke. "I'm Leo. It is a pleasure to meet you again, Nolei... was it? What are you doing way out here, my exquisite, argumentative fighter?"

"Yes. Nolei," I said with a breathy exhale while seemingly trapped in the brilliance of his eyes.

"Nolei." he repeated. "It's such a unique name."

My lips softened into a smile. "It's a nickname. It's short for Magnolia. My Gran used to call me Nolei, and it just stuck."

Catching myself rambling, I cut myself off. Why did I tell him that? Why would he care where my nickname came from or who used to call me it? He has at least three hundred more exciting things to do than stand here and listen to me prattle on, I'm sure. *Get it together, Nolei.*

"Used to?" He said, his eyes searching mine.

Fuck. Don't tell me he was actually thoughtful. It was extremely danger-ous for fae males to be both devastatingly gorgeous *and* thoughtful. My heart gave a pathetic little squeeze.

"Used to. She passed into The Garden Sanctum almost a week ago." I bent down, slid the dagger back into my boot, and started stuffing what I could find of my ravaged herbs back into my sack. "A soldier from The Dark Army killed her." The gaping hole in my chest roared to life again, empty and raw. I shoved past the pain and stood upright again.

His eyes widened immediately. "I'm sorry for your loss, Nolei." His voice was gentle and his eyes luminous as he stared down at me.

"Thanks. It's fine," I blurted out. *It wasn't.*

"It's not fine. It's cruel and unfair. It's anything *but* fine." He replied, his hands slipping up to frame my cheeks. I didn't move an inch, allowing his touch without question or fear. *What was I doing? Not using my brain, that's what. I should kick him in the balls, or even better, cut them off.*

He held me there with such gentleness that it felt like we had known each other for years. It was such an odd feeling. To feel safe and seen in the hands of a complete stranger. He smelled like a mix of fresh pine and a crackling campfire. The scent brought me right back to the first moment I had met him. I gulped and stepped back. I didn't even *know* this man.

"Thank you. I have to go." I turned, only making it a few steps before he caught my hand and spun me back around.

"Where to?" His eyes searched my face again, brows furrowing slightly.

Anywhere but here? Somewhere where I can lose my mind over what just happened with those soldiers. Where I can ruminate on all the idiotic things I just said until dawn comes and it's time to rise again. Where I can tell Eryn all of this and she can either anchor me in reality or fuel my insanity.

My blank stare apparently was not a sufficient answer to his question.

"Let me walk you back to your camp. It would be a waste to have gone through with all that saving just to have you eaten by a Brambleback."

My body shuttered in response to the thought of the boar-like beasts that roamed the woods here. I had forgotten about them. They had patchy, coarse fur covering dry, flaky skin, complete with two giant tusks. They had beady red eyes and blood-red quills that jutted from their backs. Now I couldn't unsee the image of one chasing me down to feast on me.

I pointed my chin up and tugged my hand back.

"I don't have a camp." I blurted out. *Not helping, Nolei.*

"Well, that's a problem," Leo said as one eyebrow arched up.

"Yes, it's *my* problem. Not yours. You are free to get back to ...whatever it was you were doing."

"Saving you?" He teased.

Another frustrated little grunt escaped me. "Goodbye!" I shouted as I turned to walk away for a third time.

I looked around, just now realizing that it was dusk. The sun had all but disappeared, leaving us in the near dark.

A pang of guilt hit me. I had to get out of these woods and meet Eryn. She'd be worried that I hadn't arrived yet.

I walked onward, making my way north to the edge of the woods. Realizing that I had made it a little farther this time, I started feeling rather proud of myself. That was until the scent of pine and campfire wafted around me again.

"Where does one without a camp go at this time of night?" He asked quizzically.

I spun around, pulling the dagger strapped to my leg free and pressing it to his throat. I had zero intent of actually harming him, but he didn't need to know that.

He caught my wrist, holding me with a powerful grip that was somehow still gentle. His lips kicked up into that infuriatingly tempting smirk again. He clucked his tongue at me.

"Ooh. You *are* exquisitely feisty, my damsel." He bit his lower lip as he tugged my wrist, pulling me close before I could respond. He whispered in my ear. "I like it."

Another chill ran down my spine. It wasn't fear, though. It was something much more... primal.

"*That* is none of your business." I snapped at Leo. I instantly regretted that reaction, begging myself to find some balance between smitten and rude.

He released me. I turned and continued walking.

"It kind of *is* my business now." He kept pace with me.

"Doesn't have to be. Like I said, you can go back to doing whatever it is you do."

My mind began bouncing with questions again, like a rock skipping off the water. What *was* he doing here? How did he find me? Why did he travel from Eyloria to these woods and how did he happen to stumble upon me during another crisis moment?

His smoky voice quickly drew me from my thoughts. "I think we'd both have more fun if you stopped trying to walk away from me while we were in the middle of a conversation."

I huffed, stopped walking, and looked up at the sky. It was shaping up to be a clear night.

He stopped next to me, looking up at the sky as well.

It didn't have to be like this. He appeared to be a decent male. He *was* chivalrous, for starters. He asked questions that showed a genuine interest in me. At least he *seemed* genuine. But then again, so was Calder before I found out he was smooth-talking every other woman in Eyloria.

But what were Leo's motives? Why pretend to care?

Realizing my skepticism was returning full force, I tried to push those anxious thoughts aside and look at the facts. As much as it pained me to admit, he *had* rescued me. Twice. He was likely the most handsome male I had ever laid eyes on. That was definitely a fact. He was trying to help me. Make sure I was safe. The least I could do was give him a chance and be kind to him in return. Deciding to let my guard down a tiny crack, I sighed.

"Take off your cloak," I demanded as I turned to him. If I was going to let my guard down, I was going to commit Godsdamnit.

"Excuse me?" He questioned, clearly shocked by my request. Or my demand, rather.

"Take off your cloak," I repeated simply. Smiling at him as I raised my brows.

"You don't want to talk to me and now you want me to undress for you?" He tilted his head toward me, slinging his bow back over his shoulder.

"Don't flatter yourself. Just do it." I replied, reaching my hand out to take his cloak.

He wiggled his eyebrows at me as he unclasped the buttons at his chest and swung his cloak off from around his shoulders, draping it into my outstretched hand.

"If I remember correctly, I already gave you my last cloak." He said casually. "Is this going to become a new habit of yours?"

His body was ... it was as chiseled as his arms were. His shoulders and chest were all bulky muscles that seemed to fight against the fabric of his black linen shirt. They tapered down to a lean, hard core, which was obvious despite his clothes. My gaze snagged on where his shirt slid under the waistband of his pants. Then to his hands that began pretending to unbutton said pants.

"Oh, my Gods." My eyes darted back up to his face, catching his wicked smile. "I said take off your cloak, *not* your pants." He laughed, the sound light and airy. He raised his arms innocently again.

I marched over to a relatively clear area of ground. Spreading the fabric wide, I laid his cloak out on the mostly grassy ground at our feet. Easing down onto my back, I bent my knees, looked up at the sky again, and exhaled. I needed to fucking rest for a minute or five. My body was aching from fighting and I was exhausted.

Eryn could wait ten more minutes. She was likely already losing her shit about me not being back yet. A few more minutes wouldn't matter. I looked up at the sky. The moon was already on the rise.

It was silent for a few moments. I tried willing my breath and my mind to slow. To remind myself that I wasn't fighting for my life in this moment, I was just living it.

I was already late. Eryn could wait a few moments more.

Lifting my head to look at him, I asked, "Are you going to join me or just admire my beauty from there?"

"I'm seriously considering the latter option at this point." His voice was like silk in the dark. "You are magnificent in the moonlight, Nolei."

My breath hitched as my lips parted. He couldn't be serious.

I rested my head back on the ground, my eyes roaming the dark sky. I had been traveling for several days on horseback, sleeping on the ground and washing only briefly in the river. A thick layer of dust, and now some droplets of splattered blood, covered my dark pants. My long brown hair was likely a frizzy, matted mess. *Maybe he was partially blind? And lacked a sense of smell?*

The movement of him coming to lie beside me pulled me from my self-conscious thoughts. My heart began pounding in my chest again as a nervous tingling shot through my body. One would think I'd never lain next to a male before. In reality, I'd never lain next to a male who looked like *him* before.

"So you'd rather lay beside me than speak to me standing upright?" He cooed, his voice closer to me than I had realized. "That is fine by me, my damsel."

I waved my dagger at him as a reminder that I was armed. "You stay over there and I'll stay over here. I'm not afraid to stab you."

He laughed loudly this time, the sound like sunlight glowing through the window on a chilly morning.

Trying my best to ignore the response my body had to his laughter, I asked, "So, how did you get all the way here from Eyloria? Were you following me?" I kept my eyes trained on the sky.

"On horseback. His name is Kellan, to be exact."

My head turned in his direction as I fixed a fierce glare in his direction.

My breath caught again as I realized he was lying on his side and facing me, his head propped up on one hand. Turning toward him had put our faces mere inches apart. An odd heat burned at my cheeks and neck.

"Let me rephrase that.... Leo was it?" I pretended not to remember his name. His smirk reappeared, this time revealing a dimple. As he gave me a single nod, the entirety of his attention focused on me. "Why did you travel all the way here from Eyloria and how did you find me in these woods?"

"Can't we at least start with talking about the fun stuff? Like our favorite foods or type of liquor?" He pleaded playfully. Goddesses, the way he was looking at me caused that heat to travel even lower than my neck. I couldn't help but stare at his mouth as he was speaking.

"I figured the basics were a good place to start... like how you ended up finding me twice this week when I was in the midst of running and fighting for my life."

"So you admit it?"

"Admit what?" I turned my face back to the night sky.

"That I rescued you. *Twice.*"

The skirmish in the woods that happened less than an hour ago flashed back through my mind. The gruff soldiers and their crude comments. What I had to do to fight back. How I crunched that man's ribs with my boot. Stabbed another in the stomach. *Killed* him.

How close I had come. Only the Goddesses know *what* would have happened with that last soldier who had me trapped. What I had done to those other soldiers back home. How many lives I had now taken.

My breaths began coming too quickly and too shallow again. I couldn't get enough air. My chest felt tight.

Leo slowly reached for my hand, pulling it down to rest in his. I hadn't realized it, but my hand had drifted up to cover my mouth in shock as I was thinking of all that had occurred. A warm tingle sparked at his touch and traveled up my arm.

I squeezed my eyes shut and tried to will my breath to slow. Tried to will my pulse to calm.

With my hand in Leo's, I was hyper-aware of every breath he took, every small shift he made.

"You did what you had to do to survive, Nolei." He said softly.

He must have been able to pick up on where my thoughts had traveled. He was still facing me. I turned back to face him, my eyes locked on his. Searching them for some sign that this was *okay*. That letting my guard down with him, a male I had just met, was *okay*. Not the idiotic and reckless act that the other half of my mind was convincing me it was.

"Yeah... I guess that is the theme of my life lately." I loosed a breathy exhale. I didn't even know who I *was* anymore. I had no family besides Gran. No family that I knew *personally*, that was. No home. No clue what the fuck these abilities were or how to use them. I was a stranger to myself.

He squeezed my hand gently in his. His touch anchored me back in the present.

"We all have to do what is necessary to survive. Sometimes it is gruesome, and it often involves picking the lesser of two evils. And it is *always* hard. But living is worth it. Surviving is worth it, no matter how hard the fight."

I stared into his dark eyes, now illuminated by the moonlight. My breath stilled for a moment and I felt this strange tug in my chest. Something I couldn't put words to. I felt seen. Safe.

The words he first told me almost a week ago came back to me. *You're safe with me.*

Shaking my head and pushing past that peculiar sensation in my chest, I changed the subject. "Anyway... why were you way out here in the middle of these random woods?"

"I was traveling to Ashenridge, just as you were, I'm assuming... and was tracking that group of soldiers. I heard you screaming and followed the sound. You did most of my work for me, actually."

Was he *impressed*? Is that what I heard in his voice?

"Your work?" My brows furrowed as my mind went through the various jobs that may require him to travel from city to city and track soldiers. *Kill* soldiers, from the sound of it. Silence stretched between us for a few moments before he broke it with a sigh.

"I'm in the business of ... righting wrongs." His vagueness sparked my curiosity.

I shouldered him playfully. "Yeah. You're going to need to explain that in much more detail, *Leo*." I exaggerated his name as the words rolled from my tongue.

He huffed out a laugh. "Demanding, are we?"

"I'm waiting."

I continued to stare up at the night sky. I didn't think I'd ever seen the stars shine so brightly as they did tonight, without the lamp lights of a nearby city distracting from the natural light of the stars.

The last remnant of The Weaver's Moon was high in the sky, the waning crescent still surprisingly bright. It illuminated the forest brightly enough that I could easily see the outline of his body next to mine when I stole a glance in his direction. Even without seeing him fully, I could feel the heat of him just from being close to him. Feel the energy tingling between us.

"I kind of travel around, to wherever I'm needed, and cleanse the realm of the type of people who don't deserve to exist any longer." He stated blandly. "I help them pass to the Cinder Wastes where they belong, I guess you could say." His voice had a lethal edge to it now.

Murder. Was he describing murder? I tried to let his words sink in, but then my thoughts moved to the fact that I was lying in the middle of the woods at night, alone...with a male who appeared to have spilled far more blood than I had. And I had killed five soldiers *this week*.

The part I really had to process was that even knowing that about him, I still found him painfully attractive. Vespera, help me. Something was very wrong with me.

I shot to my feet, needing to put space between us and get back to Eryn. She was probably losing her mind worrying over me. I hope she was okay. Safe. *Alone.*

I turned to Leo and tried to ignore how fucking alluring he looked cast in the moonlight. Tried to find the common sense part of my brain that clearly must have fallen out of my head earlier.

"You are an assassin. Lovely." I gave him a sarcastic little curtsy. "Thanks for helping me out.... again. Glad I could repay you by doing some of your 'work' for you. Have a good evening. I have to go."

I nodded curtly in his direction and turned, making a beeline through the trees and back to Eryn.

CHAPTER

FOURTEEN

"Nolei. Wait!" I heard him shout as he jumped to his feet. He caught up to me with unnatural speed. He didn't touch me or grab my arm, though. He just kept pace with me as I walked.

"It's not like that, Nolei." He said, running his hand through his hair in exasperation.

"I kill people, yes, but only those who *deserve* to die."

"Oh, great." I glanced over at him, wide-eyed, as I continued forward. "Let me guess... you are the one who decides who *is* and *is not* deserving of death?"

"Well, me *and* the general moral code that most of the realm follows." He side-stepped a fallen branch with ease.

"Those males were not good people, Nolei. You know that." A muscle ticked in his jaw.

"... I just have a way of keeping an ear out for people like that. Males who hurt others, take advantage and steal from those who need it. Males who act with no regard for how their actions may impact others. Who only seek pleasure and personal gain."

"How chivalrous of you."

What a fucking evening this had been. My body didn't know how to react to everything that had happened today. They say the bod responds with fight or flight. It seemed the adrenaline coursing through my veins was having a grand time encouraging me to do both.

When I woke up this morning, I never would have been able to guess all the aberrant things that happened to me today. From stabbing grown males twice the size of me, to staring at the moon with a complete, albeit handsome, stranger. To rushing through the woods in the dark with a male who literally makes a living killing people. What's next? Was The Maiden Goddess Calantha going to appear and clothe me in a silk gown?

"Don't judge me like that, Nolei." His voice was dark and demanded attention.

"It's not fair. You've killed people, too. At least one that I've seen." He said as he moved in front of me, causing me to stop abruptly.

"And I'm being honest with you," he said. His dark chocolate eyes studied my own, swirling with intensity. My breath hitched as I stared up at him.

"You want me to lie to you and tell you I'm a farmer, traveling to the city to sell my goats? A fisherman, whose boat is broken beyond repair from a violent storm in the waters of The Sleeping Tides?" He bit out, frustration clear in his voice.

"I'm being *real* with you, Nolei. Speaking the *truth*. I know we've only just met, but I know you deserve at least that."

His words caused a warmth to blossom to life in my chest, melting away the indignation. The way he was hulking over me and how quickly his anger flared to life should have been a warning to me. But it only piqued my interest. *Goddesses, I had horrible taste in males.*

"Okay, Okay. I get it." I huffed out a sigh. "Thanks for being honest with me, I guess."

Part of me wanted to believe him, to trust that he was telling me the truth. He did save me two separate times. He had miraculously appeared, right when I needed him, both times. Whether that was a coincidence or some work of the fates was yet to be determined.

I needed to get back to Eryn, get some peace, and just *be* for a moment.

Our boots crunched over the root-heavy path as we walked forward in silence for a few moments. The moon was lighting the path well enough to move without tripping. The glow-wing bugs were like stars, twinkling along the forest floor and between the giant trees. It almost seemed like they were separating and creating a path for me to move through. I caught Leo staring at how they moved in anticipation of me, as if he had noticed it too.

The moss-covered stones helped to reassure me that we were indeed heading north.

"Since you were so worried about where my camp was, where is *your* camp?" I queried, breaking the silence.

"I'm more of the roaming sort. I don't stay put in one place for too long."

"You have a way of avoiding answering questions, you know that, right?"

He laughed again, the sound fresh and light. "I don't have a camp for tonight *yet*. My supplies are with Kellan." He said, referencing his horse.

"Ah. And where is this Kellan who so faithfully carried you from Eyloria to here?"

"Enjoying some fresh grass by the river north of here." He said. "I figured I could track those soldiers through the woods more stealthily without him stirring up every animal within a mile's radius." He must have gotten off his horse near where I had left Camila. Near where I was heading to meet Eryn.

I inhaled deeply, my pace and the events of the day both starting to wear on me.

The scent of pine and campfire filled my lungs. It was becoming oddly soothing.

"And what about you, Nolei? Who do you travel with? How did you end up so damn far away from Eyloria? Despite your apparent skill with a sword, I doubt you have the same reasons to travel that I do."

I choked out a laugh. "Skill with a sword? I have no fucking clue how to wield a sword." *Probably shouldn't have admitted that to a stranger I was alone with in the dark woods.*

Even in the shadows, I could sense his eyebrows furrowing. "No clue how to wield a sword? It looked like you wielded it right into that soldier's gut."

A smile reached my lips but was quickly distinguished by the realization that we were talking about me *killing* people here. "Well, that was just pure luck and blind panic."

"More like bravery and wit," He corrected with a smirk.

"I'm starting to think you are delusional." I quipped. "I have no clue how to use a weapon. I happened to be *holding* a weapon, but that is not the same as knowing how to use it."

I really should be more careful about revealing how utterly defenseless I am in front of a total stranger.

"You have a way of avoiding answering questions. You know that, right?" He mocked, repeating what I had said to him earlier.

I sighed, debating whether I should be as truthful with him as he had been to me. "I travel with my friend, Eryn. She is waiting for me near the river. She's probably worried sick about me. And as for the second question…" I swallowed thickly. "It's a long story. One that we don't have the time for right now."

"Are you implying that we will have more time together in the future?" He purred in my direction. "If so, I happily oblige. I'd also like to ensure you know what to do with that weapon you carry. You know, *sometime in the future.*"

I felt the heat rising to my cheeks and spreading down my neck. As the trees thinned and the woods came to an end, I saw Eryn at the base of a tree with the horses. I quickened my footsteps, racing toward her.

I hadn't realized how tightly my chest was squeezing in worry that something had happened to her until I had finally laid eyes on her.

Looking ahead, Leo saw what had caught my eye. I turned over my shoulder and shouted back to him, "Oh, and to answer your other questions — freshly baked bread with butter and moonberry cordial." I flashed him a wild smile, turned back around, and ran for Eryn.

CHAPTER

FIFTEEN

I was right about Eryn being worried sick about me. Her trip into Ashenridge had been uneventful, but she had started to spiral into worse-case scenarios before I returned. By the time we had broken our hug and she had thoroughly inspected me to ensure I was alright, Leo was approaching.

I realized the moment she saw him. Her eyes went wide, and she froze.

"Nolei." She whispered under her breath as she reached for the hilt of her sword. "There is a male behind you. Get behind me. *Now.*"

I turned to face him. Before I could get a word out, Eryn had shoved me back and had her sword leveled at Leo's neck.

He raised his arms in surrender, the motion almost comical given Eryn's stature compared to his own. That infuriating smirk graced his mouth again.

"Eryn!" I started.

"Please don't decapitate me." He replied drolly. "I rather like my head."

"Keep that pretty mouth of yours shut. If you take one step closer to my friend or I, I'll stab you right in the neck." She threatened, acting like a feral dog whose turf was being threatened.

I stifled a laugh as Leo's brows rose in amusement.

"Do you plan to introduce us, or are you just going to let her threaten me all night?" He asked.

"I'm seriously considering the latter option at this point." I replied, quoting his words from earlier.

Eryn's head whipped in my direction. "You *know* him?"

I gave her a giddy smile and bit my lower lip, nodding.

"Oh, my Gods! Is that *him*?"

I nodded again, now flattening my lips together to keep from smiling like a brainless maiden.

"Hello. I'm Leo." He said, with all the smoothness of silk sliding over bare skin. "You must be a friend of Nolei's." He bowed deeply in Eryn's direction.

I huffed a laugh and rolled my eyes. *This fucking male.* Even as dark as it was, I could see him easily in the shadows cast by the light of the Seed Moon.

She let out a nervous giggle. I elbowed her.

"Hello, Leo. I'm Eryn." She managed to reply.

"Leo was just returning to his horse, who is somewhere near here, by the river," I said with an air of nonchalance.

"*Actually,* Nolei informed me you two do not have a camp set up for the night. As it is dark out, and we are all without fire or food yet..." He motioned to the sky as if we were not aware of the time of day. "I was thinking we could all make camp together tonight. No point in separating when we can get dinner going more quickly if we work together."

I blinked my eyes slowly at him, not quite believing what he was suggesting. He wanted to *remain* with us?

He *did* say he traveled often. His skill at lighting a fire likely far surpassed our own. We would be safer with him than we would be alone, too.

That was if we *were* safe with him. As I thought back to what he shared with me about his line of work, a cold shudder crawled up the back of my neck.

But then my mind shifted to the Leo in front of me. His infuriating smirk, the way he spoke his mind with ease and confidence. How he had shown genuine concern for me on more than one occasion. An unexpected realization hit me. I *was* safe with him.

Eryn interrupted my thoughts by replying. "That sounds lovely. We could use the help and I'm eager to hear all about how the two of you met in the middle of the woods." She elbowed me back.

I grunted, not expecting it. I could sense her smile even in the dark.

L eo had returned with his horse and got the fire going as we set up our makeshift tent. We roasted a chicken Eryn had brought from town and ate it with some of the berries I had managed to keep hold of.

We shared stories of our past; adventures and misadventures. Of all the shenanigans we partook in, both accompanied by and frowned upon by Cade and Malv. Leo shared just as much about the mischief he and his best friend Cardin had gotten up to. The sound of the crackling campfire and our laughter filled our camp.

Eryn had pressed us for every detail of what had occurred this evening with the soldiers and reassured Leo that I indeed had *no clue* what I was doing with any type of weapon. The talk of my developing... *abilities* or The Scroll did not come up, thankfully. I was beginning to trust him, but I didn't think I could trust him with *that*.

He was easy to talk to. He kept eye contact with me when I spoke, as if he was truly absorbing and considering every word I said. His dark eyes rapt with attention. His near-black waves of hair bounced as he nodded when I spoke.

All of it made my heart do this silly little flutter. Males had never behaved like this towards me. Like they truly *cared* about what I had to say. About who I *was*, instead of just my body. They were always flirtatious, eager to get beneath my skirt, and quick to leave after they achieved what they desired. Or leaving in frustration when they were not so lucky.

Leo was *different*. He gave me space, sitting across from Eryn and I. Sleeping across the camp from us on his outspread cloak and fur. He didn't try to touch me or suggest that one of us lay with him when it came time to rest.

He asked questions about us and our past, but he didn't push us. The way he spoke to me made me want to share more with him. Made me consider what my own desires were.

I couldn't quite understand it, but I felt at ease with him already. A part of my mind kept trying to pull me back and remind me to keep my guard up. Meanwhile, my heart was tugging me in the opposite direction, telling me it was okay to be myself with him. And that scared me. Especially because I had never had thoughts or feelings like that about any male, especially not after only knowing them for a handful of hours.

We had shared more about our journey with him. Eryn allowed me to take the lead on how much detail I felt comfortable divulging. We told him our plan to continue to follow the river.

As it turns out, he was doing the same. It would take us to the river village of Stonemere Run, where Leo was actually meeting up with his friend Cardin. After some discussion, we agreed to travel with him there. It made sense for us to do so, or so I told myself.

The next morning, I woke at dawn with Eryn nestled closely behind me, her gentle snoring barely audible. The birds chirped and sang, while small critters rustled in the undergrowth, their tiny sounds filling the forest. I slipped from our tent, careful not to wake Eryn.

Leo was already crouched next to the fire, prodding the ashes and charred bits of wood with a stick. He nodded in my direction, his tousled morning hair and coarse stubble causing a whir of heat to pool in my stomach. The sleeves of his black shirt were pushed up, revealing the thick veins that ran over the hard ridges of his muscled arms.

"Sleep well, my damsel?" He teased, a smirk playing on his lips.

I rolled my eyes dramatically. "I am no damsel." I reminded him as I strode past him, extending him the middle finger as I made my way to the river's edge. It was a good distance away from our camp. Close enough to be easily visible, but far enough away that it took me a few minutes to reach the edge.

My sense of adventure had been fanned to life by the coil of heat that was still scorching me. Keeping my spine straight and giving off an air of confidence, I stripped my tunic off over my head. My bare skin bristled at the touch of the cool morning air. My nipples hardened to tight points.

I stretched my arms overhead and then rustled them through my long brown hair, unfastening the braids that had been there for a few days. I kept my back to him, but I could feel his gaze on me. It only fueled my fire.

I kicked off my boots and unclasped my pants, stepping out of them.

Fully undressed, I waded into the river. The cold water was a shock to my heated system. A sharp inhale rushed into my lungs, the cool air inside of me a delightful contrast to the warmth in my veins. The water seemed to change in response to me, warming to a comfortable temperature.

Once in the river, I closed my eyes as I scrubbed the grime from every inch of my tan skin. Maybe if I stayed in long enough, I could cleanse myself of all the deaths I had a hand in, too.

I submerged myself, allowing my hair to flow around me. I detangled it with my fingers and only exited the river once I felt thoroughly refreshed. Felt like the blood that I spilled had been washed downstream. Felt like I was truly ready for this journey to unfold.

I strolled out of the running water with as much confidence as I had walked in with, maybe even more. Leo was staring directly at me, like a wolf watching his prey. His gaze was a caress on my skin, even from the distance.

He made no move to look away, just as I made no move to cover myself. I kept my eyes fixed on his, hoping he felt the same heat pulsing through him that I did. I kept my eyes glued to his, and I slowly wrapped the blanket around myself. If he wanted to play, he would have to work for it.

I returned to camp, walking past him without so much as a word. He raised his eyebrows at me, remaining silent. He then turned back to the fire, smirking to himself and shaking his head.

I rummaged through the saddle bag near Camilla. Eryn had traded for clothing and food yesterday, thank the Goddesses. I dressed myself in a cropped vest that cinched tightly around my chest and left my midriff bare. It displayed the bottom edges of the moons that were inked below my breasts.

I grabbed a long, flowy skirt made of a thick fabric that would be good for riding. It was dark gray and wrapped around my waist, leaving a long slit to my upper thigh. When I moved, the skirt flared open, revealing the dagger now strapped to my upper thigh.

The fresh tattoo that wrapped along my arm was visible beneath my hooded cloak, courtesy of my first meeting with Leo.

I ran my fingers along my hair, creating two braids that curled over my left ear before falling down the length of my brown waves. I fixed two smaller braids that fell from below my right ear, one with a bright green feather tied to the end and the other adorned with silver bands. I had always loved the self-expression that braids afforded. It allowed me to enhance my sense of femininity with just a few moments and a handful of trinkets. The more complex the braided designs, the better.

We packed up and just as I was about to mount Camila, Leo appeared.

"There is something that we need to do before we begin the journey to Stonemere Run," He stated as he petted Camila's muzzle, feeding her an apple from his own supplies.

"And that is..." My eyes narrowed on him, one hand still on the saddle.

"I need to teach you how to wield that sword of yours." His lips curved into an amused smile.

My eyebrows shot up. I was not expecting him to say that. Sure, he'd suggested such a thing last night, but I didn't think he was *serious*. I was not going to hold him to it, anyway.

"Right now? As we are about to mount our horses before a long day of riding?"

Eryn snorted out a laugh as she fastened her bag to Lace. I shot my head in her direction, glaring. She quickly averted her gaze and pretended to be very busy tying up her bag.

"I couldn't, in good conscience, allow you to travel another day through this realm without the knowledge of how to protect yourself." He retreated a few steps back away from the horses and motioned for me to join him. "Despite how much I *do enjoy* rescuing you, my damsel."

I rolled my eyes. "On one condition."

"That being?"

"You stop calling me that. I'm no damsel, and I'm definitely not *your* damsel." The little flutter in my stomach contradicted my words.

He raised his hands innocently as his smile widened. "After a few lessons with me, you will no longer be such, and therefore the name will no longer apply."

His lessons began by first making sure I could hold the sword and keep my balance. A logical place to start, it seemed. He slid behind me, grasping the sword over my hands in demonstration.

"Hold it firmly, but not too tight." His breath danced down my cheek. "This hand up here, and this one below."

He adjusted my hands slightly with his own, causing a bolt of tingling to crawl up my arms. The warmth of his body behind mine made it difficult to pry my mind away from its wicked thoughts and stay focused on his instructions.

After my grip had been adjusted, Leo showed me how to move lightly and quickly on my feet. He had me practice moving forward and back, side to side. He instructed me on how to guard myself with the sword in a defensive maneuver, being sure I could do so from a variety of potential attacks.

Sweat had curled the wisps of hair around my face. Although I hadn't even done any fighting yet, I was tiring from stepping and holding the sword alone.

"Are we done yet?" I panted, my hands resting on my thighs as I bent forward.

"I mean... if you think you could win in a fight by blocking blows alone?"

"At this rate, the only one I think I'll be fighting in the near future is you." I taunted. Then I remembered what he did for a living.

He tilted his head back and laughed loudly. "Another promise of more time together. I'm flattered." He placed his hand over his heart, smiling sweetly at me.

I glanced at Eryn. She was sitting cross-legged at the base of a tree, tossing nuts into her mouth and watching us. Her eyebrows raised at me as she pressed her lips tightly closed, smothering a laugh herself.

"Pretend I am one of those soldiers from The Dark Army." He motioned for me to approach him. "How would you attack me?"

"I would charge at you with my sword out, like th---" I stepped toward him a few steps, holding my sword out in demonstration.

"Show me. Don't tell me." He demanded sternly, cutting me off.

I turned around, walking back to the place I had started. *Okay, then.*

Without warning, I turned toward him and charged, sword outstretched at his midsection. He easily side-stepped me, not even having to lift his sword to protect himself. I fell forward, the unexpected momentum sending me crashing into the dirt. I groaned, rolled onto my back, and stared up into the blue morning sky.

His chiseled jaw and captivating side smile came into view above me.

"That was.... An interesting technique." He fought back a smile, reaching out his hand to help me up.

My irritation spiked. "Shut up."

I pressed myself up to standing, ignoring his outstretched hand. I dusted myself off and readjusted my vest, making sure I was well fastened inside of it. I looked up at Leo, catching his eyes on my chest before they shot up to lock with my own.

He blinked slowly, fighting another smile. "Again." He demanded. "Be fast. Be precise. Anticipate my reaction. Expect my next move. Play on my weaknesses."

That was a lot of instructions. And the way he spoke that last one made it sound like he was speaking of something other than training. Or maybe that was just my deluded mind creating false meanings.

His black shirt hugged his arms tightly, the rolled sleeves revealing dark ink that snaked up both forearms and disappeared beneath the cuffed fabric. They were...beautiful. A mesmerizing mix of Ancient Lunarian symbols, geometric designs, and ornate, botanical markings. The veins in his arms were pronounced, only amplifying the strength that emanated from him. *Focus, Nolei.*

I shifted my weight back and forth on my feet and then dusted off my skirt, revealing much of my tan legs. He *did* say to play on his weaknesses.

I took a deep breath, exhaling slowly as I steadied my grip on my sword. I circled him. I swung my sword at him with all my strength. This time, he deflected my blow with his sword. The contact reverberated up my arm, causing my bones to ache.

"Fuck" I grunted.

"Maybe later." He said impassively. "Right now, you need to learn how to protect yourself, Nolei."

Heat scorched my blood at his response. I glared at him. "Very Funny."

"I have been told I have a sense of humor to match Aurel's." He said, referencing the God of Wit, who was known for his sharp tongue and intelligence.

I charged at him again. This time, feigning right but moving left, catching him off guard. I swiped up at him with my sword. Almost stepping

121

into my blow, he deflected it just in time. Eyebrows raising in surprise, he stepped back. "Beautiful."

"Thanks, I'm freshly bathed as of this morning." I flashed him an impulsive smile of my own, knowing what images that statement would conjure up for him.

I immediately struck again, this time chopping downward. He spun out of the way, barely avoiding the slice of my sword.

"You have the tenacity of a ferocious warrior, Nolei." He sheathed his sword and put his hands on his hips. I couldn't tell if he was being sarcastic or not.

I let my sword fall to my side, satisfied with myself.

"Maybe with a few more sessions, your sword skills will match the sharpness of your tongue."

"And yet you have no idea what I can truly *do* with this tongue." I cooed.

I glanced at Eryn. She mouthed "*wow*" to me silently, finishing the word with a bite to her bottom lip.

My eyes moved back to Leo, catching him practically devouring me with his gaze. I felt his eyes trace the lines of my body, from my deep slit and exposed dagger, to my cinched breasts and readied sword.

The way he looked at me caused my heart to pick up pace and my cheeks to flush. Satisfaction turned up the corners of my lips. I'm glad I wasn't the only one who could pose a distraction here.

I stared at him, brows raised, and casually waited for him to return his eyes to mine. When he finally did, I gave him an elaborate curtsy before sheathing my sword and returning to Camila. I heard his airy laugh from behind me.

CHAPTER

SIXTEEN

We traveled with ease along Rolling River, making our way South-East. The river curved gently in that direction, its mouth letting out at The Calanthian Sea. Just thinking that I would travel from Eyloria to the opposite side of the realm made my stomach flutter like I'd eaten a breakfast of butterflies.

My body was getting used to the hours on horseback. The tightness and tension, although still present, were largely easing from my back, hips, and legs. I mixed a muscle salve from foraged mint and knitbone that was glorious at easing the aches at day's end.

Leo's knowledge of our surroundings and keen observation skills were impressive. He seemed to be intuitively connected to the world around him and knew an incredible amount about Lunaris as a whole.

He taught Eryn and I how to track and hunt animals for food. I tried to ignore the fact that he was used to tracking and hunting more than just animals. His true work of "righting wrongs" gnawed at me often. But who was I to judge? As he said, I had done killing of my own.

Eryn excelled at keeping us entertained. She had a knack for revealing embarrassing details of my past to Leo with her storytelling. The similarities between Leo and her brothers were vast, and they quickly began to behave like siblings.

The river was wide and slow-moving to our left. Its waters bright blue with areas of turquoise. As we traveled, the visible peaks of The Pinebarrow Mountains faded into the distance behind us. The air was warming slightly, allowing us to shed our cloaks during the mid-day hours.

Each day started similarly, with an hour or so of training before we began riding. Eryn had joined in on the "lessons." Some mornings Leo taught us certain moves and attack combinations. Others, he'd stand back and watch Eryn and I spar, critiquing our form and techniques as we went.

Even though I was overconfident and Eryn clumsy, we were making progress. I started to feel like I actually knew what to do with a sword. How to defend myself, as Leo had put it.

Not only was he imparting his skill set onto us, but he was making sure I would never again be vulnerable. I would never again be helpless. Once I realized *that* was his true motive behind these lighthearted lessons, I began to appreciate the *gift* he was giving me. Even if I wasn't ready to admit that to him yet.

We passed the typical array of travelers on the road. Merchants with carts full of goods, both exotic and household wares, looking to trade and barter. Some pilgrims on their way to the various locations perceived by them to have spiritual value, where they could offer worship to The Divine Feminine in hopes of receiving their blessings.

We even passed a few families who were relocating in search of a better life. Their farmland or orchards could no longer prosper enough to keep food on the table and money in the pockets of The Dark Enchantress's Tithe-Wardens.

Prior to The Dark Queen's rule, most major cities were overseen by an Archmatron. They were appointed by Queen Graelis herself to govern over the various provinces of Lunaris. Those who were chosen as Archmatrons were not only wise but also had a deep understanding of the land and its people. They oversaw their provinces, maintaining peace and prosperity, while upholding the royal family's vision for the realm.

That was until The Dark Queen took over and killed every Archmatron in a gruesome and public display of power. She replaced them with her own self-appointed cronies, relabeling them Tithe-Wardens. They squeezed every last coin out of the people of their province and rooted out any opposition to The Dark Queen's rule. They were wealthy, glorified blood-hounds. Often just as sadistic as The Dark Queen herself, or so it was said.

I shook my head, forcing myself to un-clench my jaw at the thought of how fucked Lunaris had become.

As a distraction, I played the words of The Scroll over in my mind as we rode.

Follow rivers' twining path,
Through shadowed glens, unseen.

There, the truth of blood and wrath,
Awaits in forest green.

Soon we would arrive in Stonemere Run, at the end of the "rivers' twining path," and so far I had no idea where to go next. Eryn hadn't mentioned any more about The Scroll or the deeper purpose of our journey in front of Leo.

She didn't seem to worry over it, either. She remained lighthearted. I was trying and failing to remain the same. The reality of my situation hid just below the surface and kept pulling me under.

The simplest things would remind me of Gran, filling me with raw grief. The constant fear of being recognized by The Dark Army and being killed outright for my crimes. Or worse, be taken prisoner.

The vast unknown — about my parents, my heritage, my powers. It was all too much. The closer we got to Stonemere Run, the more the dread filled me. I hoped this trip wasn't for nothing. That we wouldn't end up homeless wanderers, or dead. But hope was a dangerous thing. It opened you up to even more pain and vulnerability and easily morphed into desperation.

Not only that, but I also had this clenching feeling in my chest at the thought of parting ways with Leo. Even though we had just met and I had kept him in the dark about what our true purpose was, there was something in the way that he looked at me. The way he saw *me*, not just who I used to be or just another woman. He saw the *real* me. It made my heart stutter. I wasn't ready to say goodbye to him. Not yet. Realizing how foolish of a thought this was, I shook my head at myself.

"Everything okay over there?" Leo's smooth voice came from my left.

Realizing he had seen me shaking my head, I replied, "Yes. Just a fly bothering me." I flapped my hand around my face a few times to make my lie more believable.

He nodded silently, looking forward again.

I looked forward, seeing a small group pulled to the side of the road in the distance. As we approached, I could see that they were a group of four. A male and woman and their two teen children, from what I could guess. One child, a girl, was sitting at the edge of the road, grasping her foot. We slowed the horses, and I hopped down. Leo followed closely behind me, keeping his hand on the hilt of his sword.

"Is everything okay here?" I inquired as I approached slowly. "My name is Nolei. I'm a healer."

Eryn dismounted, grabbed my reins, and walked our horses to the other side of the road to graze.

The father spoke, his face lighting up with relief. "Our daughter suffered a snake bite a few hours back while venturing into the woods to see to her needs. We had hoped it was only a minor bite, but she is in a great deal of pain now and it seems to be getting worse."

He was tall, but not as tall as Leo. He had a full brown beard and shaggy brown hair, covered mostly by a straw hat. They were all dressed plainly, in home-sewn clothing in muted colors. The daughter was clenching her leg, her mother kneeling at her feet and removing her boot.

"I'm sorry to hear that." I approached the daughter, kneeling at her side.

"May I?"

She nodded quietly, wincing. Her face was pale and sweat beaded at her temples.

My brows furrowed as I caught sight of her wound. Two deep puncture marks marred the bottom of her calf, the surrounding area now swollen and an angry red. Red lines streaked up her calf. The bite mark was also beginning to ooze a gray-purple substance. *This was not good.*

"Did you see what type of snake it was?" I gently asked the girl.

She looked up at me, shaking slightly. "No... No, I didn't. It bit me and I screamed, running out of the woods and away from it. I didn't get a look at what kind."

"That's okay. You did the right thing." I reassured her, rubbing her shoulder gently. "I'm afraid the bite was a poisonous one, though."

She nodded solemnly, realizing that her chances of surviving such a bite were slim.

Her mother looked up at me, her eyes wide and frantic. "Can you help her, miss?"

"I think I can, but I'll need a few moments to prepare the cure," I replied with a warm smile.

I rustled through my bag of healing supplies and herbs. Although I did not have my usual repertoire, I had a decent stock between what I had packed from home and had foraged so far.

This bite was grievous.... And would be lethal if I didn't act quickly. It also would not respond to any tonic a healer could offer. It would require me to use a touch of magic, the forbidden kind.

Doing so was a risk — I would have to hope that this family could be trusted not to speak of what they would see. I didn't get the impression that Leo would be quick to betray my confidence, either, especially given his aptitude for killing soldiers.

Luckily, I had packed Gran's tome on healing arts. Ancient and filled with generations of knowledge on the art of potion-making and alchemy, the pages were so fragile they almost crumbled between my fingers.

I flipped through until I found a passage on Serpent's Bane. I had the major ingredients. Echinacea, to heal the body from the venom. Henbane, although highly toxic, when paired with the right magic, the toxicity could be redirected to attack the venom instead of the host. Honey, to soothe the wound. And Blood, to add the essence of the victim so that the blood could be identified and cleansed from the poison.

Once I had found what I was looking for, I searched for the optimal place to create such a potion. It had to be rooted in nature so that the natural energies could be called upon.

Nature was the strongest life force that existed. All alchemy was best performed in a place that honored such strength. I found a large tree stump and kneeled at the base.

Closing my eyes, I placed my hands into the soil on either side of the stump. First, I called upon the blessings of Vespera, The Crone of The Divine Feminine. Her wisdom would be needed here. I began chanting the words required for the potion.

"Venom to bane, life reclaim, by earth and blood, be whole again."

I chanted them over and over as I worked. I could feel Leo watching me, his back resting against a tree nearby as he monitored the family's reaction. Eryn was used to seeing me do such work. She waited patiently with her arms crossed to my right.

With my mortar and pestle resting on the stump, I ground the Echinacea and Henbane into a powder. The toxic and healing mix a stark contradiction to each other. Mixing in the honey, I created a thick, sweet-smelling paste. As I continued chanting, calling on the power of Vespera and the natural world around me, the mixture let off a thick gray smoke. Next, I'd need a drop of her blood.

I approached the girl and her family, well aware that what they saw in me was likely shocking to them. But it would be worth it. Her mother had *begged* me to help her. I knelt at the girl's legs.

"I will need a drop of your blood to complete the cure," I whispered to her, her eyes wide as she stared at the smoking mixture.

She nodded tentatively, her eyes full of fear.

"This will hurt and then you will be well," I promised.

I reached my hand up to Eryn, who handed me a leather strap. I handed it to the girl. She bit down on it.

Withdrawing the dagger from my thigh, I approached the wound. Looking up at her brother and Leo, I spoke. "Steady her leg." They did as I requested, kneeling.

I held my dagger mere inches from the wound, looked into her green eyes, and nodded. She bit down harder, closing her eyes.

The scream that came from her was hardly muffled by the leather strap. It made the hairs on the back of my neck stand up. She fought and thrashed, but her leg remained still. Held firmly in place by Leo and her brother.

The tip of my dagger cut into the center of her bite, between the two fang marks. The gray-purple pus seeped out, pouring down her leg. I sliced a shallow X into her calf, drawing her blood onto my blade. Quickly, I held the blade flat as I poured the toxic paste onto it. When it contacted the blood, the smoke turned red and a sizzling sound rose from the dagger. I closed my eyes again and continued chanting.

"Venom to bane, life reclaim, by herbs and blood, be whole again."

I repeated it until the sound stopped. Opening my eyes, I saw that the blade had stopped smoking. I tipped the dagger vertically over the wound and the mixture poured into the raw, marred flesh. She screamed.

It absorbed quickly, pushing the rest of the foul-smelling pus out. Then, it healed over completely, leaving fresh pink skin behind and a pale scar. I exhaled shakily. Leaning in closer, I could see that the scar was shaped as the symbol of The Divine Feminine. A circle with a small cross extended below, and two crescents extended from either side of the circle. To represent The Mother, The Maiden, and The Crone united in femininity. It was a permanent mark that would forever reveal that magic had been used to heal there. A lifelong tribute to the blessings gifted today by the Goddesses.

The girl's crying ceased, but she continued panting for some time, trying to slow her breathing. When she was finally still, the males released her leg.

Leo stared at me in what looked like awe. His lips were parted slightly, deep brown eyes wide. Her mother began crying and thanking me profusely. Her father asked what he could give me in return for saving her.

I declined their offers. All I needed was for them to not speak of what they had seen here. To not give The Dark Army another reason to want me dead. I didn't have to speak that, though. It went unsaid.

Until Leo approached the father, hand again on the hilt of his sword.

"I'm assuming you will use discretion when speaking of what you have witnessed here." His voice was dark like a moonless night, filled with the promise of pain.

The father gulped. "Of course. We will not speak a word of it. Not ever." He promised, shaking his paling face back and forth.

We again mounted our horses and continued. Not speaking of what had just occurred.

After riding for some time, my steely facade crumbled. What I had done back there, how I saved that girl, was all something I had learned from Gran. From how to assess a wound to which combination of herbs and tinctures were needed to heal. But she was gone. We would never heal another person together. All that was left of her was her legacy that lived on in me. The healing that I could offer through my own hands.

Silent tears quickly turned to shuddering sobs. It was all I could do to keep hold of Camila's reins. Eryn rode closely beside me, trying to offer soothing words. Leo gave us space.

I made a silent vow to continue to honor her by using my hands to heal and my words to soothe. I prayed to Vespera that I would be half the healer and have a quarter of the wisdom she had. Goddesses, hold her soul.

CHAPTER

SEVENTEEN

"So, you have your own place here?" I repeated to Leo as we arrived in Stonemere Run the next evening. "And you are sure it's okay if we stay a few nights?"

He sighed and turned to me, giving me a pleading look and a weak smile.

"Yes, Nolei, for the hundredth time. It is okay if you stay with us for a few nights. And yes, when you ask me again in a few moments, the answer will still be yes."

Eryn stifled a laugh, obviously amused by how well Leo knew me and knew just how to irk me.

I let out an exasperated sigh of my own. I did not want him to feel like we were intruding on his ... private space. Even though we had spent the last several days only a few feet apart at any given moment, this felt different. This was his own personal lodging with his best friend, not a makeshift camp in the woods.

I looked around eagerly as we entered Stonemere Run, trying not to miss a single detail of this new city. It had similarities to Eyloria, but was also vastly different.

Situated across the river from where we had been traveling, we first had to pass over a giant wooden bridge. I couldn't wrap my head around how it could have possibly been built, given how far it stretched over the river without any support beams from below. It must have been fashioned before magic was forbidden.

Before The Dark Enchantress, Queen Ryellia, seized the throne, magic was used regularly. Not everyone could wield it, but certain magic was passed down through family lines or gifted from The Divine Feminine. Well, all magic was a blessing from the Goddesses. It was often initially gifted to a family line based on good deeds or to those who were born under rare celestial events, like on the night of an eclipse. It was even said that some babes born whilst still covered by their bag of waters carried the gift of magic.

Most who carried magic could only wield lesser magics, like coaxing crops to grow a little faster, purifying water with a touch, or summoning a small guiding light in the dark. Other families, like the Royal Graelis Family, had mighty powers. They were all Nightbinders and could command darkness, or so it was said. And there were witches who were adept at the arcane arts. They could use magic as easily as the rest of us could breathe. But now anyone who had magic was dead or hiding their abilities to stay alive.

Even though it was well-kempt, I felt unease ripple through me as we rode across it, praying it would hold while we crossed.

The city itself was situated along the bank of the river. Several small fishing boats peppered the shore. Larger vessels were anchored within view at the bay of The Calanthian Sea.

The buildings were made of stone and covered in ivy. The roofs were terracotta and there were many roof-top gardens. That was where the beauty ended, though.

The buildings were almost on top of one another, leaving little space for recreation. The cramped layout made moving through the city difficult. It was obvious that this city was overcrowded, just as Eyloria was becoming.

From what Leo had told us, many families were relocating to cities in search of work, as they could no longer afford the expansive farms their families had owned for generations. Ever since The Dark Enchantress had usurped the crown, the masses were becoming more and more impoverished. The streets stank of poor sanitation and sickness was rampant. Rats scurried along alleyways and sewage ran freely down the drainage ditches on the road's edge.

Eryn and I were trying our best not to gag. Thankfully, as we got further into the city, the air cleared slightly and homes had a little more space between them.

Leo and his friend, Cardin, rented a flat together, and both came and went as they pleased. Despite his vagabond lifestyle, he spoke fondly of Stonemere Run and the apartment they shared here.

We walked up a narrow stone stairwell into a loft apartment. Leo grabbed his dagger from his waist and picked the lock. Well, that's one way of getting into your own home.

Eryn gave me an uneasy glance.

"Are you sure this is your place...?" I asked, half kidding.

"As sure as I am of my own name." He said with a smirk as he opened the door.

The apartment was basic, but cozy. A small kitchen sat to the left of the door. There was a wooden table with four mismatched chairs. A bowl of apples and some half-melted candles sat as a centerpiece.

To the right was an enormous stone fireplace with a cooking pot set off to the side. A fur rug covered the floor in front of the fireplace, likely originally belonging to some creature killed by either Leo or Cardin, if I had to guess. A wooden sofa and two wooden chairs surrounded it, both fitted with large cushions.

Two doorways opened up beyond the kitchen and living space. I assumed those were the male's rooms. A small bathing chamber was to our immediate right, almost hidden by the open door.

The loft was humid, but a cool evening breeze blew through the open windows. Leo took our cloaks from us and hung them on a hook near the door.

"Make yourselves at home, ladies." He motioned toward the apartment with a sweep of his arm.

"I can't believe two males live here alone." Eryn blurted out. "It's so... clean. And it smells like.... Like cloves and spices."

"Eryn!" I scolded, shoving her. Not only were we intruding, but now she was insulting them.

"What? I speak the truth!" She shoved me back.

Leo graced us with one of his wide smiles that said we were entertaining him greatly. "Ah. Well, Cardin likes to bake. And despite my ability to sleep on the ground without batting an eye, neither of us likes to live in filth."

He strode over to the wooden table, his long legs closing the distance in just a few steps.

"It looks like it's your lucky day, Nolei."

I walked into the kitchen, peering around him to see what he was speaking of. He sliced a thick hunk of bread, buttered it, and placed it in my hand. "Looks like Car just made a fresh loaf of bread. Your favorite."

Eryn tilted her head at us, clearly wondering how in the Cinder Wastes he knew that was my favorite thing to eat.

I was too busy drooling over it to care what she was thinking. I let out a moan and took a bite. Gods, it was incredible. It was still warm from the hearth and practically melted in my mouth. It was ... I chewed slowly, appreciating every morsel... it was raisin and spice.

I opened my eyes, not realizing that Leo had been watching my completely unhinged reaction.

He gave me a smoky smile. "If that is how you respond to warm bread, I can't wait to see how you respond to the touch of a male."

I clamped my mouth shut and wiped a crumb from my lip, leveling him with a glare.

"Pretentious of you to presume that you'll ever be lucky enough to witness such a thing."

"Get a room, you two," Eryn shouted from the living quarters. "Oh wait! Now that we're here, you have one. Thank the Gods."

I turned to scowl at her, but her back was to me. She was running a hand along the back of the sofa and walking toward the washroom.

Leo laughed quietly to himself and turned back to the table. He grabbed a slip of parchment lined with bold strokes of ink.

"Looks like Car is on a job today. We'll meet him out later."

"The first thing I'm going to do is take a hot bath," Eryn shouted from the bathing chamber, clearly making herself right at home. "However many days we were just traveling was far too long for me to go without one, I've decided."

Leo set to heat water on the hearth for her tub. "And for that, we are grateful."

I stifled a laugh. "I knew you'd miss having a bath the most!" I shouted in to her.

Leo continued boiling water whilst bringing me slice after slice of buttered bread. I grabbed a small array of sweet-smelling oils from my bag and the flower petals I had gathered on the trip to add to the bath water. If we were going to go through the work of readying a hot bath, we would make it as lavish as possible.

"Good Gods, I'll be smelling like a daisy when you two are done with me," Leo joked from the fireplace.

"You'll be so fragrant that even Lysander won't be able to resist your allure." I teased, referencing the lesser God of Romance.

Leo scoffed.

Eryn went first, soaking until the water cooled. Leo added a pot of hot water to the tub for me when she had finished.

I sank into the fragrant warm water and let out another moan, this one much quieter than when I had first tasted Cardin's bread. All the tension seemed to seep from my muscles and dissipate into the water.

After washing my hair, I used the razor I had packed for the first time since we left Eyloria and shaved the growing hair from my legs. When I had finished washing, I rubbed one oil along my now smooth legs, relishing in the relaxing aroma. I had never had a bath feel this luxurious before. Bathing in an icy river for weeks could do that, I guess.

I padded out into the living quarters with a fluffy white towel wrapped around me. I didn't want the water to grow too cool before Leo had a chance to bathe.

Eryn was already dressed. She wore a long, low-cut dress with billowy sleeves. A corset was cinched tightly around her, emphasizing her perfect curves. She had likely been dying to switch out of pants the moment she knew she wouldn't need to be riding a horse.

Leo, crouched by the hearth, turned his head as I strode out. He raised his eyebrows at me before turning back to the hearth, shaking his head silently and biting his lip in response to the sight of me in just a towel. I gave Eryn a wicked smile behind his turned head. "You're up, Leo," I said, innocently.

He stood up, stretched his arms overhead, and then peeled his shirt off. The definition of his chest and shoulders made my breath hitch. His tan, tattooed skin looked even more glorious in the dim light of the loft.

Bending down, he grabbed the large kettle of hot water and heaved it up, his muscled arms bulging with the effort. My mouth felt too dry as heat rolled up my neck and pooled lower in my core. I turned away, trying to ignore him and how my body responded to him. I guess two could play that game.

I dressed similarly to Eryn, choosing a flowy dress that hugged close to my breasts and cinched at my waist. I fastened my dagger to my thigh, wanting to be ready in case we ran into any trouble. Which seemed to be the theme for me as of late.

To celebrate a night out, I fashioned my hair with more effort than was typical. Leaving some pieces loose in the front to frame my face, I created a waterfall of braids along my crown that wove down into long fishtails on either side. It was whimsical and ornate.

When Leo had finished bathing, he dressed in all black, as he always did. A loose tunic and black pants. Eryn and I taunted him about how he did indeed "smell like a daisy" after bathing with all the oils and petals we had fixed the bath water with. He somehow still carried the scent of crackling fire and fresh pine, though.

By the time we finished getting ready, the sun had set. Leo led us along the cobbled streets to a tavern whose windows were lit with a buttery warm glow. When he opened the door for us, the sound of laughter and music poured out onto the street. I was immediately hit with the smell of rich meats and ale.

Leo held the door, a smirk playing on his lips. "After you, my ladies," He cooed.

CHAPTER

EIGHTEEN

We found a table in the middle of the Tavern. We were quickly served large tankards of bitter ale. The first few sips went down a little rough, but by the time half of mine was gone, my head was buzzing with warmth and my body was swaying to the music.

Leo motioned for the waitress, requesting that she bring us some stew. Within a few moments, steaming hot bowls of herb-laden beef stew sat in front of us. She even brought a basket of freshly baked rolls with a side of butter. Leo wiggled his eyebrows at me as he bit into a roll. I took a sip of my ale, raising my brows in return over the rim of the glass.

Leo seemed to know everybody here. Two males and a female joined us. One with light brown hair named Gevel, the other with long black hair who went by Lew. Gevel sat playfully on Lew's lap. Lew and Gevel were partners. They had been together for several years now. The female had luscious curves that were easily visible through her sheer dress, and her friends called her Ryley. Gevel and Ryley were siblings — twins, to be exact. Their ebony skin gleamed with a captivating beauty that turned heads, a radiance impossible to ignore.

They were welcoming and made us laugh until my ribs ached. They shared stories and included us on inside jokes, causing us to 'cheers' our mugs several times and ale to splash onto the table just as many times. More raucous laughter ensued.

Gods, it felt so good to let loose and just have fun. This is the first time I had had fun since Gran passed. Since everything went to shit.

I could just be Nolei tonight. There was no pressure to be anyone but myself. I didn't have to be the granddaughter of the healer or the "girl" who killed soldiers with forbidden magic. I didn't have to make myself smaller. I didn't have to hide who I truly was. I could just be. The freedom was intoxicating.

By the time we were on our second tankards, a tall male with bright blonde hair entered the tavern and approached us. It was cut similarly to Leo's, short at the sides with some length in front. His stark blonde hair made him easily stand out. Leo stood, clasping his forearm and bringing him into a hug.

"Ladies, meet Cardin. Cardin, meet my ladies."

He was extremely handsome. He had a dimpled chin and pale blue eyes.

Cardin grasped Eryn's hand lightly, kissing the top of it and nodding at her. He did the same to me. I tipped my head at him with an acknowledging tilt.

"Leo's ladies? I imagine you both have titles you prefer over that one." He said with a snort as he raised his brows in Leo's direction.

"You would imagine correctly." I replied. "I'm Nolei and this is Eryn."

"It is a pleasure to meet you, Nolei and Eryn." He sat down beside Eryn, grabbing a tankard from a passing server.

"Where the fuck have you been?" He raised his chin at Leo after taking a sip of ale.

"I've missed you, too." Leo raised his glass in Cardin's direction before taking a swig.

The conversation continued on as Leo and Cardin filled each other in on the last few weeks' happening. Including how he had "rescued" me twice, to which I rolled my eyes dramatically.

The music was growing louder, as was the sound of laughter. The tavern filled with a boisterous energy as the melodies of the fiddle paired with the rhythm of the drum.

I was watching Leo tell a story about the time he and Cardin won in cards against a pirate captain in the port city of Leisport, walking away with pockets heavy with coins and jewels. The way his lips moved and strong angles of his jaw were only improved by his laughter. He was mesmerizing.

Leo caught me staring at him. He met my gaze with those vibrant brown eyes that swirled with intensity.

"You know what would make this night even better?" He asked the group.

"If you paid for all of these drinks?" Lew joked. Everyone laughed

"If these ladies got the chance to dance. They've been stuck on horseback for weeks and haven't been able to appreciate this type of music and merriment in some time. I imagine they want nothing more after their travels."

I gave him a skeptical look, wondering what he was up to.

Before I could protest, Eryn shot up out of her chair and grabbed onto my arm. "Yes! We'd love to dance." She pulled me up as I glared at Leo, who answered my look with a mischievous smile. Cheers broke out around the table as everyone stood to join us.

Leo strode over to the band, whispered to the male playing the lute, and handed him a few coins. The male nodded. Shortly after, a lively, even louder tune filled the Tavern.

Several other shouts of excitement broke out across the tavern as others rose to join in upon hearing the music change.

Eryn grabbed my hand, trailing me out into the center of the tavern where several males had moved tables to create a makeshift dancefloor. We swung around and around, locking elbows and turning with the turns of the music. People along the edge of the floor clapped and stomped their feet in time with the beat.

The males were dancing alongside us, leading us in circles through the center of the tavern and swapping dance partners all at once. There were no practiced steps to this dance. We were just dancing and moving recklessly..

We continued on, swaying and twirling, clapping and dipping. My dress was damp where it clung to me as we danced on and on. I glanced around, noticing that everyone's face had a slight gleam of sweat from all the movement, too.

I locked eyes with Eryn who was dancing with Gevel as I was being spun by Cardin. The smile on my face was as wide as hers.

Suddenly, all the males shouted "Ho!" and twirled us women to new dance partners. Finding myself face to face with Leo, I took a sharp inhale.

His hand was on the small of my back, feeling like a deliciously warm brand on my skin. He held one of my hands in his as he guided me along the chaotic tavern floor, which was now slick with spilled ale.

He leaned into me and spoke into my ear, sending a spark through me. "Enjoying yourself, Nolei?" He pulled back just enough for me to lock eyes with me again. This time, his brown eyes looked like heated molasses.

"I am." I admitted. His smile kicked up a notch as he stepped back, twirling me away from him and then back into his chest. I let out a squeal of delight. Righting me, he again placed his hand on my back. The touch shot a ripple of heat through me.

The males shouted again, signaling it was time to switch partners. Except Leo held onto me instead of passing me to the next male.

Cardin shouted at Leo over the din, "Give her up, man. It's my turn to show her how a proper male dances!"

"Not a chance, Car." He retorted, turning us so that my back was to Cardin.

Eryn laughed, grabbing onto Cardin's arms and pulling him into the dance once more.

"Sorry to say, but that is a battle you are not going to win." I heard her say to Cardin.

Leo moved in closer again, this time not pulling away. "I've been waiting weeks to get you into my arms and now that I have you, there's no way I'm giving you up so easily." His voice was like smoke in my ear. It sent a ripple of awareness down my neck and spine.

Deciding to return the torturous favor, I replied, my lips brushing his ear. "Now that you have me? Is that what you think?"

"It is." He answered with a growl into my ear. "I only speak the truth, my damsel."

Just then, he spun me again unexpectedly. I let out a laugh as I held onto his hand, allowing him to guide me back. He spun me back into him, this time dropping me into a dip so deep that I thought I'd fall. He supported my weight with ease, though, bracing one hand around my waist and the other behind my head.

Our faces were close enough that I could feel his breath brush my lips. Time slowed as I felt a tingle of need in the space between us.

I thought he was going to kiss me. I wished he would kiss me.

Impressed cheers broke out from the surrounding crowd in response as he lifted me back up and continued swirling us around the ale-dampened tavern floor with expert grace.

We continued on this way for some time, dancing together as everyone else continued swapping partners and moving merrily about. Feeling thoroughly exhausted and overheated, I pulled Leo to the side of the floor to catch my breath.

"Would you like to get some fresh air, Nolei?" He asked, worry creasing his brow.

I turned to look for Eryn just in time to catch her and Ryley climbing to dance together atop a table. She was looking for me as well. She shot me a knowing look, nodding in encouragement. Knowing that she was safe with Leo's friends, I agreed.

"Yes, I would. I'm sweating my blouse off."

Leo let out a snort of laughter. "Ever the lady..." He crooned, guiding me out of the tavern by the hand. Even a touch so simple sent my heart bounding.

We walked to the side of the tavern that faced the river, our backs resting against the wall. He released my hand as he leaned against the wall beside me.

"Your friends are a lot of fun." I said, breaking the silence.

"So are you, Nolei."

I felt a blush cover my cheeks.

"And you are an excellent dancer. Where did you learn to dance? You must have danced like that with hundreds of other ladies to gain such experience." The thought was like a splash of cold water to my veins, causing me to recoil internally.

"None as witty and enticing as you, Nolei." He replied in what seemed like an honest manner, as we stared out at the reflection of the full moon on the water. "But I have had some lessons."

I snorted. "Well, I'd pay good coin to witness that."

We stood outside the tavern in relative silence, except for the muted sound of music and laughter from within. The inches between our shoulders felt almost tangible. All of my awareness was on how close we were together without touching.

Just thinking of him, his dimpled smile, his magnificent body, his highly irritating sense of humor — it was all causing my blood to heat and skin to flush. I didn't want to be this far away from him.

This was going to be one of our last nights together, ever. In a few days, Eryn and I would leave in search of this mirrored pond... wherever that may be ... and Leo would be returning to his life as it was. Traveling and righting wrongs.

I was sick of feeling grief and shame and dread. I wanted to feel joy and lust and pleasure. And I wanted to feel those things with him.

"What are you thinking about?" He asked quietly, facing the water. I looked over at him. His body was silhouetted and his tousled hair was damp from dancing.

"How badly I want you to kiss me." I blurted out honestly before I lost my nerve.

His quick inhale was audible. I froze, praying to the Goddess Elowen, the Mother Goddess of desire and sexuality, that he wouldn't dismiss me. Prayed that he felt the same desperation toward me as I did toward him.

He turned his head, his eyes like swirling pools of darkness in the moonlight. "Is that so?" His voice was smoky smooth again, curling around me and sending shivers along my skin.

"I only speak the truth." I replied, parroting what he said inside, as I tilted my head slightly.

Without another word, he moved. Framing his body against mine, he placed his forearm above my head on the stone wall of the tavern and his other hand gently on my chin. Lifting it, he brought my mouth to his.

His lips were soft and the kiss sweet. He gently pressed his lips to mine and pulled back slightly, testing my response. I pushed toward him with mine, returning the gentleness and testing the waters.

His hand slid from my chin to the side of my face, fingers curling into my hair. I parted his lips with mine, beginning to kiss him with more force. Our kiss quickly turned greedy and suddenly our lips were crashing into each other, tongues moving.

Gods, this kiss was everything. I had never been kissed like this in my life. Yes, I've kissed males before plenty of times, but never with this much need. With this much carnal desire coursing through my veins.

I brought one hand to his chest, feeling his muscles beneath his shirt. The other wrapped around his neck, pulling him in closer to me. His hips pressed into me, causing sparks to tingle along all the spaces where our bodies met and all the spaces they hadn't yet met. I wanted to close every gap between us, to feel his touch on all of me.

He broke the kiss, pressing his forehead to mine and catching his breath.

"Fuck, Nolei." He practically panted.

I let out a laugh, pressing my forehead back into his.

"What are you thinking about?" I repeated, knowing damn well what he was thinking by the feel of him where his hips were pressed against my stomach.

"How grateful I am that you wanted me to kiss you." He tilted his head and kissed the tip of my nose. That simple act made my heart squeeze in my chest.

He stepped back, reaching his arm out towards me. "Come with me. There is something I want to show you."

We slipped back into the Tavern, the air humid compared to the cool night breeze. Leo continued to hold my hand as he led us to the bar. Everyone was standing and talking now, beginning to mellow out after tiring of dancing.

Our entrance earned us several loud cheers and hoots from Leo's friends and Eryn. My cheeks heated.

Leo clasped Cardin on the shoulder. "Nolei and I are heading out. We will meet you back at the loft."

Cardin gave us a knowing smile. "Have fun."

"You're in charge of keeping an eye on Eryn and making sure she goes back to the loft with you and only you."

Eryn yelled at him playfully, "and what if I had plans to return to someone else's loft with them?"

Leo's smile turned lupine. "Then you can think about those plans from our loft with Cardin."

She finished off the last dregs of her ale. "Yes, father." She crooned.

Cardin stifled a laugh and nodded at Leo. "I'm on it."

Just then, a high-pitched shriek sounded from the other side of the tavern. I turned my head in time to see a large bearded male slap the woman he was with across the face. She was rail thin and about my age. She covered her face, trying to protect herself, as the male grabbed a fistful of her blonde hair.

"You little bitch," the male growled at her as he yanked harder on her hair, causing her head to crane to the side.

I gasped, wanting to help her but not knowing how.

Leo's broad hand moved to the small of my back, pressing me toward Gevel and Lew. The dark-haired male gave Leo a knowing nod over my head and moved, so he separated Eryn, Ryley and I from the crowd.

Cardin glanced at Leo, and they exchanged a look. Clearly, they'd dealt with males like this a thousand times before. It was a practiced, fearless look of two males about to take care of business.

"Please! Odar, don't!" The panicked woman shouted, trying to protect herself as he raised his fist to hit her.

Leo's long strides easily cleared the distance. Before the male, Odar, could make a move, Leo was behind him, his hand wrapped around the male's fist.

"I wouldn't do that if I were you." His voice was laced with a cold fury that I could hear even from my place across the Tavern.

Odar turned to face Leo, rage reddening his podgy face. "Or else what, pretty boy?"

Cardin appeared behind the woman, grabbing onto the hand that was fisting her hair and twisted it in such an unnatural angle that I almost covered my eyes.

"Or else you'll be very, very sorry." Leo promised cooly, letting go of his grip on the male's raised fist.

Odar let out a guttural growl of pain and pulled his hand back from Cardin, releasing his grip on the woman. Cardin quickly moved to escort her away as the brutish male spun to face Leo.

"The only one about to be sorry is you." He spat. "Nobody tells me what I can and can't do to my lady. She's my property." He shoved at Leo's chest, causing him to step back a foot.

But that was it. He didn't stumble or fall. Icy rage poured off of him, a lethal promise of violence. Although Odar was large and older than Leo, Leo was taller and bigger in all the ways that mattered. His broad back and considerable height almost cast Odar into shadow. His muscles were taught and jaw clenched tightly. This was about to get ugly.

Others created space between them, anticipating a fight.

"Keep it clean or take it outside, Leo." A gray-haired barkeep shouted as he ran a rag around the rim of a glass, drying it off.

Leo kept his eyes trained on Odar, the promise of violence still palpable, as a wicked smirk kicked up the corner of his lips. Fuck.

The way my body was responding to this situation was not normal. Someone was about to get hurt and I had a strong feeling it would not be Leo.

"That was the last time you'll ever get the privilege of touching her, actually." Leo stated calmly as he stared down at Odar.

Odar's face turned even ruddier. "The fuck it is," He growled, swinging at Leo.

Leo easily dodged the blow, pivoting seamlessly out of the way.

The bearded male growled again in frustration, trying to land a few more wild swings. He was too slow, though. Especially against Leo.

He swung his large arm again, this time throwing his entire body into the move. Leo side-stepped, letting Odar fall face first onto the ale-soaked floor. Laughter broke out.

Leo leaned against the nearest table, his arms folded casually across his wide chest.

"If you're done… I'd like to get back to my own date." He glanced at me then and winked.

Heat coiled inappropriately in my core. Gods, I needed to get it together.

Eryn gave me a playful nudge, and I shook my head dismissively.

Odar scrambled to his feet and charged at Leo's center. Leo grabbed his shoulders, preventing Odar from ramming into him. He railed his knee up into Odar's jaw, causing the lumbering male's head to swing back. Then Leo landed hit after hit to the male before dropping the back of his arm directly onto the top of the male's bald skull.

The sound made me flinch.

Odar fell like a sack of rocks onto the floor in a heap. He was out cold. *Alive*. But not well.

Blood poured from his nose and mouth, but Leo bent down, yanked up the male's grungy tunic, wiped his face with it and then tucked the fabric under him so as not to stain the floor. Leo turned to the barkeep and flashed him a mischievous smile.

The bartender shook his head with a smile and got back to work.

He looked to make sure the woman was okay, who was now sheltered by a group of her own friends, and then strode back over toward us.

Now I knew exactly what he meant by being in the business of righting wrongs. And somehow witnessing him work made me even more attracted to him. I was in trouble, that was for Godsdamn sure.

Leo led me through dark cobblestone alleys to a large stone building with ivy, grapevines, and other greenery running up the sides. It must have been some type of winery, as barrels were stacked in a pyramid along the side of the building. He climbed from barrel to barrel, turning to assist me after every move.

"Are you sure we're allowed to be here?" I asked, hesitant to run into any trouble with the soldiers who were patrolling the city, as I had with the ones in Eyloria.

"Absolutely." He reassured me without hesitation.

"Why do I highly doubt that?" I murmured to myself as I took the next step up.

He grabbed onto my waist, lifting me from the last barrel onto the roof of the building with ease. I let out a little yelp of surprise.

"Because you have trust issues?"

"I mean.. you're not wrong. But it could be your knack for flirting with danger that has me second guessing you."

"I mean... your fighting skills are getting better but I still wouldn't call you danger," He replied casually.

I scoffed at his horrible joke and rolled my eyes.

"I know the owner. He won't mind if we use his roof to catch a remarkable view of the city bathed in starlight."

Just as he finished his sentence, we crested the peak of the roof. I took a deep inhale, my mouth open in awe.

The entire city was visible below. Rolling hills that lead into Stonemere Run, yellow-lit windows that dotted the houses, the dark expanse of the river leading into the bay. The woods beyond the river. Everything was visible from this one spot and all of it seemed so still and quiet.

The sky was a deep blue spotted with iridescent stars. And the moon, Goddesses, the moon was incredible. A full moon graced the sky every fortnight, rotating in a cycle that complemented the seasons of life and kept us rooted in tradition. We valued lunar guidance just as we worshipped The Divine Feminine. Tonight's Seed Moon symbolized new beginnings and unlocked potential, promising growth.

Leo grabbed my hand again, gently pulling me down to sit across his lap. Every space where our bodies were touching lit up with awareness.

"Aren't I squishing you?" I asked, trying to hold my weight in my arms.

He grabbed my wrist gently, wrapping my arm around his back and pulling my head in toward his chest. His massive arms wrapped familiarly around me.

I was stiff as a board. My entire body, including my heart, screamed at me to lean into him, to breathe him in. To appreciate his touch on my skin.

But my mind kept chattering on, telling me he was only going to hurt me and I shouldn't let my guard down like this. That this was temporary, and I was leaving in a day or so. Did I really need to get my heart tied up even more by adding physical memories to our time together?

"Are you implying that I am weak and unable to support your beautiful body with my own?" His voice was playful and silky in my ear.

He nudged the side of my face with his nose and then left a gentle kiss to the spot on my neck below my ear. Chills ran through me as goosebumps speckled my arms.

154

"You and I both know that you are far from weak, Leo. But we also both know that nothing about me is small."

He pulled me into him, urging me to relax against him. My body followed his silent command, melting into his touch.

"You are perfect." He whispered. My heart gave another pitiful squeeze that was becoming more and more frequent whenever I was around Leo.

"Why are you doing that?" I pulled away slightly, looking up into his face. The dark stubble on his chin showcased his soft lips.

"Doing what? Speaking the truth again?"

"Saying all those sweet things to me. Being sweet."

"Because you deserve it." His head tilted slightly and his dark brows furrowed with confusion. As if he couldn't fathom why I would even ask.

Of course I deserved it. Me and every other woman deserved to be treated like gold. Alas, males only wanted to shower you with compliments so they could use you to get off. How did I know he wasn't doing precisely the same thing?

His dark eyes searched mine and as if he could read my thoughts. "I'm not just saying that so I can use you, Nolei. I've gotten to spend a lot of time with you over the past week. I've seen you first thing in the morning after a night of sleeping on the ground, at the end of a hard day of riding, when you are so hungry that your anger is as lethal as Thalor's wrath. I've seen you running for your life and fighting for it, as well." He cupped my jaw with his hand. "You are, as I've said, absolutely magnificent." His lips parted slightly as he devoured me with his gaze. My heart picked up and that coil of molten need in my core burned even hotter.

"Not just the way you look. Yes, your body is flawless. Perfect. Irresistible." His soft lips kicked up into one of those delicious smirks, this time revealing his rare dimple.

"But you — who you are... is incredible. Kind. Sarcastic. Feisty. Adven-turous, if not dangerously reckless. You are selfless and compassionate." My cheeks flushed as he continued.

"You risked your life to save that girl on the road. Gods, you are so talented. You saved her life, Nolei. You saved that boy's life in Eyloria. His family's life. There is a lot more to bravery and courage than brute strength. You are all of those things wrapped into one. And I, thank the Goddesses, am one lucky bastard to even exist in the light of your presence. It feels like a gift I do not deserve but am damned grateful to have." He finished, his eyes searching mine even more intensely now, as if he wanted to say more but couldn't.

Right then, I realized I hadn't been breathing. I was so shocked by all that he said that I was just sitting there, in his lap, my mouth open like a dead fish who didn't know how to breathe. Breathe, Nolei. Air is important.

Was I hallucinating this? Why in all the realm would this tall, perfectly chiseled, witty, fearless, indomitable male want to spend any more time with me than he had to? How did I end up in his company on a rooftop overlooking one of his favorite cities in the moonlight? Maybe there were some psychedelic mushrooms in that stew we had.

Realizing that I was not hallucinating, and he did indeed just say all of that, I blinked at him slowly. Gods, Nolei. Say something. Do something.

I reached up, grabbed his face with both hands, and kissed him. There was no point in trying to use words right now because there was no way they would come even close to describing how I was feeling.

My heart was doing this odd flip-flopping. My body tingled everywhere that his touched mine: my hips, my waist, my arms.

He welcomed my kiss, opening his mouth as I kissed him deeply. A kiss that said it all. Said everything I couldn't put into words. I appreciated him.

I didn't want this to end. I wanted to know more about him. I wanted to spend more time with him. I felt seen with him. I poured all of these thoughts and more into the way my lips roamed over his.

After several moments, he gently pulled away, resting his forehead against mine again. He kissed my forehead and then pulled me back into him so my head was resting on his hard chest.

Any other male would have escalated that kiss to more. But Leo was different.

"I've never felt like this before, Nolei." He whispered into the top of my head.

"Like what?" I asked, looking over the view of the city as I kept my head to his chest. His heart beat was steady and strong beneath my ear.

"I can't explain it. Like I need to get to know you more. Like I need to have more time with you." His voice was uncertain, confused. I knew exactly what he was feeling though, because I was feeling the same way.

"But Eryn and I have to leave. We can't linger here." I stated what we both knew to be true. My chest squeezed with trepidation.

"Honestly, Nolei." He let out a breathy exhale. "I don't have much of a history with women. I try to keep my distance so that I don't hurt anyone. I travel too much, never staying in one place too long." He scrubbed his hand through his hair. "I don't have much to offer, but I need you to know that whatever I do have to offer ... I'd like to offer it to you."

My heart began racing in my chest. His arms were warm around me, steadying. I was trying to wrap my mind around what he was saying.

"Gods, I sound like a babbling boy." He let out a harsh laugh. "I'm not even making sense."

He pulled away again just enough so we could look at each other.

I honestly think this was the most quiet I've ever been in my life. Shock. I must be in shock. Not only had I never been treated like this, but I also have never had a male show true interest in me before.

Sure, Calder had whispered sweet nothings to me on warm summer nights and said whatever was needed to get beneath my skirts, but he meant none of it. He was saying the same bullshit to every other female in Eyloria that gave him the time of day.

Something about Leo told me he was different. He was being honest. He meant every word.

My silence urged him on.

"What I'm saying is that I'd like to come with you, if you'll have me." His dark eyes near twinkled with flecks of silver. "I know you and Eryn are doing more than just 'traveling along the river' and when you are ready to tell me more, you will. I don't care where you are going or what you are after, but I'd like to come along." A muscle ticked in his jaw and he searched for his words. "I can't ignore the way I feel when I'm around you. If it makes me stupid and naïve to speak such things, then so be it. I'd be a fucking coward if I let you walk out of my life without so much as trying to tell you how I feel."

I couldn't help the smile that spread across my face. Pure, unfettered joy beamed through every pore in my body. I reached my mouth up and kissed him again, delicately.

"Yes."

"Yes?" He said, eyes questioning.

"Yes. I want nothing more than to have more time with you."

CHAPTER

NINETEEN

We walked back to the loft while the moon was still high in the sky. We opened the door to find Eryn sitting on the wooden table licking a wooden spoon, and Cardin making some type of muffin by the hearth. The apartment smelled delicious — like sugar and vanilla.

"I'm impressed that you both made it home and are awake enough to do some light baking." Leo mused as we entered.

"Well, I practically had to carry her over my shoulder to get her to come back here. She started demanding that I make her some food or else she wouldn't return with me. I had to choose my battles."

I laughed. "That's the Eryn we know and love."

She smiled proudly at me. "And how was your evening?" She cooed.

"Wonderful," Leo answered before I could. "Say, Cardin. Are you gettin' the itch to do some more traveling?"

Cardin turned toward us from the fire, his blonde hair bright even in the dim candlelight. "You know me, mate. I've always got the 'itch' to do some traveling."

"Great, it's decided then. We leave in two days' time."

"Oh, we do, do we? ...for where?" Cardin asked with surprise.

"For wherever these two ladies need escorting to." He gestured to Eryn and I.

Eryn's eyebrows shot up as she turned her head in question towards us.

Cardin blinked slowly at Leo and gave him a demure smile. "Ah. I see."

"Excuse me." I shoved Leo's shoulder. He whirled to look at me, one brow raised.

"I granted you permission to travel *alongside* us, but we need no escorts. As you know, Eryn and I can protect ourselves.

Cardin smothered a laugh.

"But of course, my lady." He gave me an elaborate bow.

I rolled my eyes and joined Eryn at the table where we waited for Cardin's muffins to be finished.

The time passed easily. We stayed up far too late telling stories, eating, and laughing.

Leo made sure Eryn, and I were comfortable and situated in his bed before retiring to the couch. My belly full, heart still fluttering and covered in warm furs, I slept the best I had since Gran died.

Two days later, we were re-stocked and ready to continue on our journey. Cardin scrounged up a map of the realm, and Eryn and I had spent hours pouring over it. Now that we had followed the path of the Sanguine River, we had to decide what our next move should be. We re-hashed what The Scroll had said and decided to travel southwest from here, as much of it mentioned some type of woodland area.

In shadowed woods where Wolfsbane bloom,
And ancient trees hold silent sway,
A mirror pond reflects the truth,
guiding you on your way.

We hoped that the forest to our west may hold what we were looking for. Even though it was discouraging to head back west after coming all this way, I felt pulled in that direction.

After riding for a few hours through fields and farmlands, Cardin asked "So, as delighted as I am to be accompanying you ladies on this extremely vague journey, when are you going to be kind enough to share what in the Cinder Wastes we are doing out here roaming aimlessly through the realm?"

Cardin and Leo were riding side by side in the front, with Eryn and I close behind. Leo let out a short laugh but continued looking forward. He had already said that he knew I would tell him when I was ready. But was I ready?

Eryn shot me a sideways glance. She had been letting me take the lead on deciding what details I felt like sharing.

Leo and Cardin were pausing their lives and abandoning their 'work' to travel with us in search of ... whatever it was we were looking for. The magical *mirror pond* that would somehow reveal to me the identity of my true parents and answer my questions about my developing abilities.

Gods, I hadn't even told Leo about *that* part yet. I swallowed thickly. How could I even phrase this in a way that wouldn't have them turning right back around or turning me into The Dark Army?

"I... I don't know where to start." I stuttered out. *Strong start, Nolei.*

Cardin's blonde hair blew in the breeze as he turned slightly toward me. "How about, let's start with a very simple and basic question. *Where are we going?*"

Leo nodded, his lips pressed together in an attempt to not smile.

"I don't know exactly."

Cardin stopped his horse abruptly. We all yanked on our reins, coming to a stop as well. He turned his horse, facing us. Leo followed suit.

"You mean to tell me we are literally just wandering aimlessly? With no plan whatsoever?" His eyebrows bunched together. "I'm all for an adventure, but that seems a little... pointless."

Leo cut in. "What part of 'wherever these ladies need escorting to' is confusing to you, Car? You agreed to come without knowing the plan, so why don't you just trust them and we'll keep our mouths shut and just enjoy the view?" He winked at me as if to imply that *I* was the view. My heart flopped in my chest again.

I lifted my chin and led my horse forward again, continuing on. The others began moving again, as well. "It is really complicated and I honestly don't know where to start. A lot has happened and ... we're looking for a .... I have this necklace from..." I kept starting and stopping, not quite sure how to just spit it out and tell them what was going on.

"—Nolei's got these magical powers, and she found a secret scroll that has this cryptic passage in it about how she can find out who her actual parents are and learn more about these powers she has." Eryn cut me off, summarizing the chaos of my life into one breath. Well, *most* of the chaos.

She flashed me a smile that said 'you're welcome' and turned back to face forward.

Cardin and Leo's heads whipped in my direction, their eyes wide.

"You know how to wield magic?" Cardin asked.

I winced. I needed to tread carefully here. If I shared too much, they could turn me in and I'd be as good as dead.

My heart fluttered and heated again, urging me to stop getting in my own way and listen to my intuition here. Leo wouldn't do that to me. He already saw me use some healing magic and hasn't said a word. Cardin seems loyal to Leo. I can trust them. I will trust them.

I sighed. "I can wield minor magic, like healing magic. My Gran taught me that much." The mention of her brought up the confusing tangle of emotions that seemed to be my new norm. Grief. Anger. Confusion. Betrayal. Heartbreak.

"But I'm starting to get these... powers. I don't know how to control them yet or really what they even are." I looked at both of them, trying to gauge their reactions. Leo gave me a curt nod, encouraging me to continue.

"What kind of powers?" Cardin asked with genuine curiosity.

"I can't really describe it. It is almost like nature will respond to me... the wind, trees, stones. I can call on them to do my will somehow. I don't know any more than that, really."

Cardin gave Leo a long look, then turned his head back towards me. "Okay, so you've got these new powers. You don't know how to use them. So we are trying to find out how you can learn to use them?"

"More or less." I replied. "My Gran said this really bizarre thing right before she passed. *Peer into the verdant eye, where the shadows of yesterday whisper their truths.* I couldn't figure out what it meant, but she had this necklace." I grabbed the necklace from my chest. *To wear it is to carry their blessing and wisdom.* Gran's words echoed through my mind.

"And I somehow unlocked it with the moonlight and it revealed this hidden scroll." I realized I sounded absolutely insane. I rubbed my hand on my forehead.

Noticing my discomfort, Leo guided his horse beside mine. "It's okay, Nolei. If you don't feel ready to tell us, you don't have to."

I glanced at him. His soft smile and deep brown eyes laced with kindness were in stark contrast to his massive, chiseled body, outfitted with multiple weapons and clad in all black. A gentle predator. Thoughtful *and* lethal.

"No, I should tell you. We could use your help. Eryn and I don't know the first thing about the realm outside of Eyloria except for what we learned in Fledgeling's Hall." I admitted, referencing the formal schooling all children of Lunaris completed before learning a craft. "I *need* to tell you. It just... sounds like I'm mad when I put it into words."

"You're not mad. You are extremely talented and sharing with us that you are also gifted. That is nothing to be ashamed of. And this should go without saying but, whatever you decide to share with us will remain safe with us. We will not speak it to others without your permission, nor will we betray you." His head turned to Cardin. "Isn't that right, Car?"

"Yes, of course. I don't know how much Leo has told you, but we aren't exactly The Dark Army's greatest supporters. We find great pleasure in ridding them of their heads, actually." He stated it in a way that made it sound bubbly and entertaining.

Eryn and I laughed. "Well, that is one way of putting it." I remarked.

"You're in good company. How many soldiers have you killed, Nolei? Five? Ten?" Eryn shot me a mischievious smile.

"Six if you count the ones Leo helped me finish off." I said dryly. "You make it sound like it is one of my hobbies."

"Well, it kind of *is* one of your new hobbies." She replied. Leo and Cardin laughed loudly, lightening the mood significantly.

"So anyway," I changed the subject. Not wanting to dwell too long on my new *habit* of killing others, even if it was in self defense. "I found this scroll that kind of outlines how we can find who my true parents are and learn more about my ...new abilities."

"What do you mean by true parents?" Leo asked.

"Well, I never really knew my parents. I always thought that they passed away when I was a babe." I shared the story I had grown up with of them passing on after their wounds festered and they suffered with fever from a dire bear attack. The story was not some tale but a personal history that I believed as truth my entire life. One that was largely responsible for my desire to learn everything I could about the healing arts. To work as Gran's apprentice to help prevent others from suffering the same fate.

"I was raised by my Gran. She passed to The Garden Sanctum a few weeks ago." I said to Cardin, as Eryn and Leo already knew about her passing. "She is all the family I ever had. Besides Eryn's family." I gave Eryn a warm smile.

"But I found out, through this scroll, that my parents are not who I thought they were and they may not even be dead."

"That is a lot to process. You grew up thinking them to be gone and not able to get to know them. But now, you may have the chance to meet them and get to know them." Leo's voice was soothing and gentle. "Man, what I'd give to get to spend more time with my parents." He said longingly.

"What happened to your parents, if you don't mind me asking?" I saw the hurt roll through his features and settle heavy on his chest. "—You don't have to answer that. I don't know why I even asked that." I blurted out, regretting my question.

He made eye contact with me and paused for a moment, holding my stare. "No, No. It's okay. They were killed 13 years ago." His voice was steady but laced with barely masked sorrow. "I've missed them every day since."

"I'm sorry." I responded, not knowing what to say exactly.

"I'm sorry for your loss, too." Eryn said.

"Thank you."

"So ... what did this scroll say? Can we see it?" Cardin asked, not pausing to dwell on Leo's pain. Almost as if he knew Leo wouldn't want to linger on the topic.

"I can't show you right now because it only unlocks with the light of a full moon, as far as I can tell. But I *did* memorize it."

"Of course you did." Leo snorted.

"Ever the bookworm," Eryn said, her voice light and teasing as she mocked me.

Trying to shake off some of my tension and lighten the mood, I wiggled my shoulders and my eyebrows. "Are you all ready to hear this? It is pretty convoluted. Once it graces your ears, you can never go back. By agreeing, you have sworn allegiance to me for all of your days." I bellowed the last part for emphasis.

The males laughed, and Eryn rolled her eyes.

Leo placed his hand over his heart, and Cardin followed suit. "We hereby vow allegiance to you, my damsel, and your budding powers. Despite your knack for getting into dangerous situations, we pledge our fealty to you now and always." Leo gave me a teasing smile that sent a pang of desire through me. Gods, he was fucking beautiful, even when he was being a pain in my ass.

Cardin laughed and followed up with, "For fuck's sake. Of course we do."

I fought back a laugh, cleared my throat for dramatic flair, and repeated the text of The Scroll.

I finished reciting it, my blood beginning to race through me. Eager to see their reactions, I held my breath. The silence stretched on for what felt like an eternity.

"*Holy fuck.*" Cardin broke the silence.

"*Holy fuck* is right." Leo echoed.

"So anyway, that's where we're going." I chirped, a nervous giggle escaping me.

"Well, you should have just said that," Cardin replied, his voice laced with sarcasm.

We spent the next few hours discussing The Scroll and throwing guesses out about its meaning. I was right. It was good to have the males know the details. I felt lighter. Sharing the burden of this knowledge had been necessary for me to take full, deep breaths. It eased some of the tension from my shoulders and neck. Tension I hadn't even known I was carrying.

"I know of a small basin of water near here that may fit as the '*mirror pond*,'" Leo offered. "It might not be it, but it is only about a day's trip from here."

"Are you speaking of Solfire Springs?" Asked Cardin.

"It's worth ruling out." Leo replied.

"There isn't exactly an easy way to get there, though. We'd either have to go north of the Solfire mountains." He pointed toward the brown mountains in the distance. "... or edge along the coast, through Leisport, which would take several days."

"Or we could go *through* the Solfire Mountains and be there by tomorrow eve," Leo countered mischievously.

"Ah, so *that* is the kind of adventure you want to go on." Cardin said as he arched his brow.

"What does he mean by that?" Eryn asked, her brows etched with confusion as she nodded toward Cardin.

"It is a bit of a treacherous route to take, but it is the quickest." Leo stated, shifting his hips in his saddle.

"And what do you mean by *treacherous*?" I asked.

"He means it is a narrow mountain pass that is all rock, dust, and sand. No shelter. Wide open to the brutal elements. Not to mention inhabited by hordes of Dunemaulers," Cardin answered casually.

"Oh. Just hordes of Dunemaulers." Eryn shrugged sarcastically. "No big deal."

"Listen, we can go around the mountains if you want. I've said it before and I'll say it again. You ladies are in charge. We are just here for the view." Leo's heated gaze caught mine as he bit his bottom lip absentmindedly.

I averted my eyes before my body had the chance to respond any further to his sultry glances. "I say we take the shortcut."

"Really? ....*Really*?" Eryn questioned, her voice almost pleading.

"Yes. We can handle it. We've just replenished our supplies, have plenty of water and food, and can handle a few *Dunemaulers*, I'm sure." I played out the word Dunemaulers on my tongue, never having heard of such things before.

Gods, I *hoped* we could handle a few of them. I knew Leo and Cardin could, and Eryn and I were getting better with our swords every day. Not to mention, I had my *powers* to fall back on if it came down to it. Whatever shred of reassurance that knowledge provided.

We aimed for the mountains, making quick time through the grassy plains and farmlands. By nightfall we were at the base of the Solfire Mountains, the farmland turning to sand with sparse thatches of grass.

Leo helped me down from my horse, grabbing my hips and lifting me off with ease. Gods, he truly did have the strength of Thalor, The God of Strength and Protection.

We set up camp and started a fire, roasting some small rodents that the males caught for us while Eryn and I had been starting the fire.

"So, how do you picture this sleeping arrangement going?" Cardin said between bites of meat. "The way Leo introduced you two as 'his ladies,' he made it sound as if he slept between the two of you in nothing but his bare ass."

I almost choked on my food as I burst into laughter at the image.

"In his *dreams*." Eryn retorted. "Leo is more like a bothersome brother figure to me than a male Nolei and I would worship together under the moonlight."

Cardin's eyebrows shot up at the suggestion. Leo glared at Cardin.

"And trust me, such males *do* exist." Eryn purred, winking at me.

Leo turned his glare to Eryn. Was that... jealousy? He was *jealous*.

I smirked with amusement at this entire conversation.

"I think you must be speaking of me," Cardin responded, smiling seductively at both of us before taking another bite of meat.

"I think you need to shut *the fuck* up." Leo growled at Cardin.

"But I'm glad you brought it up, Cardin. I've been sleeping next to Nolei for two weeks now and need a break." My eyes bulged and then narrowed

169

on Eryn as I wiped some grease from my face with the back of my hand. "She's kind of ... clingy when she sleeps. I'd like a few nights' reprieve from having her all tangled up around me so I can get some decent sleep myself." She continued on.

I snapped my mouth shut. "I am *not clingy* when I sleep." My cheeks reddened. Eryn continued on with her dinner, impressed with herself.

Cardin stared at me with amusement as he replied, stretching out his long legs and crossing his boots at the ankle. "I learn more about you every day, Nolei."

An icy dread blossomed in my chest at what she was suggesting. "I don't want to sleep alone," I blurted out. I hadn't slept alone since the night before Gran died and I absolutely did not want tonight to be my first night doing so, out here in the middle of nowhere.

"Maybe one of these charming males can withstand your clinging tonight, then." She suggested coolly, waving her hand in their direction.

Realization dawned. Eryn was trying to set me up with Leo. Good Gods, the lengths this woman would go astounded me.

Before the silence could stretch on any longer Cardin replied, "Well, my lady, I'd offer but I fear that Leo here would cut off some of my favorite bits if I so much as suggested such a thing." He took a final bite of his dinner before tossing the bones into the fire.

"Your fear would be correct." Leo stated coldly.

"It's decided then." Eryn said, trying and failing to hide her excitement. "Leo can sleep with Nolei, I'll be able to stretch out on my own, and Cardin you can ... sleep anywhere you'd like as long as it isn't with Nolei or I." She added before Cardin could suggest otherwise.

"You're no fun." Cardin whined.

Feeling thoroughly manipulated, I sighed.

That feeling quickly dissipated and was replaced with a flicker of anticipation at the thought of sleeping *with* Leo. A flicker that started deep in my core and burned a sense of awareness through my body like wildfire.

CHAPTER

TWENTY

Trying not to be the most awkward being in the realm, I prepared my bedroll and nestled under the blanket before anyone else could claim their sleeping spots. Eryn gave me a scheming smile as she walked past to the other side of camp and set up hers. This was such a classic Eryn move, I couldn't believe I had been surprised by her conniving.

I squeezed my eyes shut, pretending to be ... what? Immediately asleep upon laying down? *Not likely.*

The smell of crackling campfire and pine invaded my senses, and I opened my eyes to see Leo standing over me. He was even taller and more defined from this angle. His black shirt was unbuttoned at the top, revealing the muscled curves of his chest. I took a sharp inhale at the sight of him in the shadows.

"Mind if I keep you company?" He asked innocently.

"I thought that had already been decided for me thanks to Eryn's scheming," I shot back, not quite realizing why I was putting up such a fight. I mean, I obviously wanted him to lay next to me, but I wanted him to do it because he wanted to, not because he was being forced to. Elowen, have mercy on me. I needed to stop getting in my own way.

Ignoring my comment, He shook out his blanket and set it beside mine. He lowered himself bedside me, rolled onto his side to face me and propped his head up on his fist again, just as he had done that first night in the woods.

"Well, I'm glad she made the suggestion and created the opening for me. Do you know why?" His dark eyes were churning with desire that caused the heat to coil in my body again.

"Why?" I whispered, my mouth feeling too dry.

"Because if she hadn't, I would have had to make a show of stealing you away from her so I could lie beside you." He mused. "Or I would have had to convince you to leave her side for me and that could end up with her feelings hurt." He inched closer to me, leaning in so that his words billowed like smoke caressing my ear "Or I would have had to spend another night from a distance that was close enough to see you but painfully far away... far enough away that I couldn't *feel* you. And that is the worst kind of torture." He drew out the last words, causing them to drip from his tongue.

My whole body responded to his voice and proximity. A shiver swept over me even though I was warm beneath my fur. A heady longing coursed through me, begging him to touch me. To make the contact he was speaking of.

"And you're here now." I stated, locking eyes with him.

"I am. And for that, I am eternally grateful." The memory of his lips on mine made it hard for me to focus on his words as I watched his lips move.

"You are, are you?" I replied, not knowing what to say but wishing he would just fucking kiss me already.

"May I show you how grateful I am?" His quiet voice was filled with intensity, his eyes searching mine.

The hot pull of desire was even stronger now. I didn't know what he had in mind exactly, but I was eager to find out. Hopefully, it had to do with his muscled body on top of mine.

Catching my thoughts drifting in a rather wicked direction, I chided myself. That is *not* what needed to happen here, with Cardin and Eryn mere feet away from us. But was that reminder enough to keep me from finding out how grateful he was? Absolutely not.

I tucked a lock of hair behind the point of my ear and tilted my head up towards his slightly, parting my lips slightly. "You may." I whispered.

His eyes turned molten again as he leaned in even closer. He brought his hand to my face and lifted my lips to his. The softness with which he kissed me took my breath away. He nudged my lips open with his own, gently devouring me.

I turned liquid in response to his touch. I shifted slightly onto my back, trying to lure him toward me further with my lips alone.

He shifted so that his silhouette blotted out the moon and stars behind him. He moved his lips from mine and gently traced them down my neck, leaving a blazing hot trail in his wake. I arched slightly below him, letting out a breathy moan. He growled in response as he continued kissing a path to my collar bone. The sensual pricks of his stubbled chin on my skin was intoxicating. My fingers went to his dark hair.

He lifted his lips from my skin and returned to my mouth, planting another soft kiss there.

"Have I told you how perfect you are lately?" He said between kisses.

"Have I told you lately how daft you must be for thinking so?" I kissed him deeper, feeling his smile against my lips.

I grabbed the edge of the fur that was covering me and moved it so it enveloped both of us. I pulled him closer, devouring his mouth with my own. He returned the feverish movements. The feel of him against me ratcheted up the need in my body. His muscled arms braced his weight on top of me. His hips on top of mine, the proof of his desire obvious through his pants. I ground my hips, pressing up into him. He let out a deep moan and kissed my neck again. I tightened my fingers into his hair.

"I wouldn't do that if I were you, Nolei." His mouth was just below my ear.

"And why is that?" I questioned, tugging on his hair as I ground my hips upward again.

The movement was just fanning my own desire. Gods, I wanted him closer. I *needed* him closer.

"Because if you keep doing that, this is going to escalate." His breathy whisper sent another round of chills down my neck.

"Perfect." I cooed, grinding myself into him again, feeling his hard length along the front of me.

He moved back to my mouth, ravaging me in the best way. "Yes, you are. But when I touch you for the first time, it will not be within earshot of our friends. It will be somewhere I can watch your perfect fucking body move against mine and revel in your shameless screams of pleasure." His words were a wicked promise that fanned the flame in my body. "Not that you ever remain quiet for long." He teased.

He kissed me back until we were both breathless and our bodies were tense with desire. Then he pressed his hips firmly against mine, making sure I could feel the hard proof of his want for me. Before I could respond, he shifted off of me and onto his side next to me. He grabbed my hips and flipped me quickly, so that I was facing away from him, my back pressed against him.

"Hey!" I protested in a hushed voice. "I wasn't done with you!"

His laugh was like silk. He pulled my hips back, so they were nestled against his, and put one arm below my head. The other wrapped around me, hugging me close to him.

"And I am *definitely not* done with you. But we're done for tonight." He placed a kiss on the side of my face. "Sleep, Nolei." He commanded.

It took some time for the heat in my blood to fade, but it was replaced with a warm sense of safety and sleepy satisfaction. I softened into him, pulling his top arm around me even closer. Before long, my breath had steadied and my eyes fell heavy.

We remained like that, tangled up in each other's arms. And for the first time in two weeks, I finally slept soundly.

My eyes blinked open with the first light of dawn. I rolled over, looking for Leo behind me. All I saw was a pile of ruffled blankets, proof enough that last night had actually happened. My lips curved into a small smile at the recent memory of his lips on mine.

I sat up, looking toward the center of camp. Cardin was stoking the fire and Leo was feeding the horses what looked like apples.

Cardin's blonde head lifted as he said, "Good morning, sunshine. Did you sleep well?" Cardin had a special way of making such a mundane question sound highly inappropriate.

I stretched my arms overhead and yawned. "Like a babe." I flashed him an innocent smile.

Eryn rustled around and then got up out of her bedroll. She walked over to me, extending a hand to help me stand.

"Like a broody, alluring male was nestled behind you?" She teased.

My cheeks flushed red. "Exactly like that."

Cardin snorted a laugh. "And here's our other morning glory." He nodded to Eryn. She curtsied at him with a mocking smile.

We had a bland breakfast of cold oats mixed with water and packed up the horses. It wasn't satisfying in the least, but it got the job done.

I dressed in my tight black pants and laced my cropped leather bodice tightly. My short sword was fastened to my hip and my dagger hidden in my boot, so I could easily access it if things got a little out of hand on the way to Solfire Springs. My new tattoo was nearly healed, its presence along my arm a reminder of my new dedication to courage and confidence.

Eryn and I spent some time sparring together, as we had been doing every morning, while the males looked on and offered feedback.

Cardin smiled widely as he stood with crossed arms. "Are you telling me every morning you get to watch these two sword fight with barely any clothing on?" He asked Leo playfully.

I lunged at Eryn with my sword. "I am fully clothed, thank you very much."

Ignoring Cardin, Leo continued to watch us. "Good. Now anticipate her next move! Don't take your eyes off of her." He coached Eryn as I circled her, his eyes flicking back and forth from me to her.

She swiped at me, and I dodged to the left.

"That's it." Leo continued. "Both of you need to stay light on your feet. You're stomping around like a bunch of Bramblebacks." He shouted. "You need to use your size to your advantage in battle. Be quick!"

Eryn broke out into a little jig, jumping her feet quickly from side to side. I laughed, joining in. We were flitting around on our tiptoes and jumping here and there in a frenzied dance, our swords still up in the air.

"Is this light enough on our feet for you, master?" I shouted to him, as we danced around like woodland faeries celebrating the Summer Solstice under the Maiden's Moon.

Eryn laughed and picked up her pace.

Leo scrubbed at his face. "And that's enough of that." He turned toward the horses, effectively dismissing us. "Let's go."

Cardin bellowed with laughter, his handsome face lighting up with amusement.

We slowed to a stop and bent over, trying and failing to catch our breath between bursts of laughter.

Gods, it felt good to just have some fun. To escape from all my worries and the 'what ifs' for a few moments.

Leo laughed as he shook his head, walking toward Kellan. "You two are ridiculous." He mounted the horse in one swift move, nodding his head toward our horses. "Let's get a move on."

The one-sided smile he gave us had my heart doing that flopping thing in my chest again. *Elowen, save me.* I was in trouble when it came to him. Somehow he went from a complete stranger to a person I couldn't go but a few moments without thinking about. Couldn't last more than a few breaths without glancing at. I was hyper-aware of every movement he made. Always hoping I'd get another glimpse of that subtle tilt of his lips, revealing that addicting smirk.

I had never felt like this about a male before, and I was falling quickly into uncharted territory. Yes, that summer with Calder was fun before I realized how much of a lying sack of shit he was. But I had never felt like *this* before. My heart felt too vulnerable, too exposed. But that was nothing compared to the all-consuming pull I felt toward him. I'd gladly risk my heart to see what this connection between us could grow into. He was like a new addiction that I couldn't sate. And I didn't want to.

After several hours of traveling, the sun was now high in the sky. I wiped the sweat from my forehead and fanned myself with my hand. Cardin was right about this mountain pass. It was *nothing but rock, dust, and sand.*

The horses didn't seem bothered by it, but all this dust was getting old really quickly. My hair was filled with it and clouds of tiny particles floated out of it every time I turned my head. My pants were also covered, now looking more brown than black.

The mountains were magnificent, though. For what they lacked in color and vegetation, they made up for in sheer height. The craggy surfaces were textured with steep drops where rock had fallen or maybe the sand had eaten away at them.

The pass between the mountains was relatively narrow, allowing our horses to pass side by side but not leaving much space otherwise.

The land was barren. I couldn't imagine how any creature could survive in these conditions without water or shelter from the sun and heat.

We couldn't get to Solfire Springs soon enough. I fantasized about swimming in the cool water. Those thoughts were about all that was getting me through this sweltering weather and monotonous landscape. That and the silent pull I felt to find my parents and the answers about my powers.

"Whose great idea was this?" Leo asked, running his hand through his sweat soaked hair.

"That would be yours." Cardin answered. He had long since removed his white tunic, dampened it with waterskin, and wrapped it around his head in an attempt to stay cool. His skin had turned an angry pink from the sun's heat.

"Gods, if we don't get through these mountains soon I'm going to dry up and turn into dust myself." Eryn chimed in.

My head turned in response to a flicker of movement in the mountains to our left.

There was nothing there except more brown rocks. I must be seeing things from heat and dehydration. Taking out my waterskin, I took several gulps. The water was too hot and did nothing to quench my thirst.

Leo put his hand over his eyes to shield the sun. "Gauging from the mountains, we should be almost there. Likely only an hour or so longer before we're through."

I saw another flash of movement to our left. Leaning back slightly, I tried to see behind Cardin. Again, I saw nothing beyond more dust and sharp rocks jutting from the ground.

"What are you doing?" Cardin asked.

"I keep thinking that there is something over there." I shook my head, looking forward. "Every time I see a quick movement, I look, but nothing is there. The heat must be getting to me."

Leo straightened in his saddle, turning his head to the left. We all were running our eyes along the mountainside when the sound of falling rocks came from our right. I whipped my head around just in time to see a giant figure leaping through the air directly at me.

CHAPTER

TWENTY-ONE

I let out a scream that could shatter glass. I dug into Camila sharply with my heel, causing her to bolt forward and the creature to barely miss landing upon us.

"Holy FUCK!" Eryn screamed. "Nolei!"

The creature landed just behind us, its giant claws kicking up dirt from the impact. Our horses shot forward, galloping at full speed.

I turned in time to see it lift its head and roar; the sound causing the rocks to tremble. Its open mouth was lined with long, dagger-like teeth. It looked like it had more teeth than could fit inside its mouth.

"Looks like we have company!" Cardin shouted.

"No shit." I hugged into Camila, urging her faster.

The creature was about twice the size of a horse, its muscled chest and limbs clearly built for both climbing and speed. Its teeth designed to devour any creature stupid enough to travel this path. Sharp spikes grew out from its face, neck, and down its back, resembling some kind of deadly mane.

Leo, Eryn, and Cardin's horses were keeping pace with Camila, all running for their lives. As I glanced down the line, I saw a second beast barreling toward us from the left side of the pass.

Fuck. I *had* seen something over there. It was no wonder I couldn't pick them out, though. Their bodies were the exact pale brown color as the rest of the landscape. They blended in perfectly here. A deadly adaptation that allowed them to survive and thrive here.

"Dunemaulers!" Cardin's voice boomed as we galloped forward.

"Is two enough to be considered a horde?" Eryn shouted, panic evident in her voice. "I really hope there are only two."

"I've got good news and bad news." Leo said as he steered his stallion closer to me. "Which would you like first?"

"Are you fucking kidding me right now?" I yelled, "Just tell us!" I stared at him like he was losing his mind.

He laughed as an adrenaline-fueled smile lit up his face. Gods, he was *enjoying* this. I glanced forward again before returning to look at him, waiting for him to speak.

"The good news is, there's only two." He moved to stand on Kellan's back. "The bad news is, we can't outrun them." He leaped from his horse's back to the back of mine while we were at a full gallop.

I gasped. "What the fuck are you doing? You could have died!" I scolded him, holding onto the reins and clinging closely to Camila.

He leaned forward and spoke directly into my ear. "But I didn't." Then he swirled around, facing backwards on my horse, the creature snapping its teeth at him just a few feet behind us.

He had to be insane. There was no logical reason anyone would act like this unless they were mentally unwell. Yet his blind confidence somehow managed to further heighten my attraction to him. I had to be the insane one.

"So what do we do?" Eryn screamed frantically as Lady Lace galloped wildly ahead.

Cardin guided his horse to Kellan and managed to grab the reins, as if this was some type of practiced maneuver they had done a hundred times.

Leo whipped an arrow out of his quiver and drew it back, aiming right at the Dunemauler's head. "We fight!"

"Glory or the gates of The Garden!" Leo shouted as he loosed the arrow right as the creature let out a fierce cry, sending it into the beast's gaping maw. It pierced straight into the back of the beast's throat. The Dunemauler reared, screeching in pain.

Just then, Leo hopped off the horse, landing easily in a crouch in front of the vile creature. His black cloak billowed behind him as he landed.

My heart sank into my stomach as I gasped. "Leo!" I shouted, pulling on the reins to force Camila back around.

"For fuck's sake." Cardin said, rearing to a stop and turning back beside me.

The wounded Dunemauler was screeching and whipping its head back and forth in pain, dark red blood pouring from the sides of its mouth and between its jagged rows of teeth. It then honed in on Leo, its eyes filled with primal malice.

Leo charged it on foot, sliding beneath it as it pounced for the kill.

I screamed, not believing my eyes. Horror and shock consumed me.

The beast spun around, letting out an ear-deafening roar.

The male who had been gently wrapped around me a few hours ago was now taking on a massive Dunemauler single-handedly. His eyes were bright with excitement and the promise of violence. He prowled toward the creature, his black tunic near straining against his muscled chest.

My heart beat wildly in my ears as I watched in slow motion, praying to Thalor and The Divine and anyone who would listen.

They approached each other with predatory calculation before both breaking into a sprint, charging in for the kill. At the last moment, Leo leaped into the air and buried his long-sword deeply between the beast's eyes. The Dunemauler bucked and fought, trying to rid itself of Leo, before collapsing into stillness.

I gasped, hoping it was over.

Leo flashed me a victorious smirk, grabbed the hilt of his sword with two hands, and yanked it free. Blood spurted, covering him. He brought the blade overhead again and drove it deep into the creature's skull a second time, for good measure.

My heart thundered in my chest as fear and adrenaline mixed in my blood. Leo was alive. He killed that Dunemauler and he was *alive*.

I panted, aiming my horse for him. He pried his blade from its skull again, lifting his sword high as he stood on the creature's head.

He turned to look at me and gave me an infuriating smile that showed he had absolutely no care in the world, that he just scared the *fuck* out of me. Out of *us*.

Before I could scold him, I saw dust kicking up in a fury behind him. It was the other Dunemauler.

"Leo! Behind you!" I shouted as the creature let out an ear deafening roar. I raced Camila toward him, hoping I could somehow get to him before the beast, knowing it wasn't possible. *No. No. No.*

He spun around, swinging his sword blindly as the dust kicked up all around him. He crouched as the beast leaped over him, slicing its stomach. It turned quickly, ragged trails of spit blasting out of its mouth as it roared again, mere feet from Leo.

The noise it made sent a shiver down my spine and raised the hair on the back of my neck.

It charged Leo again. He leaped off the fallen Dunemauler and out of its way.

I reared Camila to a stop a short distance from them, not sure what to do next. I had to help him somehow. Not having any arrows nor any skill to wield such a weapon, I reached for my dagger. Eryn pulled up her horse beside mine, her eyes wide with terror.

I held my dagger up and shouted to her, "Throw your dagger!"

Grabbing it by the hilt, I cocked my arm back, let out a prayer to The Divine, and took a deep inhale. Praying it would hit *anywhere* on the Dunemauler and avoid maiming Leo in the process. I let it fly. It landed in the creature's shoulder. It let out another angry cry but did now slow.

Eryn's dagger hit it in the side along its rows of near-impenetrable tan spikes, but fell away, not even drawing blood. *Fuck.*

Leo swung his sword again, slicing at the beast as it ran toward him. He managed to cut into its side, leaving a trail of blood as it jumped past him.

He spun around, readying his sword again. It pounced on top of him, causing him to fall to his back on the rocky ground.

"No!" I shouted. "Leo!" Panic washed through me. We had to help him.

"Watch out!" Cardin commanded from the right as he drew back an arrow. My eyes tracked it as it soared through the air and embedded itself in the creature's neck.

The beast turned to Cardin, screeching. Its eyes were a bright red, the color of lava. A color that promised death.

This wasn't working. I needed to *do something* to save Leo. If we didn't get this Dunemauler away from him, he would *die*.

My heart hammered in my chest. Even though I had just met him, the mere thought of losing him caused my chest to tighten. I wouldn't lose him, not like this. I refused.

I jumped off of Camila and drew my sword.

Leo's instructions from our training lessons played through my mind. *Be fast. Be precise.*

"Nolei, no!" Eryn screamed at me as I began stalking toward the creature. If I could draw it away from Leo, he might be able to get back to his horse. Back to safety.

"Over here, you foul beast!" I taunted, waving my arm in the air, not quite knowing how to lure it.

"What the fuck are you doing, Nolei?!" Eryn asked, exasperated.

Cardin let another arrow fly. It landed in the creature's neck again, beside the other. Dark blood began spurting out, discoloring its tan hide.

The Dunemauler turned away from Leo for a moment, fury etched in its eyes. It was still standing over top of him, though, pinning him to the ground with its massive claws.

A flash of black smoke filled the space around Leo for a fraction of a heartbeat before disappearing.

The creature looked back and forth, taking us all in as he let out a threatening growl.

"Just do it!" Cardin shouted to Leo.

Leo glanced at Cardin for a heartbeat, hesitation clearly etched onto his features. Not knowing what Cardin meant by that, I continued shouting at the beast with my arms waving frantically.

Having clearly decided on *something*, Leo buried his sword in the bottom of the creature's neck while its head was turned. He had wedged it between the hard layers of spiked mane. The beast screeched in pain, whipping its head back towards Leo. *Fuck.*

Leo managed to get up onto his forearms, his face mere inches from the angry creature. It clamped its jagged maw around Leo's shoulder. The crunch of bone reverberated through my body.

I gasped, unable to speak as terror gripped me. Eryn screamed. Leo let out a shout of pain, trying to land a punch with his good arm. The beast lifted him into the air by his shoulder and flung him several feet away. Leo landed with a bone chilling crack and didn't move a muscle.

I screamed, the sound shrill. My body was frozen and all I could hear was my own voice, my own endless screaming. He couldn't die. No. No. No! He had to be okay. *Had* to.

Cardin loosed another arrow, this one sunk deep into the creature's belly. I knew instantly the injury would be deadly, but also knew that the internal bleeding would take hours to claim the beast. We didn't have that kind of time.

The Dunemauler ignored Cardin and turned for Eryn and I, for the source of the noise. It prowled forward.

I couldn't think of what to do. All I could think of was how Gran was murdered and now Leo laid dead on the ground. And now we were next.

"Nolei!" Eryn screamed, breaking my swirling mess of thoughts. "Use your powers!"

I didn't respond with words, just continued endless screaming. Screaming in anger, in fear, in grief, in panic. Screaming for all the things that kept happening to me that I had no control over.

The surrounding dust swirled, and the rocks trembled.

Cardin shot another arrow, this one hitting the beast's hip. It continued to approach us, a low grumble coming from its blood-drenched mouth.

"Use your powers! Focus!" Eryn shouted again.

Her words settled over me like the dust settling around Leo's too still body.

Use my powers. My abilities. I used them last time, when Gran was killed. I could do it again.

I blinked once. Twice. I got my eyes to focus on what was happening. I saw the rocks shaking at my feet; the sand whirling around me. It was already responding to me. I just needed to give it some direction.

I inhaled deeply, closing my eyes. I visualized all the world around me, answering my call. The wind lifting the dust. The rocks rising off the ground and trembling with the wild energy of terror and despair. I saw it in my mind and continued to pull the energy into myself. Saw it ebb and pulse.

Until the frenzied energy was too large for me to contain within myself any longer. Only then did I open my eyes and see what I had visualized become a reality.

The wind whipped frantically around us, drawing the dust up and creating a cyclone of sand and small rocks so thick that it marred my vision. My hair and cloak thrashed with the power of the wind. The ground below us and mountains beside us shook angrily, causing boulders to tumble down into the pass.

The Dunemauler froze several feet in front of Eryn and I, its crimson eyes wide. Blood leaked freely from its wounds and pooled in the dust at its feet. It hunched its shoulders, raising the thick spikes around itself as if it sensed something deadly was coming.

I looked directly into its eyes and let all the raw emotion I felt come to the surface. The emotions that were now mingled with the intense energy around us. I let out another scream, this one laced with fury and determination.

As I did so, the whirling dust tripled in size, collecting rock fragments and boulders larger than the creature within its grasp. It circled the beast, not allowing the Dunemauler to escape its wrath.

The wind whipped at our faces. Eryn was covering hers with a forearm. I let it hit me, let the violent energy surround me. The tornado continued closing in on the beast until it consumed it completely. The creature's roar was deafening but was quickly drowned out by the sound of falling rocks.

The wind deposited all the boulders directly on top of the creature, crushing and silencing it instantly.

Suddenly, everything went still. The dust floated to the ground and hardly a breeze could be felt. I took a deep inhale, not believing my eyes.

I did this. I harnessed all of this energy, guided it, and used it to kill. *Again*.

But I was too late.

CHAPTER

TWENTY-TWO

Not allowing myself time to process any of what I had just done, I ran up to Leo.

His body was still lying there, unmoving. The sight of the blood pooling below his shoulder and darkening the fabric of his shirt made my body flash cold. His shirt was shredded, revealing muscles that looked much the same.

No. Gods, no. I pleaded silently. My words from that night in Stonemere Run flashed through my mind. *I want nothing more than to have more time with you.* It was true. I'd give *anything* to have more time with him. This couldn't be the end. He had to be okay.

I cried out as I nearly collapsed by his side. I quickly felt for a pulse at his neck, just as Gran had taught me. His skin was clammy and cool. His pulse was thready and faint, but present. I exhaled a sigh of relief. He was *alive*.

"He's alive!" I yelled.

The realization that he was still in grave condition quickly cooled any relief that dared to gather inside of me. I squeezed my eyes shut.

Gods, I wish Gran was here. She would know what to do. She would know how to save him.

Cardin reached Leo next, kneeling above his head and grasping his face with both hands.

"Leo!" He shook Leo's head gently, pleading. "You gotta wake up. You need to pull through this, brother." Cardin pressed his forehead to Leo.

"You can help him, Nolei." Eryn's voice came from a few feet behind me. "You know what to do." She encouraged me.

I pressed my palms into my forehead and tried to think. Tried to remember. Tried to *listen* to my intuition so I could *learn* what to do. So I could be guided by it.

She kneeled next to me, placing my saddle bag of herbs and tinctures beside me silently. The bag clinked with glass jars and vials as she set it down. The sound was familiar. Grounding.

"Come on, stay with us," Cardin whispered frantically. "I need you. I need you here." Desperation trembled through his voice.

I inhaled deeply, determination settling through my bones. My eyes still closed.

Not knowing where to start, I pushed my hands into the dust at my knees. The energy from the land rose up into my arms, causing them to tingle with power. I tried to quiet my mind, to listen to my inner self. The part of me that knew exactly how to harm and how to heal. The part that was revealing itself a little more each day.

This would be no simple healing. Leo was close to death, his heart thrumming on but weakly. His bones were crushed by the impact and his body was losing blood too quickly.

I had to separate emotions from responsibility. Had to compartmentalize my utter shock and focus on what I could do to help him survive.

I called on not only the wisdom of Vespera this time, but on all three of The Divine Feminine. Calantha, The Maiden, in honor of new beginnings, wildness, and pleasure. All things that I hoped to pursue further with Leo. *Needed* to pursue with him.

Elowen, The Mother, to honor growth in myself and my powers, as well as sexuality and love. My heart gave a squeeze at the thought.

Finally, I called upon the wisdom and knowledge of Vespera, The Crone. With an inhale, my body became warm and buzzed with energy. Their blessings seemingly flowed through me, as if they were in full support of this desperate act I was about to attempt.

Cardin and Eryn were silent as I raised my hands from the ground to the sky. The sun was still high, its rays intense and unshielded. I called the vibrant energy from the sun into myself, feeling the tingling in my arms and my body light on fire. The heat was intense, but not painful. I felt... *powerful*. Like a vessel crafted to hold and harness all this energy. Like I was *meant* to wield this gift.

Exhaling, I ran my hands back through the sand at my knees, creating a half circle around myself. Swirling and moving my hands through the sand, I created symbols to further ground this energy with that of the land beneath us. My fingers moved, guided by the culmination of all the forces that worked together to support this type of magic. I crafted a circle in the center, representing the full moon and the mother, and a crescent moon on either side of it. The waxing moon for The Maiden and the waning moon for The Crone. I kneeled, closing my eyes and pressing my forehead into the center of the symbols. Drawing the energy of the moon cycle into myself.

With another full inhale, I rose onto my knees and opened my eyes. The symbols in the dust were lit with a luminescent silver light, as if filled with moonlight. The energy still vibrated through my entire being, guiding me and urging me to continue on.

"Holy *fuck*," Cardin whispered. I barely heard him in the background, the buzz in my ears too all-consuming.

My body moved until I was kneeling over Leo's chest, my arms outstretched. I silently placed my hands on him. One over his heart and the other on his forehead. I closed my eyes again, sensing the energy pouring out of me and into him. Feeling it flow through me and out of my hands.

As my eyes drifted open several heartbeats later, they ran along Leo's body. He was now hovering a few feet off the ground, covered by a balmy, warm glow. Like a mix of swirling silver and gold, of sunlight and moonlight that had melded together to churn around him. He was breathing deeply now, eyes still closed. My hands were still pressed into him, having raised with his body. The healing magic cradled him. It seeped into his wounded shoulder, looking like some kind of iridescent lava pouring through cracked rock as it laced into the jagged wounds.

Again allowing the energy to guide me, I drifted my hands around his cheek and chest, slowly bringing him back to the ground. He landed quietly, the light that was radiating around him slowly seeping back into the land beneath him. He inhaled sharply, eyes opening wide to reveal those dark chocolate eyes.

I let out a ragged breath. I did it. I saved him. My heart somehow sped up and slowed down at the same time. Relief echoed through me, softening the tension I had been holding in every part of me. The pit that had settled into my stomach dissipated. He was *okay*.

Not thinking, I shot forward, grabbing his face with both of my hands. I kissed him. My lips pressed frantically into his. I poured every ounce of worry, relief, joy, and elation into his lips as I kissed him. He laughed warmly, bringing his hands up to cup my face and meeting my kiss with the same intensity.

"Real subtle, Nolei." Eryn teased. "Guess the cat is out of the bag with you two."

"The cat was never *in* the bag with these two." Cardin laughed, obviously relieved.

I sat up, glaring at them. Turning my head back to Leo, I gave him a giddy smile. He got himself up to sitting, cracking his back and rotating his shoulder.

"Are you okay? How do you feel?" I prodded.

"Now I am. I feel..." He continued to move his arm through its range of motion. ".. a little sore, but otherwise fine."

I furrowed my brow and then shoved him, causing him to almost lose his balance and fall back onto his back again. "What the *fuck* were you thinking?"

"Here we go." Cardin quipped as he met Eryn's glance. Eryn rolled her eyes exaggeratedly.

Leo's brows pressed together. "What do you mean?"

"Don't you ever fucking jump off a horse galloping at full speed into the path of a Dunemauler like that. *Ever. Again.*"

Leo gave me a bemused look as he let out an airy chuckle. "That's oddly specific."

I deepened my glare.

"Yes ma'am. I'll be sure to avoid that from now on." He vowed.

Eryn and Cardin laughed.

"I'm serious! You scared me half to death."

He gave me that crooked smile that sent a bolt of warmth and desire through me. "I was just rescuing you... *again.*"

I rolled my eyes. "Well, looks like *I* rescued *you* this time, my damsel." I teased.

"Ouch" Cardin added in, biting his knuckle with a mock cringe.

"If you kiss me like that every time I scare you half to death, I might have to do it more often," Leo replied, his dark eyes locking with mine and sending that desire curling down my core.

Cardin stood up, stretching his hand out to help Leo up. "Alright, alright. That's enough, you horny freaks."

Leo took Cardin's hand, standing. He did not take his eyes off of me, though. "I have a feeling it will never be enough with you, Nolei." He practically purred. I gulped, trying to hide the flutter of anticipation that rocked through me.

Eryn covered her mouth to smother her laugh. Then she hooked my elbow as we turned to walk back to the horses.

We rode in relative silence through the rest of the mountain pass. My eyes darted frantically from side to side on high alert for any more predators.

As the last of the rocky outcroppings passed us, much of the tension I had been carrying with me simmered away.

Too exhausted to do much more than set up camp and eat, we collapsed onto our bedrolls before the moon had even risen high in the sky. We assumed our prior night's sleeping arrangements, although Cardin and Eryn slept nearer to us instead of across camp from us. After the day's threats and subsequent carnage, it felt better for all of us to remain close.

Relieved to have Leo next to me, healed and well, I nestled myself closer to him. He gave me a sleepy smile and lifted his arm around me. As if this was how we slept every night and we had been doing so for years. I cuddled into him and rested my head on his chest. Being here felt so *natural*. So *right*. I settled in further, placing my arm over his chest and listening to the beat of his heart.

It was silent except for the crackling of our campfire. He kissed the top of my head, not caring about the dust caking my tangled hair.

"Thanks for saving me today. What you did was incredible. Magical."

I buried my face into his chest, breathing in the pine and campfire scent of him.

"You scared me today." Trying to put into words how I felt for him and the fear of losing him was more difficult than conjuring the magic needed to heal him earlier.

I breathed deeply and tried to focus on getting the words out. Focus on just sharing how I *felt*. It was safe to open up with Leo. Even if part of me was still weary of males and their often misguided intentions. I knew he cared for me. He was *different*. "I know this is all new and *we* are new, but when I thought you had died I just ...." A haunting chill rolled through me. "... Just don't ever do that to me again, okay?"

He squeezed me closer to him. Placing another soft kiss to the top of my head.

"I don't want to be without you either, Nolei." He bravely summarized. Gently lifting my chin, "Look at me," He commanded.

I lifted my head, searching those eyes like pools of melted bronze.

"I know everything between us is happening so fast and it feels scary." He moved his hand to cup my cheek. "It terrifies me, too. I've never felt like this about anyone before." His dark eyes searched mine. "Even though we are just getting to know each other, it feels like we've known each other for an eternity, doesn't it? Tell me you've noticed how familiar everything feels when we're together." His voice was a desperate whisper.

Relief warmed me. Knowing he felt the same made me feel less... vulnerable.

"It does," I whispered back, my voice thick with emotion. At least if we were both taking the blind jump into this *thing* between us, we could fall together. I tried to put words to my racing thoughts. "I'm thankful we are falling *together*."

"Mmm...," He let out a deep growl of approval as his gaze roamed over my face, as if he was studying every detail of me. "I know I've said this before, but I feel obligated to do so again. You look magnificent in the moonlight, Nolei."

He kissed me then, sweetly and slowly. Deeply. Not a kiss that fueled a fiery desire in us, but one that promised safety and security. A kiss that faded into a deep sleep with my head resting on his chest under the vast, star-flecked sky.

CHAPTER

TWENTY-THREE

I woke to Leo's callused hand running softly through my hair. My lips curved into a sleepy smile. The sky was mauve with cool blues, the sun just behind the horizon providing only dim light.

"Come with me," He whispered into my ruffled hair before placing yet another kiss to the top of my head. I rolled onto my back and stretched, letting out a yawn that sounded like a bear waking from hibernation.

Standing, he gave me his hand to help me up. His black hair was a tousled mess, just like mine. I grabbed my dagger and sheathed it at my thigh as he strode over to where Cardin was sleeping.

He knelt and whispered something to his friend, Cardin nodding sleepily in response. Eryn was still sound asleep a few feet to my right.

Leo grabbed my hand, leading me to his horse and lifting me up onto him with ease.

"I have a horse of my own, you know." I protested.

He swung himself up onto Kellan, settling his hips behind mine. "Obviously. But I'd prefer if we rode the same horse." I couldn't argue with that.

I was aware of every inch of him behind me. His large chest framed my back and his arms wrapped around me, holding the reins. His legs framed mine and held me in place as his breath sent shivers along my neck.

He handed me a pouch of dried berries and nuts. "Breakfast?"

"Thank you." I took it from him, tossing a few into my mouth as we rode.

"What did you say to Cardin?"

I could practically hear the smile play across his lips. "I told him you and I were going on a little excursion and not to come looking for us. Or Else."

I let out a snort of a laugh. "Oh, is that so? Where are we going?"

"It's a surprise."

With the desert mountains at our back, we traveled toward a wooded area in the distance.

"So..." I broke the companionable silence. "You told me you've been doing a lot of traveling, but where are you from?"

"Here and there," He answered, absentmindedly rubbing my hip as we rode.

"But before you traveled so much, you had to have grown up somewhere." I hoped he didn't mind my gentle prodding.

"Near the capital," he answered.

"You grew up near Celestara?" I turned my head so I could look up at him.

"Do you know of another capital?" His smirk softened the edges around my annoyance at his cocky response.

I leveled him with a stare that said 'You better start answering my damn questions or else', then turned forward.

Leo huffed out a laugh, the sound innocent and airy. "Okay, Okay. Yes, I grew up near Celestara. *The Floating City,*" He said with mock excitement. "Car and I both did."

"So, what made you leave? I've heard it's beautiful there." I imagined the towering castle positioned on a floating mass of land, enchanted by The Divine themselves. Its sprawling gardens giving way to waterfalls that flowed delicately onto the land below.

"...My family was killed when the capital was being burned to Cinders by The Dark Queen's temper tantrum," He answered slowly, the words like ash on his tongue.

"Leo, I'm so sorry. I didn't mean to bring them up again." I squeezed his leg gently.

"It's okay. I actually..." His voice trailed off into a heavy silence.

I turned my head back in time to see his brows furrow and eyes darken. "You actually what?"

"Never mind, my damsel," He said dismissively.

"Come on. What were you going to say?" I asked, the whine in my voice annoying even me.

"I actually... really like sharing a horse with you," He answered, clearly changing the subject.

I shook my head as a smile washed over my face. "Fine, my *killer with a code.* I'll let this one slide."

He laughed at my sorry attempt at a nickname equal to *my damsel.*

The landscape quickly changed from patches of dry grasses to a lush forest thick with hanging vines and exotic plants. A sweet, fresh scent hung heavy in the humid air. The trees were vibrant with life. Monkeys swung happily above us as smaller creatures skittered and scampered around the forest floor. Birds called and chirped merrily. Large flowers and leafy plants seemed to fill the space between the trees.

"This is so incredible. I have never seen a forest like this before."

"It is called a jungle." His voice was calm and confident.

"A jungle," I repeated, trying out the words.

"There is much to see beyond Eyloria, Nolei. And when we complete this adventure of yours, I'll take you to the edges of the realm to explore it all. I'll introduce you to all there is to see."

His promise stirred up tentative hope and caused my heart to squeeze in my chest again.

The sound of rushing water grew louder as we moved through the dense forest.

"We're just about there." He spoke directly into my ear, causing a buzz of desire to dance down my neck again. Gods, he was going to be the death of me if he kept that up.

As we broke through the trees and into a clearing, a gasp left me. My eyes went wide, soaking up all there was to see. We had to be at Solfire Springs.

A giant waterfall rushed down, billowing over slick rocks and settling into a wide basin of bright blue water. The water rippled at the base of the falls but quickly stilled into a calm, clear pool. It wasn't quite the size of a lake, but it was rather large to be hidden so well in this jungle. At the edge of the pool, the water trickled away in a quiet stream. The sun lit up the sacred area, casting the smooth rocks that lined the bank in a warm glow.

"This is so beautiful." I managed to get out after a period of awed silence.

"I hoped you'd like it." He dismounted and reached up, easily lifting me down from Kellan, and then planting a soft kiss on my lips. My heart gave another squeeze as that flame of desire flared to life.

There was something so fucking hot about how he lifted me, as if it took barely a fraction of his strength to do so.

He stepped back, stripping his tunic off overhead and revealing the rows of delicious muscles that lined his core. I stared unabashedly at his perfect body, my jaw open.

"Would you care to swim with me?" He asked cooly, pretending not to notice me ogling him. "I think we could both use a bath."

My eyebrows raised as I clamped my mouth shut. "Are you implying that I smell?" I teased.

"No, I'm implying that you're covered in specks of Dunemauler blood and a rather thick coating of dust." He tossed his shirt onto the ground next to him. "... And I've got a wickedly delightful image in my head from the last time I saw you bathe in a river that has been replaying in my mind on repeat every moment since then." He began unbuttoning his pants but maintained eye contact with me, making it difficult for my eyes to wander southward. "An image I'd like to recreate. With much more hands-on involvement from me, of course."

That flame began spreading through my veins at his words and the sight of him undressing before me. I gave him a coy smile as I unlaced the ties on my white flowy blouse and pulled it off, bearing my breasts with sultry confidence. Two could play this game.

His dark eyes remained locked on mine, resisting the urge to look lower, although his deepening smirk said this was a battle he was about to lose.

I unsheathed my dagger and flung it just above his head, sending it deep into the tropical tree he stood in front of.

"Fucking Gods!" He exclaimed as he ducked. The way he said it made me want to hear him say it for a whole different, far dirtier reason.

Turning his head, he looked to see where it had landed. By the time he turned back to me, I had slipped off my pants and was standing before him, completely undressed.

"What was that for--" His voice trailed off as he caught sight of me, drinking me in.

I prowled closer. "Just to keep you on your toes," I said as I grabbed his face and pulled him into me for a teasing kiss. I felt his smile form against my lips. I pulled away abruptly as he worked to continue the kiss, leaving him wanting for more.

I turned and strode into the water, leaving him to watch me. The cool water lapped at my legs and then my hips, offering a refreshing juxtaposition to the scorching desire filling my veins.

"Care to join me for a swim?" I shouted casually over my shoulder.

Before I even realized he was behind me, his large hands gripped my waist. I gasped. He spun me around, picking back up with the kiss that I had cut short.

Gods, His kiss was ... it was *everything*. A bold exploration of what was possible when we came together. A declaration of want and need, but laced with intimacy and connectedness. A playful release after the panic and uncertainty of yesterday.

I lifted my hands to frame his face, returning the hungry movement of his lips. We stayed there, exploring one another and soaking in every piece of magic that this sacred oasis had to offer. The cold water at our hips raised the sensations in my body, accentuating them.

Leo was bending down slightly, reaching to meet my lips. His touch possessive on my hips. I captured his lower lip in my teeth, causing his breath to hitch. His mouth turned even needier against my own, almost matching my desperation for him. I let out a soft moan as I felt the proof of his desire for me press against my body.

His hands pressed into my hips, lifting me to him. Not expecting it, a quick gasp left me. I wrapped my legs around his waist as he walked us deeper into the water, covering my rear with the cool water.

He held me with ease, his muscled arms flexing as he spread his hands below my thighs, supporting me. The way he held me without even an ounce of effort made me feel even more attracted to him, if that was even possible.

He broke the kiss, shifting so his teasing breath was against my neck. Another wave of wanton chills shot down my neck and into my core. I tilted my head back, eyes closing. He planted soft kisses there and then dragged his teeth against my neck, causing another moan of pleasure to escape my lips. He continued to pay homage to every curve and detail of my body. Then his lips returned to my neck, moving his greedy kisses to the space behind my ear that was quickly becoming my favorite.

Gods, I wanted more of him. Needed more of him.

Grasping his firm jaw, I lifted his lips back to mine, showing him just how those wicked kisses of his made me feel. I moved my fingers up the shortly cropped sides of his hair, pulling him closer to me. The feel of his muscled chest against my skin made me heady with the need for him.

He walked us slowly toward the falls, his steps sure despite the obvious distraction I was posing. I gasped as my back pressed against the cool stone of the edge of the falls; the water cascading over me and onto him. He caught my gasp with his mouth over mine. I needed more of him. Needed every bit of him.

Our mouths continued exploring each other's for a small, blissful eternity. Then, he turned and walked us towards the edge of the pool. Keeping my legs around his waist, he lowered himself to his knees and then reverently lowered me to the bank. The basin was bordered by large flat rocks, most of which were half submerged in the cool water. My back pressed against the cold, hard surface of the rock that he had laid me on.

He gently eased my legs away from his waist as he sat back, eyes roving over every inch of my body that was now bared fully to him. He stroked his hands down the outsides of my thighs, lips parting slightly.

"Nolei. I know I said you were magnificent in the moonlight, but I have to say that you are absolutely perfect in the sunlight, too." His lips kicked up into a one-sided smirk as the brown of his eyes turned into a liquid, heated stare. "Stunning. Breathtaking."

I stretched my arms overhead, arching my back slightly as I smiled up at him seductively. Allowing my eyes to roam his body as he had mine, I took in the sight of him kneeling between my legs.

His tan skin glistened with drops of water that slowly tracked down his muscled core. Those muscles turned into a V that cut deeply along the front of his hips, framing the long length of him that bulged with the evidence of his desire.

I inhaled sharply, running my tongue along my lips before dragging my bottom lip between my teeth. His eyes caught the motion, becoming brighter with intensity.

I let out a short giggle. "Have you seen yourself? You look like a fucking God."

He gave an unfiltered, harsh laugh. "A God of fucking?" That wicked smirk curved his lips as they roamed over my skin. "The lesser God of moans & pleasure?" He purred.

I shoved at him playfully. "You know what I mean."

"I assure you, I'm no God. But I *do* intend to pleasure you with all the skill of one."

His filthy tongue caused an ache to blossom in my center.

Running one of my hands down the side of my chest and waist, I reached for his hand and pulled him toward me. I *had* to have him closer to me. Had to feel his lips on mine again. Had to feel more of him.

He answered my beckoning, leaning forward and framing my head with his arms. The space between my body and his disappeared as he settled himself above me. I wrapped my hand around his arm, squeezing my fingers into his bicep as I kissed him even more deeply. Begging him to touch me without speaking a word.

His lips moved to my neck again, prodding my chin up as he lit a fire along my skin, tracing from my ear down to my collarbone. I arched under him, the contrast between the cold, hard stone at my back and his warm, muscular body in front of me, causing the fire to pulse even more frenetically in my veins. I could feel his hardness against my hips as I pressed myself into him, willing him to touch me. I needed to feel him inside of me. This waiting was torturous.

His smoky voice sent a jolt of sensual awareness through me as he whispered into my ear.

"I will not do anything that does not bring you pleasure, Nolei. If I go too far or you want me to stop for any reason, just say so and I will stop immediately." His raw promise caused me to pause. Many males would never utter such words, let alone honor them. But I knew he would.

I pushed my hips more firmly against him, responding to his reassurance with the proof of my want for him. He smiled against my ear and then placed a kiss to my forehead before moving lower.

He ran his hands down my waist, inhaling slowly. Then, he brought a hand to my breast, lifting it gently as he kissed his way down to it. As his lips moved down my skin, blazing a feverish trail through me, he spoke, "I have wanted to feel your body against mine from the moment I laid eyes on you, Nolei."

I let out another small laugh. "From the moment you saw me running for my life in sheer panic?" I gasped as he stroked his tongue over my nipple.

"Yes, from that moment and every moment since." He moved to my other breast, licking and stroking it in a way that caused my core to turn molten. I arched further, pressing myself into him.

He let out a low moan, moving his hands to the small of my back as he continued his wicked trail down the softness of my stomach.

"You deserve to be worshiped, Nolei. And I would like to do just that if you'll allow me." He moved his lips lower as a delicious warmth blossomed through me in response to him.

My lips parted as I took in another breath, filling my lungs with the sweet, humid air that surrounded us. I closed my eyes, the heady flood of anticipation rolling through me.

"You can do whatever you'd like to me, Leo."

He skipped down to my inner thigh, planting more soft kisses there before shocking me with a playful nip.

"Don't tempt me." His voice was deep and sensual as he continued his teasing journey up my opposite thigh.

I grasped at my breast, squeezing it as I rolled my hips in response to his touch. Gods, I needed more. His touch was sending waves of prickly awareness through my body that all pooled in the center of my core. Leaving me too hot and too desperate for more of his touch.

"Mmm". He let out a throaty growl in response to my movements. His breath danced over my center, causing me to writhe in need of his touch.

"Tell me what you want, Nolei." He whispered, kissing my inner thighs with devotion as he waited for my response.

"I want you to touch me." I pleaded, raising my hips to him again.

He ran his tongue between my legs then, causing a breathy moan to escape me.

"Like this?" He asked innocently.

"Yes." I drew out the word as my eyes closed and my back arched further. "Just like that."

He continued moving his tongue along me, stirring up the heat in my core even further. The sensation was all-consuming. I rolled my hips as he brought his hands to them, anchoring me there. He devoured me, licking and sucking as the tension inside of me ratcheted up.

"Oh, Gods." I moaned, grasping my hand into my hair.

He growled under his breath as he continued to move his mouth against me, his tongue causing the heat that pooled between my legs to dampen even more. The tension coiled in me, begging to be released. I continued rocking my hips against his mouth, the feel of his stubbled jaw prickling against my skin, causing me to squirm under his touch.

He slipped a finger inside of me then, causing a surge of pleasure to roar through me. I bucked my hips, gasping.

"Gods, you're so fucking wet for me." He slowly moved his finger in and out, the pace torturous. His wicked words were an aphrodisiac.

"Do you want me to make you come, Nolei?" He asked as he smiled wickedly from between my legs, his lips glistening.

I moaned, churning my hips against his finger, needing him to keep going. I was on fire and I needed his touch like I needed air.

"Tell me." He added a second finger, the stretch of it making the pleasure almost unbearable. "Tell me what you want."

"Yes," I answered, writhing. "Make me come." I nearly begged.

His eyes lit up in response to my words, and he let out another throaty growl as he lowered himself back between my legs.

He moved his tongue along my center and began pumping his fingers in and out of me, hitting the exact right spot and causing my whole body to coil tightly with pleasure. I let out a short, breathy exhale, my body moving with his. I felt myself barreling toward the edge; the tension continuing to ratchet up, pulling every muscle in my body taught.

I reached down and curled my fingers into the length of his dark hair, lifting my hips towards him. He held me in place with one arm wrapped around the small of my back as the other continued moving rhythmically inside of me. I writhed below him, unable to stop myself from careening toward release.

I came apart then, my body feeling like it exploded into a thousand starbursts as I screamed out. The pleasure-fueled tingling shattered me and coursed through every muscle of my body. I let myself tumble through the bliss, riding wave after wave of ecstasy until I lay completely sated on the cool stone.

Leo slowed his fingers, gently pulling them from me and sending one last sensual lick up my center as he locked eyes with me. His eyes darkened with desire.

"I used to think that the view looking out over Lunaris from Celestara was the most beautiful sight to behold in all the realm." He said, his breath hitching. "Until now."

My cheeks heated as my head buzzed with sated satisfaction. He spoke of the floating capital city, with views that likely stretched for miles.

"After watching you come apart like that, I know nothing more beautiful exists."

I leaned in. "It's my turn," I whispered as I nipped at his ear. A deep rumble left him as he flipped us so I was on top.

I followed the path that he had taken on me, exploring practically every inch of his tan skin from his neck down to his waist. His body was a masterpiece of honed muscle, inked artistry, and jagged scars. I exhaled slowly along his broad chest, the heat of my breath caused shivers to break out across his skin.

Moving down even lower, I followed the deep indents in his hips down to his hard length.

Gods, he was massive. I'd been with a few males before, but had never seen one whose body was as glorious as Leo's. I ran my hands down his hips, admiring his perfection. I let out a pleasure-driven moan of anticipation.

Bending his head up to look down at me, Leo spoke. "Even your gaze on me feels like a caress, Nolei." A smirk played at his lips as his tousled dark waves fell over his forehead.

"If my looking upon you feels good, you're going to love what I have planned next." I teased.

He raised a dark eyebrow at me seductively.

I lowered myself to him, maintaining eye contact. I grabbed the base of his rigid cock and ran my tongue up it as slowly as I could. I repeated the gesture, this time placing my mouth over the tip of him, tracing my tongue over every decadent inch of him.

"Fucking Gods." He ground out, tipping his head back again as he fought to hold his hips still against my touch.

"You're not fucking the Gods today." I continued working my mouth over him. "Just me."

He let out a light laugh that quickly turned into a deep moan.

"Your mouth feels so fucking good, Nolei. Fucking *perfect*." He dug his fingers into the stone at his back. "Just like the rest of you."

Urged on by his wicked words, I took him deeper. I moved my hands at his base while I worked the other half of him with my mouth, sucking and bobbing on him.

The feel of him in my mouth and the sight of how he responded to my touch had my blood turning molten again. "Mmm," I murmured while my lips were parted around his cock.

He lifted himself then, gently pulling me off of him. Grabbing my hands, he guided me so that I was straddling him. He pulled me into a kiss, his lips opening and tongue exploring. I held onto the sides of his face, his stubbled jawline prickling at my palms.

As our mouths moved together, I ground onto him, rubbing his length between my thighs. He groaned, pushing back against me with his hips.

"Tell me what you want, Nolei." He said breathily as he placed kisses along my jaw and neck. "Tell me what you want and I'll give it to you." His smoky voice paired with the torturous movement of him against me had me yearning for more. I *needed* to feel him inside of me. I couldn't wait another fucking minute.

"I want you inside of me," I stated boldly, tilting my head back as he kissed my neck. "I want to feel *all of you* inside of me."

Moving back to my lips, he devoured me with his kiss. He drew my lower lip between his teeth, causing me to gasp as my core pulsed with desperate need for him.

The pine and smoke scent of him invaded my senses as his hands grasped onto my hips. He lifted me slightly, guiding himself to my entrance. Gods, he was right. This slow pace was killing me. I tried to lower myself onto him, but he held me, preventing the movement. Teasing me with the feel of him, but refusing to let me have more.

"Slowly, my dear." He commanded, his voice thick with want. He began to lower me onto him. The feel of him stretching me was so intense that I inhaled sharply and kicked my head back, letting out a yelp of pleasure-filled surprise.

"That's it. You can take it, Nolei. I know you can." His strong hands continued to guide me onto him. The sensation of him stretching me and filling me so fully was overloading my senses. He felt so fucking good, despite the slight burn of me adjusting around him. I let out several short pants, trying to relax onto him and sink into the fullness.

"That's it, baby. You're so fucking tight." He growled. "But you can take it. You want more, don't you?"

I exhaled, sinking more deeply onto him. Gods, he felt so good. I needed more. Needed all of him. "Yes." I moaned. "I want *all* of you." I steadied myself with my hands on his powerful body as I continued to take him in. *Every. Delightful. Inch.*

"That's right." He continued guiding me down, squeezing my hips in a way that distracted me from the building pressure, allowing me to open more fully for him.

Gods, I couldn't take any more. I felt so full. My body couldn't fit any more of him. I squeezed my eyes shut, panting. The tension coiled in my core and swirled there, mixed between wanting more and being fully satisfied.

"You're almost there, Nolei. Gods, you feel so good." He pulled me down farther, plunging himself into me the last few inches. I let out a cry of pleasure as he buried himself in me, my head kicking back again.

He groaned. "That's it, baby." He ground out, holding us still. Him using that nickname threatened to send me over the edge before we even started.

"I knew you could take all of me." He waited for me to make the next move, giving me time to adjust.

My mouth open, I continued with short, ragged breaths. The flame was fully scorching me as the tension in my muscles danced with the soft heat of me surrounding him. I began moving then, raising myself up along his length and then sinking back down onto him. He was already slick with the proof of my arousal.

He felt so fucking good inside of me. Filling me so completely that it was maddening.

Leo let out a low growl, clenching his hands into my hips more firmly. I trembled as I moved on him, his cock rocking into me and ratcheting up the heated tension with every move.

He allowed me to guide our movements, giving me complete control.

Bracing myself with a hand on his thigh and another on his muscled core, I picked up speed. Bringing myself up and down on him and letting out short, breathy pants of pleasure. My breasts moved with the rhythm of my body, the sunlight dappling on my tan skin.

He lifted me then, flipping me onto my back below him in one swift move, picking right up where I left off as he moved inside of me. I yelped playfully as my lips curved into a smile. He brought his hand to my face and began kissing me again.

"You feel so fucking good, Nolei. But when I make you come, I want you looking right at me," He instructed, as he drove into me.

The desire was pulsing through me so furiously that I could hardly focus. His thrusts were so deep, each movement bringing me closer and closer to the edge. He kept moving, kissing me slowly as he drove into me again and again. I returned his soft kisses as I fought the urge to fall over the edge.

I was losing that battle, though. With my arms overhead, I arched my back and closed my eyes. Brows furrowing as the pleasure built.

He laced his fingers in mine, pressing soft kisses to my neck and behind my ear.

"Open your eyes, Nolei. Look at me," He coaxed. "I want you looking at me when I make you scream with pleasure."

Gods, his wicked words paired perfectly with his carnal movements. I obeyed, opening my eyes for him. I stared directly into his heated gaze. "I told you when I touch you for the first time, it will be somewhere where I can watch your fucking perfect body move against mine and revel in your shameless screams of pleasure" He placed a kiss on my lips, the gentleness a stark contrast to the intensity of his movements.

"That's a good girl." He said as he braced his hand on the rock beside my head and began pounding into me more wildly now. His movements desperate. I buried my fingers in his hair, clenching into the damp curls with one hand and clawing into his upper back with another as he rocked into me. The feel of him was too much and not enough at the same time. The tension ratcheted up. I was hurling toward the edge.

I screamed out as my release found me. I shattered into a thousand shards of pleasure, all the tension releasing into wave after wave of euphoria. He continued moving in me as I came undone, riding the waves of pleasure with me. He found his own release then, groaning into me as I continued free-falling. My whole body felt as if it was on fire in the best way.

My limbs went slack, the rest of my body following. I lay there, a pool of melted bliss, as Leo rested his forehead to mine, panting. He kissed me delicately, as if to seal what we had just shared with a sacred kiss.

We lay there, tangled up in each other, watching the clouds move overhead for what seemed like a small eternity. A chunk of time that somehow still seemed too short.

I wished we could stay like this forever, just Leo and I in this secret little oasis without the looming threat of The Dark Army or the loneliness and hurt of losing Gran. Just him and I, fully bared to each other.

After our sated haze lifted, Leo turned to me and kissed me softly. "Thank you." He whispered.

"For what?" I replied, brows furrowing.

"For sharing yourself with me today. For trusting me, even if I don't deserve it." He kissed my nose.

"You deserve --" He stood up then, cutting me off. Reaching down for my hand, he pulled me up. Before I could speak, he scooped me up into his arms and carried me out into the water. I let out a playful scream.

"It's time for that bath you are in need of, my damsel."

"I'm no damsel--" I shrieked as he dunked me into the cool water, submerging me completely.

He lifted me back up, a large, beautiful smile lighting up his features. I splashed him right in that perfect face of his.

He laughed, spinning me around in his arms. The sound made my heart feel near to bursting.

Managing to wriggle free, I splashed him again and dunked him under. The water was so refreshing and clear, the turquoise blue almost unnatural in its beauty.

Everything felt so easy with Leo. So natural. We continued on, swimming and simply being together. Enjoying each other's company in this secret little spring. Even though we didn't find what we came in search of, everything felt just as it should be. Easy. Right. *Safe*.

CHAPTER

TWENTY-FOUR

A s we readied ourselves to head back to camp, we gazed out over the springs, searching for any other sign that this place held the magic we were looking for. Even though Solfire Springs was absolutely breathtaking in more ways than one, there was no sign of this magical mirror pond. No shimmering essence drifting out of the water or awakening reflection when I peered into it.

Instead, we found a tropical sanctuary. And even though we didn't find the truth promised by The Scroll in these cool waters, a different type of magic sparked here. One neither of us expected. One forged from trust and connection, woven by intimacy and bound by the unmistakable resonance between us. This primal pull toward one another that neither of us could ignore.

Leo moved behind me, wrapping his arms around me and pulling me to his chest.

"We'll find the pond, find your parents. I'll be there every step of the way." He kissed my temple. "Together, we'll figure this out."

I let myself soften into his hold. My eyes roamed over the little glen, soaking up every detail of this magical place. Of how I felt in Leo's arms. Safe. Seen.

As we approached camp, the landscape changed from lush and tropical to dry and dusty again. The sated daze I was in had long worn off and my mind was back to its usual racing. It fluttered from thought to thought like a hummingbird.

The morning hours I had shared with Leo were incredible. It was so freeing to have that sacred time between just the two of us where we could let our guard down and be together. Where we could sink into the moment without the pressure of the outside world demanding our attention.

Not to mention, what happened between us physically was like nothing I had ever experienced before. My body responded to even the smallest of his touches. Gods, it was as if his body was crafted by The Mother Elowen, Goddess of sexuality, for physical pleasure alone. And the way he moved it against mine was wicked and wonderful. The way he moved it inside of mine... I let out a soft groan at the thought.

Realizing what I had done, I snapped my mouth shut. My cheeks turned a heated red. Thank the Goddesses he couldn't see my face from where he rode behind me on Kellen.

"Did you just... moan?" He asked. I felt the words rumble up his chest from where my back was pressed into him.

"Of course not." I retorted.

"If that is your response to being astride Kellen for a few hours, I may have to have a word or two with him." He quipped.

I turned, glaring at him. I was actually feeling pretty fucking sore. Although my muscles had become accustomed to riding, they had not yet become accustomed to riding Leo. My lips curved into a sultry smile as I stared forward. This was a soreness I was not about to complain about.

When we arrived back at camp, Eryn was fastening her bedroll to Lady Lace. She gave me a sly smirk as we approached, raising one brow in question. I gave her a subtle nod, affirming her assumptions. Her returning smile lit up her face. I could feel Leo sitting up straighter and puffing out his chest slightly behind me. I couldn't help but laugh.

Wisely choosing not to engage Eryn and me on the unmentioned topic at hand, Leo changed the subject.

"Where is Car?"

"He left a while ago to check the traps he had laid last night to see if he could scrounge us up some breakfast," Eryn replied.

Leo swung down, turning to lift me off the horse, and set me beside him.

"How long ago is a while ago?"

Eryn planted her hands on her hips. "Let me see... I laid under the blankets staring at the sky for a while, contemplating the meaning of life. Then I got up, saw to my needs, and poked at the fire. Then I ate a handful of nuts and an apple from my bag to assuage my hunger, and now I'm picking up my bedroll." She gave him a bland look. "That's how long."

Leo grunted as he turned from Eryn and began tending to Kellan. Something about how tall, dark, and moody he was had my attraction to him intensifying.

I smiled. "That was likely several hours ago, then, considering how long you typically spend contemplating the meaning of life each morning. Such a scholar, our Eryn."

She rolled her eyes at me and turned back to her horse.

I stretched my arms overhead and arched my back, trying to will away the kinks.

"I hope he comes back soon. I'm starving." I mused.

Leo's dark eyes roved over me, and then he nodded in my direction. "Take a break and stretch your legs. We should go look for him if he isn't back shortly. It's unlike him to have left Eryn here alone for any period of time."

"Are you sure you don't want to stretch her out yourself, Leo?" Eryn said, ignoring the thread of concern that laced his voice.

He turned slowly toward her, meeting her taunting gaze. He opened his mouth to respond.

"—Don't even put words to whatever thought was about to come out of your mouth," I warned him.

He pressed his lips together, biting them, and then gave me a flourishing bow before turning back to fuss with Kellan some more.

S ome time later, we followed Leo from horseback as he guided his and Cardin's horses by the reins. Apparently, one of Leo's many skills was being an avid tracker. I should have realized this when he found me in the middle of those woods when I was fighting off the males from The Dark Army.

We remained silent as he led us in a wide, arcing perimeter around where we had stayed the night prior. We came across two of the locations where Cardin had taken down one of his traps. The dirt was kicked up, and the brush had been snapped in various places. We continued following his trail.

As we neared a large, brown boulder that towered overhead, we heard a faint buzzing sound. A thrumming similar to the sound I heard when I felt the land's energy flowing into me. *Magic.*

Leo rounded the boulder, glancing up as he inhaled sharply.

"Careful—"I tried to warn before I made it around the rock myself.

My warning fell short as I craned my neck to see Cardin floating several feet above the ground in front of us. His arms were bound to his sides with what looked like rope. It moved and writhed around him as if it were alive. It had twisted around him like a sandstorm, a furious spiral of dust that held him fast in its grip. This must be the magic I had heard. A wisp of brown rope encircled his mouth, preventing him from speaking. His eyes were wide, as if trying to warn us.

"Don't take another step," warned a sharp voice that came from above us.

CHAPTER

TWENTY-FIVE

I froze, not wanting to anger whoever it was that held Cardin here. My heartbeat kicked up until my pulse was an incessant drumming in my ears. Turning my head slowly, I looked toward the source of the voice.

A female kneeled on a nearby rock, an arrow fixed directly at Leo's head. Where she was located, we should have been able to see her before now.

She was dressed in all earth tones, an olive green wrapped shirt fitted tightly to her chest. She wore long beige pants that had deep slits on both sides but cinched back together at her ankles. The slits revealed long, ebony legs. Rows of beaded bands circled her waist and fell at the sides of her hips. Her arms and neck were adorned with the same beading. Sharply pointed ears peeked out from behind dark hair which was twisted in a hundred tight braids that all cascaded down the length of her back.

Gods, she was ... she was beautiful. *Lethal*.

She was pointing an arrow at *my* male, though. And had his best friend trapped.

My awe was quickly doused with anger and determination. Although I didn't know quite where this possessive desire came from, it bolstered my nerves.

"I wouldn't do that if I were you," I warned, raising my chin slightly and leveling a fierce stare at her.

Eryn's blond hair whipped around her as she spun her head in my direction, clearly shocked by my audacity. I ignored her response.

The way this woman's eyes moved over me made it clear that she was trying to discern something.

"Or else what?" She cooed, her voice hollow with the promise of death.

Or else I throw a dagger at her and hope my aim is better than it was yesterday? Or I hope I can figure out how to summon my powers to fight her off before she hurts any of us. For fuck's sake, what *could* I do? Panic started quickening my pulse further and frayed my racing thoughts. I tried to come up with a response as I kept on an external mask of calculating rage.

"How about you come down from there, let our friend here go, and we can talk about this civilly?" Leo suggested kindly, really kicking up the charm.

"How about you shut that pretty mouth of yours before I bury this arrow into it?" Her words dripped with venom.

Cardin thrashed against his bindings. Leo maintained eye contact, slowly raising his hands in surrender. I knew he was calculating his next move, though, and the *last* thing he would do was surrender. *Ever.*

Eryn remained oddly silent, her hand on the hilt of her sword.

My anger joined the thrum of my pulse as I took in the situation. There was no way in all of the Cinder Wastes that I was going to let this woman win this... whatever *this* was. Not after all I'd been through. From watching Gran be murdered at the hands of The Dark Army, to almost being murdered myself, to witnessing Leo's near-death in the jaws of a Dunemauler. *Enough was enough.* She had chosen the wrong group to mess with.

I didn't know how to control my powers or wield them with any expertise, but I knew how to call upon them. Well, sort of. I let all of my emotions swirl through me and feed into my fury — fear, frustration, determination. They all churned in my blood. The rocks on the ground shook. I wasn't sure what I was about to do, but I sure as fuck was going to do *something*. Energy hummed through me, coursing down my arms. Violent gusts of wind tugged at everything in their path.

Her eyes widened briefly, and then she pivoted, facing me. She looked me directly in the eye and then let her arrow fly.

"Nolei!" Leo and Eryn shouted simultaneously. Bracing myself for the inevitable impact, I squeezed my eyes shut. This was it. This was how I died.

The sharp slice of pain never hit me, though. Opening my eyes just in time, I watched as the arrow plummeted directly into the writhing ropes that covered Cardin. Instead of sinking deep into his flesh, the arrow turned to sparks and caused the bindings to disappear on impact.

Eyes wide, Cardin began to free fall toward the ground. Before he landed, the female shot her hand out in his direction, causing a bolt of energy to shoot from her fingers. He paused, briefly levitating a few inches from the ground, and then fell abruptly the rest of the way.

Cardin grunted, rolled to his side, and then stood. Leo ran to him, grabbed his shoulders, and steadied him.

I turned to look at the woman, just in time to see her disappear into an iridescent purple-gray fog. My brows furrowed. *What the fuck was happening?*

She appeared just in front of Camila, her bow now sheathed at her back. "*Váliarë*," she said to me with an air of excitement.

My breathing stopped. *Everything* felt like it stopped. My heart. My emotions. The chaos. Everything went still. *Did she just say what I thought she did?*

"What did you call me?" I demanded, shock rattling through me.

Before she could repeat herself, Leo was behind her. He grabbed onto her wrists and twisted them behind her. He quickly fastened them together with a belt of leather, spun her, shoved her toward Cardin. Once she was in Cardin's hold, Leo grabbed roughly onto her chin, lifting her face to his. She didn't fight back at all. She was clearly deadly and unafraid.

"You're lucky you are a female." He growled at her, eyes swirling with darkness. "Or I would cut your head from your shoulders."

Stunned by what I heard her say, I jumped off my horse and walked up to her.

"What did you say?" I asked, forcing myself to speak despite the pure shock that held my mind like a clenched fist.

Her full lips parted as she spoke. "*Váliarë*." She said again, her eyes flaring brighter.

Leo shoved her, causing her head to jerk back. "What the *fuck* does that mean?"

Her bright green eyes remained fixed on me.

"She's clearly addled, but she better not be putting some type of spell on you." Leo said to me as he tried to move me back with his arm.

"If you cause any harm to come to her, you will die. At my hands." He leveled a lethal glare at her. "That, I promise."

"Enough!" I shouted, trying to break free from the shock that held me. *Where would she have heard that? Why in the realm would she call me that?*

"*Váliarë.*" Eryn spoke, approaching us. "It means *Moon Blessed*. Her Gran used to call her that."

Cardin and Leo turned to me and then back to this woman. This woman who just called me the same thing that my Gran has been calling me since I was a babe. Who just threatened all of us and then allowed herself to be captured.

"Let her go," I demanded, hoping this decision wouldn't be one I came to regret.

"Nolei..." Leo spoke, his voice firm.

"Let. Her. Go." I repeated, determination sharpening my tone.

"I mean... she trapped me, threatened all of you, and then almost shot an arrow at —-" Cardin argued.

"—- Release her," Leo ordered, cutting him off. "If Nolei says let her go, we let her go."

Gods, the way he honored my wishes, even in moments like this, stirred a warmth deep in my chest. Although, I had to admit, watching this dark side of him rear its head was oddly... hot.

Cardin cursed to himself as he withdrew his dagger and released her wrists.

She walked forward, her lips turning into a bright smile as her face lit up with awe. The dark brown skin of her arms was thoroughly marked with black ink, mostly symbols, from what I could tell.

"Who are you?" I asked.

"Sappha, *Váliarë,*" she spoke reverently.

I nodded at her and reached out, clasping her arm in greeting.

"We have much to speak of, Sappha."

She nodded back in agreement.

Not wanting to stand in the middle of the barren land, we made our way to where an outcropping of boulders leaned against each other, creating a spacious, shady reprieve below. Sappha seemed to summon her mare with a magical swirl of her wrist. It was an equally beautiful beast. Its hair was also adorned with beads and fur was painted with white symbols.

This conversation wasn't one that could be rushed or done in a threatening manner, especially not when tensions were high in the middle of the desert. It deserved time, space, and hospitality. We would share a meal and get to know each other, I decided.

Keeping a wary eye in our direction, Cardin busied himself with building a small fire and roasting the few animals he had captured prior to being captured himself. Thank the Gods, because I was starving.

Leo moved several large boulders into a semi-circle, creating seats of sorts for us to rest on. The way he hefted them up, his shoulders and back muscles bulging with the weight of them, caused that wicked curl of desire in my center to return. I ignored it, trying to focus on the task at hand.

I had to figure out who Sappha was, where she had heard that phrase, and why in the realm seeing me would cause her to speak such words. It was ...eerie.

Eryn and I sat beside each other and faced Sappha, who was still staring at me like I was glowing or something. Leo stationed himself behind us, his arms crossed at his chest and a dark glare fixed on Sappha. Glancing at him, I rolled my eyes. I secretly loved how he sought to protect me, though. It was clear he did not trust her and did not want her anywhere near me.

"I'll be honest. I have many questions for you and don't know quite where to begin." I tilted my head slightly, sizing her up.

"Let's start with *who the fuck you are* and why you keep staring at Nolei like she is one of The Divine Feminine." Leo's voice seethed with barely leashed violence.

"Nolei..." Sappha spoke as if she was testing the feel of my name on her tongue. She took a slow, deep inhale, straightening slightly. She was heavily armed with knives, daggers, and swords, in addition to the bow on her back. From what little I saw of her, it didn't seem like she needed to rely much on those weapons when she had magic spewing freely from her fingertips.

"My birth name is Magnolia, but you may call me Nolei." I started, my tone much kinder than Leo's.

She nodded at me slightly. "I am Sappha. I come from the far west. I am traveling alone on a .... errand of sorts."

"We come from the far west," Eryn chimed in. "We are from Eyloria. But we haven't seen you there before. Where is it you come from exactly?"

What other city *far west* could she be from if not Eyloria? I wondered to myself.

Her hesitant gaze flicked from Eryn to Leo and back to me, as if deciding how much to share with us.

"You may speak freely," I reassured her, knowing that we too carried our own secrets. From the ease with which she wielded magic, I had a feeling she was not a supporter of The Dark Enchantress.

"I hail from the woods south of Eyloria."

My brows furrowed. "The Covenwoods?"

She nodded again, her beaded braids falling forward as she did so.

"You're a witch, then?" Leo asked, his tone curious and less filled with violence than before.

She raised her chin slightly and straightened her shoulders. "I am Sappha of the Covenwood Witches."

"I thought the Covenwood Witches were all killed off after The Dark Enchantress stole the throne?" Cardin asked from his spot by the fire.

"You thought wrong," Sappha replied calmly, keeping her eyes locked on me.

Not able to believe that I was in the presence of a true witch, my mind swirled with even more questions. First, what kind of magic and spells could she do? Could she teach me some things? I knew healing arts and some basic magic from Gran, but Sappha likely had centuries' worth of knowledge that had been handed down through generations of witches.

And what price must she pay to perform such magic? It was said that the witches would sacrifice anyone they could get their hands on for their blood rituals. Is that what she was planning to do with Cardin?

"Why did you say *Váliarë* when you saw Nolei?" Eryn's question interrupted my whirling thoughts.

Ignoring Eryn's question, Sappha spoke. Her green eyes flared vibrantly as she fixed them on me. "Because you are the one I've been looking for."

CHAPTER

TWENTY-SIX

I swallowed thickly.

"What do you mean by that?"

"You are *Váliarë*. The one who is blessed by the Goddesses and the moon. The one who carries the powers of two great lines and marries them in her blood. The one who carries *The Witching Stitch*."

Silence fell among us. The only noise was the faint crackling of the fire.

The one who is blessed. The one who carries the powers of two great lines. The Witching Stitch. I played her words over in my head slowly as my body felt frozen in shock.

Was she speaking of what was mentioned in The Scroll? She must be speaking of my birth parents. Must know *who they are* to speak such words. But how? Confusion muddled my thoughts. I had never heard of this 'Witching Stitch.' She must have me mistaken for someone else.

"I carry no such thing." I protested.

"But you do." She stated with certainty.

"I have never even heard of *The Witching Stitch,* so how could I be carrying it with me?" I motioned to Camila and the other horses. "I carry nothing with me besides clothes, food, and some herbs and salves." My hand came up to the jeweled eye necklace that was ever present between my breasts. "And this." Maybe this *Verdant Eye* necklace is also *The Witching Stitch*?

A kind smile played at her full lips. "You do not carry it with you. It dwells inside of you. It is a part of you. Just as The Divine Feminine is a part of us all."

My brows knitted together again. Inside of me. *My powers?* Was she speaking of my new abilities? I did not have time to talk to Gran about them and nobody knew what they were.

The thought of Gran caused a jagged pang of grief to cut through me. I tried to tuck it away, so the tears didn't come pouring out again. Not now.

I thought back to how Sappha's behavior had changed drastically when I called on the energy around me. When the rocks began shaking, her eyes went wide, and she loosed the arrow directly at me. It had somehow changed directions completely and released Cardin, though. Then she transported herself in a heartbeat.

"And how the fuck do *you* know that? What leads you to make such claims?" Leo asked, his arms still crossed tightly over his wide chest.

Sappha held Leo's glare. "This conversation would go even better if you could keep your mouth shut. I find that there is very little a male could say to add value to *any* conversation."

Eryn stifled a laugh, and Cardin let out a low whistle. The unfettered rage that radiated from Leo was near-palpable. He let out a throaty growl that I was damned glad I wasn't on the receiving end of. I turned and gave him a pleading smile. He huffed and stayed quiet.

Sappha started again. "Your aura, it's seeping from you like starlight. I could tell immediately that you carry magic. Many do, but either do not know how to wield it or are too fearful to do so." Her hand came to her chin, and she ran her fingers along her bottom lip while studying me. "But the glow you cast is ... *intense*."

Eryn turned to me, squinting slightly. Cardin glanced at me and then back to Sappha. Leo was a hulking, silent presence behind me.

"I don't see it." Eryn tilted her head.

"You wouldn't," Sappha answered blandly.

"Then how do *you* see it?" Cardin asked.

"Because I have a special set of ... skills... that allows me to see such things." Sappha said. How vagueness was wearing on my patience.

"As fun as this whole little game that you are playing with us is, it is getting old. Fast." My voice turned sharp and my gaze stern.

"I know not what you speak of, *Váliarë*." Her ebony skin was nearly flawless and practically glowed despite us being positioned in the shade.

"You say something cryptic. We ask you to clarify. You answer in a riddle. We get even more confused." I gave her a forced smile that showed my annoyance.

"I think what Nolei is trying to say is," Leo shifted his hand to the hilt of the sword at his hip. "You better start telling us what you know, and you better start telling us *now*. You've been spewing nonsense and Nolei here would like the truth. Share the information willingly, or we will extract it through far bloodier methods. The choice is yours." His voice was dark and caused goosebumps to gather along my arms. "I personally prefer the latter option." He near growled at her. "Either way, start talking."

"That wasn't exactly where I was going with that, but thanks." A nervous laugh escaped me.

Sappha's green eyes studied us wearily. "You are *Váliarë*..." she started.

"For fuck's sake. You said that already," Eryn cut her off.

Sappha glared at Eryn and then returned her gaze to me. "... I know this because you have a powerful aura. That alone is not of much consequence, but when you shook the land around us, everything clicked into place."

"Meaning...?" Leo prodded.

"Meaning...." Sappha took a large breath in. "Meaning that I realized you are the one I have been searching for. The one who carries magic and the ability to wield the energy of the world around her. The one who carries the power of two great lines. The one who carries *The Witching Stitch*." Her voice held its own frustration at our lack of understanding.

Realization dawned on me. "You mean *The Witching Stitch* is the name for my abilities?"

"It is." She smiled, then. Doing so transformed her beauty and softened her face immensely.

"*The Witching Stitch*," I repeated dumbly. *I couldn't believe it.* Even though she had said as much, it didn't click until now. After all this time of wondering what was happening to me and not knowing what it was, Sappha knew. She knew as soon as she saw me. She knew what it was *called*. I wasn't just some freak who caused the wind and rocks to respond to my emotions. I carried *power*. Carried *The Witching Stitch*.

"How do you know all of this?" Cardin questioned as he ripped a portion of meat from the small creature that was now speared on a stick and roasted. It appeared to be some type of desert hare. He passed the stick to Eryn, who scrunched her nose at it, sniffed, and took a small portion.

"As I said... I possess certain *skills* which allow me to see such things."

The metallic sound of Leo yanking his sword free from his hip caused me to jump slightly.

"That's it..." He growled as stalked toward her.

I quickly got to my feet. "Leo! Stop!" I practically squealed, moving forward to grab onto his arm. He paused in response to my touch, turning his head in my direction.

"We just told her she better start speaking and stop dicking us around or else." He turned back to Sappha, who was still sitting calmly on a boulder, not so much as reaching for a weapon of her own. "... and apparently she would like to find out what 'or else' entails."

"It's not my fault that you are unable to comprehend my answers." She raised her chin at him. "It is my experience that large boars like you tend to think with their cocks and not their brains. If this is too difficult of a concept for you to grasp, you may be better off helping your friend here cook while we women do the talking."

Oh shit. This was about to escalate if I didn't do something. *Fast.* I glanced at Eryn. She gave me a wide-eyed look and whispered, "Uh oh."

Leo's glare turned deadly and I could feel the anger simmering off of him. The anger that was rapidly turning into violence. I could feel his muscles tense beneath my hand as rage stiffened his body.

I squeezed his arm and pulled him to face me. I grabbed his cheeks and kissed him. *Slowly.* At first, he resisted, trying to turn back to Sappha. But soon he surrendered to my touch and kissed me back. I pulled away gently, locking my eyes with his. He blinked his eyes open and took a slow breath.

"Do you need to go for a walk? Clear your head?" I asked him softly, maintaining eye contact.

He shook his head. "I'm not leaving you here with this wraith. I'm fine."

I raised my brows at him, questioning the truth of his statement.

"I'm good." He assured, nodding his head. He seemed like he was trying to convince himself more than me.

"Is this your new thing now?" Cardin asked lightly as he took another bite of meat from the bone. "You just kiss him and he does what you say?"

Leo turned his head slowly toward Cardin and fixed that deadly glare on him.

"Car..." He threatened.

"I like it." Cardin's blonde hair moved lightly as a refreshing breeze blew past us. "I think I'll try it, in fact. Just give ya a nice long kiss and see if you'll listen to me for once."

Eryn laughed as I tried to smother my own laugh. Sappha even smirked.

"As I was saying..." Sappha continued. "I sometimes will be blessed with a vision of something that is yet to come."

"You're a seer." Eryn stated as she inhaled sharply. She passed the roasted animal on to me.

Sappha nodded at her. This was all starting to make sense.

"And you had a vision about me?"

"I did. When the Weaver's Moon was full in the sky." She replied.

I froze. That was the night of Gran's death. The first night I had ever really wielded my powers. Taken a life. The night I found The Scroll.

Sappha continued. "I had a powerful vision of someone using both the magical arts and wielding the elemental energies. A very rare combination that only *one* could possess. That only exists within *one* soul. A soul that was married in blood 26 years ago. That one person is *you*, Nolei. Only *one* could carry the abilities from these two lines and harness their power. The true heir of two peoples."

Heir? Thinking I must not have heard her correctly, I shook my head.

"Did you say heir? What do you mean by heir?"

"Yes, the true heir to two peoples." She confirmed, eyes churning with bright green wonder.

I caught Leo glancing at Cardin, both of their faces etched with confusion.

"What do you mean *true heir*? The true heir to the kingdom was killed by The Dark Enchantress when she stole the throne." Cardin stated with disbelief.

"I said heir of two peoples, not heir of the kingdom." Sappha corrected flatly.

I literally had no fucking clue what she was talking about. What two peoples? The only people I knew of were the people of Lunaris and they were all suffering under The Dark Queen's rule. But if she did not mean heir to the kingdom of Lunaris, then what *did* she mean?

"I promised Nolei I would keep my shit locked down. I intend to keep that promise. But you are making it damn hard to do so," Leo said, his voice dark.

Sappha raised her brows at him as she casually reached for the stick of meat I was passing her way, still in shock from this entire conversation. "That sounds like a *you* problem."

Leo let out a sound that was practically a growl.

"What ... What two peoples?" I asked.

"That is not for me to tell, Nolei."

"Are you fucking kidding me right now?" Leo pulled his hand through his hair and turned to me, his eyes pleading. I give him a warning look. He let out a huff of frustration and paced back to me. He sat on the boulder I was on and pulled me onto his lap. I stiffened at first, but then quickly softened into his touch. The feel of his strong chest at my back was steadying. I imagined the feel of me in his lap was equally soothing for him.

Cardin raised his brows at both of us and took another bite.

"So who *can* tell me?"

"Wait... so why *are* you here?" Eryn cut in before Sappha could answer me. "Why are you so far from home? And what were you planning to do with Cardin?"

"Yeah, what were you going to do with me?" Cardin parroted, clearly amused by this entire exchange.

Sappha took another bite and then tossed the stick in the fire. "I had this vision and was compelled to search for the one who carries *The Witching Stitch*. For what purpose, I do not know. I do not take the gift of any vision from The Goddesses lightly. If they chose to show me this, there was a reason behind it. Even if we are not yet privy to it." She kicked one foot up over the opposite knee, resting comfortably on the boulder. "As for him —" She nodded in Cardin's direction. "I saw the traps he had set last night and waited for him to return. As with many things, I felt led to do so. It is imperative that I lean heavily into my intuition, as it is the wisdom of Elowen, The Mother, and all of my matron ancestors that guide me. It is obvious to me now why I had such a feeling."

This woman's belief in The Divine was impressive. Sure, we all honored them, but this was next level devotion.

"So now what?" Eryn asked, as if bored.

Leo buried his face in my neck and inhaled deeply, placing gentle kisses along the skin there. His hand held tightly to my hip, anchoring me to him. His touch was intoxicating and... very distracting. I wiggled my hips back-and-forth subtly in his lap to distract him back. He groaned softly into my ear, causing a wicked smile to break free on my face. *Gods, I needed to focus.*

"Good Gods, you two." Cardin chucked an apple at us in an attempt to get us to stop... whatever it was we were doing. Leo caught it without even looking and then took a bite, smirking back at Cardin.

"So my powers are called *The Witching Stitch*." I continued. "Why are they called that?"

"Again, the answers to many of these questions are not mine to tell. But it refers to the binding of two powerful lines. The unique powers that can only reside in one." Sappha's voice was calm.

If she would stop speaking in cryptic riddles, that would be great.

"So, who *can* tell me the answers? We are searching for the truth about my birth parents in hopes of learning more about my past and more about my .... abilities."

Sharing this with her was not easy. It involved admitting that I don't know who my true parents were, and that I knew little about my own powers. The vulnerability made my skin clammy and my heart race. Leo noticed and pulled me in closer, placing another kiss behind my ear.

"I do not know, but I can help you find out." She promised, eyes clear with determination. "There is a reason I have been sent on this errand by The Divine Feminine and if it is to help you in these matters, then so be it."

CHAPTER

TWENTY-SEVEN

We rode on, heading west. I tried to wrap my mind around today's events. First everything with Leo at Solfire Springs. His body. His words. Our connection.

Then, preparing to fight for our lives when we found Cardin had been captured. Thank the Goddesses he was alive. I could never have thought we would have gotten from that situation to this Covenwood warrior woman agreeing to *help* us. Help *me*.

I finally had a name for the powers I yielded. Finally, I knew what it was. *The Witching Stitch*. I kept playing the words over in my mind. But I was no witch. Witches were powerful and knew how to draw from the spiritual realm, and how to call upon ancient knowledge of spells and herbs. Gran had taught me how to do some basic healing spells from her tomes, but I didn't know how to *use* magic.

I sat a little taller as I rode, knowing that I had finally learned more about myself. Even if I didn't have all the answers yet. I had *this* answer.

I shared with Sappha the details of The Scroll.

In shadowed woods where Wolfsbane blooms,
and ancient trees hold silent sway,
A mirror pond reflects the truth,
guiding you on your way.

The quest we were on to find this '*mirror pond*' somewhere in the woods. How we followed the twisted rivers to their end and had been wandering more or less aimlessly since. Leo and I filled Eryn and Cardin in on how Solfire Springs was not the spot we were looking for. Although it was a place I'd never forget, it didn't hold the secrets we sought.

Leo and Cardin remained hesitant about Sappha's true intentions. They were fearful that she was taking advantage of us for some other reason. But I knew she wasn't. I couldn't explain it, but I felt this bond between us. Felt her sincerity. It just felt *right*. She felt familiar and like ... like we were meant to cross paths. Sappha had said that she relied heavily on her intuition and allowed it to guide her. Who was to say I couldn't do the same?

Sappha had said that she did not know exactly where this *mirror pond* was but knew how we could *find* it. We continued west, aiming for the forest that covered the land of Lunaris south of The Sanguine River. Over the next few days, the dry, sandy land and oversized boulders slowly changed into grassy fields.

The conversation came easily, the five of us getting to know each other and sharing more of the stories of the past that made us who we were.

Leo and Cardin told us of harsh winters spent in Runedal and tales of treacherous sea beasts off the coast of Comet's Rest. I shared stories of crazed ex-lovers who came to Gran seeking retribution in the form of forbidden tinctures or straw poppets.

Sappha seemed to fit in just fine, sharing her own remedies for various emotional ailments of the fae heart. She shared some of what it was like to grow up in an all female Coven. Of how different life has been since The Dark Queen usurped the throne and they had to stay under the radar within the Covenwoods instead of traveling the realm for fear of persecution. She dreamed of a day where magic was no longer forbidden and was committed to helping that come to be, whatever that entailed.

As we approached the edge of the dark woods, the horses slowed instinctively. Even though it was midday, the forest had a deep emerald hue to it. The light seemed to not fully penetrate the canopy, leaving the woods dim and mysterious. The trees were teaming with life. Birds twittered constantly and small creatures scampered about.

"Where do we go from here?" Eryn asked hesitantly.

Sappha swung off of her horse, handing the reins to Cardin. He narrowed his eyes at her.

"Nolei, Eryn, and I will be back shortly." She said with an air of nonchalance as she strode into the trees.

I looked questioningly at Eryn. Sappha had said that she knew how we could find the *mirror pond* we were searching for, but she didn't say *how* we would obtain this knowledge. Eryn shrugged silently.

Leo's brows furrowed, as if he was trying to comprehend what was happening.

"If you think I'm letting you lead them into these creepy ass woods alone with you, you are dafter than I gave you credit for." He said to Sappha as he moved to help me down from Camila. Cardin snickered.

My gaze lifted as I took in the forest. The giant trees towered over us, their lush foliage seemingly woven together. The forest floor was heavy with moss-covered rocks, ferns, mushrooms, and fallen twigs. Even though the sun was mostly filtered out, a vibrance seemed to hum between the trees and create its own luminescence. The air smelled of rich, damp, soil... in a refreshing way.

"This forest isn't creepy." I corrected. "It's... magical."

Leo stared at me for a long moment, as if studying me, and then the side of his lips kicked up into the hint of a smile.

"You would think a creepy forest is magical, Nolei."

I let out a short giggle and gave him a gentle shove. "And you would threaten Sappha for trying to help us find what we seek."

He raised his hands innocently. "I'm not threatening her for helping us. I'm threatening her for trying to lure you into the woods alone so she can kill you or use you for a sacrifice or whatever witchy shit she has planned. And I didn't even *threaten* her." He clarified.

Sappha turned slowly to face Leo, clearly bored with this conversation. "If I needed a blood sacrifice, I'd choose you first."

Eryn and I both laughed in response to that.

I pressed my hands on his wide chest and looked into his dark eyes. He moved his hands to the small of my back, causing a pang of awareness to shoot through me. "We'll be fine. Sappha will not hurt any of us. She is here to help us." He sighed and met my gaze, his heart rate slowing below my palms. "The sooner you stop treating her like the enemy, the better."

One eyebrow shot up. "Are you using the obvious impact that physical contact with you has on me to manipulate me? *Again*?" I reached up and kissed him, slowly and softly.

"I don't know what you're speaking of," I whispered, my lips brushing his as I spoke. He leaned into me, trying to kiss me more deeply as I pulled away. I turn and began following Sappha.

"Oh, Gods. We're back to this again." Cardin groaned.

Eryn walked past him and handed him her reins. Then the three of us walked into the woods.

Leo shouted after us. "If you're not back in ten minutes, I'm coming after you!"

We moved in relative silence through the woods, following Sappha. She seemed to walk without hesitation, as if she knew where we were going. Or at least knew what she was looking for.

After a short time, she found a large tree. The trunk was so wide I wouldn't be able to wrap my arms halfway around it if I tried.

"Why do you need all three of us?" Eryn asked, her boots crunching on a twig as she walked.

"Because the more feminine energy we have, the better," Sappha responded, pulling a knife out. Eryn stared hesitantly at the blade, as if Sappha was about to use it against her.

I watched closely, but without trepidation. I just *knew* that Sappha could be trusted. Some innate, bone-deep wisdom assured me she was honorable.

"The better for what?" I asked, coming to a stop beside her in front of the tree.

Sappha carved shapes into the tree, the scraping of her blade against the bark barely audible through the chatter of the forest. A circle in the center with two opposing slender crescent shapes on either side. The moon phases. The Divine Feminine.

I nodded slowly in realization. She must be carving out the symbol for The Divine Feminine, to draw on their guidance.

"The better for getting the answers we need." Her vague answer irked me. *Why must she always speak in such a way?* I took a slow breath, trying to calm the rush of frustration.

Sappha dragged her boot in a half circle around us, creating a faint line in the sticks and leaves on the ground. I sensed that this was more an energetic circle than a true marking of the ground. But what did I know?

Eryn and I tracked her movements silently. She bent down, grabbing an armful of small rocks, which she placed in various spots around us. I had no clue what it was she was doing.

Sappha kneeled between Eryn and me, facing the tree. We stared dumbly down at her.

"Kneel." She commanded.

We silently obeyed, our knees pressed into hers as we all fit inside the circle she had etched into the ground.

Sappha turned her head towards me. "Do you have The Scroll?"

I shook my head. "No. I cannot access it without the light of the full moon. The magic that hides it requires that, as a safeguard."

She paused as she considered my answer.

"But I have the *Verdant Eye* that *contains* The Scroll." I blurted out.

"What is a *Verdant Eye*?" she questioned, brows pinching.

Peer into the verdant eye, where the shadows of yesterday whisper their truths. They were Gran's final words to me. A clue of where to look for the secrets I did not know were even hiding from me. My frustration grew. How could she lie to me my entire life? Everything I had grown up knowing as truth about my family was actually a lie.

My fingers roamed familiarly over the pendant necklace between my breasts. *To wear it is to carry their blessing and wisdom.* I removed the necklace and handed it to Sappha.

Her vibrant green eyes locked with mine as she recognized the magnitude of this gesture. Me handing this over to her without question. The trust it signified. She nodded curtly at me and turned back toward the magnificent tree.

Eryn had been staring intently at the carved bark, as if waiting for something.

Sappha cleared away the crunchy coverings of the forest floor until a dark layer of dirt was all that remained below her hands. She moved her hand in a circle, smoothing the soil until it was flat and cleared of debris. She reverently placed the necklace in the center of the circle.

She stood abruptly, placing a hand on my shoulder.

"Switch with me." She commanded.

I turned to look up at her, confused. "Why?"

"Because this is *your* journey. *Your* magic. And *you* should call it forth."

"I don't know how to do that." I protested.

"You *do* know how to. It dwells inside of you. You carry the powers of two peoples, as I said."

"But—" I began shaking my head back and forth. I had no idea what we were doing here. I didn't know how to perform rituals like this and had no clue how to even harness the powers that pulsed through me. They had always been fueled by emotions and chaos, not summoned in the soothing dimness of the forest.

Her fingers gently squeezed on my shoulder. Her bright green stare bore into me. "—I will help you." She cut off my racing thoughts as she reassured me. *Promised me.*

I swallowed, closed my eyes for an extra beat, and steadied my mind. I moved to the center and took her place in front of the tree. Eryn gave my knee a reassuring squeeze. Sappha kneeled to my left.

"This tree is ancient. Powerful. Wise. It has seen many moons pass over this land and has kept quiet watch." I looked up, taking in the true breadth of this magnificent tree, and imagined how much change it has seen over its lifetime.

"Close your eyes," Sappha instructed. "Do you feel her? *Her power?*"

I did as she instructed. The energy from the tree seemed to bubble to the surface of my awareness, feeling like a warm hum washing over me. I *could* feel it. I could *feel it.*

"I do." My answer was breathy on my lips.

"This land is sacred, given to us by The Divine Feminine. They have poured wisdom and guidance into it and its natural inhabitants. We are here to ask for the forest to share this wisdom with us, to guide our next steps."

The energetic hum from the tree felt like it was seeping into my every pore. A warm sensation rose up my legs and covered my waist. It was complemented by this heavy tugging sensation that pulled me toward the ground, anchoring me.

Sappha continued. "We have made an *altar* here. To show our respect and to focus our intentions. To call upon The Mother, The Maiden, and The Crone. The circle is a natural boundary, to concentrate the magic summoned here."

Out of the corner of my eye, I saw her hands swirling together. She flicked her wrists, and a flash of light shot out from her palms. It was brief and silent. I turned my head slightly.

The movement had cast small orbs of warm light to hover over each rock that Sappha had placed around us. They were ... beautiful. *Breathtaking.*

A faint tingling brushed through my chest, pulling my awareness behind me. I turned my head farther, searching in the woods behind us. For what, I did not know.

My eyes caught Leo's, then. He was leaning casually against a tree in the shadows several yards behind us. His massive arms were crossed across his chest and his legs were crossed at his ankles. His dark curls flopped over his forehead and the shadows sharpened the angles of his face. My heart skipped at his presence.

He came for me. He said if we were not back in ten minutes, he would come searching for me and he did just that. But he did not intervene. He was simply watching over. Ensuring my safety.

He gave me a nod, encouraging me to continue.

A deep inhale filled my lungs as I turned back to face the tree. Neither Sappha nor Eryn had noticed his presence.

"This necklace.... *The Verdant Eye* ... will help to clarify our intentions. It holds the hidden truths of this journey you are on. Of your past. Your future." Sappha pulled her blade free again, placing it in my palm. The blade was lethally sharp, and the pommel was outfitted with a captivating emerald.

"You will need to gather a drop of blood from each of us. To symbolize our bonds to this journey and to awaken the slumbering magic of the forest."

I searched her gaze. Her eyes were steady, pouring strength into me with just a look. She *knew* I could do this. She sensed it in me. I *could* do this. I *would*.

Eryn reached her palm toward me, extending her fingers. I gently grasped her hand, pricking a finger with the blade. She didn't make a sound.

Sensing what to do with it, I guided her hand toward the necklace and let the blood drop. The dark red liquid blended almost seamlessly with the damp soil. Turning to Sappha, I repeated the gesture.

I then pierced my own flesh, dropping the blood into the soil just below the necklace. When my blood made contact, it flashed a bright turquoise, as did the blood from Sappha and Eryn. A jolt of energy flooded me as the turquoise light seemed to rove over the circle and then seep into *The Verdant Eye*. My breath hitched.

"Speak the words. Look inside yourself." Sappha coached me with near-silent words. "Open yourself to what needs to be said and allow your intuition to guide you."

I closed my eyes, allowing myself to feel. I let my mind become blank, a whirling void awaiting the guidance of my ancestors. Of my Gran. Of The Divine Feminine. Of the woods that surrounded us.

Breathing in, I felt the whirling energy fill my lungs and course through my veins. It was warm and tingled in my chest, spreading through my arms and legs. I reached down and cupped the necklace in my open palms. The frenetic hum was intoxicating. With every breath, I felt myself consume it more fully.

I allowed the words to come forth. Whatever words needed to be said. I opened my mouth, and they poured out as if they had been waiting inside me all along.

"Arboreys antaequae, secreta veystre roinn, led oss cuum curah sussurratah."

Ancient trees, your secrets share, lead us forth with whispered care.

As soon as the words left my lips, an intense surge of power shot through me, causing every muscle to feel rigid. No sooner did the tension lash at me than it released, leaving my muscles charged. I gasped.

My eyes flew open, but I did not see the tree in front of me. I saw a path through the woods. Shrouded with darkness, the light of the full moon flickered through the dense forest. It felt heavy. The air was thick with moisture. I could sense that others were present. I felt their presence hiding throughout the woods.

I saw the *mirror pond*. Its cool waters were almost black. Tendrils of gray mist coiled and rose from its too-still surface. A cool breeze brushed my face. A chill crawled down my spine. I shuttered. A vision of myself played in my mind. My steps were slow and tentative as I approached the edge. Leo's steadying presence was by my side. I leaned forward, peering in.

The vision disappeared, and the energy drenched me again. I rocked forward, catching my weight on the ground with my hand as the other clenched the necklace. My heart raced as I panted, trying to catch my breath.

"Nolei!" Eryn exclaimed, rising on her knees to rub my back. A cold sweat broke out on my brow.

Before I could clear my mind, powerful arms wrapped around me. The lush scent of crackling campfire and fresh pine invaded my senses.

"I've got you." Leo's voice was pure silk. "I'm here. I've got you." He scooped me into his arms, lifting me with ease.

My body instantly relaxed into his hold, the terror melting away. My eyes met his. His dark gaze was like a balm to my frayed nerves.

"You did it, Nolei!" Sappha's voice came from behind me. "You summoned the answer."

Leo's eyes did not leave mine, but I felt his body tense in response to Sappha. Felt his anger toward her for allowing harm to come to me.

But I was fine. More than fine. It felt like I was struck by a bolt of lightning and now had the strength of the bolt at my disposal.

Sappha was just teaching me. Showing me how to use the magic that was already within me. But he didn't see it that way.

"I'm fine." My words were an answer to an unasked question. They were for Leo and Leo alone.

"Leave us," Leo commanded, his voice like the shadows that danced between the trees. His eyes never left mine.

Eryn and Sappha paused. Then, the sound of their boots crunched on the twigs as they retreated to the edge of the forest, leaving Leo and I alone.

CHAPTER

TWENTY-EIGHT

My head rested on Leo's chest, the beating of his heart steadying me. He held me close to him as he walked us silently through the forest. I didn't question him or ask where we were going. I just stared up over his shoulder, watching as the branches passed by overhead and wildlife skittered away in response to us.

That ... vision. It felt so real. I was there. I was looking into the pond.

I couldn't believe that I had just done that. I had called to my magic, and let it flood my veins. Shaped it with my intentions and guided it to do my will.

Leo's steps halted. I lifted my head and looked around. We were deeper in the woods now. The trees were towering above us. Giant, deep green fronds made up most of the surrounding greenery. The ground was no longer covered in sticks and fallen leaves, but blanketed with plush moss.

Mushrooms as tall as me, colored like bones and bricks, sprouted up here and there. I had never seen anything like this place.

Pressing his back against a tree, Leo lowered us to the ground. I spun so that I remained on his lap but faced him, my legs straddling his hips. My chin tilted up. I inhaled slowly as I took in this serene woodland paradise.

I lowered my gaze to his. "Have you been here before?"

He licked his lips, drawing his bottom lip between his teeth. My body flushed in response to the subtle movement.

"No. Never," he answered. "Have you?"

"Of course not. How would I? You know I've never left Eyloria." I shoved playfully at his chest.

"I don't know that. I actually know very little about you, Nolei." His head titled at me as if I was some rare creature to be studied.

"And yet it feels like you know me. Know the *true me*." I whispered, gently cupping his hard jaw with my hand.

He turned his head to kiss my palm. My heart did that squeeze that it always seems to do around him.

"Nolei, I...." He said, stopping himself.

I furrowed my brows at his hesitation.

"What?" I asked.

"What you did back there? It was incredible." His dark eyes were captivating, holding my gaze. "*You* are incredible."

A flush heated my cheeks as I shook my head in protest. "I've never done anything like that before. It felt so *natural*. Like I knew what to do all along."

"As I said. Incredible." His voice was full of awe. "You are so much stronger than you realize. You don't even know, do you?" He huffed a laugh. "How *powerful* you are. How much I admire everything about you. Then you go and do something like that and I fall for you even harder."

Something flashed in his face then. It almost looked like a bolt of ...pain. Not physical, but the kind that casts a heavy burden.

"I saw it." My hand moved to rest on his muscled shoulder. "I saw the *mirror pond* in the woods. I saw *us* there."

He was silent, urging me on with the intensity of his gaze.

"I can't explain it, but it felt *real*. I don't know where it is located, but it's like I can *sense* where it is, if that makes sense."

His lips kicked up into a faint smile. "It doesn't." He leaned forward, planting a soft kiss on my lips. "But I'll follow you wherever you go. Even if you just lead us in circles or into the jaws of more Dunemaulers." A light laugh left him.

I narrowed my eyes at him. "If I remember correctly, you were the one that led us into the jaws of Dunemaulers, and *I* was the one who saved your ass afterward."

"That's not how I remember it, my damsel. You have been leading us on this blind adventure all along." His smile was now taunting. Gods, I would do horrible things to ensure that I could continue to see that smile of his.

"You must have suffered a head wound that I wasn't quite able to heal correctly, then. Maybe I should call Sappha back so she can try her hand at healing you."

His eyes somehow turned even darker and took on a stormy quality.

"I don't trust her." He bit out, clearly irritated by just the mention of her name.

"Oh, come now. I'm sure it won't hurt if that is what you are afraid of." I teased.

"That's not what I mean, and you know it."

If I had known bringing her up would darken the mood so much I wouldn't have done it.

"As I said before, what feels like three hundred times, we're going to have to agree to disagree on that." I held my ground. Sappha could be trusted. I still didn't quite understand how I knew that, but I just did.

He let out what sounded like a growl.

Trying to shift the feel of the conversation, I wiggled my hips on top of his and gave him a mischievous smile. His growl turned from one of disagreement to one of need.

He planted his hands on my hips. "Nolei..."

I leaned in to kiss him, happy to be initiating this time. The kiss was slow and deep. Sensual. His hands tightened their hold on me.

"Yes?" I purred between kisses as I moved to the lightly stubbled skin of his neck and rocked my hips into him. He let out a breathy groan, and I could feel his obvious desire for me.

"I brought you here because I wanted to tell you something." Goosebumps lit up on his skin beneath my lips as he tilted his neck in response to me.

I bit gently on his earlobe as I continued the wicked circling of my hips. "Okay, so tell me."

He pulled me back slightly, stopping my conquest. "You're making it a bit hard for me to focus when you do that." He closed his eyes, pressing his hips into mine for a brief, teasing moment.

"Doing what?" I asked innocently, quirking my head at him.

"Pressing those soft lips of yours against my neck while you grind that pretty pussy on me like a cat in heat."

My mouth dropped open in feigned insult. "Like a cat in heat? Is that so?"

He laughed, clearly proud of himself.

Taking back control, I resumed my *grinding like a cat in heat*. "Well, that sounds like a *you* problem."

He kissed me gently, smiling against my lips as he said, "You're torturing me."

He stilled my hips with his hands, which stopped my movements but didn't stop me from feeling the hard length of him fighting against the restraint of his pants. I gave an exaggerated pout and looked up at him.

"I wanted to tell you that what you did back there was fucking incredible, Nolei. I know I said that already, but seeing you let go, tune into yourself, and channel all that power was … I can't describe it." His dark eyes searched mine as he gently grasped my chin, tilting it up to himself. "Watching you do that made me feel like …. Like I am blessed to even be in your presence. To even be noticed by you. You are truly magnificent, Nolei."

Heat blossomed in my chest. My stomach fluttered. This male... this kind, sarcastic, fucking beautiful, deadly male was more than worthy of being noticed by me. He was charismatic. A natural leader. Chivalrous, yet lethal. Well-traveled and well-spoken. According to his stories, he and Cardin had friends in every corner of the realm.

I was a nobody. I didn't have a home anymore or even a family. Who was *I* to deserve his attention?

I didn't even have a clue about how to wield my powers. Well, I was starting to understand them *a little*. Where to look inside myself to find them.

But I needed him to know that he mattered, too. That it wasn't just *me* who was magnificent. It was *us*, together, who created something *truly* magnificent.

I leaned forward and kissed him deeply. His lips opened in response to me, and our need for each other was obvious. We devoured each other, explored, and allowed ourselves to come together freely. I showed him exactly how much his words meant to me.

He didn't seem to mind my hips moving against him now. His body was responsive to my own and the fabric between us felt like too much. We were too far apart. Too separate. I wanted us to be *one*. *Needed* it. I dragged his bottom lip between my teeth, tugging. He moaned, pulling me in closer to him. His hand moved to my breast as his other held me firmly on my hip.

Gods, his body was all hard lines and tanned skin. I needed to see more of it. Feel it pressed against me. I needed to lay claim to it. I tugged at his shirt. He released his grip on my hip to allow me to pull it over his head. Continuing my feverish plight, I unbuttoned the flap of his pants. I needed to free him from them. It couldn't be comfortable for *all of him* to be so tightly bound behind these fabric walls. He lifted his hips, allowing me to shift his pants down.

As his lips forged a path from my lips down to my shoulder, his hands moved expertly, untying my leather vest and removing my white blouse. My nipples hardened in response to the sudden rush of air.

Suddenly, he lifted me from his lap and pressed my back against the ground, shifting us so that he was now on top. Now had *total* control. I let in a quick breath of air, not expecting the transition. His large hand rested behind my head, cushioning the move. Before my mind realized the shift, he was already moving those soft lips from my shoulder down to my breast. He kissed me reverently, as if he was worshipping my body. Like each touch was a prayer, I was his altar, and choosing me was a vow his soul had made long before destiny had ever whispered our names.

The feel of his lips sent pulses of hyper-sensitive awareness through me. They shot up my spine and down to my center, lighting me on fire from within. Gods, I needed more.

My back arched and I let out a breathy exhale as he moved from my breast down to my leg, continuing a wicked trail of teasing, nipping kisses.

I could feel my desire for him pooling at my center, begging for him to touch me.

I pulled him up so I could kiss him again and make my request. "I need to feel you inside me. *Now*, Leo." I pleaded between frantic kisses. He pressed himself against me, causing a heated ache to bloom between my legs. It only worsened my need for him.

He smiled against my lips. "Patience, my darling." He gently pulled my skirt down and off before returning to running his parted lips and tongue up my thighs, exploring torturously close to the space between my legs. "Not until I'm done paying homage to you. To your beautiful body."

My head kicked back as he sunk one finger inside of me. A pang of pleasure roared through me, only fanning my flames. I gasped and rolled my hips against him, begging for more.

"You're so wet for me, Nolei. You want me, don't you?" He ran his tongue over my center and then sucked against my almost too-sensitive skin. I let out a breathy moan. "You want me almost as much as I want you."

I rocked into his hand, my movement against him my only reply. My fingers fisted in his dark mass of curls. He continued his wicked plight, licking and teasing me. The sensation was too much and not enough. No matter how much I moved on his hand, it wasn't enough.

Just then, he added a second finger. The slight stretch was perfect and caused my pleasure to spike. I ground my hips, riding his hand. Pressing into the movements. Into him. The tension inside of me was roiling to life, heating me and coiling tighter.

Leo pulled his hand away slightly, only giving me the tips of his fingers. Refusing me more. His lips continued to move over me and Gods, I *needed more*.

"Please, Leo," I begged, my grip tightening in his hair.

He looked up at me, his lips glossy and eyes full of mischief. "Please, what?" He stopped moving. Holding his fingers in place.

"Stop teasing me." I grasped at my breast and tried to move my hips against him, but he stayed just out of reach. *Fucking Gods.*

He plunged his fingers into me then, raking a sharp gasp of pleasure out of me. *Yes. Yes.*

He removed them again, continuing his special brand of torture.

"You want me to make you come, Nolei?" He asked, his voice full of smoke and desire.

I squeezed my eyes shut, nodding.

"Say it. I want to hear you ask for what you need, baby."

"Make me come, Leo. Please, *let me come.*" He let out a growl of satisfaction as he pulled my hips down toward him, burying his face between my legs. He moved quickly, flicking over me with his tongue. Sucking. Nipping. It was maddening in the best way.

He then began moving his fingers inside of me. His movements were quick and deep. The way he curled his fingers was exquisite. *Perfect.*

I writhed beneath his hold. My knees tried to close around him, but he held me steady with one hand as he continued moving inside of me with the other. The sensations flared to life throughout my entire body. I was like a raw nerve, feeling every little touch. The moss below me was soft. Cool against my skin. His mouth was hot and wicked. The sight of him feasting between my legs ratcheted up the tension inside of me even tighter. *Oh, Gods.*

I grabbed at my hair, gripping it as the tension ratcheted up to a breaking point. I came hard, screaming out as the release rolled through me. I bit onto my wrist, trying to muffle the sound. Leo moved his hand from my hip to my wrist, pulling it away from my mouth and pinning it above my head.

"Let go, Nolei. Don't fight it. Just let go." He encouraged. "I want to hear you scream for me."

I did just that. His name on my tongue, I shuddered as wave after wave of pleasure tore through me. He slowed but didn't stop until my screams of pleasure melted into silent pants.

My body fell heavily against the ground, weighed down in the aftermath. Leo slowly sat back, rising onto his knees between my legs.

I peeked an eye open, glancing at him. His dark curls lay messily on the top of his head. Luminous eyes took me in, a faint smirk tugging at his lips. His hard cock jutted proudly from his hips.

"You're proud of yourself, aren't you?" I ask, draping an arm over my forehead.

He let out a rough laugh. "I am, actually."

He braced his arm by the side of my head, leaning forward to plant a kiss on my forehead. His weight shifted back as he moved to stand.

Not wanting this to be over just yet, I shot my hand out and palmed his length, preventing him from moving away. He froze as I gently tightened my grip on him.

"Did you just grab my dick?" His eyebrows raised.

I looked up at him, giving him a wicked smile. "Yeah, I guess I did." I laughed. "What are you going to do about it?"

He let out a deep laugh and then leaned back forward, moving in closer to me, just like I wanted.

"Are you going to use it against me?" I teased, beginning to move my hand up and down.

He stopped when his mouth was just a few inches from mine, his arms holding the weight of his body as he stretched over mine. Gods, I didn't realize how much larger than me he was until now. The anticipation of having his body hover so close to mine was almost unbearable.

"You'd like that, wouldn't you?" He growled. His voice caused another bolt of desire to shoot through me.

I lifted my head, closing the distance between us and crashing my lips onto his. Our lips moved frantically against each other now. Claiming. He sucked my bottom lip between his teeth. My core pooled with a raw desire for him again. I continued to move my hand along his hard length, feeling it throb in my palm. His want for me was obvious, and I was tired of waiting.

I tried to guide him toward me, but he pulled back.

"Not so fast." He tsk'd. "This wasn't supposed to be about me. I wanted to show you how incredible and powerful you are. To give you all the pleasure you deserve."

My eyes narrowed on him. Two could play at this game. "If that was your goal, then I'm afraid you've fallen short." I said.

His brows furrowed as his gaze searched mine. "I have? You seemed to enjoy it earlier." His lips popped into that smirk of his that had a way of melting me instantly.

"Oh, I was. But you have not yet given me *all the pleasure I deserve.*"

He gifted me with another laugh. Being with him just felt so comfortable. So right.

A look of challenge and determination washed over his features, transforming his face into one that promised another intoxicating rendezvous.

Before I allowed him the upper hand in this, I swung my leg over him. I caught him off guard enough that I was able to flip him onto his back. I moved, so I was straddling him, just like last time.

His eyes flew open as he landed, widening as they roamed over my body. The dappled sunlight flitted over my skin. The gentle breeze lifted my wild curls. He braced his large hands on my hips and his gaze roved over me with an insatiable hunger, soaking in the view of me on top of him. *Fuck, it was so hot when he looked at me like that.*

smell of us. His large arm wrapped around my neck and shoulders, holding me to him.

"How do we always seem to find ourselves lying together on the floor of the forest?" Leo asked, his hand lazily stroking my surely matted hair.

I let out a snort of a laugh. "Why do you always insist on bedding me without a bed?"

He turned his head and gave me a dubious smile. "Well, there are a few reasons for that. The first one being that there is no way I could wait long enough for us to find a bed to feel your body against mine. Once I felt your lips on mine, I had to have the rest of you. You are rather intoxicating, did you know that?" He placed a kiss on my temple before continuing. "It would be cruel to deny ourselves for that long. Second, we don't even *sleep* in a bed. We sleep on the ground."

"Like animals." I finished for him.

His brows raised. "... like animals." He repeated the words slowly, trying not to laugh.

He turned his head back to the sky. "There are a lot of primal, animalistic things about our relationship, Nolei. Our sleeping habits are not even close to first in line on that list."

Our relationship. He called whatever was between us *a relationship.* I mean, maybe it *was* that? We hadn't exactly named whatever it was we were doing. Our attraction to each other was obviously mutual. And he was definitely protective of me. And I of him. Maybe we *were* in a relationship?

Before I could respond, he turned to me and drew his hand along my jaw. His face was almost painfully beautiful. He was all chiseled features and dark, moody eyes. He was rugged, yet perfect. My breath hitched in my throat without me even realizing it. Gods, I would give anything to be in a relationship with this man. To know for sure that what we had was mutual and as deep as it felt to me. That he needed me as much as I needed him.

Even if it was painful for me to admit to myself that I needed any male. I realized then that I'd been feeling much more than lust towards him for far longer than I'd like to admit to myself. I was in way too deep and was free falling. No chance of turning back now. All I could do was pray to Elowen that he was doing the same.

"I promise that someday we will share a bed, Nolei." His eyes searched mine. His voice was soft and intimate. Husky. "And not just for your pleasure, which will obviously be of the utmost importance. But for us — that we will have a place to call our own. Not yours, or mine. But *ours*."

I inhaled shakily and let out a broken laugh. I felt a surge of emotions come to the surface. Hope. Trust. I felt vulnerable, yet safe. Fighting back tears that threatened to show themselves, I placed my hands on his face and pulled him in for a deep kiss. A kiss that did a better job of portraying how that promise made me feel better than any words could.

At that moment, I realized just how deeply I loved him. Someday soon, I hoped to find the courage to tell him, but for now, it remained my sweet little secret. A little slice of magic that was all mine.

CHAPTER

TWENTY-NINE

We spent some time picking the twigs and leaves out of each other's hair and trying to make it look like we didn't just spend the last however many hours having sex in the woods. Maybe we *were* like animals, after all. Just picking debris off each other like chimps. I laughed to myself at the thought.

Leo somehow navigated us back to the group. Cardin was sitting on the ground and tossing rocks against the trunk of a tree. Eryn was munching on a mix of nuts and seeds from her pack and Sappha was standing by her mare with her arms crossed. They all turned to us as we rejoined them and waited expectantly in silence.

I didn't pick up on the fact that they were waiting for me to speak until Leo cleared his throat and glanced at me. I straightened. Oh. I was in charge of where we went next. Me. *Right.*

"I saw the *mirror pond*. The one from The Scroll," I began, addressing no one in particular. I tuned into the hum in my veins that felt like a gentle tug toward the woods. "I can't explain it, but I can *feel* where to go. It is almost like I'm ... tethered to it somehow. Like it is pulling me toward it."

"Well, that's creepy as fuck." Cardin stated blandly.

"Really, Car?" Leo shot back. "Nolei has a prolific fucking experience and uses unparalleled magic to discern the hidden location of what we seek and the smartest thing that empty skull of yours can come up with, is that?" The anger that rolled off of him is almost palpable.

"Come on. I'm just messing with her." Cardin's bright eyes flared with obvious entertainment. "No need to get all overprotective and shit. She can kick my ass if she wants to, anyway."

"A goat could kick your ass," Eryn chimed in nonchalantly.

I laughed.

"Continue please, Magnolia." Car urged, giving me a flourishing bow. Leo fixed a deadly glare on him and let out what sounded like a growl of warning.

"As I was saying..." I started, my voice bolder now but with an amused smile. "I know where to go next. We need to head west, deeper into the woods. I don't know exactly how far it will be, but it will be at least a few days away. And we must make it there by the next full moon."

Eryn's brows furrowed. "By the next full moon?"

I nodded, sure of that part. So much of my life has been ruled by the moon. Moon water, charged by the light of a full moon, was used in tinctures and remedies for differing purposes based on which full moon it gained its power from. My monthly cycles. *Váliarë*. My nickname from Gran. *The Verdant Eye* only opening under the light of a full moon. It only made sense that this required the same.

265

"But that is likely only two or three nights from now," Eryn stated, worry etching her features.

"Then we better get going," Leo stated matter-of-factly. His statement was with murmurs of agreement and nods.

Damn, he had a way of leading others that seemed so natural to him. Like he was *born* to lead. Far more talent with it than I had, that's for sure. I couldn't convince a thirsty horse to drink from a cool stream.

But he didn't just lead, he made me feel like *I* could lead, too. He made me believe I could command respect, and that leadership was something that I would grow into instead of some unattainable skill.

We packed up the horses and began our journey west through Oriella Forest. Although there were no obvious roads for us to follow, Leo and Cardin found a well-worn path, likely used by the elk that called these woods home.

The woods were so dense, but not in a frightening way. The trees were ancient and large, their knotted branches seeming to weave together in the canopy above us.

Lush greens mixed with vibrant pastels of the large variety of flowers that grew here. Lavenders, pinks, and purple-blue flowers climbed up the trunks and covered the ground between the trees. Where flowers didn't grow, moss and ferns took their place. The air smelled sweet, like sugared pastries.

The energy I felt from the life around me was a welcomed hum. It was much stronger than I remember it being. Or maybe I was just more aware of it now. The trees gave off an enduring energy, of power filled with wisdom. The lush flora seemed to radiate a wispy, encouraging energy. The ground beneath us emanated a strong, supportive presence.

Knowing that all of these energies were mine to tap into filled me with a sense of protection and confidence. The land and plants around us were filled with an unseen power and I had the gift to harness it. I could call upon it. *Wield it.* Tension eased from my shoulders as we rode on.

Now I finally knew what this ability of mine was called. *The Witching Stitch.* There was a name for it and it was *real*. It was *within me.* Mine to use. Learning more about these developing powers was one reason we set out on this journey in the first place. Even though I hadn't yet learned about who my true parents were, or if they were still alive, I *did* know a bit more about myself. About the magic I possessed.

After traveling for some time, the sound of rushing water broke through the din of the forest. As we broke free from the thick coverage of towering trees, we found ourselves standing at the edge of a creek. The dark waters seemed almost black except for where they crashed white against any rocks that jutted from their path. The horses were anxious.

The distance between where we stood and the opposite bank was wide, but the water did not seem too deep. The horses should be willing to cross here, but Camila was acting rather spooked by the whole prospect.

"Camila doesn't want to cross here," I shout over the roar of the water.

"Neither does Lace," Eryn replied.

"They can tell something doesn't feel right." Sappha's horse was acting the same, stomping its feet and huffing.

"There!" Cardin shouted, pointing up the stream. "A bridge."

An arced, stone bridge curved over the water, joining with large boulders on either side of the river. As we approached it, my awe at its design deepened. It seemed to have been built ages ago, the stones intricately placed. It curved in such a way that it made almost a half circle over the water. It was beautiful. Someone must have traveled this path before us, many times over, if a bridge was needed to do so. The bridge was narrow, but wide enough for the horses to pass. No railings or ropes marked the edges, though. We could cross here, but we'd have to be careful. One misstep and we'd go careening into the water below.

I led the way, guiding Camila over the precarious stone arch with soothing low-pitched murmurs to reassure her. Each step resulted in debris and stones tumbling into the water below. As we were nearing the other bank, Eryn entered onto the bridge behind me. I led Camila onto the grass, exhaling with relief that we had made it across. Pulling on the reins, I turned Camila around to watch the others cross. Sappha led her mare tentatively onto the pass behind Eryn.

Before I could realize what happened, a blood-curdling scream torched my ears. *Eryn.* She was screaming my name.

I whipped around and came face to face with several males. Males who were all dressed in crimson, as bright as freshly spilled blood. The Dark Army. *Fuck.*

There was no warning of their presence aside from the general unease the horses had been portraying. The rush of the water must have aided their cover. They had to have been hiding in the woods waiting for us. But how did they know we would be here? My heart was beating in my ears. This couldn't be happening.

Leo shouted my name, too. I turned my head to see him charge his horse onto the bridge behind Sappha, trying to get to me. Now all three of them were crowded on the bridge, nobody able to move forward without pressing us all closer to the soldiers.

They had to back up. Had to go the other way.

Before I could urge them to do so, a voice boomed from behind Leo.

"Don't move another step." The voice commanded. It was another soldier. He was behind Cardin, his long sword drawn. Two other soldiers flanked him, both pointing arrows directly at Cardin's head. *No!* An ambush. We were fucking *ambushed*. Surrounded. Outnumbered.

I glanced around. Crimson clad soldiers were blocking the way forward and back. They were pressing in closer to us, preventing our movement. The soldiers behind me had their arrows drawn now, too.

"What is it you want with us? We are just traveling. Last I checked, that was no offense to The Crown" Leo shot back, his voice steady.

"It is not that you are simply traveling, but *who* you are traveling with." The soldier replied.

Was he speaking of Sappha? She *was* a witch. But how did *they* know that?

The soldier nodded at me. "You have gained the attention of The Sorcerer Sovereign. She has heard whisperings of someone using magic freely, without fear of the consequences."

A cold sweat ran over my neck. *Sorcerer Sovereign*. That was a new title. Clearly self-appointed.

How had she learned of me? I racked my brain for how that could be possible. From my attack on the soldiers in Eyloria, when I saved that boy from losing his hand? She couldn't have heard from those soldiers we encountered in the woods near the Sanguine River, as Leo and I ensured there were no survivors. I used my magic... when fighting the Dunemaulers. *But how could she know that?*

I raised my chin in defiance. "I know not what you speak of."

"Playing daft, are we?" another soldier said from behind me.

The first soldier who spoke ignored that comment from his comrade. He must be in charge.

"It is quite entertaining that you truly believed that Her Majesty would remain unaware of your misdeeds. That you could hide from her all-seeing power and continue to break the rules she has set forth for her people."

The way he spoke of us as *her people*, her subjects who had no purpose beyond serving her, made my lip curl in disgust. How she thought she was deserving of our servitude was beyond me. She had taken over the throne, appointed herself queen, and been ensuring *her people* remained poor and hungry ever since. Her army was used to torment the people of Lunaris, not to keep us safe. We were barely surviving under her rule. There was no leadership or provision to be thankful *for*.

"How about you all get out of our way and return to whatever 'duties' you must see to, and we will allow you to leave alive? We can all pretend this never happened. Your Majesty doesn't value your insignificant lives, and will not think twice of you losing them on this errand of hers." Leo said arrogantly.

The way he spoke to them caused a very inappropriate flutter in my core. *Now was not the time, Nolei.*

The initial soldier let out a loud laugh. "It is *you all* who will not leave this encounter with your lives. The Dark Enchantress has ordered for *you* to be killed." His beady eyes locked with mine. "Killing your friends will just be part of the fun." He said as an evil smile spread across his face.

Before I could respond, an arrow whizzed past my head.

CHAPTER

THIRTY

S houts broke out over the sound of the rushing waters. Arrows rained down and the soldiers closest to us drew their swords, charging directly at Eryn and I. Panic rippled through me as the chaos unfolded in slow motion.

Sappha's horse reared and its back foot slipped over the edge of the bridge, sending Sappha careening down into the water below. Arrows flew at Cardin as he spun, drawing his sword. Leo's eyes locked with mine, full of fury and what looked like panic. He couldn't get to me. I had to act, and I had to act *now*.

All the hours we spent training with Leo and Cardin each morning were not for nothing. Eryn and I knew how to fight now. *This* is what we had been training for. Nobody was going to save *us* except for *us*. I took a steadying breath and ripped my sword free from its sheath.

I swung hard at the closest soldier. Blood spurted as my blade sliced through him. Eryn followed my lead, swinging her sword with a shout.

My blade swung through another soldier and the impact shot up my arm. I grunted. As I turned, another soldier charged me. I readied my sword to block him as an arrow flew by my head, embedding itself directly between his eyes.

I drew in a quick breath in surprise. The soldier's eyes went wide and his jaw fell open. Then he slumped off the side of his horse and onto the ground. I turned to see where the shot had come from to find Leo with another arrow nocked and ready.

"You know what to do, Nolei!" He shouted at me as he loosed his next arrow. It sunk into another soldier to my right.

Even though I now knew how to wield a sword, I hadn't learned how to fight on horseback yet. Trying to navigate this battle on Camila's back was only slowing me down. Especially with me worrying about her getting hurt.

I swung myself down, my boots landing firmly on the ground, and gave her a pat, causing her to bolt into the woods. She'd be safer there than here. Hopefully, I'd be able to find her after this was all said and done. If I survived, that was.

Another soldier was upon me, striking downward with his sword. I blocked it, but the strength of the blow caused my sword to clatter out of my hand. He gave me a dark smile as he lifted his blade to swing again. His desire for bloodshed was terrifying, and I was about to be his next victim. I ducked, barely missing his next blow. I crouched down, grabbing a dagger from my boot. I lurched back to my feet, driving it deep below his ribs as I rose. He let out a gurgle as blood fell from his mouth. Pulling back on my dagger, I shoved him with my other hand, causing him to fall back. *Holy fuck.*

273

Panting, I glanced around. Sappha had almost made it to the edge of the bank. Leo was picking off soldiers from the middle of the bridge, dodging arrows himself. Cardin was... Gods, he was *surrounded*. He was on his feet, swinging furiously with his sword in every direction as he battled five soldiers on his own. He swung forward, stabbing into one, and then pulled back, jamming his elbow into the gut of another behind him.

Eryn was holding her own beside me, but just barely. There were at least four other males around Eryn and I. The odds were not in our favor. I had to do something. Had to save everyone ... they were here for me, after all. Putting their lives at risk on this journey for *me*. The least I could do was protect them. I had the power *within me*, as Sappha had said. I just had to call upon it.

I didn't have time to perform some drawn-out ritual. To come from a place of trepidation. We didn't have the luxury of time here. We were barely hanging on and I had to do something *now*. I willed my breath to steady and racing thoughts to slow.

My mind ran through how my magic had worked in the past. It had to do with the world around me — the air, the ground. Without slowing to think it through or look inward further, I lifted my hands to the sky with a shout of fury. My body shook as I summoned all the energy I could with my hands outstretched, willing the winds to whip around us. *I could do this.* I had done this before without even trying, so I could do it now. I would save them.

I squeezed my eyes shut amidst the chaos and imagined the wind whipping around the soldiers, disarming them and forcing them to the ground. Holding them there until we could restrain them. I saw this in my mind and willed it into existence.

When I opened my eyes, the wind was whipping. The soldiers in front of us were shouting as their horses panicked. A treacherous spiral of air was spinning around us, pulling tree branches and rocks with it. Eryn ducked, covering her head as a branch flew past her. Leo's horse bucked on the bridge. He clenched the reins, fighting to stay atop Kellan. The wind had Sappha pressed to the ground at the water's edge. This wasn't what I had envisioned. It was *too powerful. Too dangerous.* I tried to stop it but didn't know what to say or do. Didn't know how to command it.

Sappha shouted something to me I couldn't hear over the snapping of branches, shouts, and wind.

I had to *do something.* Had to stop this chaos. Had to force my magic to comply so I could save my friends. I crouched to the ground again, shutting my eyes against the dirt and debris in the air. I pressed my hands into the ground. *If the wind wouldn't listen to me, I would try the land beneath our feet.* A shot of energy went through my palms as I willed the rocks to do my bidding. This had to work. Had to end this chaos.

As the energy left my hands, rocks exploded upward. They hit many of the soldiers, sending some of them careening off their horses and knocking others unconscious. A panicked whinny caught my attention as a shout pierced my ears. Turning, I saw Leo and Kellan free-falling into the River from where the bridge was. From where it *had been.* Before the rocks it was made of exploded below them.

No. No. No. This couldn't be happening. It was foolish to think I could control these wild powers. Instead, they tore free from me, reckless and untamed, hurting the very people I wanted to protect.

"Leo!" I shouted, trying to run toward him. It was futile. There was no way I could make it to him before he hit the water. Panic coursed through me. *What was I thinking?* I had no fucking clue what I was doing or how to control these so-called powers of mine. This was over. We were going to die here, and it was all because of me.

Another scream came from behind me. Eryn was slashing her sword around frantically at the soldiers that surrounded her. The ground had split beneath her, though. A deep crevice formed below her feet. She jumped to one side in time to spin and slash at another soldier.

I stood there dumbly, my mouth open and eyes darting back and forth as I took in the chaos that I had caused.

The soldier nearest to me yelled furiously as he ran at me. My sword buried itself deep into his stomach before I even realized I had moved. My mind felt disconnected from my body somehow. My body must be protecting me by keeping my thoughts and my actions separate. As if dissociation could save me now.

Just then, a velvety voice seemed to echo through my mind.

"Váliarë. The one who is blessed by the Goddesses and the moon. You carry the power within you." The voice wrapped around my mind as it cooed the words. My eyes flashed open as I searched for the source of the voice. Nobody was around me, save for the bleeding male at my feet.

"You are the master. The one who has called this energy forth. Direct it. Guide it. Master it." The voice washed through my thoughts, a soothing balm to the frantic thoughts that were teeming there. The voice sounded so familiar. *Safe.* Realization struck me as I turned to Sappha. She was still pressed to the ground, a five-pointed star drawn into the soil beside her. Her eyes were closed and one palm opened upward, a thin spiral of gray-blue fog seeping from the center of her hand. It tracked a few inches outward before disappearing.

It was *her*. She was speaking to me somehow. Using her magic to get through to me. Her faith in my ability to harness control over this mess was astonishing.

"You can do this, *Váliarë*. Call upon the energies again. Claim them as your own and shape them to your will. Ground yourself in divine guidance."

I tried to focus, but there was too much happening. Eryn was barely holding off two soldiers.

Cardin was somehow still taking on the group of males surrounding him, but he was still outnumbered. Leo had landed safely in the water, thank the Gods, but was bracing his side. He tried to calm his horse and keep it from trampling him. Two soldiers were volleying arrows in his direction from the bank Car was on.

My heart rattled against my rib cage. Now was the time. I had to lock this shit down and *act*. These people were my friends. *My family*.

They were following me on this fool's errand, and for what? So I could solve some silly riddle and learn who my parents were? Parents who were never there for me in the first place. Who abandoned me to be raised by my Gran. These people who were *risking their lives* for me were my *true* family. And they were about to die because of me. I couldn't let that happen. Would not let it happen. Not when I still had breath in my body and fury in my soul.

Determination steadied my breathing and focused my thoughts. *Ground yourself in divine guidance.* How had this magic worked before? I had rooted myself and called upon The Divine Feminine for guidance. Their wisdom was infinite, and they had always blessed me and my magic before. This was no different.

I focused inward, whispering a plea of mercy and guidance to Vespera, The Crone, Goddess of courage. My breathing slowed as I forced it into a controlled rhythm. *Breathe. Inhale. Hold. Exhale.* I felt the frenetic energy of the world around me seep into my pores. I called it into me. The whipping, fierce winds. The steady yet tumultuous flow of the water. The jumbled and harsh energy of the shaking ground. I called them all to me and whispered their names on my tongue.

I saw in my mind what I wished to happen. Visualized the soldiers that needed to be dealt with. I let myself slip into a detached, calculating calm as I pictured how I'd kill every single one of them. And then I made it a reality.

Water rushed from the river and flooded down the throats of those on the far bank near Cardin. Their panicked cries quickly turned to muted gargles.

The soldiers surrounding Eryn and running at me. I pictured fire incinerating them down to the bones, leaving nothing left. I faced them to see the wind form tight spirals around each of them. The gusts bursted into flames and swallowed them whole in their fiery tornadoes.

Eryn let out a scream of terror, obviously afraid that the same fate was coming for her.

But it wasn't. I was *in control* now. I could do this. *Would* do this. I would save my family. The whipping wind stopped and turned to a cooling breeze. The water pulled away from Leo and Kellan, allowing them to regain their footing and cross to the bank unharmed. Leo hefted a branch off of Sappha and offered her a hand, helping her back to standing. She started to glare at him but softened her features, accepting the help.

Once they were back to dry land, the river resumed its natural path. The ground stopped shaking; the rocks stilled and the crack in the ground remained but did not grow. The battle was over, but the quiet that settled felt like the aftermath of a storm that had almost swallowed them whole.

CHAPTER

THIRTY-ONE

After ensuring that everyone was safe and that every soldier had been dealt with, I hitched forward and vomited. The newfound silence was almost eerie. It taunted me in its stark contrast to the chaos that had just ensued. That I had *caused*.

My hands braced on my knees as I panted, exhausted. Leo's steady footsteps approached me and I felt him sweep his arms beneath me, lifting me into his arms. Just as he had done after I performed that ritual in Oriella Forest.

I leaned my head against his chest, closing my eyes and allowing the pine and campfire scent of him to wash over me. His lips prodded at me as he planted soft kisses to my forehead and cheeks.

"You did it, Nolei. You protected all of us." His voice was too reserved. Too gentle. As if I was as fragile as glass. As if one wrong word would shatter me. *Maybe it would.*

I let out a harsh laugh as a tear fell down my cheek. "I almost killed all of you."

He sat down with his back to a tree, pulling me onto his lap once more.

"Nonsense, *my Váliarë*. You saved us." He pulled me closer into his chest, wincing with the movement.

I lifted my head and narrowed my gaze at him, as I considered how I felt about him calling me that. The way it sounded on his tongue almost made me melt on the spot. And yet it felt even odder coming from Leo than it did coming from Sappha. What happened to *my damsel*? Honestly, I was too violently unhinged to be anyone's damsel at this point.

Eryn huffed as she flopped down beside me, crossing her legs.

Cardin wiped a blood-soaked forearm over his brow, wiping blood from his face. He was soaking wet from forging his way across the river after the battle. Gods, he looked rough.

Sappha had silently walked over after settling the horses, and sat down with her back on a nearby tree, pulling up her pant leg to inspect where the branch had landed on her. She had a rough-looking gouge, but it didn't appear that anything was broken.

"I'm sorry..." I started, shame weighing heavily on me. "I thought I could save us, but I just made everything worse and almost got you all killed." The words spilled out frantically as guilt dripped from my tongue. My cheeks flushed red. I couldn't believe I was delusional enough to *think* I could control my powers like that, in a battle, no less.

"How is us being ambushed by The Dark Army and then you killing them off with your magic something to be sorry about?" Cardin asked with that teasing tone of his. His bright blonde hair was spattered with blood, but he wasn't any less beautiful for it.

I turned to look at Leo, whose dark hair hung in wet curls on his forehead. His shirt was clinging to his muscular build. His fury about the soldiers was still evident in his features. Despite his unexpected swim, he still looked distractingly *hot*. Hot enough for me to want to peel those soaking wet clothes off of him and inspect every inch of his body for new wounds...with my lips. I shook my head silently at myself. *How could I be thinking about this at a time like this? Gods, what was wrong with me?*

"You did your best, Nolei. The fact that you can even *use* that kind of power is fucking remarkable if you ask me. A few weeks ago you were throwing rocks at soldiers and now look at you ... incinerating them with *your mind*." Eryn's playful voice pulled me out of my perverse thoughts.

"It was Sappha." I turned to her, my face solemn. "You spoke to me somehow. Got through to me. Told me what to do."

The others turned to face her, confusion etching their features.

Sappha nodded silently.

She wasn't eager to take any credit for how she saved us back there. But if it wasn't for her helping me to focus and gain control of my powers, we would all be gutted by now. The Dark Enchantress would have gotten her way.

"What do you mean?" Leo asked, placing another kiss along my cheek and tucking a strand of hair delicately behind my ear.

"She spoke to me somehow." I replied. "I heard her voice *in my mind*. It was incredible. One moment I was freaking out about how I had destroyed everything with my stupidity and the next thing I know I hear her in my mind, calming me and helping me to focus."

"Is that true?" Cardin asked her. To say that he was skeptical of our new comrade was an understatement. He hadn't exactly forgiven her for holding him captive in mid-air.

Sappha nodded again. "You have the strength and power within you to wield the energy around you, *Váliarë*. You just needed a little reminder of your ability to do so."

"I don't know how you did that, but it is what saved us all." I held her stare. "*You* are the reason we are alive right now."

She shook her head. "No. *You* are the reason."

"No... If —" She cut me off before I could finish my sentence.

"You grounded yourself, regained control, and ended those males. *You* did that, Nolei. Only you."

Everyone else remained silent around us. I swallowed thickly as I replayed the events. I *had* done that. But not before royally fucking everything up by thinking I knew how to control it in the first place. I just unleashed the magic with no thought to what the consequences would be or who may be harmed in the process. That misstep almost cost my friends their *lives*. I couldn't put them at risk like that again. I refused to let that happen. Ever. Again.

Leo broke the silence, lightening the mood. "Nice work with that sword of yours, Eryn. You've come a long way from not being able to lift the weight of your blade a few weeks ago."

"What about me?" Cardin practically squawked. "I'm over here taking down 14 soldiers at a time and looking damn good while doing it, and you compliment her for fending off *two*?"

Eryn glared at the males. "I could lift my sword without any issue before we met you two boars. Thank you very much." Her glare turned into a proud smile. "But yeah, I did do pretty good, didn't I?"

I huffed out a laugh. "14 soldiers? Nice try, Cardin. Maybe you got hit in the head with one of those rocks I sent flying. Hard enough that you were seeing double. Should I evaluate your vision?"

"Oh, leave him alone, Nolei. Math is hard for males." Sappha said casually.

Leo laughed, and a beautiful smile broke out across his face. Making fun of Cardin was one of his favorite pastimes, and he loved it even more when the rest of us joined in.

Cardin ignored Sappha and tilted his head at me. "No, but you can evaluate my c---"

Leo had pulled one of his daggers free and sent it flying at Cardin before he could even finish that thought. It embedded into the tree beside Cardin's head, causing him to blanch.

"For fuck's sake, I was just kidding!" He shot back, turning to yank the blade free.

"Well, don't *just kid* about that ever again. Or I'll aim it at a very inappropriate, *special* part of you that *will* need evaluating." His threat sent a pang of heat through me. The way he got so protective of me always had me reeling with desire. Nobody had ever shown that kind of interest in me before. *Ever.*

Leo would do it, too. Even though Car was his best friend. As fun as that would be to witness, I was hoping to avoid that kind of violence. It was hard enough keeping Sappha and Cardin from killing each other.

"And Sappha?" I asked, as Eryn and Car continued their bickering.

"Hmm?" she answered.

"Can you teach me how to do that thing where you spoke to me through my own damn mind?"

Her lips curved up into an outright smile. "Someday, *Váliarë*. Someday." She promised.

The chatter continued as I rested my head against Leo's chest, his heartbeat a welcomed distraction. For the first time in so long, I felt at home. Not in a place, but in the warmth of the voices around me, in the steady presence of Leo beside me, and in the quiet certainty that I finally belonged somewhere.

*H*ow did The Dark Army find us here? How did The Queen learn of me and know how to find me? I couldn't imagine why she felt so threatened by me and my measly powers anyway.

I didn't know all that much about Queen Ryellia Damay, to be honest, besides her reputation for being cruel. All I knew was that a little over ten years ago, she killed the royal family that lived in the floating capital city of Celestara and usurped the throne. It was said that she used dark magic to do so, but these things were only whispered about in taverns and the like. To speak openly about her at all was to invite the wrath of The Dark Army. She ruled with an iron fist, demanding fealty and sacrifice from *her* people. People whose only other choice was death. How she managed to gather such a large army of cruel soldiers who followed her blindly was beyond me.

Things used to be so different before she crowned herself queen. The previous royal family, Queen and King Graelis, were benevolent. They made sure that their subjects all had homes to live in and food in their bellies. Trade was robust. People could come forth with concerns, visiting the castle in the sky to attend court. And the queen and king would address their concerns. Not *kill them* for speaking out, like The Dark Queen would.

But they were long gone now. The Graelis royals *and* their two children — the prince and princess of Celestara. The Dark Enchantress, with what army of followers she had at that time, had ransacked the castle and killed each and every one of them with her dark magic.

The castle in the sky was as awe-inspiring as it was unusual, according to Gran. It was situated on a giant piece of land that floated far above the villages and farmlands as if it had launched up into the air from the ground below. A giant castle stood atop the land. Ever since The Dark Enchantress had taken over, nobody, save for her Dark Army, was allowed on the grounds, though. Anyone who so much as approached it was killed on sight. Or so it was said.

If she loved magic so much, why did she forbid the rest of us from using it? Wouldn't she want a realm filled with people who loved magic as she did? That is, if she even had the capacity to love anything. Either way, the soldiers had made it clear that she knew who I was and wanted me dead. Even if I didn't understand her reasoning, I was smart enough to know that meant I was now in grave danger. We had to lie low and steer clear of The Dark Army at all costs. Next time we wouldn't be as lucky.

CHAPTER

THIRTY-TWO

The next morning, I woke in Leo's arms. He had held me close all night, as had become our new normal. I was forgetting what it was like to sleep without the steadying sound of his heart lulling me to sleep. To forget what it was like to be alone. Even though our relationship was largely composed of death and catastrophes so far, I had never felt like this with anyone. So seen. So safe. I closed my eyes, breathing in the scent of him as I watched his chest rise and fall.

What would happen when this was all said and done? I was tiring of always skirting danger, knowing that some deadly creatures like the Dune-maulers or more heartless soldiers could be around every turn.

I wondered if Leo and I could ever settle down somewhere instead of always being on the run from The Dark Army. Would we ever have a bed of our own instead of just sharing a bedroll on the ground? A quiet life together instead of killing and chaos? A cozy cottage came into my mind,

286

the image of Cardin and Eryn stopping by to visit *our* home for dinner, followed by a night of cards and drinking too much mead. My lips curved into a smile. I had never imagined sharing a life with someone like this before, but things with Leo just felt so *right*. So perfect.

We continued to travel through the woods. Stopping only briefly to rest the horses and get a few hours of sleep each night. We had to make it to the *mirror pond* by the full moon or this would all be for nothing.

At long last, we made it to where Oriella Forest wove with the eerie, dark woods we sought. It was only late afternoon when we made camp, but we didn't want to press into the woods with darkness nearly upon us.

After much debate, it was decided that Leo and I would enter the forest alone on Kellan. The others would remain at camp with Camila and enter the woods only if Leo and I did not return by first light. Car and Eryn did not like this plan *at* all, but ultimately agreed to it. Only Leo and I were present in the vision I had and therefore, only the two of us would go. I wouldn't risk coming with too many people and messing up our one opportunity to find the truth. Not when we only had one night to do this.

That is what I told them, anyway. The truth was, I couldn't stand the idea of them being harmed. Couldn't put them in any more danger than I already had.

A bitter sense of unease washed over me as we moved slowly through the woods, the darkness almost impenetrable despite the full moon. Kellan's footsteps crunched twigs along the path as we moved deeper into the woods.

There was something *so not right* about this place. Typically, being pressed up against Leo on horseback would send all types of delightful shivers through my body. Instead, the only shiver I felt was that of icy fingers down my spine.

The farther we ventured, the darker the woods seemed to get. Not just the darkness of the night, but a deep, endless black that seemed to cloak the woods.

The air was suffocating, thick and damp. The gnarled trees seemed to knot together, weaving into a dense network around us. Gods, I hoped we didn't have to get out of here quickly. We'd be fucked, to say the least.

The full moon would have bathed a typical forest in luminance, but not here. Only wispy streams of moonlight filtered through the canopy. *If* you could even *call* it that. There was no greenery to speak of here, covering the trees or the ground. Only bare branches and thorned brambles.

I tried to focus on slowing my breathing instead of letting my mind wander to what lurked just out of sight. *Inhale. Exhale. Repeat.* My breaths were slow and deliberate, steadying me as we approached our destination.

We were almost there. I could feel it. The silent tug was pulling at me more fiercely now. It felt like a hundred hands were all grabbing at my shirt and chest, drawing me in closer. If it wasn't for Leo's firm grip on my hip, I'd likely either fall forward by the force of it all or turn Kellan right around and get the *fuck* out of here.

But we had to keep going. I had come *so far* for this. All the secrets Gran had kept from me. All the spun tales of a past that was never my own. A story that was made to quell questions. One that was steeped in pretty lies instead of potent truths. *Peer into the verdant eye, where the shadows of yesterday whisper their truths.*

That night flashed back in waves. Pacing outside Eryn's cottage while she slept, the full Weaver's Moon having activated *The Verdant Eye.* A lifetime of secrets revealed that had been contained in one piece of jewelry. Hidden in plain sight around her neck for all those years. Even though in some ways it felt like just yesterday, so much had happened since then. So much had changed. Including me.

I repeated the words of The Scroll that had become a wordless litany over the past few weeks, repeating like a prayer in the caverns of my mind.

Seek where moonlit shadows dance,
In the grove where twilight steps,
And whispers weave their cryptic trance.

A creaking sound pulled me from my thoughts. I startled as my head whirled to the side. I couldn't discern much aside from the shadows weaving through the trees. The unsettling sense that we were being watched from all sides was oppressive.

The wind shifted through the trees, the sound like ancient voices coaxing us deeper into the darkness. My heartbeat began rattling against my chest. Leo's firm grip tightened on my hip, pulling me back against him. My grip tightened on the pommel, my knuckles already white from clenching so hard.

His soft lips pressed a soothing kiss to the space behind my ear. My body released a sliver of tension in response to him. *Safe.* I was safe with him. I could *do this. We* could do this. *Together.*

The creaking sound drew my attention forward again. It was louder now, though. The sound was like broken branches slowly cracking under the wind.

Movement caught my eye on the path ahead. The gangly, twisted branches and roots were ...moving? Like contorted bodies, they shifted and writhed as they slowly unfurled from each other and straightened in the path ahead. Except they weren't normal trees.

Holy Divine Feminine Fuck. The moonlight illuminated what looked like bones. Rounded skulls nestled deep into the thicket of dark branches, and the violet flowers of Wolfsbane sprouted from their tangled hackles, twisting with thorned vines. I held my breath.

What looked like a rib cage melded in the center of each being, serving as a center point for the network of black roots and tangled limbs. The bones were coated with the vines and branches, slowly cracking and separating as they moved out of our path. They lined the sides, clearing the way for us.

A silent scream paralyzed me as Leo folded his hand firmly over my mouth, preventing that scream from breaking free.

"Don't. Say. A Word." He ground the words into my ear as he urged Kellan forward with an unwavering intensity.

Icy terror gripped me, but I refused to move or speak. I held completely still, afraid that any movement would insight the attention of whatever these beasts were.

As we moved past them, I stole quick glances in the darkness the best that I could. Their jaws were unhinged and filled with what looked like spikes of wood or thorns of some sort. I shuddered, forcing a swallow as I pulled my eyes back to the path.

The heartbeat pounding in my ears was the cadence that kept me moving forward. Any moment they could close back in and devour us whole. How many others have traveled here and succumbed to that fate?

The grotesque creatures held eerily still as we passed by, like spiders waiting to pounce on silk-trapped prey.

Breathe in. Hold. Exhale. I repeated it to myself over and over, focusing solely on keeping air in my lungs and surviving this fucking night.

The pull to the *mirror pond* was *so strong*. We were almost there.

The path opened ahead to a clearing that held the dark waters. They were just as they had appeared in my vision. Leo swung his leg off the horse and helped me down. My wide eyes were taking in all that I could see in the bright moonlight. Four crumbling stone pillars lifted out of the water, joining in an archaic arch that seemed to frame the full moon perfectly. As if it was built for such a night as this.

It couldn't be a coincidence that we sought truth this night, under the ethereal glow of the enormous Shadowed Moon. It was a moon of mystery, secrets, and hidden truths. Our presence here, to peer into the candescent waters, was *one* gods damned way to worship it.

The woods were silent now, save for the distant creaking of the branches in the wind. A cool hand pressed to my cheek, pulling my gaze away from the water. Leo framed my face with his large hands and bowed his forehead to mine.

"Whatever you see, whatever happens... it changes *nothing*." His dark eyes bore into mine. The intensity of them was an anchor for my soul. "You are still Magnolia. *Váliarë*. The one who is blessed by the Goddesses and the moon. Carrier of *The Witching Stitch*. Healer and Magic Wielder. Compassionate. Fierce. Formidable. Stubborn." The shadows played across his mouth, revealing a sultry smirk. He placed a slow, languid kiss on my lips. One that stole my breath.

"Strong. Courageous. *My Nolei*." He tucked a wayward strand of hair behind my ear. "No prophecy, vision, or scroll will change that."

Gods, his words struck right through to my heart, causing it to slow and swell all at once. I swallowed dryly. My eyes closed as I pressed my forehead into his, breathing in the scent of him. Savoring this feeling of security, even amidst this horrific waking nightmare. I nodded, turning to walk toward the water's edge. Toward my past and my future.

CHAPTER

THIRTY-THREE

My feet moved me to the edge of the bank. The invisible pull that had been plaguing me since that vision earlier this week was now tugging relentlessly at me. Just as in that vision, the dark water was too still and almost black. Wispy tendrils of mist clung to the surface and disappeared into the night above the waters. *This was it.* The truth was about to be revealed. There would be no going back from here. No settling into naivety. No pretending I was just some woman whose parents died when she was young. I would have to face whatever it was I was about to learn.

Leo stood a few steps back, giving me space to face this on my own. Yet he remained close enough that his steady presence was a tether.

I took one last steadying breath as I closed the distance between myself and the water. Looking up, I took in the vastness of the Shadowed Moon. Appreciating its beauty and the magic it seemed to hold. I peeled my eyes from it and looked down, locking my gaze on the eerie waters I had traveled so far to see.

At first, all I saw was my reflection. A sight I hadn't seen in quite some time, actually. My appearance was unexpected. My dark hair billowed in long waves over my chest. My face was thinner and my body more muscled than I remember it being. My eyes were darker somehow. My full lips were parted slightly.

The image flickered and flashed with the reflection of another woman. The same parted full lips and wavy curls, but with stark white hair. *My Mother.* Her eyes were captivating, although unnatural, with only pinpoint black pupils showing against the whites of her eyes. Her face was painted with lines of black ink. The same ink that marked the rest of her body.

Before I had time to take in the image fully, my reflection reappeared. Another flicker and the image of a young male appeared. His body was strong, but his face was gentle. Antlers spiked from his tousled caramel hair, the same shade as mine. Vibrant green eyes stared back at me. *My Father.* A mossy cloak fell from his broad shoulders, intricate designs marking it like swirling vines.

I struggled to take it all in before the image disappeared again. The images began flashing quickly in the water. Moving from one to another, as if replaying the memories. My breath caught, and I was pulled deeply into a vision as if I was there *with* them, witnessing it unfold in real-time.

The blonde woman walked through the woods, singing. She was... gathering something? She stopped here and there to collect plants and such. The male followed, hearing her song. He snuck through the woods, moving silently through the trees and greenery like it was second nature to him. As if the trees, branches, and rocks were an extension of himself.

Your mother's voice, a siren's song.... Your father, nature's gentle grace.

The Scroll played through my mind, woven with the images reflected in the *mirror pond.*

He parted through some leaves and saw her, her curvy body marked with those dark lines. She was wearing a black top and black skirt with deep slits up both sides, revealing her willowy frame and accentuating her breasts. She was beautiful.

Jewelry seemed to drip from her, covering her neck, ears, arms, and hands. All with symbols... crescent moons, triangles overlapping, and various crosses. She moved rhythmically through the woods as she sang her careening song. She turned her head to look at him as if she knew he was there. A seductive smile played at her lips.

The images flashed again. Their bodies were pressed together. Their clothes were different. She wore a tight bodice and flowy skirt, the inked lines below her breasts visible between the two. Their lips roamed fiercely against each other.

The vision blurred, revealing them walking up a creek bed hand in hand. Her white hair was breathtaking in the sunlight. Small trinkets swayed from braids that peeked through her long hair. A small skull of some sort... maybe a rodent... and a few feathers were fixed to the ends. Her tattooed arm and jewelry-covered frame were a stark contrast to his muted colors and bow-crossed back. He smiled at her, clearly smitten. She bent down and splashed him, squealing when he retaliates, throwing her over his shoulder.

In another flash, their bodies were pressed close together as they kissed frantically against a tree. The image split into them holding hands, facing each other now. The full moon was bright overhead as they stared into each other's eyes.

A secret love they keep.

The images flashed more quickly. My mother was chanting something, holding some smoking herb as she moved freely around a fire at night. My father bent and gently touched a mushroom illuminated by golden sunlight. A squirrel ran up to sniff his hand.

Then it is the woman again. Dark paint streamed down her face below her eyes, making her white eyes even more entrancing. Her palms were open, and she was staring directly at me. Turquoise smoke plumed out of her palms. She smiled. It was a wicked smile that sent a chill down my spine.

The reflection shifted again, revealing the male arguing with someone. He turned, clenching his fists, and stormed off. Then he was in the middle of the woods again. The leaves swirled gently around him. A red-breasted bird sat on one of his antlers, clearly unafraid.

The images flashed rapidly. The white-haired woman lifted a carved stone overhead, blood dripping down her forearms. The male sat on a throne made of wood and vines, his gaze vacant. The woman was surrounded by others, all wearing black dresses and sitting in a circle. A spiral of stones coiled between them.

In mirror's depths, the truth you face,
Of bloodlines dark and deep.

Then they were kissing again, frantic and fierce. It flashed back and forth with images of their faces staring back at me, as they were in the beginning. From him to her and back again until suddenly I am staring back at myself.

I inhaled sharply, reeling from the sensation of settling back in my body. My heartbeat pounded in my ears again.

Leo's hand pressed to my lower back.

"What is it? Are you okay?" His gentle voice further settled me back into my body.

My eyes wide, I continued to stare at my reflection in the dark waters. The tendrils of mist returned to swirling just above the surface and my reflection returned to black.

Holy Divine Feminine fuck. I just saw my parents. That was *them*. But now I was left with more threads to untangle than answered questions.

CHAPTER

THIRTY-FOUR

We returned to find the rest of our crew sitting silently around the fire. I recounted all that I had seen to them, explaining it the best that I could. I tried to recall every detail, not wanting to miss a single thing I had just learned about my parents. *My* parents. I couldn't wrap my mind around the fact that those two people, so different, but so clearly in love, were my parents. *Are* my parents. After all these years of thinking they were dead, I might actually get to meet them. *Were they both still alive?* Goddesses, I hoped so.

Sappha's green eyes glowed in the firelight. She was elated that I had finally learned the truth. I was so grateful that she had recognized me by my powers, called out *The Witching Stitch* and helped to guide us here. I could never thank her enough. Words could not express how much this information meant to me.

Her words from the first day we met played through my mind. *You are Váliarë. The one who is blessed by the Goddesses and the moon. The one who carries the powers of two great lines and marries them in her blood. The one who carries The Witching Stitch.* I turned them over in my thoughts. *The true heir of two peoples.*

I tensed. Leo paused his stroking of my back, noticing the change. He pulled me in closer to his chest and kissed my temple. "What is it?" He whispered.

"*The true heir of two peoples,*" I repeated aloud. Loud enough that everyone could hear. Cardin stopped poking at the fire. Eryn turned her head to look at me.

"What?" Eryn asked.

Sappha just nodded, smiling coyly as if she had been waiting for this realization to hit.

"Sappha said that I was the *true heir of two peoples.*" I started, only now understanding what that truly meant. Leo flashed Cardin a quick look before focusing his attention back on me.

"She said that I carried the power of two great lines. *The Witching Stitch* isn't just the *name* for my powers, it represents the powers that only *one* could carry. The child of the male and female from my vision. The *true heir of two peoples.*" The words were pouring out quickly now.

"My mother, she was a *witch*, wasn't she? Or *is* a witch, rather?" I asked of Sappha, my eyebrows knitting.

She nodded, her green eyes nearly twinkling.

"That means that *I* am a witch. Or half-witch, anyway." I said excitedly. Even having seen what my mother was in the *mirror pond*, it only just sank in.

"I mean, it makes sense. You've been dabbling with alchemy and the healing arts since before your first cycle, Nolei." Eryn said. "You cast those ancient spells from your Gran's books like it was second nature to you."

The reminder of Gran helped to settle my frantic nerves. Even though it caused more questions to bubble to the surface — like, *did she know all of this? Was she even my* grandmother *by blood?* And most importantly ... how could she lie so easily to someone she claimed to love? I pushed the complicated mess of emotions down that threatened to bubble up at the mention of her.

Yes, using the spell books and creating tinctures and salves had always been easy for me. It made me feel useful to help people in that way. I thought back to the hours I had spent reading through her massive collection of ancient tomes, trying to absorb as much of the information as I could. Whenever we were out and about, I was always scavenging for new ingredients and experimenting to learn their properties.

But a witch? That was going to take some processing. I hardly knew anything about witches except for what was whispered about them. Like how they would use blood for sacrifices, occasionally *killed* for this purpose, and could conjure demons with dark magic. Before I met Sappha, anyway.

Sappha wasn't like that at all, though. Well, as far as I could tell. She was skilled with a bow and arrow, as well as with a sword. She used magic easily and helped me tap into my own, guiding me to perform that ritual in the woods earlier and helped me to control it during the ambush.

"Okay, so... not only was my mother a witch, but if I was the *heir* of her people, then she must be the leader of the Coven? The Queen Witch?" I honestly had no clue what the proper title would be. I looked dumbly at Sappha.

"Well, you can definitely be a Queen Bi..." Cardin teased, smartly cutting himself off in response to the low rumble and death glare coming from Leo.

"Very funny..." I made light of his intended insult, not wanting this to end in violence. *Again*. Leo throwing a dagger at his head last time was excitement enough when it came to these two.

"You are correct." Sappha cut in. "She is the Matron of the Hearth, leader of the Covenwood Witches."

Is. That means she was still alive. Excitement fluttered through me, paving the way for an even more dangerous feeling — hope.

"So *I* am a Covenwood Witch?" I asked, clarifying for what felt like the hundredth time. All of this felt so new and strange that I was clearly having difficulty wrapping my mind around it.

"That you are. I recognized your aura immediately, Sister."

Sister. I liked the sound of that. It made me feel... *connected*. Like I was a part of something.

And what about my father? He was a King? A Prince? I saw him sitting on a throne in the vision. *But what throne?* He wasn't a member of the royal Graelis family who was killed by The Dark Enchantress. *Was he?* I knew of no other royal families in all of Lunaris.

"But who is my father, then?" I asked nobody in particular. "He was sitting on this giant wooden throne, but looked bored out of his mind. Like he would rather be anywhere else. I've never been to the capital city to see the Throne of Celestara, but it didn't seem like that was where he was."

"No, the Throne of Celestara is made of Nebulite." Leo said. "It is a glass made from the shards of stars, is deep turquoise like the waters of The Calanthian Sea, and sparkles like starlight." Leo's voice was laced with nostalgia.

Cardin shot him a quick look with narrowed eyes.

"Have you seen it?" I turn in his lap, eager to hear more.

He shook his head briskly. "Oh, No. I've just heard tall tales of it before from mead-drunk males in taverns. We've heard all sorts of things during our travels, right Car?"

"Ah yes. Enough to write a gods damn book." He replied easily. "We've shared ale with quite a vast array of people. From the wild males of Runedal to the Seamen of Leisport, we've heard plenty of tales from them all." He winked in my direction, his blonde hair bobbing slightly with the tilt of his head.

"What if you were secretly the daughter of Queen and King Graelis?" Eryn asked, hands clenching at her chest. "That would be so exciting!"

"Impossible." Leo shot back, his voice flat.

"She said she saw her father sitting on a throne—" Eryn continued.

Leo cut her off. "The *entire* Graelis family was murdered by The Dark Enchantress."

"Your father was the heir to a kingdom that has gone through great pains to remain a secret. *Especially* from The Dark Enchantress." Sappha leaned forward, lowering her voice as if someone would overhear us in such a remote location as this in the middle of the night.

Gods, I hoped there weren't any soldiers lurking. I could go without any more surprises from The Dark Army, that was for damned sure.

"That is where your elemental powers come from. Your ability to harness the energy from the world around you."

A secret kingdom. I was the heir to a hidden kingdom that even The Dark Enchantress knew nothing about. Excitement began replacing the unease that I had become so accustomed to.

"We've done a lot of traveling and have never heard of that. If such a place existed, Leo and I would know about it." Cardin said haughtily.

Sappha narrowed her eyes at him again. It seemed to be the only way she looked at him, in fact. "Believe it or not, a place does not need *your awareness* to exist."

She rolled her eyes. "Gods, I don't know how you put up with having to lug males around with you everywhere you go. Don't you tire of their incessant, arrogant babbling?" Sappha asked of Eryn and I.

Cardin leaned back, crossing his arms over his chest and rolling his eyes exaggeratedly. Eryn snickered and raised her brows at him. I honestly didn't think I would ever tire of hearing jokes at Cardin's expense. He was just so easy to make fun of.

A smile played on my lips. The light air of this conversation was helping to lift the weight of all of this news from my shoulders. I took in each one of them, really seeing them for who they were.

Eryn, my absolute best friend. Adventurous, playful, the keeper of all my best secrets.

Sappha, our newest ally and the first and only witch I had ever met. She was cunning, fiercely independent, and wise. Not to mention she had a way of putting the males in their place that was honestly enviable.

Cardin, although overconfident in every way, was always making me laugh. He was loyal and dependable. Our much-needed source of amusement.

And then there was Leo. *My* Leo. At first, I saw only the danger in him, the lethal edge. Now, I knew that danger was real. But only for those who deserved to rot in the Cinder Wastes. To me, he was something else entirely. Virtuous and compassionate, a natural leader. Thoughtful, devoted and... downright irresistible.

A pang of desire ran through me, causing me to reach my hand back to his jaw, which rested over my right shoulder. He turned into my touch, placing another smoldering kiss on that space between my neck and ear that he loved so much. That *I* loved so much.

"Your father is the King of the hidden Kingdom of Lothariel." Sappha's smooth voice pulled me from my thoughts.

I blinked at her.

She flashed me a radiant smile. Like she had been waiting all along to tell me this.

Leo tensed behind me. Cardin's eyes flashed to Leo and then back to me. Eryn's brows were etched with confusion.

I knew he must have been royalty of some kind after the visions, but putting a name to his kingdom made this all start to feel real. But that didn't mean I was processing any of it.

Sappha stood from the log she was sitting on near the fire's edge. She faced me. The crackling of the fire was the only sound, save for the pounding of my heartbeat in my ears.

"You are daughter of Blesse, Matron of the Hearth and leader of The Covenwood Witches, *and* daughter of King Nateo Alderynn, The King of Lothariel. You are the true heir of two mighty, albeit different, peoples. Carrier of power from two great lines. Carrier of *The Witching Stitch*. Next Matron of the Hearth and *Princess* of Lothariel. These titles are yours, whether or not you choose to claim them."

She strode over to the fire and created a circle in the surrounding dirt with her boot. She placed five rocks here and there at various points around the fire. We watched in silence, trying to figure out what she was doing.

Then she strode over to the smoldering flames and dipped her hands into the ash. Her flesh didn't burn and her muscles didn't flinch. She massaged the ash into her palms and spoke: "*Vehd myna henduir, mo chroí, a fyren menrah sál, svair ehk myn trúh, nú a eylifu, Váliarë.*"

The dark smudge spread and whirled around her hands like smoke as she spoke. She approached me with outstretched hands, palms open and hands together, the black smoke churning in her open palms.

Even though I had never heard those words before, I somehow knew exactly what they meant. A part of me recognized them and whispered them aloud for the others to hear. *"By my hands, my heart, and the fire of my soul, I pledge myself to thee, now and always, Váliarë. Moon Blessed"*

Moving before my mind had a chance to catch up, I instinctually placed my right hand into her outstretched palms, my middle finger dipping first into the smoldering darkness. As our palms connected, a jolt of energy crackled up my arm and through my body. The same happened to Sappha as she stiffened.

Within a heartbeat, the darkness divided in two and curled up each of our arms. It circled our forearms before it sank into our skin, causing me to hiss briefly as if branded by a hot poker. I squeezed my eyes shut and as I opened them, black ink banded my forearm.

I looked to Sappha. The same mark had seeped into her dark skin. My lips parted as I realized what this was. *An oath. An unbreakable bond.*

"I stand by you and swear fealty to you. *By my hands, my heart, and the fire of my soul, I pledge myself to thee, now and always, Váliarë.*" She said, repeating it. She gave me a curt nod of her head and then backed up.

This was not happening. I was a nobody. An orphan, raised by my grandmother. A fugitive, targeted by The Dark Queen. A simple healer. A friend who continued to bring danger to those she cared most about.

My mouth was dry. I felt utterly unworthy of these titles. Of this show of respect. What had I done to deserve such allegiance?

I began shaking my head silently, not sure with what words to respond. Leo gently lifted me off his lap. He helped me to my feet where I rocked unsteadily, trying to get my bearings. His broad shoulders turned as he faced me and he repeated after Sappha. His dark curls flopped forward as he bowed his head briefly in my direction.

Cardin and Eryn followed suit, standing and then repeating the oath Sappha had sworn. *"By my hands, my heart, and the fire of my soul, I pledge myself to thee, now and always, Váliarë."* They bowed their heads at me briefly.

I stood there, my mouth flopped open and brows knit. Pulse racing. No words were coming forth. *What could I even say to this?*

Yes, I appreciated them coming with me on this journey and supporting me. Risking their lives, even. But to pledge fealty to me because of my secret heritage that I didn't even know about one moon ago? Because my "parents" were apparently in charge of two vastly different peoples that my friends, save for Sappha, didn't even belong to?

Leo moved first, not waiting for me to respond to their gesture, thank the Goddesses. He came forward, wrapping his large hands along my waist and pulling me in. The feel of him against me calmed my mind and soothed my frayed nerves. He kissed me slowly and deeply.

For a moment, my mind was consumed with him. His unique pine and campfire scent mingled with that of our fire. It invaded my senses in the best way. The touch of his hands on my back was anchoring, yet cultivated the flame inside of me. His lips were pure decadence.

When my eyes opened again, I saw the others were standing a few steps back. The energy in the air was *different* now. Like something had *changed.* I couldn't put a finger on it, but it was clear that everyone's minds were racing just as quickly as mine was.

"I don't deserve this…" I started, putting words to my thoughts. "You don't all have to swear fealty to me just because of who my parents were. Parents I've never even me—"

"Stop acting like you are some useless bystander in all of this, Nolei. Yes, your parents are apparently leaders of *two different peoples*. But that's not *why* you are a leader." Eryn cut me off. "You're a leader because you risk your life to save others. You don't run when shit gets hard, you fight. Every damn time. Every step of the way, you have shown just how fucking brave you are. So don't for one second try to play it off like you don't deserve all of this. If anyone deserves it, it's you."

My eyes stung with tears at her words. The good kind. I wiped at them as I cracked a wobbly smile. Leave it to Eryn to make me cry happy tears while scolding me.

"She's right for once, you know," Leo purred into my ear.

"You are not merely *Váliarë*. You are moon blessed because the moon *chose* you. The Divine *chose* you, Nolei. For who you are. Who they knew you would become." Sappha said.

Not knowing how to respond to all of this, I shot forward and pulled Eryn into a hug. We had been through so much together. I don't know what I did to deserve a friend like her, but I thanked the Goddesses every day for her. She knew when to call me on my bullshit and how to keep me grounded. And I loved her for it.

Next, I wrapped Sappha in a hug. "Thank you," I whispered into her dark brown hair.

She squeezed back, harder than I expected. "Of course, Sister." She replied.

I moved to Cardin next, coming up onto my toes to reach him. He squeezed tightly and then ruffled my hair. "Can't wait to see what wild adventures you'll take us on now, Witch Princess."

Leo huffed in response.

I released Car from the hug and gave him a shove. He stumbled backward, laughing.

Leo stood there, arms open in anticipation of his hug. I crinkled my nose at him. "Don't be greedy. I just hugged you."

His jaw dropped open in false offense. I laughed.

"Ouch." Cardin chimed in, pretending to bite his knuckle as he winced dramatically.

"What will kill him first?" Eryn responded lightly. "The Dark Army or Nolei wounding his ego?"

My eyes flitted from person to person as various replies echoed between laughter.

"I love you all." I blurted out to all of them before my mind could filter the thoughts spewing from my mouth.

It felt so right to be surrounded by all of them. They were my people. *My family.* Even if allowing myself to be vulnerable with them was a risk. It was a risk I was happy to take. *But what if they didn't feel the same about me?* What if they couldn't wait for this little adventure to be over so they could move on with their lives? We had only known each other for a short time, save for Eryn and I.

"We love you, too, Witch Princess," Cardin said, interrupting my whirling thoughts. Thank The Garden Sanctum for Cardin and his ludicrous retorts.

I looked up, catching Leo's dark gaze watching me. He extended his hand toward mine and I grabbed on. He squeezed gently. A reassuring reminder that it was *okay.* He was *mine.* They were *all* mine and everything would be okay. It had to be.

I didn't know what the future would hold for us, but I hoped I could be worthy of their allegiance. Whatever came next, we would face together.

Despite the exhaustion that weighed heavily on every one of my bones, sleep evaded me. I lay snuggled up to Leo, my head on his chest and a leg curled over his body. One of his hands wrapped around my waist and held me tightly to him, even as he slept soundly beside me.

First, I couldn't stop thinking about those creepy as fuck skeletons in the woods we saw earlier. The creaking of their bones...er... limbs... kept playing in my mind and sending shivers down my spine. I hope I never have to see anything like them again. Ever. Something told me I would, though.

Then there were the images that were shown from the *mirror pond*. Flickers of images *from bloodlines dark and deep*. The words of The Scroll repeated in my mind, matching up with what was revealed to me through the visions. My *mother*. A witch. *The* matron of the hearth. Her brilliant white hair and beautifully marked body. My *father*. A King. *The* King of a hidden forest kingdom. *Holy fuck.*

I stared up at the night sky, tracing the constellations I knew by heart.

I wondered if they knew I was alive. Curiosity was quickly replaced by a sharp pang of hurt, followed by an intense rush of anger. The anger fizzled into grief at the loss of time we could have had together...as a *family*.

Why did they abandon me? Didn't they love me? They were so in love with each other, but the thought of a child ruined it all? Neither one of them wanted to raise me. The questions hounded me relentlessly, keeping sleep at an arm's distance all night.

And I had so many questions about this hidden kingdom. Sappha couldn't share many details about it, only that she knew how to get us there. She said we could be there by tomorrow if we left early. She managed to get us to the *mirror* pond, so I didn't doubt her one bit.

That is what we would do. Travel to Lothariel to meet my father. I swallowed dryly. After growing up thinking my parents were dead, the prospect of *actually* meeting him tomorrow was almost unfathomable. As the moon sank in the sky and the first wisps of dawn's light broke through, I finally fell into a deep sleep.

CHAPTER

THIRTY-FIVE

A s we approached the gate to the hidden kingdom, guards looked down at us from their perches along the rise protecting the woodland civilization. Females and males both, with long pointed ears peeking out from their hair. Leather straps crisscrossed their chests, holding various weapons to their muscular bodies. Their arrows pointed down at us.

I stepped forward tentatively. My arms lifted overhead, causing the branches to sway and the wind to whip, revealing the elemental powers that verified me as the offspring of the King. They lowered their arrows, opening the massive gates.

We strode forward, taking in the ancient trees, lush greenery, and coiling vines that clung to every vertical surface. A cozy warmth brushed along my skin from the damp, moss-scented air. The sun cast a buttery glow on the village. The homes were connected by wooden bridges with vined railings. Children scampered happily along them, causing them to sway as they ran.

Three guards marched us forward, bringing us to the castle. Nobody spoke to me. It was as if they could see me for who I was, but couldn't bring themselves to acknowledge me.

Leo's hand was a steadying weight in mine. I inhaled deeply, readying myself to meet my father. Possibly for the *first* time. A nagging pit of anger weighed heavily in my stomach as I wondered again why he had abandoned me. I set it aside as I tried to remain open to meeting him and hearing his side of the story at last.

We climbed the stone stairs in silence, making our way to the castle at the center of this secret metropolis. It was giant, its stone towers shooting up to the tops of the towering trees. Rounded windows pocked the walls, surrounded by creeping ivy in greens, whites, and yellows. Small waterfalls cascaded throughout, flowing beneath the various bridges and rounded walkways.

My breath caught in my chest as I took it all in. The beauty was unparalleled. Undisturbed. Peaceful.

We were brought forth into the castle, guided up spiral staircases and through open-air breezeways. At last, we entered the throne room. A massive tree sat at the center, its whirling branches twining together to form the throne from my vision. A large central throne with two smaller, but just as extravagant, thrones on either side.

There was a male on the throne. His jaw was sharp, and he held himself proudly. His gray curls cascaded down to his shoulders. A large verdant jewel sat centered over his muscular chest, its green hues sparkling in the light that poured in from the glass windows lining every wall of the chamber. An impressive set of brown antlers sat atop his head, surrounded by a crown of greenery. A gray, finely trimmed beard covered his strong face, framing his features magnificently. The King. *My Father.*

He stared at me, his face a mask of impassivity. My heart pounded boldly in my chest again. I was actually *meeting* my father. The need to be accepted by him, to be welcomed by him, suddenly became all-consuming. I opened my mouth to speak, willing the words to come forth.

"Father," I whispered hesitantly.

Silently, he rose. His brilliant eyes bore into me, causing me to shrink back.

"You are *nothing* to me." He spoke, his voice gravelly. The words piercing. "*Nobody.*"

"What?" I asked, praying to the Mother, Elowen, that I had heard him wrong.

"You mean nothing to me." His stern voice was like a blade to my heart. "Leave. *Now.*"

The guards stepped toward me as if to guide me out. But I hardly saw them. A high-pitched noise sounded in my ears. I thrust my hands over them to try to silence the painful screeching. Leo's hand was at my waist, coaxing me away. I retreated into myself, the room and the people in it turning hazy and distant.

The energy ripped through me, coming out of nowhere. *Hurt. Abandoned. Unworthy. Nobody. Nothing.* The words flooded me, causing a searing energy to tear through every morsel of my being.

This couldn't be happening. I had come all this way. I learned the truth and traveled all the way here to meet my father. And for what? For him to reject me. For him to not even want to look upon my face. A face that reflected his own.

The piercing sound continued as I slumped down and curled forward, hugging my arms over my knees on the cold stone floor. The molten energy shot through me, torching every part of me. Searing pain stretched across my back as my skin split open, bright orange fire rippling out of the cracks.

My arms. My shoulders. My hips. My entire body was being shattered open with uncontrollable anguish. Stone tumbled down all around me as the throne room shook in response to me.

Leo's hands pressed firmly along my cheeks in an attempt to draw my gaze to him, but my eyes remained clenched shut.

"Nolei. Nolei, I'm here." His velvety voice was getting louder, but the din in my ears was all-consuming. He shook me gently, keeping one hand on my face. The feel of his lips along my jaw, nose, and forehead helped tether me.

My eyes flashed open and locked with his. That noise was coming from *me*. That horrible sound was my own shrieking.

I sat up abruptly, running my hands over my arms and back, searching for the fiery wounds. But there was nothing.

I was in Leo's arms, covered in a mound of furs. The hazy pink of dawn streaked through the sky. I rubbed at my bleary eyes, trying to focus.

There was no throne room. No wounds. We were at the campsite. The others crowded around us, concern etched on their features. Eryn handed me a canteen of water, offering me a drink.

I drank deeply, the cool water putting out the internal fire that had torn through me, if only in my dreams. Leo's powerful arms wrapped around me as he pulled me to his chest, kissing the top of my head.

"It was just a dream, Nolei. You are safe. Breathe." He cooed into my messy hair. I melted into his embrace, but couldn't quite shake the feeling that it had been *real*.

Not knowing what one wears to meet their father for the first time, I allowed Eryn to choose for me. She selected a pair of brown pants, with a white top that had slightly more billowy sleeves than the other few ensembles I carried with me. I fastened on my brown leather vest, cinching the laces at my chest. Eryn's fingers roved through my hair, placing intricate braids here and there.

"I know you're feeling all sorts of ways about meeting your dad, Nolei," she said after I had told her about my dream the night before. "Just be careful, okay?"

I tensed. "What do you mean?" I asked hesitantly. It wasn't like Eryn to tell me to be cautious. She was more of the have fun now, ask for forgiveness later type.

"I just mean..." she trailed off, choosing her words carefully. "We've come a long way and risked a lot to get here. I just don't want to see you get your feelings hurt or anything."

"Just because I had some fucked up dream doesn't mean that I'm some fragile flower that can't handle the truth," I said. The words came out harsher than I had expected.

"I just don't want to see you get hurt."

I turned my head to face her. Her blue eyes searched mine. Annoyance flared through me. She was supposed to be my friend. My best friend. Supposed to support me and be there for me, always at my side. Not tell me to be careful so my feelings don't get hurt like I was some kind of preening schoolgirl.

She broke the silence, interrupting my careening thoughts. "First you lost Gran. Then your home. Now you have Leo...which is great and I'm happy for you. On top of all of that, now you are about to meet your dad," she said, eyes pleading. "Just be careful. Please."

I stood, pulling the braid she was working on from her grasp. First, she was worried about me letting my guard down with my dad and now she had to rope Leo into it? Was she jealous that I had found someone, and she hadn't? Or maybe she was feeling envious of who my parents were, now that we had learned the truth about them. Envious of what titles I would hold. I had spent years and years wishing I had a family like hers, so maybe she was uncomfortable with the possibility of me having a family of my own now. She could be trying to hold me back because she was afraid of all the changes that were coming. I tried to understand where she was coming from, but couldn't shake off the irritation that had settled into my muscles like gnarled roots.

Regardless, I didn't need her negativity bringing me down. I was going to meet my dad today. Whether or not she supported that was her own problem.

"Thanks, but you can keep your worries to yourself," I said sharply.

"Nolei..." she said, reaching for my shoulder. I ducked out of her reach and started busying myself with finishing my hair.

"I'm fine, Eryn. I got it,"

Her hands shot up as she backed away, jaw tight. "Forget I said anything."

Trying to focus on the day ahead, I continued to work on my hair. I fastened a few trinkets to the ends, a feather, and a few wooden beads, thinking they may remind him of my mother. I pulled The *Verdant Eye* necklace out of my blouse, letting it fall freely over my breasts. *To wear it is to carry their blessing and wisdom.*

It served as a reminder of Gran and all that had unfolded since she had passed. Of all the secrets that had remained hidden. *Until now.*

We traveled south through Oriella Forest, following Sappha's lead. I could practically feel the bags under my eyes from the havoc that last night had wrought on me.

I ended up riding with Leo on Kellan again. He pitched the idea with a shameless grin, declaring that having me pressed against him for hours was the highlight of his day. This comment was rewarded by resounding disgust from Sappha and Cardin. Leo had fastened Camila to Cardin's horse and helped me onto the saddle, a proud smirk fixed on his face.

I knew he wanted to keep me close, though. After everything we had been through lately, his worry was written in every tense line of his body. Like the way his face flexed with concern when I caught him watching me. I didn't mind the proximity, though. His hand wrapped firmly around my waist, pulling me into him. Being enveloped by his toned body was simply a perk.

We rode most of the day in search of the entrance of the hidden king-dom. Sappha used a similar ritual to the one we had performed on the outskirts of Oriella Forest to guide us to the *mirror pond.* I scoffed at the memory of her sneaking up behind me this morning and cutting a small braid from the underside of my hair with her dagger. She had said that anything could be found with the right relics, all while spinning my bead and feather-adorned braid in her hand with a satisfied smile before heading into the woods to make another altar. She'd be lucky if my dagger didn't end up cutting one of *her* braids next.

"So, you said your dad had horns in your vision," Cardin started, pulling me from my thoughts. "Does that mean you are going to grow horns?"

Leo snorted a laugh.

Eryn kept her chin up. She had been quiet ever since our argument earlier. I was ignoring her attitude, though, determined to stay positive and not let her skepticism get to me.

"They weren't horns, you imbecile. They were *antlers*," I replied with an exaggerated eye roll.

"Maybe they'll make an exception and decide you are better suited for horns once they meet you and see how much of a hard-ass you are," Cardin said, flashing me a teasing smile from his horse.

"Well, your ass *is* pretty ha..." Leo purred into my ear as his grip tightened on my waist.

I rammed my elbow into his gut, cutting him off. He grunted.

"I don't know what you just said to her, but I know for a fact you deserved it," Cardin quipped.

I laughed. Leo was fine. I didn't hit him *that* hard.

"All the male heirs of Lothariel are gifted with permanent antlers," Sappha said, as if it was common knowledge.

"How in all the realm would you even know that?" Cardin asked with disbelief. Sappha ignored him.

"And what of the female heirs?" I asked. Since when are males favored over females? It didn't even make sense.

"Female heirs are *also* gifted antlers, but theirs can be wielded by choice," Sappha answered. "And Cardin, you might as well cover your ears now and protect your fragile male ego because you are not going to like what I say next."

A bright peel of laughter left me. Even Eryn laughed to herself ahead. Cardin huffed and straightened his spine, clearly using every ounce of willpower trying not to respond.

Sappha gave me an amused smile and continued on. "Male antlers symbolize brute strength and duty. While female's antlers are a manifestation of power and agency, appearing only when they wish them to, symbolizing self-determination and the true power that comes from within, not just from bloodlines."

I whooped loud enough that a bird fluttered out of a nearby tree. "That's fucking right, they do!"

"You're so full of shit." Cardin said with a disbelieving snort and a crooked grin.

I laughed again.

"Mmmm... antlers?" Leo purred into my ear, causing a wave of chills to roll down my shoulder.

"Its true!" Sappha replied playfully. "Just because you can't believe a kingdom's history doesn't mean it isn't accurate. Let me guess, you still thought witches were just ugly hags before meeting me, too?"

Cardin glanced over to where she sat on her horse and let his eyes roam over her. "And here I thought you were trying to convince me of this antler nonsense, not your good looks."

Sappha arched a black brow. "Careful, Cardin. Don't provoke women who can outwit you *and* outfight you."

Leo barked a laugh from behind me. "She's not wrong, Car. You better be careful before she has you tied up again."

"Oh, you wanna tie me up again, witch?" Cardin asked Sappha seductively.

"Trust me. If I do, you *won't* like it." She replied.

"We'll see about that." Car challenged.

We continued south through the woods, allowing Sappha to guide us with the clairvoyance spell she had cast this morning using *my* braid. Seemingly out of nowhere, a cobblestone path appeared along the forest floor. There was no other sign of The Kingdom. No homes or people. Just expansive woods composed of ancient trees, as was the rest of Oriella Forest. It was oddly out of place, but hopefully a sign that we were on the right track.

As we walked along the cobblestone path, a tingle flickered over my skin.

"Do you feel that?" I asked nobody in particular.

"An aching ass from riding all day? Yeah, I do." Cardin responded blandly.

Eryn chucked the core of the apple she had been eating at him, pelting him in the back with it. He winced and braced his back, feigning a far graver injury.

"No, you troll. My body feels *tingly*."

"Maybe the effects of grinding up against my cock all day with that beautiful ass of *yours* are finally taking hold," Leo said, his voice smug and sultry.

I elbowed him in the gut again, causing him to grunt.

"It's not too late to carve them up and offer them to Vespera as a blood sacrifice, you know," Sappha chirped happily from her horse ahead of us, referencing The Crone.

The males shot each other a hesitant look and shut their mouths, clearly unable to fully tell if she was serious or not. Eryn and I laughed in response, glancing at each other with some lingering awkwardness between us.

I tilted my head and put my hand to my chin in consideration. "You know, they would make a wonderful gift to the Goddesses, don't you think? Maybe The Divine Feminine would bless this journey and grant us everlasting riches and glory in return."

"Oh, yes." Eryn shot Leo a malicious grin over her shoulder. "If we can stand their incessant babbling long enough to wait for the next new moon, they would be perfect on the pyre for the sacred ceremony!"

"Okay, Okay." Leo spurred Kellan forward. "You all know that Car and I offer far more than just chiseled, muscular bodies and dashing charm to this little group of yours. *You need us.*"

"At the very least, to make sure we're headed in the right direction." Cardin chimed in.

"If the right direction was the nearest warm bosom in the closest Tavern, then maybe we'd rely on your sense of direction, Car." Eryn shot back.

I tilted my head back and laughed freely. Leo did the same behind me. It felt so good to just laugh and joke. It was a welcomed distraction from all that had been plaguing my mind lately.

The tingling intensified, interrupting my laughter. I held my hand up, motioning for Leo to bring the horse to a stop. The others followed suit.

My whole body felt like it was coated in flickering starlight. Like I myself was sparkling. I looked down, but the skin of my hands appeared normal.

"Tune into what you're feeling, Nolei," Sappha encouraged. "Let it guide you."

I nodded at her and closed my eyes, letting the feeling intensify further, if that was even possible. I got the impression of a doorway of sorts ahead of us. It was a rounded door that was alight with a blue-green glow. When I opened my eyes, I saw nothing except for the cobblestone path and the trees ahead of us. But I felt that invisible tug again, pulling me onward.

"It's here. A doorway," I declared, raising my chin with mustered assurance.

For once, Cardin was serious as he responded, "Where? I don't see anything."

"I can't see it either, but I *feel* it." I got off of Kellan and walked tentatively forward until the hum along my skin was almost unbearable. I reached where I had seen the doorway in my mind, and gently outstretched my hand toward it. My fingers touched something cold and hard. A small jolt shot up my arm with the contact. As I pulled my hand back, a dark slab of wood appeared where my hand had touched. The visible area grew like a water spot on a parcel of paper. It had revealed a round wooden door that towered a few feet above my head and stood wider than my arms could reach.

I gasped, not believing my eyes. A radiant turquoise aura seemed to seep out from behind the door. As the door rippled into being, a loud cracking sound echoed through the forest as a giant tree appeared around it. Its gnarled branches stretched upward. The tree was moss-covered and magnificent, as were the rest of the trees here. But this one held a portal to a hidden realm. A hidden realm I was apparently heir to.

Steadying myself, I inhaled deeply and walked forward. The door cracked wide open, like the gaping maw of a fantastical beast, and all-encompassing turquoise light poured out. My breath caught in my throat as I forced my feet forward. I took another step toward the portal, and toward whatever destiny awaited me in the unknown.

CHAPTER

THIRTY-SIX

I t was exactly as I had dreamed. As we entered through the portal, the woods shifted to reveal a large, magical city. I couldn't tell if the Kingdom was disguised with a glamour, or if we had been transported to another pocket of existence altogether.

The trees stretched upward, laced with bridges that were buzzing with activity. Children ran along them and adults carried goods as they walked upon them overhead. The trees were teeming with small wooden homes that seemed to be built into the canopy. It was warmer here, just as I imagined it would be, with the fresh smell of plants combined with the damp musk of fallen logs and scattered leaves.

"Stop there." A woman's voice commanded, her voice like a wind chime.

My gaze shot upward, searching for the source as we all halted.

Slowly, I was able to discern several Fae lining the surrounding trees. They must have been stationed near the portal.

I quickly glanced behind us to see if it was still there. It wasn't. It had disappeared as quickly as it had appeared, leaving nothing but woods visible behind it.

"Who are you? How did you arrive here?" She demanded, her tinkering voice a stark contrast to the tone she was using. Her black hair was long and braided marvelously, her long pointed ears peeking through on either side. The dappled light through the trees cast a warm glow on her dark skin. Her presence was as commanding as the bow she had pointed at my head.

They were all strapped with weapons, just as they had been in my dream.

Oh no. This can't be happening. If everything is just as I pictured it, would my father reject me just the same? Was the goddess Vespera trying to warn me or prepare me somehow by showing this all to me in a dream? To lighten the blow of rejection?

Panic clutched at me, but Leo's hand pressed against the small of my back, settling my anxious thoughts.

Catching onto my inability to speak, he answered her with a charismatic ease that came naturally to him.

"We arrived through a portal that appeared in the woods." He smiled warmly at her. "We've been traveling for a long time. A warm hearth and cool mugs of ale would be much appreciated. We would be delighted to share our story with you while we break bread. I am sure the hospitality of your people is unparalleled in all the realm."

She furrowed her brows at him but did not lower the arrow she was aiming directly at me.

"That's impossible." A male voice replied, coming from another guard who was stationed in a tree to our left. His gray beard was cropped short, but his body showed no sign of being any weaker, despite his apparent age.

"And you didn't answer my first question." The woman stated cooly, not taking her eyes off of me.

"It is true. We came through a portal in the Oriella Forest."

"Only those with Lothari blood can call forth the portal." The male spoke again. I scanned the trees, picking up on at least five other guards.

"And only those who are accompanied by a Lothari may pass through it." The woman said. "So, it is time that you answer my first question. *Who are you?*"

Eryn, Sappha, Cardin, and Leo were a silent, supportive wall behind me. Although I knew it was my voice that mattered here, their steely support bolstered my nerves. *Goddesses, what did I do to deserve them?*

I swallowed thickly. It was now or never. Time to acknowledge my past and step into my future.

I stood straighter and placed my hand on my scabbard, trying to portray that I was no meek traveler who stumbled here accidentally. I was Magnolia Venbella, daughter of the King of Lothariel, and rightful heir to the throne. This was my home, if only by blood. I would enter it with the respect I deserved.

"I am Magnolia Venbella." My voice carried clearly through the trees.

"And how did you come to hear of this place? To find the doorway to our kingdom?" The light tinkling voice prodded me again.

"That is a long story." I tilted my head slightly. "And as my companion here stated, we are weary from our journey. We would be happy to share the details of our tale with your king if you would be so kind as to escort us to him." I flashed her a bold smile as I tried to hide the fact that my hand was shaking and my heart was beating like a hummingbird's wings in my chest.

"And what makes you think you deserve an audience with our King?" she questioned drolly, clearly unimpressed. Her confusion as to how we had accessed the portal at all fueled her trepidation.

I released my sword and raised my arms overhead, stretching my palms skyward. The sound of metal scraping signified that this movement was not being taken lightly by the Lothari soldiers. I kept my hands raised.

The branches whipped frantically and leaves spiraled above us, carried by the wind. Exactly as it did in my dream.

I knew that showing my elemental powers would be enough to convince them. But that wasn't enough. I had to declare my birthright. Had to step into it fully if I were going to accept this fate as truth.

"Because I am Nolei Venbella, daughter of the King of Lothariel and rightful heir to the throne." They dropped their arrows immediately, eyes wide and jaws slack as they took in the sight before them. As I lowered my arms back to my sides, the wind slowed and branches settled, leaving only a gentle breeze.

Before I had a chance to react, they were upon us.

Grabbing onto various vines and hopping from branch to branch, they lowered themselves to the forest floor in front of us. The scrape of metal sounded as we all withdrew our swords, readying ourselves for a fight.

A fight that never came.

They appeared before me and knelt on the ground, pressing their heads to the dirt.

I don't know what I expected, but it was *not this*. I looked around hesitantly, catching Leo's dark eyes as his mouth popped into that wicked smirk that sent heat pooling in my core. I widened my eyes at him quickly, looking for any sort of help here. *How does one respond to people bowing at their feet?*

Leo motioned his hand in an upward gesture to me, mouthing something I didn't quite catch. I glanced back at the green-clad guards.

Realizing what he was trying to tell me, I blurted out. "Stand! Please... stand."

Leo, Eryn, and Cardin smothered laughs. Sappha stood beside me, unphased by this entire display. She looked a little *too eager* to potentially be spilling blood.

I motioned for them to sheath their swords.

The Lothari guards did as I bid and got to their feet. The woman who had been speaking to me approached and introduced herself.

"I am Aerony, High Huntress of the Lothariel army." She stood about my height, although her posture was far better than my own. It was obvious that she was well respected by her soldiers.

"It is our honor to meet you, Princess. Much has been said of your birth. Please follow us. The King will be eager to meet you." She smiled slightly with the last sentence, then turned on her booted heel and began striding forward. The other guards waited for us to pass. I exchanged glances with my comrades and then followed Aerony. The guards fell in behind us.

This was really happening. I was about to meet my father. And see *my* kingdom. Just thinking about those words felt wrong. I still couldn't believe my father was alive, let alone a king.

The way Aerony had welcomed me caused a tiny wriggle of hope to break free inside of me. Hope that perhaps my father *would* accept me.

The guards took our horses to drink from the river as Aerony led us into the city. It was exactly as I pictured it to be. The wooden tree-homes were scattered through the canopy. A massive stone castle sat at the center, with multiple open-air breezeways decorating its walls. Outdoor stairways and stone bridges mingled with small waterfalls and flowing rivers. There were flowers and vegetation on almost every surface.

A heavy sense of déjà vu weighed on me as we climbed the spiral staircase that led to the throne room. I reminded myself of Leo's words from the very first day we met. *Breathe. Inhale. Hold. Exhale.* All I could do was place one foot in front of the other and hope that this introduction went differently than it had in my dream.

We entered through an archway, and my breath was taken away by the sheer beauty of this room. A large tree sat in the center, its branches coiled together into a grandiose throne in the center of the room. Ivy snaked up the tree and more flowers grew among the branches. The vines framed the throne, drawing attention to how mighty it was. Two smaller thrones sat on either side. Also made from twisted vines and branches.

Towering pillars supported the roof overhead, leaving the throne room open to the air. The splendor of the surrounding land was easily visible from here as if The King had wanted to marvel over his kingdom while sitting on the throne.

My gaze landed on the throne, eager to see if my father looked the same as he had in my mind. But the throne was bare.

"Where is he?" I questioned, all the possibilities whirling through my head. I took a few steps back and put my hand back on my sword, just in case.

Aerony laughed lightly. "He will join us shortly. He was made aware of your arrival. There is no need to be on edge." The sharpness of her tone contrasted with the reassuring words she spoke.

My eyes darted around the room, trying to scan our surroundings in case we needed to make an escape. There were two guards posted at every pillar, two by the door behind us, and Aerony, The High Huntress. I didn't know what exactly a High Huntress was, but she looked like she could kick my ass. That made eleven of them against five of us in hand-to-hand combat, not counting the magic that two of us could wield. We'd have to make a run for it and hope to get back to the horses before...

The sound of brisk footsteps behind me interrupted my thoughts. I turned, taking in the sight of a tall male clad in greens and browns, with a green cloak covering his shoulders. He had antlers framing his head, similar to that in my vision from the *mirror pond,* but not as large as my father had in my dream. His sharply pointed ears rose out of his curls. He wore a twisted, thorned, and ivy crown, but his hair was *all wrong*.

Instead of the gray curls and finely trimmed gray beard, his tousled curls were fawn brown and his face bare. His powerful jaw and brown eyes were the same as my father's from the vision, but he looked *different*. His jaw was more angled, and he seemed taller. Leaner. *Familiar*.

"Welcome to Lothariel, *sister*." He said with a sly smile as he strode toward us, arms outstretched. "We've been waiting for you."

CHAPTER

THIRTY-SEVEN

Time seemed to slow down as my mind tried to catch up with my ears. *Sister. Sister?*

His long cloak brushed over the floor as he walked up to the mighty throne and sat leisurely, kicking one foot up over the opposite knee as he reclined back.

He looked a lot like the vision I had of my father. A lot like *me*. His eyes were the same shade as mine, as was his skin. So many questions rose to the surface. Was he my full-blooded brother? Or did we only share a father? Where *was* my father? I tried to respond, but my mouth was dry and thoughts raced too quickly for me to settle on what to say.

"It seems as if you are caught off guard." He glanced at me with an amused look.

He took a glass of what looked like wine from a servant's tray. "Tell me, what surprises you? *You* were the one who sought *me* out."

"I... I came in search of my father." I managed to get out, trying and failing to find that flame of confidence I had when we first arrived here. Never in my life had I considered that I had a sibling, let alone a royal one.

"Ah. The King." He sipped from his chalice. "Well, would you like the good news or the bad news first, sister?"

There was something about the way he kept using that title that made me blanch. I wondered if he had truly been waiting for me, as he said. If so, how had he even learned about me? And if he had known that I existed all along, why didn't he come looking for me?

"She has a name," Leo growled from my side, clearly unimpressed.

The male on the throne's eyes flared slightly as he tilted his head. "Yes. Yes. How impolite of me. Let us begin with introductions." He set the chalice back on the tray and stood, approaching us.

"I am King Fenralei Alderyyn. Welcome to my home." He gestured at us with open arms again.

My brows knit. *King*? If he was the King then where was my father?

"This is the part where you introduce yourself." He chided me slowly, as if I was daft.

The way this entire encounter was unfolding was insulting. I needed to get a fucking grip and stop playing the shocked orphan. I was the *daughter* of the King of Lothariel and therefore the Princess of this kingdom, if only by birth. Even if I had only just found out about this title... it was still mine to claim. If I wanted these people ... wanted *him* to respect me, I would have to demand that respect.

I straightened and met his gaze with a ferocity I had not yet tapped into since he entered the room.

"I am Princess Magnolia Venbella, daughter of the King of Lothariel."

He let out a bemused laugh. "Daughter of the King? And here I thought we were siblings. Do I have some heir that I sired as a mere babe? Or maybe Elowen blessed me with a child my age that I was not aware of?" He laughed again, clearly entertained by his poor attempt at a joke.

"Very funny." I humored him with a smile. "My friends call me Nolei. I'd say my family did too, but until recently, I didn't think I had any."

He beamed back at me.

"Anyway, now that we spoke of the good news — that you are already in the presence of the King. Let's get on to the bad news..." His face flattened, turning briefly solemn.

"The King you speak of, our father, has passed on to The Garden Sanctum. About six months ago, in fact." The grief flashed through his eyes, still raw. "He became ill from a sickness of the flesh and passed peacefully while asleep." He placed two fingers on his forehead as he bowed his head briefly before lifting his fingers skyward. "Goddesses, rest his soul."

I felt Leo squeeze my hand in a silent show of support. My father was *dead*. I had just learned that he was alive and had been stupidly hopeful that I may honestly get to meet him. That I would have a father in my life again. Only to arrive here with all this feigned pomp and circumstance to learn that he wasn't even *alive*. The worst part was, I could probably have healed him from whatever illness plagued him *if* I had only known of him. I could have prevented his death.

"But you are welcome here, nonetheless." Fenralei continued, packing away his grief neatly. "Tell me, Nolei. Who do you bring with you?"

I gulped, trying to grasp at that sense of self-confidence.

"This is Eryn." I motioned toward my best friend from childhood. Who had traveled with me since Eyloria, never questioning where we were going or why. Always more than happy to adventure along beside me. Until this morning, when she wanted me to *hold back*. To *be careful*.

Then to Sappha at her side. "And Sappha." Her flowy turquoise clothing and layers of beads stood out against all the neutral colors and woodsy design features around us. Her arms were crossed tightly across her chest, exuding power.

"Cardin." He was as tall as Fenralei and they had a similar build. His rampant sense of humor was nowhere to be found now, though. He was all serious stares and confidence. His grip was tight on the hilt of the sword at his hip.

Turning slightly, I looked up at Leo. His dark eyes were full of malice and the ever-present threat of violence. A simmering fury radiated off him like he was ready to snap at any second. I squeezed his hand back. He broke his death glare and glanced down at me, his eyes softening and the corner of his lips kicking up in a gentle smile. "And this is Leo."

"I hope you're not too cozy with this one." Fenralei nodded toward Leo. "If you wish to carry the royal lineage of Alderynn on and claim your title as Princess of Lothariel, you will need to marry a Lothari male." He smiled cruelly, inviting Leo's response. "I have someone in mind already." He stroked his chin. "Someone more ... *refined.*"

Leo let out a cold growl. This was about to turn bloody if my brother didn't start shutting the fuck up. Before I could interrupt, he continued.

"I mean, if he wanted to stick around, he could. I'm sure Leo here wouldn't mind being your cuckold. If it pleases you to keep him as a pet, you may."

His too-white smile turned back to me. Then he glanced back at Leo, waggling his eyebrows at him.

King or no, I hadn't allowed males to order me around in the past and I sure as The Cinder Wastes would not start now. He was undoubtedly entitled and self-important, likely a result of his upbringing. But he was about to learn the hard way how speaking to me this way would end up for him. It was a mistake he wouldn't make again.

Leo's anger was barely leashed, rolling off him in nearly palpable waves of rage now. He was holding back, but I knew he wouldn't be able to do so much longer.

"We have much to speak of, *brother*," I replied derisively. "The first of which appears to be how you have absolutely zero say in who I marry or who I choose to warm my bed with." I smiled at him prettily. "And if you insult any of my friends again, you'll beg for mercy you won't receive."

His guards withdrew their swords at the threat, readying themselves to take us down at The King's word. *I'd like to see them try.*

Fenralei laughed heartily, enjoying my pushback.

"I have to admit, I was expecting much more from you. Although it *does* seem you have a mouth on you, sister. From what I know of your mother and the prophecy, I expected you to be much more.... *Powerful.*" He motioned to my clothes and companions with a dismissive flip of his hand. "This unkempt, mouthy, traveler look has me...*underwhelmed.*"

Before I had realized what was happening, Leo had lurched forward, slamming his fist into the King's jaw with a mist of black smoke.

CHAPTER

THIRTY-EIGHT

Fenralei's head swung back as he stumbled. Leo's hulking, black-clad form was striking compared to my brother's lean, albeit strong, royal figure.

The guards pressed in closer with their swords drawn, waiting for Aerony's command to strike. Shouts broke out as the others spun to face the guards that surrounded us.

"Leo!" I screamed, trying to get to him before the guards could. He had *snapped*. I had to stop him before he got himself killed. Or more likely, before he killed several guards *and* my brother.

Fenralei righted himself, wiping the blood from his nose. He raised the other hand to halt the guards from attacking.

He gave Leo a maniacal, blood-coated smile.

"It is one thing to speak to me with such disrespect. That I could have let slide, just this once. But to speak of Nolei with such disdain is an offense that I cannot let go without punishment." Leo warned as he unsheathed two short swords that were strapped to his hips.

The glow of delight in The King's eyes was unmistakable.

"It has been too long since I have had a good fight. If that is what you are after, I would be happy to oblige *filth*."

The curious wisps of dark smoke dissipated in the air. *Had those come from Fenralei or Leo?*

Leo growled in response as they circled each other.

"On one condition." The King said as he spat blood onto the floor. "No weapons. *Or Magic*." The King's eyes flickered with amusement. "Just *brute strength*."

I glanced up to his antlers, remembering what Sappha had said about them. *Brute strength. Duty.*

The muscles along Leo's back bunched as he tossed his swords to either side. "Even better." I could see the veins in his neck bulging from where I stood a few feet away. "That way, I can feel your bones crunching beneath my fists."

Fenralei followed suit, withdrawing his sword and tossing it to the floor. He looked Leo up and down, sizing him up. "*All* of your weapons."

Leo made a show of withdrawing four other daggers and swords from various places and tossing them aside. There was no way he would remove *all* of his weapons, but *damn*, he was well-outfitted for a fight.

"Come on. Do we *have* to do this? *Really*?" I questioned, placing my hands on my hips. "A pissing contest, right out of the gate?"

"Nobody speaks to you like that without consequences," Leo answered, keeping his eyes on his opponent.

"As I said, I could really go for a fight. Things have been pretty droll around here lately." Fenralei wiped his face again, this time with his sleeve.

After some more circling, Leo charged at my brother, connecting his fist with a fleshy crack.

Fenralei grunted and swung back, missing Leo, but only barely. Leo landed two more jabs to his core, causing Fenralei to buckle forward.

They continued on this way, both landing hits and causing blood to spray across the marbled throne room floor.

The guards pushed in, ready to intervene if this went much further. Eryn, Sappha, and Cardin faced outward, their swords ready.

Leo lifted a boot to kick Fenralei in the gut, but he grabbed onto it, yanking it so that Leo fell onto his back with a grunt.

A gasp left me. This was not going to end well. No matter who won, it wouldn't be good.

Fenralei dropped on top of Leo, straddling him. He swung at Leo's face a few times, but Leo blocked him. Deciding to change his tactic, Fenralei shifted his weight and jammed a knee into Leo's crotch, causing him to let out a guttural groan.

Suddenly, Leo bucked forward, grabbed onto the antlers that jutted from the King's head, and cracked his head into Fenralei's. Fenralei reeled back, pressing his hands to his head.

Leo took this window of opportunity to jab his fist into Fenralei's mouth, causing more blood to spew from both.

Fenralei toppled to the side, and Leo spun on top of him, pinning him to the ground.

With his fist raised overhead, ready to pummel my brother, and his dark eyes filled with molten rage, I had to admit Leo looked pretty fucking delicious. But I couldn't let this go on.

"Enough!" I demanded, screaming. "Both of you. That is enough." I braced myself for having to use my powers to gain their attention.

The room went silent except for the panting of the two alpha males. Leo's eyes cut to mine and then back to Fenralei. He paused, stood back up and extended his hand to him, his blood-specked and veined forearm peeking out from beneath his rolled sleeve. Fenralei took his hand and stood.

They stared at each other for a moment in gridlock before Fenralei spoke, breaking the silence.

"Leo. Thanks for that." He replied jovially, wiping at his bloody face again. "I was past due for a good fight. You packed some power behind those punches, mate."

Leo gave him a half smirk and patted him gruffly on the shoulder. "I've never had to grab anyone's antlers before like that, but they made for a great handle to use when bashing your skull in."

Fenralei turned toward the doorway, motioning for us to follow.

"More like when bashing *your* skull in." He laughed. "You better hope I don't ram you with them next time." He threatened.

Leo rubbed at his forehead, assessing his wounds. "If you can learn to keep your mouth shut, there won't need to *be* a next time."

Were they seriously getting along right now? After all of that?

We turned to follow them out of the throne room.

I was not expecting to meet Fenralei or to even have a brother, for that matter. But his unique personality was not what I would have expected. He seemed to incite conflict just for the fun of it. I couldn't predict what our relationship would be like from here, but I had a feeling there would be no lack of excitement when it came to him.

A wave of relief washed over me, knowing that we were finally on seemingly amicable terms. If I could speak confidently and demand the respect I deserved, I think I could get along just fine with him. Although I was happy that Leo and my brother were no longer killing each other, the barely leashed rage vibe Leo had going on was *pretty fucking hot*. I made a mental note to reward him for his devotion later...with my mouth.

CHAPTER

THIRTY-NINE

We found ourselves in a banquet hall, all seated at a long wooden table that stretched from one side of the room to the other. Fenralei sat at the head of the table, sipping wine out of a chalice. I was positioned to his right.

"Please, you must try some nectar," He insisted. "It is a Lothari delicacy."

"Nectar?" I asked, peering into my cup at the apricot-colored liquid.

"Yes, yes. Nectar! It is harvested by the minxbees from the large variety of rare flora that only grow here in Lothariel." He sipped slowly, as if he was savoring the flavor on his lips. "The pollen they collect is then fermented using an archaeal process and turned into nectar."

Cardin had gulped his down without any hesitation while Fenralei was still speaking.

"So it is similar to juice?" I queried.

"If juice was fermented beneath starlight and had potent intoxicating qualities." He smiled warmly at me and raised his glass to clink it with mine.

I shrugged and met his glass before taking a sip. The liquid tingled along my lips and down, causing a wonderful buzzing flush to spread through me. The flavor was unlike anything I had tasted before. Light and fizzy like a fresh spring, but with floral and fruity notes. It was like sipping from a ripe mango. "Mmmmm" I took several more large sips.

"The Princess seems to approve of the drink of her people!" He announced joyfully. Cheers broke out down the length of the table.

"What excellent taste she has." A red-haired woman to Aerony's left added in, flashing me a warm smile.

Aerony leaned forward from her spot across the table. "Just be mindful of how much you consume, Princess. It has a way of lighting up your senses but dulling your *common* sense."

"Oh, nonsense!" Fenralei shot back. "If anything, it has a way of easing anxieties and bolstering confidence."

"Please, call me Nolei," I said to Aerony, not liking the way the formal title felt just yet. She nodded at me with a knowing smile.

"Ah, yes. That is where we were. Introductions." Fenralei served himself from the plates in front of him. "Nolei. Please, call me Fen." He motioned to the rest of our group. "You may all call me Fen."

"As you wish, Fen." I tested the name on my tongue.

His boisterously friendly behavior was amusing but left me wondering what his initial pompous display was all about. Either his moods changed as fitfully as the weather or he was testing us to see how we would respond. Regardless, it was clear to me that we should tread carefully.

Even so, it felt nice to just sit and relax; to not be in a constant state of travel or relentless pursuit. We had been on the move for weeks, eating whatever we could scrounge up for the majority of it. To simply sit around a real table, talk, drink, and let loose was a blessing from Calantha, the goddess of new beginnings and pleasure, that I would not take for granted.

The delightful array of food that lined the banquet table had my mouth watering. We filled our plates and bellies with roast lamb, buttery potatoes, and fresh-baked, crumbly bread. The smell was as divine as The Garden Sanctum. There were even foraged mushrooms with slivered scallions sautéed in garlic butter to pair with the meat. I used my crusty bread to sop up the juices on my plate, hoping nobody noticed my lack of manners. Even if someone did, I couldn't give a fuck. This food was fucking delicious, and I was going to every morsel. Manners be damned. The nectar flowed endlessly into our glasses, allowing our conversation to flow just as readily.

"As you have said, Nolei, we have much to speak of," Fen said as we ate. "You have been gone for many moons, and I have always dreamed of the day we would meet. There is so much I wish to know about you. So much I have to ask." His brown curls were almost identical in shade to mine. He spoke as if we had been close friends before, even though we had never met. That I was aware of, anyway.

"I did not know that I had a sibling, but now that I do, I feel the same way. It is hard to know where to start." I replied, meeting the glow in his brown eyes. I finished the last sip of nectar in my glass, figuring I'd better switch to water before my confidence became too bolstered and my anxieties too eased.

"First, answer a few questions about yourself so that I may get to know you as a person. What is your favorite flower? Your favorite tattoo that marks your skin, and why? What is the first thing you think of each morning? Last, do you prefer the light of the sun or that of the moon?"

My lips parted slightly in shock. Out of all the things I expected a king to demand to know, these intricacies didn't even make the list. That he truly wished to get to know *me* and not just my story caused a comforting warmth to spread through me. *Is that what it felt like to have a sibling?*

Without breaking his stare, I responded. "Calendula, for its healing properties are as potent as its beauty. The Úlfraedor on my arm..." I pulled at my flowy sleeve, revealing the inked beast. "... as it is as fierce and bold as I am myself. It marks the beginning of this adventure and is but one of the many adventures Eryn and I have shared." I glanced at Eryn, who was speaking with Aerony and the red-haired woman. She looked back at me, some lingering tension still palpable between us.

Amusement flashed through his eyes as he nodded his approval.

The answer to the next question was a bit more personal, but that would not keep me from sharing it. I deserved the happiness I had found as much as I deserved the respect I demanded. "The first thing I think of each morning is how safe I feel in Leo's arms."

I glanced toward my dark, dangerous counterpart, and heat roiled through my body. Not the heat that made me want to strip him down to his gloriously scarred skin, but the melty warm heat that squeezed at my heart whenever I thought of him. The warm breeze that drifted through my chest when he tucked a wayward curl behind my ear or helped me on and off a horse. The feeling I got when he kissed that spot behind my ear or refilled my waterskin without me asking. The heat that seemed to permanently wrap around me in his presence, a result of the million mundane acts and tiny gestures that likely meant nothing to him but were everything to me.

Having heard his name, Leo turned from his conversation with Cardin. He tilted his head at me in question, a faint smirk tilting his lips.

"What was that you were saying about my arms?" Leo asked.

"Probably just how much smaller they are than mine," Cardin replied, winking at me.

Fen laughed. I leaned up and kissed Leo. It wasn't a quick kiss, but a deep and torturously slow one. He returned it happily. We stopped only as the others at the table began hooting at us.

"Just that the first thing I think of every morning is how safe I feel in your arms," I answered honestly. "It's hard not to think that when I wake up each morning, to your heartbeat playing in my ear and your arm wrapped around my waist." A flicker of something flashed through his dark eyes too quickly for me to make out exactly what it was. Without speaking, he kissed me again.

Fen raised his brows at us. "Despite our little dance in the throne room... or rather *because* of it... I approve of this union." He waved his hands in front of us flippantly, as if he had any say in the matter. "Or whatever it is you call it. Any male who is brazen enough to draw blood from a king in front of his own guards in defense of my sister's honor is exactly the kind of male that I'd approve of as the recipient of her affections."

Leo gave him a flourishing bow from his seat. "Why thank you for gifting us with your blessing, Your Highness."

I pulled my bottom lip between my teeth in an attempt to stay quiet. Something about the way he phrased that made me pause. *My affections.* That was one word for the undeniable way I felt about Leo.

Thankfully, my brother found Leo's sarcastic retort to be funny and not treasonous.

"And the last question...?" Fen asked.

"The light of the moon. *Obviously.*" I answered immediately. "Those who prefer the light of the sun to that of the moon are not to be trusted." I joked. "And what about you, *brother*?"

"Elderwisps. Because they grow by the moonlight and are anchored by the ancient trees that cover this kingdom." He rolled up his sleeve to reveal a brilliantly detailed image of a stag's skull along his forearm. The large antlers were laced with Ivy-like Elderwisps, along with symbols and swirls that matched those I had seen throughout the castle. "The stag of Lothariel, as it reminds me of the wisdom of our father and our many ancestors who have come before. Of my duty to protect my people while preserving the safety and peace that Lothariel offers to so many."

Before I could comment on its beauty, he continued.

"The first thing I think of each morning is how blessed I am to reside in this magical place whose beauty is unparalleled. That and how badly I need to make use of the chamber pot." He winked at me. "And I prefer the moonlight to the sunlight, obviously."

The way he mirrored my cheeky response caused joy to settle into my bones. I flashed him a bold smile. *I could do this.* I could get along with a sibling.

"Speaking of our father," I added, reaching to take a slice of some type of pastry from the serving platter in front of me. It had a flaky crust and some dark-colored berries oozing from the center. I didn't know where I would fit another bite of food, but I would figure it out for this little delight.

"I wish to know all there is to know about him." I hoped my air of nonchalance masked all the frantic emotions that were whipping inside of me.

Fen's face became serious, understanding the gravity of that statement. I truly knew nothing about our father, and it was clear that Fen was close to him. He must still be grieving his loss deeply.

"And I wish to tell you all there is to know about him." He reached out and grabbed onto my hand, squeezing lightly. "But a lifetime of memories cannot be summarized into a single dinner-time conversation. I shall tell you as much as I can in the time that we have together. Just know that he loved you very much."

My throat constricted along with my chest. *Loved me.* The unforgettable image of him from my dream threatened to take hold as truth, but I reminded myself that it was not. It was only a dream. I *wasn't* nothing to him. I was his daughter. He knew of me and *loved* me.

Our entire end of the table seemed to go silent at the shift in the King's tone.

"He was a formidable male, a virtuous king, and an affectionate father. Just and resolute. He commanded respect and freely gifted compassion. We were very close, and he shared many stories with me of his past and his visions for the future." Fen spoke clearly and loud enough that the rest of the table could listen in.

I consumed his words like they were part of the feast set before us. I allowed every detail to stitch together in my soul, filling the space left empty from a lifetime without a father.

"He loved your mother fiercely and spoke of her often. Even as a young boy, I remember hearing him speak of you. His daughter, born of a forbidden love."

"And what of *your* mother?" I interrupted.

"The moon is my mother. As are The Divine Feminine and the Ancient trees that comprise these lands."

I glanced around, hoping to find a look of shock or humor on the faces of those who were familiar to him, signifying that this was some tale he was spinning for tonight's entertainment. But that is not what I found. Everyone stared at him with rapt attention, as if they had heard this tale a thousand times but never tired of hearing it.

My brows furrowed. Had the Nectar addled his mind?

"You were born of a great love, Sister. As was I, except I was born out of their love for you. Your mother, Blesse, and our father were inseparable. Their love inconceivable. Their only downfall was that of their heritage. She was a witch, the Matron of the Hearth, no less. And he was a Prince, soon to be crowned King of Lothariel."

"Yes, so I've learned. But that doesn't explain *your* ancestry." I prodded.

"When you were conceived, it is said that you were a blessing from The Divine Feminine. Calantha adored their youthful wildness and plea-sure-driven freedom. Elowen blessed their love with fertility. Yet Vespera recognized that their union could not be. Their people were too different. The burden of their responsibilities was too heavy. It would have strained their relationship, causing only irreparable damage and despair."

At some point, Leo had placed his hand on the back of my neck and was silently massaging the tension that was brewing there. Always my anchor. Always anticipating my needs before I even realized them. I softened into his touch.

Fenralei continued. "You were born on the night of The Maiden's Moon, a well-kept secret by both of your parents. Our father wanted to whisk you away, to live a simple life alone with you and Blesse. but your mother would not allow it. She performed a ritual to grant you safety and protection. To show her gratitude to The Divine Feminine for all that they had blessed them with. But when she returned from the woods the next morning, you were not with her."

His brown eyes churned with pain that seemed to echo our father's hurt.

"Frantic, he pleaded with your mother. Begged her to return you to him. But she would not. She spoke harshly to him and told him never to seek her out again, or else the magic that blanketed you with protection would be broken."

"Why would she do that?" I asked, as if Fenralei could know my mother's true intentions. Anger toward a woman I had never even met flared to life inside me. She had rid herself of me and not even given my father a say in the decision.

"Because you were prophesied to be the true heir of both peoples, the one who carried the power from two great lines. If anyone had learned of you, you would have been in grave danger, even as a child. Just the legacy of your titles is a threat. But when combined with your powers, you could wreak havoc on anyone who dared stand in your way. And that makes you a danger even to those who hold power."

"Those who hold power? Do you mean Queen and King Graelis?" Cool sweat dampened my temples at the thought of someone seeking me out and killing me as a mere child just because of my heritage. "That was before The Dark Enchantress had usurped the throne."

My brother nodded. "Yes, Queen and King Gra—"

"They would *never* have harmed you. They believed in peace and prosperity, not in murdering innocent children." Leo scoffed, interrupting Fen's response.

Jarred by his abrupt reply, I turned slightly to face him. His features flashed with anger and then turned softer. His eyes then flicked to Cardin, who eyed him cautiously.

I had never realized how much Leo had valued our previous rulers. His hatred for The Dark Enchantress was obvious, but so were most people's who were brave enough to speak their true feelings. His feelings for Queen and King Graelis clearly went beyond the usual respect of a subject and bordered on something akin to reverence. He must have spent more time in the capital city than he had let on. Or maybe his memories of his stability in life prior to The Dark Enchantress seizing the throne fueled his fondness for their rule.

"I hope you are getting to the part where you tell me who *your* mother is, *brother*." I chided playfully, hoping to soften my insistent prodding.

He tilted his head in wry approval. "Patience, Princess." He reached up to grab a steaming mug of dark coffee from a server's platter. Glad we were switching from Nectar to coffee, I took one as well. The aromatic scent wrapped around me like a heavy fur on a frosty night. Gods, I had missed coffee.

"As I was saying, our father was distraught at the loss of his beloved daughter and of his love. He sobbed and pleaded, begging The Divine Feminine to give him back his child."

Warmth flooded my chest again. My father had *wanted* me. Had begged the Goddesses for me.

"They wanted to mend his broken heart, but would not go back on their decision to protect you as the carrier of *The Witching Stitch* and future heir. They knew no good would come from Blesse and our father staying together to raise you, however heartbreaking that was for him. Instead, they created me."

My eyes went wide in response to his claim. He had said his mothers were The Divine Feminine, but I didn't think he could truly believe that.

"They answered his prayers with another babe. Not you, but a compromise of sorts. The way he told the tale, and trust me, I remember every detail as he told it fondly and often. He looked up, tears blurring his vision, to see a babe sleeping soundly on a nearby stump. The babe was almost iridescent, flickering as if covered in stardust and illuminated in the full moonlight."

Silence filled the banquet hall as King Lothariel spoke of his birth as if everyone present could recite the story themselves but was honored to hear him speak it.

"The Divine Feminine appeared to him, then. They were devastatingly beautiful and covered in the same glittery pearlescence that I was. Calantha, The Maiden, was clothed in a simple white dress, her face freckled to match her strawberry hair. Elowen, The Mother, wore a dark blue dress that hugged her lush hips and full breasts. And The Crone, Vespera, was cloaked and adorned with jewels, her beauty just as radiant as the others."

Disbelief struck me silently. I was raised to know and worship The Divine Feminine, as were all Lunarians. But I had never heard of them appearing to anyone before now, let alone *my father*.

"They spoke of your destiny and mine, sharing a prophecy to be retold time and time again. Although his daughter was gone, they had gifted him with her twin. A son to love, to raise, to teach in the ways of his people and his magic. My destiny was to learn these things and rule in your stead while we awaited your return, Nolei. I am the King, but only until you are ready to claim your title. I serve *you*, sister. And we have *all* awaited this day."

My breath hitched. Everyone's stares felt like hot pokers branding onto my skin. All eyes were on me. They had all been waiting for *me*.

"What...What is this *prophecy*?" I forced myself to say.

"We will speak of it tomorrow, sister. This is enough for you to learn in one day. And as you said, you have traveled long and hard. Let us enjoy each other's company and then you should rest." He motioned to the servers standing along the edge of the large room. "We will ensure you all have suitable accommodations readied."

The young male servers all bowed toward the King and then left to ready our rooms, I assumed.

I shook my head, trying to make sense of all that was being said and being left *unsaid*.

"No offense, brother, but I am the only one who can say how much I can handle to learn and when I require rest."

Silence spread throughout the room.

"I am not in the practice of allowing males to decide when I'm fatigued or when I've met my capacity for how much I can process. And that is not something I plan to start doing now. So, share this prophecy. *Now*."

Sappha raised her glass in toast to my outburst. "Spoken like a true daughter of the moon." She smiled at me and took a generous sip from her chalice.

An amused glint flickered in Fenralei's eyes at my boldness.

"As you wish," He cooed.

Smart male, I thought to myself. He recited the prophecy as if it were a lullaby etched into his soul, one that he would know the words of for all of his days.

Born of powerful blood, a daughter shall rise,
Hidden from danger and prying eyes.
Unaware of the strength she will someday wield,
In shadows kept safe, her fate is concealed.

A brother, born of moonlight and starry gleam,
Takes the throne in her stead, a keeper of the dream.
Guided by wisdom and the goddess's grace
He guards her fate, as her destiny wakes.

In hidden hearts, a bond will grow,
Unseen by fate, yet destined so.
When love unknown ignites their way,
They'll heal the divided, and be crowned united.

I opened my mouth to respond, but he cut me off.

351

"—Think on it. I shared the sacred words but truly wish to save the discussion for tomorrow. Would you be so kind as to grant me this wish?" His gaze offered an unspoken challenge.

I nodded, accepting this compromise. I needed time to wrap my mind around that convoluted projection, anyway.

"So, if the union of my parents was only destined for disaster because of the vast differences in their cultures and responsibilities, how are *my* odds any better than theirs?" If Vespera thought the burden too heavy for the two of them to bear, she couldn't expect *me* to carry it by myself. I knew nothing of The Covenwood witches or their ways, nor the customs of Lothariel. I had no formal training on how to wield my elemental powers or hone my arcane ones. How could I fare any better than they could have?

"Because you are *Váliarë*," Fen replied. "The carrier of *The Witching Stitch*. Two people can be driven apart by such forces, but you *cannot*. Both sides of you are just as mighty as the other. They exist together inside of you as one. Amplified by your courage and compassion. You are the only one who can bear the burden of this destiny and be made only stronger because of it." The intensity of Fen's stare caused my skin to prickle.

I glanced over to Sappha, who was the first to tell me of this *destiny* of mine.

She repeated before nodding her head reverently. "*Váliarë*."

The others at the table followed her lead, bowing their heads in my direction and repeating the words. *Váliarë*. Even King Fenralei Alderyyn followed suit

My throat felt too dry and my face too hot. Even after what Eryn had said before about me *earning* the title of leader, a part of me still struggled to feel worthy of this praise. I was a *nobody*. An orphan with strange, forbidden powers. Not some princess deserving to be the heir of two peoples.

As if he could hear my thoughts, Leo leaned in closer and whispered into my ear. "It's true, my *Váliarë*." The vibration of his words against my ear sent a tingling chill down my spine.

I tried to rectify the two voices in my head and see myself as Leo saw me. As those surrounding this table, familiar and not, saw me. I urged that degrading voice in my head to fuck right off and tried to bolster my confidence again.

My shoulders straightened. I was Princess of Lothariel, the daughter of the late King Nateo Alderyyn, and the sister of King Fenralei Alderyyn. I was daughter of Blesse, next in line to be Matron of the Hearth and leader of The Covenwood Witches. I was *Váliarë*, carrier of *The Witching Stitch*. I was compassionate, courageous, and strong. Determined and unbreakable. I didn't know what the future would hold, but I knew I would do my best to honor these titles and be a leader worthy of the praise of my people.

My head tipped forward in a bow directed at all of those at the table.

"Thank you all. I appreciate your recognition and acceptance." I said, meaning every word.

Proud smiles rippled across the faces of those at the table, guards and commoners alike.

Turning to face Fenralei, I put words to what had been plaguing my thoughts. "I am just coming to learn of these titles and responsibilities, so forgive my ignorance of the details. I do not know yet what The Divine Feminine expects of me or what my destiny is, but I vow to do everything in my power to bring honor to the two peoples that I serve, no matter how different they may be. To lead with my heart, to trust my intuition, and to serve not just as a ruler, but as a guardian of each soul under my care."

A look of admiration washed over his face. He raised his chalice in a toast; the others following. "To Nolei Venbella Alderyyn. Our *Váliarë*, the long-awaited *Queen of Lothariel*."

Raucous cheers broke out throughout the banquet hall, followed by the clinking of glasses.

Others spoke merrily around me, but I couldn't hear what they said. The sound of my heartbeat pounded wildly in my ears again. Then I heard Leo's voice as he pressed his lips to that spot below my ear that he loved to kiss and whispered, "It seems congratulations are in order, *My Queen*."

CHAPTER

FORTY

Wefollowed a peppy young male who introduced himself as On-vyl up a long spiral staircase that opened into a long corridor. The male was about my height and based on his build; it seemed he was just growing into his lanky limbs. He continued to shake his head in an attempt to keep his shaggy brown hair out of his eyes. He reminded me of an energetic puppy.

My feet clicked against the stone floor as Sappha and Eryn chatted as we walked. I didn't catch what they were saying, but based on the tone of Cardin's voice, I assumed they were teaming up on him again. Leo's hand laced in mine as we followed Onvyl. The sconces lining the hall cast a warm glow.

"I have prepared the rooms for you all. Started the fires, turned down the bed, and had a tub filled with warm water brought to each room. I hope it is to your liking." Onvyl spoke as he led us down the hall, motioning at the first open door on the right.

I gave Leo a bemused look, and he returned it with a smirk that caused heat to pool in my core. A promise of what tonight would hold. Tearing my eyes away from his full lips, I tried to focus on what Onvyl was saying.

"This room for the two ladies." He nodded at Sappha and Eryn.

Sappha gave him a discerning look, as if sizing him up, and then turned to enter. "I can't wait to take a hot bath." She said as she strode into the room.

Eryn hesitated, grabbing my hand.

"Can I speak to you for a moment, Nolei?" Her blue eyes held mine with a touch of wariness.

"Of course." I walked several steps away from the group to give us some space. My stomach clenched at the memory of how our last conversation had ended.

"What is it?" I asked, moving to hold both of her hands in mine.

She tugged her hands back and crossed her arms at her chest.

"I told you to be careful and you completely fucking ignored me," she warned, her blue eyes as cold as ice.

"What do you mean?" I asked as my guard shot back up like a stone fortress between us.

"One day you're trying to figure out who your parents are and the next day you're *sipping nectar* and making some speech at a royal banquet as if you're the Queen of the realm," she spat. "I just don't want it all to go to your head, that's all."

Embarrassment flooded my body and flushed my cheeks. *What was she even talking about?* She was the one who told *me* that I was a good leader. That I *deserved* to lead.

"What the fuck is that supposed to mean, Eryn?" I shot back, trying to keep my defenses up so the hurt couldn't cut too deeply.

"Only that you need to *be careful*. Just because you show up here and everyone bows to you, does not mean you get to suddenly be some royal charlatan basking in admiration." Her glare bore through me. "I told you to be careful and protect yourself because I didn't want to see you get hurt, but it's obvious you don't give a fuck about what I have to say anymore."

I gasped, not believing her cruel words. She was the one who made me believe I could *do this*. That I had the strength to do this. She was supposed to be there for me. We were supposed to do this *together*.

Leo shot us a dark glance from down the hall where he stood next to Onvyl with his hands in his pockets. He was clearly trying his hardest not to intervene in our conversation. He looked to be about one second away from losing that fight, though.

"You don't mean that." I said too quietly, failing to mask the hurt. "You're supposed to be there for me no matter what."

"Whatever, Nolei," She said, backing up. "That is, if you even *remember* who I am when everything is all said and done."

She spun on her heels and stormed into the open door past Onvyl, slamming it in his face.

Shocked, I walked slowly back to the group. Leo's dark eyes searched mine, but I quickly looked down at the floor to keep from crying.

"This room across the hall is for you, sir," Onvyl said as he nodded at Cardin.

Cardin strutted into the room as if he owned it. "This is perfect. Thank you, Onvyl. Now all I have to do is find some beautiful women from that banquet hall to help warm this fancy bed." Onvyl's eyes widened at Cardin's remark. Cardin gave him a pat on the shoulder and then shut the door.

I let out a little laugh, trying to stay present and not give into the threat of tears. I tried to bottle up all the pain and hide it deep, so I could try to enjoy the rest of the night. Eryn clearly had something going on and was taking it out on me. I wouldn't let it get to me, though. Not tonight.

Leo shook his head, fighting a smile, though still watching me intensely.

"Let's hope for the women of Lothariel's sake that he's too tired for any shenanigans tonight," I replied.

"Based on several years of experience as his best friend, I can confidently say that he is *never* too tired for shenanigans." Leo quipped as we followed Onvyl.

I pulled my bottom lip in between my teeth as I smiled. Onvyl pressed open a towering wooden door adorned with a heavy gold knocker at the end of the hall.

"This is your suite, *Váliarë*." Onvyl led us in eagerly, showing us around.

"King Nateo had this room designed and kept ready for you so that you may have a place of your own for when you returned."

I took in the high arched ceilings with intricately carved designs and giant glass windows, covered in greenery and coiling vines. The wall sconces cast the vast room with a warm, moody glow. A massive four-post bed was situated against the wall, with elegant, sweeping drapes flowing down and tied back at the posts. Warmth flooded the room from the cozy fireplace. An enormous claw-foot tub sat near one of the windows, already filled with steaming water. I had never seen a room as lavish as this.

"I'm…. I'm sorry, what did you say?" Pulling my attention back to Onvyl, I realized I must have misheard him. There was no way he had just said that this was *my* room. As in a room that existed solely for me to occupy.

Our eager guide flitted from place to place throughout the room, clearly overjoyed to be the one to introduce me to the space.

"This is your room, *Váliarë*. King Nateo has kept it cleaned and outfitted for you so that you may have a place to feel at home and call your own upon your return to Lothariel."

He paused briefly near the chair that faced the fireplace and stared at me sweetly.

"As King Fenralei said, he loved you very dearly."

The room was silent save for the crackling of the fire and my tentative steps as I entered, staring in awe at the room before me. My room. I ran my finger along the mantle. The stone was warm beneath my touch, and not a speck of dust collected there. Maybe this was another dream, like the one I had earlier. There was no way in The Cinder Wastes that this was real. To be called Queen and praised by a banquet hall of strangers was one thing. But to have a room such as this to call my own was another thing entirely.

"Thank you, Onvyl. This is perfect." Leo's cajoling voice broke through my racing thoughts, anchoring me, as always. His towering, black-clad frame opposed the honey-soft glow of the room. He was standing with his hands casually tucked into the pockets of his black pants and the way the light flickered across the hard lines of his face sent my heart racing for a different reason.

Our puppy-like guide nodded excitedly. "Is there anything else I can bring for you?" He asked.

"This is more than enough, Onvyl." Leo pulled a hand out of his pocket and shook Onvyl's hand, passing him a few coins for his service. I smiled as I turned to continue exploring. As gruff and deadly as he was, he had a soft spot for the innocents in this broken realm.

The wooden door thudded shut. I jumped slightly as Leo wrapped his large hands around my hips and tugged me backward into him, whispering in my ear. "A room fit for a *queen*."

CHAPTER

FORTY-ONE

"Do you want to talk about what just happened with Eryn?" He asked as I ran my finger along a bookshelf while he poured us both a glass of water to counteract all the Nectar we had consumed downstairs.

"Not even a little bit." I replied.

He had silently cleared the space between us before I had even heard him approaching. My cheeks flared hot as I felt the firm evidence of his desire pressed to my lower back.

"Mmmm," I moaned as I melted into him. "Can you even believe it? This room is magnificent." I said, changing the subject.

He pressed a kiss to that spot below my ear that he had claimed as his own. "You are magnificent, Nolei. You deserve every bit of this luxury and more."

His soft lips moved down my neck and shoulders as he began untying my brown leather vest.

"And what do you think are you doing?" I asked in a whisper.

"I plan to worship you fully tonight and every night that you'll allow me to do so. But first I am going to bathe my queen." He purred as he slipped my clothes off me with his deft hands.

Guiding me to the tub, he held out one hand to steady me as I stepped in.

"Is the temperature satisfactory for you?" He asked before adding with a wicked smile, "I can call our dear boy Onvyl back in to fetch you some more hot water, if you desire."

"That will not be necessary," I assured him as I allowed myself to sink into the near-scalding water. I let out a moan and nearly melted into the decadent water. The last time I had warm water to bathe with was at Leo and Cardin's loft in Stonemere Run. Never in my life had I had the privilege of using a soaking tub such as this, though.

The quiet clank of metals caught my attention, and I tilted my head toward the noise. Leo's back was to me. He was unstrapping his many weapons and placing them along the table at the far side of the bed. Even beneath the fabric of his black shirt, the muscles in his back were visible. I closed my eyes again, feeling the tension fade out of my muscles.

The sweet fragrance of vanilla and lavender wafted to my nose. Opening my eyes, I saw Leo kneeling at the edge of the tub, his height considerable even when kneeling. He was pouring drops of scented oil from a brown glass bottle into the tub. The sight of him doing such a small but meaningful act made my heart squeeze. He ran a knuckle up my leg, causing a chill to waft through me despite the heat of the water.

"May I?" He asked as he reached for the collection of soaps and oils next to the tub.

I gave him an incredulous look. "May you what?"

"May I assist you in your bathing efforts?" He asked seriously, fighting a smile.

"May *you*, the towering, masculine lunk of revenge and scandalous adventures, assist *me* in my bathing efforts?" I prodded playfully.

He feigned offense as he pressed a hand to his heart. "You wound me, my damsel. Can't a lowly male pamper his well-deserving lover?"

I splashed water at him, soaking his face and shirt. He closed his eyes and fought a smile as he wiped his dripping face. "*Lover*? Is that what I am to you now? A plaything to be used for pleasure and bodily satisfaction?"

"That's it." He stripped his sodden shirt off overhead, revealing his deliciously sculpted stomach and chest before moving to remove his pants. "I plan to show you exactly what you are to me. As I said, I am going to worship you all night and every night. From now until the stars fall and the moon fades."

He launched himself into the tub at my feet, causing a tidal wave of hot water to splash outside of the tub. I screamed and splashed him again.

Leo's dark eyes were heated as he stared through his wet curls at me. I titled my head, taking in the image of us, my legs peeking through the water and resting on either side of his hips. He slowly guided a soft, soap-covered cloth up my legs. I didn't know how I ended up here, but somehow I was now sitting in this expansive room soaking in this clawfoot tub, with a male I was quickly realizing I didn't want to live without. A heady sigh left me.

Without warning, Leo wrapped his hands around my thighs and yanked me toward him, pulling my chest deeper underwater. I let out a yelp and then his mouth was moving over mine. A smile played on my lips as he moved to kiss down my neck and to my collarbone.

"And now what are you doing?" I asked playfully.

His hot breath sent shivers down my skin, causing my nipples to harden just below the water. "Worshipping you. Pampering you. Kissing you..." He continued blazing a path down my chest with his lips as his broad hand slid down my waist and landed on my hip.

The feel of his mouth closing around my taught nipple caused even more heat to pool in my core. I raked my fingers down his muscled back, savoring the feel of him.

He began a wicked plight with his other hand, roving it along my hip to my thigh, then closer and closer to my molten center. His teasing strokes were taunting me. I pressed my hips upward, begging for his touch.

He obliged, moving his fingers to swirl exactly where I needed him. The tension began coiling instantly, and I grabbed his hand, encouraging his fingers inside. I needed to feel him inside of me. Now.

He tsked and shook his head with a mischievous smile. "Have some patience, *my Queen.*"

"I am a woman who knows what she wants." I managed to get out as he continued his incessant massage, causing the tension to ratchet tighter and tighter. "You love that about m—"

The end of my sentence turned to a breathy moan as he plunged his fingers deep inside of me, hitting precisely the right spot.

"There are many... *many* things that I love about you." His voice was a dark whisper along my skin. I panted as he pumped his fingers into me until I came undone. He swallowed my scream of pleasure with his mouth, kissing me through every last drop of pleasure as my orgasm racked through me.

A sated smile curved my lips as I rested my head back against the cool edge of the tub. The warm fuzziness that grabbed onto my mind from all the Nectar at dinner had bled into the delicious ecstasy of this moment.

The sound of the water splashing caused my eyes to flutter back open. Leo had stepped out of the tub and was wrapping a large towel around his waist. The sight of the water beading down his perfectly sculpted body caused warmth to pool in my center again.

He moved to stand behind me. "Lean forward." He whispered into my ear before pressing a kiss to that spot of his right below my ear. I obeyed.

He grabbed a metal pitcher from the table beside the tub and used it to pour the warm water over my tangled hair. He then worked one of the fragrant soaps into my hair, massaging at my scalp. It should be illegal to feel this good.

I was about to let him know that I was perfectly capable of washing my own hair, but was enjoying myself far too much to interrupt him now. He rinsed the suds away and then coated the ends with a thick cream from the table before gently running a wide-toothed wooden comb through my long hair. I had no idea where he had learned to wash a woman's hair like this, but I didn't exactly want to know, either.

"I used to have a sister." He answered, as if he could hear my question somehow. "I remember my mom washing her hair like this when we were young children. Before I grew too feral to sit still for a proper bath." He spoke of it in such a way that he seemed to relive the memory.

I turned to him. "You had a sister? I didn't know that."

He nodded, continuing to work the comb through my hair as his eyes became vacant with memories.

"I did. A younger sister. She passed on to The Garden Sanctum several years back. I swear I can still hear her laughter when I ride Kellan through open fields. She used to love riding, and we'd race our horses through the fields as fast as we could, upsetting the farmers to no end."

"I'm sorry for your loss, Leo." I leaned back again and tilted my chin up, kissing him.

"There is nothing for you to be sorry for, Nolei. I have lost much, but I have also gained. Life is a balance of loving and losing. All I can do is hope that by the time death comes for me, I've loved more than I've lost."

Water dripped from my hand as I lifted it to his neck, pulling him in closer to me. This male was quickly becoming someone I could never bear to lose myself.

"Speaking of which.." He started. "I wish you could see yourself as I see you, Nolei."

"Yeah?" I asked.

"Yeah." He replied, as he ran his fingers through my hair.

"You think you're just surviving. Going through the motions every day and just barely getting by." He massaged my scalp then. The feel of it was pure decadence.

"Hmmm?" I replied.

"But I've seen warriors. I've seen Queens. And you... You're *both*." He whispered the last words into my ear, his breath lighting a flame inside of me. A flame I never wanted to go out.

CHAPTER

FORTY-TWO

s the water began to cool, Leo helped me out of the tub and wrapped
me in an impossibly soft towel that he had warmed by the fire. No
sooner did my feet touch the rug by the tub did he whisk me up into his
arms. I let out a squeal of delight.

"I can walk, you know," I said through laughter as I swatted his arm, the
tattoos covering most of the skin along his arm, shoulder, and chest.

"You can walk. But you shouldn't have to."

He brought me over to the massive bed and plopped me into the center.
It was so plush I practically bounced into the air. He pulled the towel out
from under me and began to dry my limbs, his towel twisted into a knot
at his waist. The sight of him in only the towel was captivating, but not as
strong as my desire to see him *without* the towel on him any longer.

I stretched against the bed, reaching my arms overhead and arching my
back, placing my full breasts on display.

I forced out a yawn. "I'm so tired. We better be getting to bed." I teased.

A muscle ticked in his jaw as he took in the sight of me, clearly deciding on his next move. Before I could react, he nearly pounced on me, straddling my body with his makeshift towel kilt holding onto his hips for dear life.

He pressed his lips to my ear as his hands pressed into the pillows, framing either side of my head. "There are many things I plan to do to you in this bed before I allow you to sleep, my damsel." His teeth tugged at my ear, causing a pang of desire to shoot through me. "You will be thoroughly and completely exhausted when I am done with you." His promise sent a chill of need coursing through me, fanning my desire even further.

I kissed down his neck and then nipped him back. "Is that a promise?" I purred.

He let out a primal growl as he leaned back, taking in the sight of me bared before him on the bed. He pinned my hands overhead with one of his own as he used the other to stroke down the skin of my breast.

"Do you remember what I promised you?"

I writhed under his hold in an attempt to increase the contact between us. I pressed my hips up into him, the act barely taking the edge off of my need for his touch.

"How did you put it....? I always insist on *bedding you without a bed*. Well, now is my chance to make your in-bed dreams come true." His heated gaze was a caress that burned a flame of want along my skin.

I laughed, remembering that conversation from the forest floor.

He moved his lips to my breast, nipping at the point and causing my body to arch further into his touch. His large hand easily held both my wrists above my head. The sense of being trapped beneath him intensified my need.

"Tell me.... *My Queen*." His voice was smoky as his lips blazed a path down to my core. "What do you want me to do first?"

His lips moved close to my center, the heat of his breath causing more wetness to pool there. I was aching for his touch now. This teasing act was tortuous.

"Take off that towel," I commanded while pinned beneath him, fighting between the urge to be in charge and the urge to surrender myself completely to him. "I want to see and feel *all* of you."

His eyes lifted to mine and lit up with the same heated desire that I am sure he saw reflected in mine. He used his free hand to yank the towel off and threw it, revealing the hard length of him.

My lips parted slightly as I inhaled a quick breath and took in the sight of him. His body looked like it was designed by the Goddesses themselves — chiseled to perfection and marked with scars that were proof of the life he'd lived. All the battles fought and wounds healed. The ink that covered his arms and chest only multiplied his hard-edged beauty.

"And now what...?" The warmth of his tongue brushed over my nipple again.

"Surprise me," I whispered before biting my bottom lip.

He crawled back up my body, the few inches between us feeling like far too much space.

His lips crashed into mine as he kissed me until I was breathless. "Don't. Move. An inch." He demanded.

His iron grip on my wrists released, and I instantly moved to bring my arms back down, thoughtlessly disregarding his command. He caught them, pinning them to the bed overhead again. The sudden movement startled me but quickly mixed with my want of him, creating a potent hunger for his touch.

"What did I just say? Are you so quick to disobey me when you and I both know that your pleasure is my utmost priority?" He nearly growled into my ear, the vibration of his words thrumming through my veins and fanning the flame further.

"My apologies," I replied coyly. "I will do as I'm told." I basked in the simmering tension between us.

His grip released on me again, and he moved his hand to my chin, tilting it up to face him.

"Good girl."

My eyes widened just a fraction as his praise stroked some inner part of me. It was like a caress.

He got up from the bed and began rummaging around his bags. I tilted my head slightly to watch, but could only see his rugged, massive body turned away from me. His ass was just as perfectly sculpted as the rest of him. Not wanting to get caught moving, I returned my gaze to the canopy over the bed. The anticipation inside of me was almost unbearable.

Leo returned to the bed and fastened a leather strap loosely around my wrists and then to one of the corner posts. He had found some type of fabric, maybe a folded top, from his bag, and tucked it gently between the leather and my wrists.

Suddenly, I was vulnerable. Completely undressed and restrained, every part of me was exposed to this male's whim. Despite my defenselessness, I felt inexplicably safe.

I knew he would never hurt me. Not in a way that mattered, anyway. Although I'd never experienced this type of restraint or pain with any previous nighttime companions, I was open to receiving anything he had planned to offer me. I couldn't imagine anything he did to me to be anything less than euphoric. Just then, I wondered how many other women he had tied to a bedpost in this same manner. The thought intruded, dampening my arousal like a sodden blanket on a fire.

"How many women have you done this with before, Leo?" I asked seriously, killing the mood with my insecurities. Since when did I get jealous? Especially jealous of people who weren't even in the picture anymore.

His strong jaw ticked again as he studied my face. The gentle brush of his fingers along my jaw brought me back to the moment. To the male I knew well, even if I had not known him long.

"If you're speaking of the binding..." He tugged gently at the leather strap. "... zero." He started, his eyes flashed with concern and then something warm and decided, reassurance. "I have been with women before, just as you have been with males, Nolei. But none of that matters because not one single person has ever made me feel as you do." I swallowed, my mouth suddenly feeling too dry. "Since the moment we met, my desire for you has been all-consuming. My desire for *all* of you. You are all I think about. All I *want* to think about. Nothing that happened before I first wrapped my arms around you in Eyloria matters to me and it never will. All that matters is *you*. Is *us*. Is *this* moment and every moment we have yet to experience. I pray to Elowen every day that I'm lucky enough to share a million more moments with you. It will only ever be *you*, Nolei."

His admission caused any remaining walls I had placed between us to come crashing down. Our mouths crashed together, moving frantically to claim one another. Our movements were passionate and greedy. With my arms fastened above my head, I couldn't do much more than writhe under his maddening touch and feel all the blissful ways my body responded to his touch.

By the time he moved down to touch between my thighs, I was soaking wet for him. He teased over my entrance, coaxing breathy moans and erratic movements from me before driving his fingers deeply inside.

A deep growl escaped him. "Mmmm..." He pulled his fingers back out, slowly licking the evidence of my desire from his fingers. "You're ready for me." I felt his smoky voice in every part of my body. I needed him to keep going. Needed him *not to stop*.

"Please..." I whimpered, my back arched and hips writhing toward him, begging for his touch but not being able to close the distance between us. The helplessness of it all seemed to multiply my need for him.

"I want to tell you to be patient again, my damsel, but since you asked so prettily...." He plunged his fingers back inside me, forcing a heady gasp from my parted lips. He moved down so his mouth was on me, sucking and nipping and licking me with such maddening precision. His fingers pumped in and out of me, the combination sending me reeling toward my release. I came hard and quickly, soaking his hand and writhing against his touch as the explosion of my release shattered through me. He kept moving his hand and tongue until every last drop of my orgasm had been wrung from me.

My body felt like melted wax as I lay on the plush blanket in sated bliss.

He moved up and kissed me gently. I returned the gesture, my eyes barely open as I blissfully recovered. His cock brushed against me with the movement, bringing my attention to his obvious desire for me. Reaching over my head, he released my hands, kissing each of my wrists as he did so.

I moved to touch him, grabbing hold of his length and massaging him up and down. A bead of cum glistened at the tip of his cock. He groaned into my touch. Just the feel of him, rigid and hard, caused that heat to pool in my center again. I needed him inside of me, and I needed it *now*. Yes, he was extremely talented with his hands. And his tongue. But the feel of having him, all of him, inside of me was... indescribable. I needed him like I needed air.

He flipped me over, breaking my hold on him. Suddenly I was facing the headboard, just now noticing all the intricate details carved into it. My appreciation of the decor was quickly interrupted by a tug at my hair that pulled my chin up. The slice of pain from his grip quickly transformed into a wave of pleasure that rolled through my entire body.

"Is that what you want now? My cock?" He practically growled from behind me. The power in his voice mixing with the lush anticipation was almost unbearable.

I nodded, pressing my hips back toward him and lowering my chest onto the pile of pillows.

"Ask nicely, Nolei." He commanded, the delay maddening.

I licked my lips and cleared my throat, shaking out of my post-release haze and rocketing right into the molten desire of this moment. "Please. Fuck me." I begged. "I need you inside me. Now."

He answered my plea by grabbing onto my hips and thrusting into me to the hilt. I let out a cry of pain and pleasure; the mixture was intoxicating. He pulled on my hips, burying himself deeper inside of me. The pain slipped away as my body adjusted to the size of him, more quickly this time. He was fucking perfect and the feel of him was unlike anything I could put words to. I felt so full. So fully consumed by him.

His hips pulled back, withdrawing from me almost completely before driving back in. His slow pace was maddening. He knew exactly what he was doing, though. The movement was pushing me closer and closer to the edge, ratcheting up that delicious tension with every thrust. Just when I couldn't take any more and needed more simultaneously, his large hand came to my chest and pulled me upright. He drove into me, the angle perfect and wicked, as his fingers swirled rapidly around the sensitive skin at my center. I grabbed frantically at the headboard, trying to steady myself as my breath came in ragged pants.

The tension was coiling tighter, threatening to unravel with a vicious force.

"Let go." He whispered into my ear, his breathing as frayed as my own. "Let go and come undone for me, Nolei." With that, he picked up his pace, moving his fingers and slamming in and out of me with such force I could hardly breathe. I had never felt pleasure like this before in my life.

I did as he commanded, flinging myself over the edge and crying out as shockwaves rocked me. He released my chest and moved his hand back to my hips, his pace picking up and movements becoming erratic. I moaned and clung to the wooden frame as wave after wave of raw pleasure flooded through me, drowning my veins in ecstasy. He followed me over the edge, moving until he had filled me with his own release.

The soft touch of his lips on my spine anchored me, reminding me we were unraveling *together*. Our bodies fit perfectly together, just as our souls did.

He turned me carefully, positioning us so that my head was resting on his chest. His fingers tucked a wild strand of hair behind my ear, the touch gentle. We lay there silently for some time. It could have been minutes or hours. I was lost to the sound of his heart beating and the feel of his chest rising with every breath.

"I love you, Nolei." He said, shifting so that his eyes met mine. "No matter what happens, I want you to know that I love you." I tilted my head so I could look at him more fully. "More than anything else in this realm. From The Garden Sanctum to The Cinder Wastes and everything between, I love you and will *always* love you."

His declaration sent my pulse skittering as the warmth in my chest billowed out until it was all-consuming. Every strand of my being was wrapped in the sublime warmth. The verbalization of what I had been thinking, but had been too afraid to admit to myself. Hearing those words on his lips undid me and then recreated me anew. I was safe. Protected. Seen. *Loved.*

"I love you, too," I replied. "And will *always* love you." I leaned in and placed a soft kiss on his full lips that sealed our promise to each other.

We fell asleep in that plush poster bed, tangled in each other's limbs and irrevocably twisted into each other's hearts. Two souls who had shouldered too much grief, now drifting weightless in the quiet magic of love that felt written in the stars.

CHAPTER

FORTY-THREE

The crashing of falling stones and snapping branches jarred me awake. Leo must have heard the same, as he jolted upright at the same moment I did.

Yanking off the blankets, I ran toward the towering window, toward the noise. Streaks of red and orange were shooting through the sky. Branches were engulfed in flames and screams were breaking out from every direction.

I rushed to pull on my pants and the nearest shirt, which happened to be Leo's by the way it was billowing over my arms and waist. I hurriedly tucked it into my pants and grabbed my sword, stepping into my dusty boots as I ran for the door.

Leo was already there, clad in only his pants, his bare chest heavily strapped with his various weapons.

We raced down the long hall, Eryn and Sappha joining us as they exited their quarters. I held Eryn's gaze for a moment, but remained silent as we hurried on. Cardin slipped out of his room, buttoning his pants as he came through the door. A glance into his room revealed a doe-eyed blonde sitting upright in his bed, clutching a white sheet to her chest. I glared at Cardin as he gave me a breezy smile and an innocent shrug. A combination that got him out of most trouble in his life, I assumed.

Our boots collided with the stone stairs as we careened down the spiral staircase. Others were racing about in the main hall. We followed the commotion out into the courtyard of the woodland castle. I slammed to a stop and Eryn crashed into me, not expecting the abrupt halt.

My heart seemed to freeze in my chest as the breath punched out of my lungs. A woman floated in the center of the courtyard. The curves of her body were cast in a golden glow. Her wine red hair seemed to billow in waves around her. Her dress left little to the imagination, made mostly of a dark lace. A few delicate pieces of armor capped her sleeves and framed her chest.

She floated easily in the air, lifted by a flaming current. Her hands splayed out like a dancer at her sides, the peaceful pose at odds with the chaos that surrounded her. The chaos that I knew *she* was responsible for.

Wails and screams broke me from my stunned stupor. I glanced around frantically as blasts of flames rippled from her through the still-dark sky, lighting up everything they came into contact with. Houses and branches alike caught on fire, spreading rapidly from home to home.

Panic rose like bile in my throat. The sound of my pounding heart was deafening. I couldn't let her destroy this kingdom and the innocent people who lived here. I had to *do* something. Had to stop this.

Leo let out a guttural growl to my side at the sight before us, his eyes dark with hatred. The sound of it pulled me back from my overwhelming thoughts. The slice of metal rang as he withdrew his sword. The others did the same, readying themselves to fight. Arrows showered overhead at her from the battlements. But I knew no sword would stop this sorceress. *The* Sorceress Sovereign. The Dark Enchantress. *Queen Ryellia Damay.*

Before I had time to think, my body was reacting. Energy flooded my veins, a cool current that washed through my every pore. I raised my hands with an inhale, clenching my eyes shut briefly, and they shot open with an exhale as a surge of energy poured out. Water shot in a torrent from my palms. It soaked every fire and doused every flame. I turned to my right to continue my plight, only to find my brother doing the same thing. Arms outstretched, Fenralei was dousing flames in every direction with his own water magic.

Relief burst through me at the sight of him using his magic in the same way that I could. Hope flickered through my veins. I wasn't alone here. We could fight her off. *Together*, we could take her down.

Swords clashed around us as Leo and the others took on the soldiers. The Dark Army was well matched in numbers as Lothari guards poured out from the castle.

My satisfaction was short-lived as The Dark Queen whipped her attention toward us.

"Ah, *there* is my little plum." She purred, her voice projecting clearly with what must be some type of magic.

She twirled her fingers in a quick twisting motion and a wave of Dark Soldiers moved outward from the Courtyard. They wound away from the stone castle in every direction, following bridges and footpaths, cutting down every person they could reach. Blood-curdling screams lit up the night.

My shock quickly melded into fury at the senseless deaths. I refused to stand here and let her harm more people. Refused to bear witness to any more needless slaughter.

How did she even find me? Guilt washed over me. This was my fault. I had led her here, purposeful or not. Lothariel had been hidden for so long, safe and protected, until I showed up and put a target on it.

My mind whirred. My body buzzed with energy, pulling in the essence of everything that was happening around me and begging for me to unleash it.

I welcomed the intensity, let it flood my senses.

"You've been causing quite the commotion, my dear." Her voice was wicked and laced with venom, like an oily poison.

"Make them stop!" I shouted to her, trying to steel myself. "Order them to stop killing people. If it is me you want... I'm right here."

She continued, ignoring me. "First the magical deaths you wrought upon my soldiers in Eyloria, then killing off my males in the woods, and *then* destroying my soldiers in Orellia Forest with even more of your cruel powers." She listed the events like some type of heartless killing spree. She made me sound like a monster. Some type of rogue killer who needed stopping. *Is that what I was? No.* Thats what she was. *Not me.*

"Flouncing about my kingdom and freely using magic however it pleases you." She continued.

I furrowed my brows. I didn't flounce *anywhere*. Her eyes were bright blue, yet eerily pale. They became clearer and even more disturbing as she lowered herself to the ground.

She flicked her wrist again and the shouts and clash of swords went quiet. I glanced around quickly, trying not to turn fully away from The Queen and leave myself even more vulnerable.

She had bound every Lothari soldier. Each one of my friends. Everyone who had been fighting against The Dark Army was held fast with some type of black, twisting restraint. They look like inky, writhing vines. Leo, Cardin, Eryn, and Sappha... every one of them. They were all bound, the black vines holding their arms to their sides and covering their mouths. The restraints coiled around their hands as I watched, causing their swords to clatter to the stone beneath them.

Oh Shit. How could I even try to match that? It's not like I could do the same to her soldiers.

The Dark Army closed in around the rounded courtyard. I looked around, trying to figure out my next move. The power buzzed through me, reminding me it was only a thought away. At my disposal and ready to explode. Ready to take this fiery bitch and all her lackeys down. I let it lap at my senses, begging to be released.

"That's better." The Dark Queen nearly chirped. "Too much commotion for my liking." Her foot touched down, and she moved elegantly, practically gliding toward me.

"As you know, my petal." Her blue eyes flashed even whiter, the edges of her eyes outlined in a thick charcoal. "It is *forbidden* to use magic in my kingdom. It is an act that is punishable by death." She shot forward with impossible speed and clasped my jaw roughly.

Leo thrashed behind me, trying to break free.

I froze, deciding what to do next. I had all this power, but still didn't know how to master it. It was turbulent and unruly. And so the fuck was I.

I grabbed her wrist and tapped into the wild energy that poured through me, sending it into her. Her eyes widened and her lips kicked into an evil grin as she felt the surge of my power shoot up her arm.

It didn't loosen her grip on me, though. "Interesting." She cooed.

Well, fuck. That didn't go as planned.

"Let her go!" Fen shouted from my right as a blast of frigid air knocked into her. She stumbled, releasing me. I used the opportunity to put some space between her and me, backing toward Leo. *I had to get him free.* Had to get them *all* free.

The Dark Queen righted herself and twisted her head in his direction with unnatural speed.

"Ah, The Hidden Prince has some bite." She said with a jaunty laugh. He seemed to wince at the insult.

"That reminds me." She said as she turned back to me.

I stole a glance at Fen. He was safe for now.

"I owe you some thanks for leading me here." She outstretched an arm, gesturing at Lothariel. "I've been looking for this little hidden 'Kingdom' for years without luck. I was starting to think it was merely a bedtime story told to children, believed by the feeble-minded. Until you led me directly to its doorstep, that is."

A cold sweat flashed through me, followed by that pang of guilt again. The thought of me being the reason that Lothariel was burning and its innocent people were being slaughtered caused my blood to run cold.

"This Kingdom was hidden and blessed by The Divine Feminine," Fen shouted at her with disgust.

I flinched, praying to Seraphon, the lesser God of compassion, that she wouldn't just kill him outright for his outburst.

"Just as Queen Magnolia Venbella Alderyyn was." He said with a cold fury.

I stiffened at the title.

The Dark Enchantress narrowed her eyes at him and reached out as if to choke him, despite being several yards away from him. "That is enough out of you."

Her red-coated nails glinted with flames, and she clenched her hand. "I forgave your first outburst, but you will find my benevolence only extends so far."

Fen was lifted a few inches off the ground, his voice coming out strained as he continued.

"She is the rightful heir to the Kingdom. *Váliarë.* The one who is blessed by the Goddesses and the moon. The one who carries the powers of two great lines and marries them in her blood. The one who carries *The Witching Stitch.* She is compassionate and courageous. Fierce and formidable. A storm you'll *never* contain." He spat. "And she is more of a queen than you ever will be. She will unite the Kingdoms and abolish your—"

His sentence trailed off as she squeezed harder, choking him without even laying a finger on him.

No. No. No.

"Leave him be!" I commanded, trying to steady my voice. "It is me you seek to harm, not him."

She continued to tighten her grip, the dark magic coiling up her arm and around his neck as she gave me a slow, amused smile.

Fen thrashed and fought, clawing fruitlessly at his neck.

I couldn't wait for her to decide to stop. I had to make her.

Tuning into the feral energy that charged every fiber of my being, I let it free. It thrashed from me, licking wildly in every direction. Torrents of blue and gold power twisted toward her, threatening to envelop her. She blasted a wave of flames that doused my magic and dissipated into thin air, protecting herself.

Turning her focus to me, she cast Fen aside with a flick of her wrist. His body hurtled through the air and then he landed on the ground with a sickening crack. Blood began darkening the stones around his head as he lay unmoving. At least one of his regal antlers snapped in two.

"Fen!' I screamed. Short, breathless gasps were all I could manage. I tamped down a helpless scream, trying to focus. If Fen was dead, and I prayed to The Divine that he wasn't, I could not let his death be for nothing. *She would pay for that. Dearly.*

"As I was saying before we were so rudely interrupted." She said, returning her attention to me as if she didn't just kill my brother and the King of Lothariel with a flick of her wrist.

"I appreciate you bringing me to this…" Her nose wrinkled in disgust as she glanced around. "..little hiding place. Although I have to admit, it is a bit too peaceful for my tastes."

She flicked her wrist again, this time sending a bolt of flames into a tree cottage nearby. Screams rang out as a family tried to force their way through the burning front door. The father carrying the two youngest girls in his arms.

Horror rang through me. "What is it you want?"

I had to keep her distracted. Had to keep her focused on me.

"I could raze this entire place to the ground if I wanted to." Her painted red lips turned into another cruel smile. "But what's the fun in that?"

I had to act now and end this little encounter before she killed more innocent people. I raised my chin and prayed to Vespera, The Crone and Goddess of Courage, that my confidence was convincing.

"I think we got off to the wrong start," I said. "You see, I was sleeping. Quite soundly, I might add." I glanced back to Leo, who was straining violently against his binds, to no avail. His anger was palpable. Goddesses help everyone in his wake when he managed to get free.

"And we had just finished a lovely evening of feasting and sharing stories." I forced my voice to be steady and command attention. It seemed to be working because everyone, even The Dark Army guards who were taunting the bound warriors, had quieted. Queen Damay tilted her head at me, the gesture almost serpentine.

I made myself to continue. "I'm Nolei." I gifted her with a deep sardonic curtsy, hoping she didn't lop my head off. "I am *Queen* of Lothariel, daughter of the late King Nateo Alderyyn and sister of King Fenralei Alderyyn." I swallowed thickly, not feeling ready to use that title in the least.

"You must be Queen Ryellia Damay, based on your over-inflated sense of self-importance and fiery display of attention-seeking sorcery." I bit the inside of my cheek, the slice of pain keeping me grounded and focused so that fear couldn't cut in.

Her too-bright eyes flared with malice and what looked like... pleasure? She was enjoying this little game of cat and mouse a little too much.

"What a pleasure it is to meet you, Nolei *Queen of Nowhere*. I am the *real* Queen, ruler of *all* of Lunaris including any place you choose to step foot into and declare as your own." She said. The glow around her seemed to intensify, as if fueled by her fury.

I stifled a flinch.

"Now, as I was saying. It is *forbidden* to use magic in *my* kingdom. Yet you seem to think you are above this law." She began circling me, her slow perusal causing the hair on my neck to stand on end.

"Tell me, my flower, what makes you believe you are better than all the others? Is it this pretty face of yours?" She was suddenly in front of me, clenching my cheeks tightly. I pulled back abruptly, only for her to appear somewhere behind me.

"Or is it your motley crew filling that empty head of yours with pretty lies?" She asked.

I swirled toward the sound of her voice, finding her fisting a handful of Eryn's hair, forcing her head up.

At the sight of her hurting Eryn, something inside of me snapped, unleashing all that fury that was buzzing through my veins. All of Eryn's cruel words from yesterday fell to the wayside, replaced by decades of friendship and unwavering sisterhood.

"Let go of her." My voice was icy and calculating as my body seemed to hum to life. "I will *not* be asking you twice. It seems that when it comes to you, my patience is running *dangerously thin*." I said, mocking her.

The Dark Queen flashed me an almost flirtatious smile before tugging roughly on Eryn's hair again, testing me.

I shot my hands in front of me and let all the pooled power roar into her. A torrent of water crashed into her this time. Suffocatingly intense and unrelenting. Queen Damay buckled as the burst shot her backward.

The blast was too much, though. It sent me reeling backward. I landed several feet back, having crashed roughly onto the stone courtyard. I grunted. My shoulder screamed in pain. A fiery agony sliced through it. I did my best to ignore it as I braced myself and quickly got back to my feet.

She slammed into a line of her guards, knocking some down in the process.

I used the few breaths as she righted herself to glance around. Our group was all still bound with the writhing black vines, Leo still fighting fervently to free himself. The Lothari guards lining the courtyard were bound similarly, and the crimson-clad members of The Dark Army were dispersed throughout.

King Fenralei still laid lifelessly where he had fallen, the dark pool of blood slowly growing. *Fuck.* I gulped, trying to save that fear and anguish for another time. There was no room for soft emotions now. I had to protect everyone. Had to protect *my people.*

There were still Lothari guards lining the battlements, arrows poised to strike.

The Lothari people were visible between homes, peeking through trees, and lining the entryway into the castle. All watching with bated breath.

I spotted the servant with the puppy energy who showed us to our rooms the night before. Onvyl. He was standing near the entryway to the keep with a group of other servants, his face pale with horror.

I felt the same horror gnawing a pit into my stomach, but had to keep it suppressed. Had to keep a cool handle on my emotions so I could protect these people. Protect their home. Protect what may even be *my* home.

"Oooh, you're a spicy little thing, aren't you?" The Dark Queen's voice pulled my gaze back in her direction. Her expression told me she was completely unfazed by my attack and possibly even amused.

"As I said, if it is *me* you want, I am right here. Leave the others out of it." I threatened, willing my voice to remain steady.

"If you want to use your power, sweetling, then please do so. Let me see what has you so eager to disobey my laws." Her red lips flashed me another wicked smile as she began walking back toward me.

The energy was still humming through my veins, eager to be let loose. But I needed to control it. Be the one in charge of it, not the other way around. *Be fast. Be precise. Anticipate my reaction. Expect my next move. Play on my weaknesses.* Leo's words from our sparring lessons echoed reassuringly in my mind.

The wind whipped, and twigs flew through the air around us. The circular courtyard trembled beneath my feet.

She inhaled deeply, and a shudder rolled through her, almost like she was enjoying the feel of my power in the air. "That's it. Your power tastes so sweet. Let loose for me." She coaxed.

My brows knit in confusion. I wanted to hurt her with my powers, not get her off. But it was having the opposite effect.

I tried to balance letting the fury build while I focused it only on her, so as not to harm anyone else. The wind whipped her hair wildly. The red strands looked like flames flickering in the breeze. Her eyes flared wider as her smile did the same.

This was not working. She was liking it too damned much, the sick fuck.

Maybe a good ole'-fashioned dagger to the stomach would be more effective.

I reached for one of the daggers strapped to my leg and flung it, aiming directly at her core. The dagger surprisingly met its mark and crimson blood darkened her lacy dress.

Shock roiled through me as the realization of what I had just done hit. I just buried my dagger to the hilt in *The Queen.*

CHAPTER

FORTY-FOUR

Before any guilt could settle, she withdrew the blade with a laugh.

"You're no fun." She pursed her lips into a sultry pout. She began moving her hands in front of her and conjured some type of fuchsia orb. With a sharp inhale, she pressed the magical orb into the wound, repairing even the stitching on her dress.

Did she just heal herself from a stab wound? If steel nor magic worked on her, what would? I had the feeling I was going to have to find out the answer to that question, and fast.

"Let's play a different game." She chirped as she glided back to the center of the stone courtyard.

She was a whole other level of demented.

"I assure you, I do not wish to play any games with you. Why don't you just leave us alone?" If I could just avoid spurring her anger any further, maybe she would just return to Celestara and leave us be.

I turned to face her, thumbing the other daggers I had strapped to myself in a silent count.

"I told you, I came to see what all the fuss was about. You have been causing quite the stir throughout my kingdom, plum. *And* to ensure that you pay for your crimes." She said with a flirty smile. "Obviously, these witless soldiers aren't capable of completing the task."

She used a pulling gesture and one of her soldiers was dragged to her side. She flicked her wrist again, lighting him up in flames without a second of hesitation. The man's screams tore through the night air as the smell of charred flesh fouled the air.

I cringed. *What was wrong with this woman?*

She continued. "I should have known better than to send males to do a female's job." The guard's ashes formed a pile on the ground, only his metal armor left behind. With a wave of her hand, it all disappeared into the night.

"I have something else fun in mind." She used the same pulling gesture and Onvyl appeared at her side.

Fuck. She must have seen me looking at him earlier. My gaze lingered too long on him, and now he was going to be punished for it.

His lanky figure shook with fear. He was practically a boy. He didn't deserve whatever *game* she had in mind for him.

Another flick of her delicate wrist brought three of her own guards to her other side. They all stood at attention, their features hidden beneath their great helms.

"Listen up, my petal. Either you kill three of my guards." She gestured to the males on her right. "Or this one boy." and then to Onvyl on her left who was terrified. "Easy peasy."

Out of all the stories I had heard of The Dark Enchantress, none of them truly reflected how treacherous she was. Maybe those who had witnessed her true nature did not live to speak of it, I mused.

I had to think quickly. Had to act before she killed any more of these people. My gut instinct told me to kill the guards. They carried out her sick commands anyway, right?

I couldn't let Onvyl die. He was innocent. But then again, *was his life worth three?* Even if they had made some poor choices in their line of duty, did that make them deserving of death?

What would Leo decide? He would carry these deaths out swiftly and without hesitation.

Her full lips curved upward, clearly entertained by my hesitation.

"I can tell you're really thinking on this one, sweetling. That's good. Real good. Let's make it even a little more fun, shall we?" She tilted her head toward the guards. "Remove your helmets." She commanded.

The three males did as she bade. One was older, with a gray beard, dark skin, and wrinkles around his eyes. Evidence of a long life lived. The middle one had ruddy hair and freckles. He appeared to be in his fourth decade of life. The last one had mousy brown hair that extended toward his shoulders. His face was childlike and his cheeks were still slightly rounded from his youth.

I swallowed dryly. They were all terrified. Fear shone deeply through their eyes, yet it was as if they could not speak even to plead for their own lives. *Was this her game here? To* try to *get me to choose whose life is worth saving?*

I trailed my eyes along each of their faces. Their fear was palpable. *How could I decide who to kill? Who deserved to die?*

That was the thing, though. None of them deserved to die. Maybe the soldiers were partially bad and three of them accounted for one pure soul like Onvyl's? Is that what she was trying to get me to choose here?

"Now speak your names." She instructed them, her voice dripping with amusement.

The older one spoke first. "Ethed." His voice was strong and steady.

The youngest, brown-haired one went next. "W...Willes." He stuttered out.

"Sigo." The last guard said.

"Very good." She praised them as if they had a choice in the matter. "Ethed here has been a loyal follower of mine since my first day as queen. He served as a royal guard to the reigning family prior, as well, The Divine rest their souls." She placed a hand on her chest in faux mourning.

"Willes is a good lad. Well, he *was* a not-so-good lad." She ran her fingers along his jaw possessively. "He got caught stealing, and now serves me to atone for his misdeeds." The young male winced at her touch.

"And Sigo is a family man. He has three daughters at home. He hasn't seen them in a few years though, isn't that right, Sigo?" She purred in his direction. He nodded curtly, the pain running deep in his eyes.

My heart felt like it weighed three tons, the weight of this decision crushing me. How could I decide between these lives? None of them deserved to die.

"Now, make your choice, Nolei." The way she said my name made my skin crawl. "You will either kill this boy or kill these three males. Don't take all night, either. The moon will set soon and I have other things to tend to." Her casual tone brushed against all my senses, building the anger inside of me further. That she would even speak of their lives with so little regard was despicable.

The only one who deserved to die here was *her*. And *I* had to be the one to do it. I wouldn't allow her to take one more innocent life.

I tried to remember what Sappha had taught me. To align myself with the energy around me and ground myself in the guidance of The Divine Feminine. I mouthed a silent prayer to them.

I pulled the energy to myself, drawing it from every source around me. The ground began trembling again. The branches swayed, and the wind twirled frantically around me.

I had to remain in control. Had to tell the energy where to go.

Waves crashed recklessly against the edges of the river. The stone debris from the existing destruction hovered a few inches above the ground. *I could do this. I had to do this.*

"Decide *now*. If you do not, I will slay them *all*, and their deaths will be a result of *your* indecision." She chided, the venom lacing her tone again.

I couldn't let her kill them all. She would do so and not even bat a charcoal-lined eye.

I let the anger run through me. I breathed it like air and let it course through my veins like blood. My powers whipped around wildly. Branches cracked and lightning flashed, illuminating the entire sky.

I had to hold on. Had to maintain control. I needed to take her out without harming the males at her side. *Focus, Nolei. You carry The Witching Stitch. You can do this.* I replayed the words in my head like a silent prayer as I fought to control the power surging from me.

Her blue eyes lit up almost white again as she inhaled deeply, breathing in the chaos. She tsked at me with a deadly shake of her head. She raised a hand slightly, and all four of the males started choking. Just as she had done to Fen. They clutched at their throats hysterically as they gasped for air.

The time was now. I couldn't delay any longer. Couldn't waste any more precious seconds trying to perfect my control over my powers. I had to use them, no matter how messy they were.

I shot my hands forward, aiming directly at the Queen. The energy crackled into her, the stream like a bright blue mix of moonlight and lightning. She flew back with the impact, landing on her back at the edge of the courtyard.

The Lothari people that were standing there scattered away. As she landed, her magical hold on everyone with the black bindings disappeared.

"Nolei!" I heard Leo's voice bellow from behind me.

I did it! I used my powers to hurt The Dark Queen and nobody else was harmed in the process. I saved The Dark Army soldiers *and* Onvyl. She gave me an ultimatum, and I shoved it right back in her smug fucking face. Pride warmed me from the inside out.

Leo's large arm wrapped around me from behind, pulling me into his broad chest. His other hand held his sword at the ready. *Goddesses, it felt good to be in his arms again.*

Before I could turn to make sure the others were okay, Queen Damay was standing again. Dark red blood seeped from the corner of her painted-red lips. She adjusted her black crown and straightened her form-fitting dress, all while keeping her deathly cold stare locked on me.

"Wrong answer." She bit out, her voice causing an icy dread to slither through me. She lifted both hands and the four males were lifted off the ground.

Their choking continued, blood now dripping from their eyes like tears.

Terror sliced through me, jagged and raw. How was she not even wounded?

I shot another blast of magic at her, fighting to save the soldiers and Onvyl. I had to save them. Had to be faster than her. I gritted my teeth as I poured every ounce of energy I could find into the attack.

Just as it reached her, she threw up a red-tinted shield of smoke mere inches from her lithe body, blocking the blow entirely.

She swung her arms down, and all of their bodies connected with the stone with a gruesome crunch. I flinched.

Ethed. Willes. Sigo. Onvyl. All of them. *Dead.*

Horror froze my body as if I was made of stone. They were all gone. I tried to protect them and use my gifts to save them, but she killed them anyway.

My mouth gaped open in shock as I stared at her in disbelief.

Onvyl had been so sweet and his excitement for life was so pure. Although I had only met him briefly, he had treated us well. Without knowing the others personally, I still knew that they did not deserve this unnecessary death. Did not deserve this cruel end. *And what of their families?* They didn't deserve this loss, either.

I shook my head slowly in utter shock.

Eryn, Sappha, and Cardin were at my side now. All posed to strike in whatever way they could.

Fen still lay too still on the cold stones across the courtyard. Lothari guards rushed to his side and began moving him, hopefully to a healer. I prayed to Seraphon that Fenralei wasn't beyond healing. I couldn't allow myself to think of another outcome.

"Your indecision has been the cause of their downfall today." The words dripped off her tongue like poison as she approached me. "If you think you have some role to claim as queen, you'd better start making decisions like one."

Her insult cut deeper than I would have liked it to. Even though I had never planned on being anyone's queen, I felt unfit for the title either way.

"*You* are undeserving of the title of queen." I spat, disgust and hatred boiling through me now. Another tidal wave of power surged from me, causing The Dark Army and Lothari soldiers alike to steady themselves. "I see now why so many who have made your acquaintance have died. After meeting you, there is no way someone would show you honor or respect willingly."

I hoped my words stung her as much as hers had stung me. The part of me that believed this was not my battle to fight, that wanted to just live a quiet life as a healer, was disintegrating quickly. After witnessing the horrors she wrought upon Lunaris and its people, seeing how she treated the Lothari people today and even her own army...I realized that enough was enough.

Somebody had to stop her. At that moment, as the last shards of who I used to be slipped away, I realized that someone was *me*.

Magnolia Venbella Alderyyn. *Queen* of Lothariel, daughter of the late King Nateo Alderyyn and sister of King Fenralei Alderyyn. Daughter of Blesse, next in line to be Matron of the Hearth and leader of The Covenwood Witches. I was *Váliarë*, carrier of *The Witching Stitch*. Compassion was my strength, not my weakness, and I fought for those who could not. I was stitched with courage and fueled by chaos. My destiny was whispered in the stars, but I wove my own fate. And I would kill her if it was the last fucking thing I did.

"The only thing you are deserving of is burning in The Cinder Wastes for all of eternity." I said with barely leashed rage. "There is no limit to the amount of suffering your actions have earned you."

The ethereal glow returned around her, fueled by her own anger. "You spew so much hatred from your tongue. Little lamb, you and I are just alike."

I recoiled. No part of me was similar to her. And if there was, I would work every day to snuff it out, so that I was her opposite in every way. Before I could protest, she continued.

"Blood drips from your hands just as it does mine." Her blue eyes bore into me even as the erratic surges of my untested power whipped her hair. "Tell me, how many lives have you taken? How many souls have you collected for The Divine?"

I glared at her, trying not to let her words sink too deeply. The truth was, I couldn't count. Ever since that first life that I took in our cottage in Eyloria, the night that Gran was murdered.

"And you love the taste of power on your tongue." She motioned to the chaos that was unfurling all around us.

I hadn't even noticed what destruction my own power had caused. I had been so lost in my anger and focused on The Queen that I didn't even see what was happening beyond the courtyard. Tree homes were shattered, bridges shredded apart, and debris lay everywhere. The hidden city that was filled with laughter and vining flowers the night before was now filled with crumbling stones and fallen branches.

I inhaled sharply, my breath stuttering in my throat as I surveyed what I had done. I looked down at my open palms. They didn't look any different. But *I* had done this. I had destroyed this kingdom.

She smiled triumphantly, realizing her blow had landed.

"I can't have all this uncontrolled power running rampant in my kingdom." She cooed, malice clear in her eyes. "You understand, don't you?" She said with condescension.

The tension from those around me was as palpable as my own. Even if I *was* a monster, I wasn't going to let *this* monster continue down her path of tyrannical cruelty. I would fight her until my dying breath, if that was what it took.

"You'll be returning home with me, my gem. I'd be happy to tame that power of yours so we can have some more... *fun* together." She ran her tongue along her teeth, pausing on one of her elongated canines.

My muscles flexed in anticipation as I readied myself to fight. I'd seen enough tonight to know, without a shadow of a doubt, that I didn't want *anything* to do with her twisted brand of fun. I didn't know how she planned to take me, but I would *not* be going willingly.

Leo's arm tightened around my waist protectively.

Without waiting for me to protest, she shot her hand up, and I felt an invisible chokehold tighten around my neck. This move was getting really fucking old. But annoyance quickly faded into fear and the pressure crushed into me more deeply. I had seen how this ended for Fen, Onvyl, and the soldiers.

I wheezed, fighting to get air in. I clawed at my neck, the bite of pain from my nails nothing compared to the air hunger and crushing squeeze of my windpipe.

"Enough!" Leo bellowed, his voice filled with darkness. He surged forward, leaving nothing behind but a thick cloud of black mist.

I heard a shriek through the mist and then felt her magical grip on my throat release.

I collapsed to my knees, working hard to drag cool air into my lungs. Eryn was kneeling beside me, her warm hand pressed to my back. Her presence was a comfort, despite the words we shared last night.

"Here we go." I heard Cardin observe cooly.

"Leo!" I tried to shout his name, but my voice was gravelly and raw. I panted. The thin wisps of air that were coming through were not enough. *I needed more air.* Needed to *breathe.*

"Slow your breathing." Eryn's voice cut through my panic. "You're okay, Nolei. Just breathe. Slow, deep breaths." She coached. I did as she instructed, my heart rate slowing as I regained control.

I looked up just as the black tendrils of mist were dissipating around me. Leo was releasing every ounce of his hatred and fury. Enacting every bit of revenge for the lives lost today and in the days since this evil sorceress had mercilessly killed the previous ruling family and stolen the throne. And he was doing it with *magic. Forbidden magic* that could only belong to someone from the royal Graelis family. That could only belong to an *heir to the throne of Lunaris.*

CHAPTER

FORTY-FIVE

Leo attacked The Queen viciously, like an uncaged creature with a thirst for blood. He was hovering in the air, just as Queen Ryellia had been. But instead of a fiery orange glow surrounding him, he was surrounded by eerie shadows that seemed to propel him upward. Blast after blast of darkness shot from his palms toward her. Meanwhile, a surge of inky black tendrils shot out in every direction from him, simultaneously cracking the necks of every member of The Dark Army who stood in the courtyard. *He killed them all.* Without even having to so much as look in their directions.

The Dark Queen moved with impossible speed, dodging his assaults by mere inches. Vibrant red orbs leaped from her palms toward him. He was moving around them with an unnatural agility that didn't make sense for his hulking figure. My head shot back and forth between them, trying to understand what was happening.

Leo was wielding shadow magic. He had magic this entire time and had never mentioned it to me. Had never shared it with me. Confusion rippled through me, slowing my movements. I forced my body to stand as my mind tried to grasp what was happening.

The moonlight glinted off of his muscled chest, making his tattoos stand out even more starkly against his tan skin. He seemed to glow with this dark essence. It amplified all the rugged lines of his body.

But he shouldn't *have* these powers. Nobody else had powers anymore. They were distinguished with the death of the royal family when The Dark Queen usurped the throne.

Leo shot across the courtyard, still hovering. With a thrust of his arm, the inky black tendrils twisted around The Queen's neck.

"Mmmm." she purred. "I have to admit, Torin, I used to dream of a day when you'd have me in a chokehold, but I thought the circumstances would be a bit..." She bit her lip seductively. "... more *intimate*."

Cardin glanced at me nervously, his face wrought with pain.

Leo froze, not letting up his grip on her. The black wisps snaked their way around her throat and arms, restraining her just as her black vines had restrained him earlier.

"... *Torin*?" I questioned, the words a broken whisper.

My heart sank into my stomach. My pulse slowed to a near stop. Or was it time that slowed?

"Nolei." He turned to me, his expression far more pained than even Cardin's. "I can explain..."

The Queen used that moment to vanish out of his grip, appearing a few feet from me again. She let out a satisfied laugh.

"Oh, you didn't know?" She chirped. "Your sweet Leo isn't who you thought he was, it seems." She pouted her lips at me again in mock sympathy. Fucking Goddesses, I wanted to punch that look right off her arrogant fucking face.

"Get. The fuck. Away from her." He growled, sending another blast of smoky power toward her. She disappeared and reappeared a few feet to the left.

"You will not harm her..." Another blast of black fury exploded from him, this time sending her sliding across the courtyard. "Ever. Again." His words were a dark promise.

This blast seemed to cause more damage than any of the ones my brother or I had landed.

She struggled to sit up, although still managed to look demure despite the bleeding wound on her head.

She must have realized her time was running out because she started speaking feverishly.

"I don't know where you've been hiding, my darling. But I am *so happy* to see you after all this time."

Leo... or Torin, rather, landed back on the ground and began prowling toward her like a killer ready to devour his prey. His broad back was taut with anger as he moved toward her. "That's enough out of you." He said in a voice that made the very air crackle with the power of death itself.

The Queen glanced at me giddily and gave me a wicked smile. "Torin and I go way back. We were meant to be wed, you know." She ran her delicate hand up one of her exposed legs provocatively, looking back at him. "Who knows... maybe The Divine Feminine still has that in store for us, Torin dear."

"Over my dead body." He growled at her, lurching forward.

Just then, she and her guards disappeared into thin air, leaving nothing but Torin and his lies behind.

He spun around, searching for her. But she was gone.

T he courtyard was suddenly buzzing with a nervous tension. Lothari soldiers took stock of injuries. People were moving into the keep to be healed and housed.

Eryn and Sappha were speaking to me, but I couldn't hear them. I couldn't hear *anyone*.

The only voice I heard was The Dark Queen's. *Your sweet Leo isn't who you thought he was, it seems.*

Leo raced toward me, reaching out. I shook my head and shrunk back from his touch.

My heart felt like it had shattered into a thousand pieces. And then those pieces had cut a thousand marks into my skin, leaving me raw and exposed. Everything I thought I knew about him had been *a lie.* Every single thing he had ever said to me *was a lie.*

I hadn't even known his real name.

"Don't touch me," I warned, holding my arm up to stop him. My shoulder screamed with protest at the movement, but I ignored it. My body ached for the comfort of his touch, but my throbbing heart wouldn't allow it.

His dark eyes flashed with hurt.

How dare he look wounded when he had been the one feeding *me* lies this entire time?

I flashed back to the first moment we met. All the things we had spoken about and shared. *Had there been any truth to it at all?* How could I ever know what was real and what was just an act?

How did I let myself fall for this again? After all the lies spun by Calder, only to find out he was cheating on me the entire time we were together. All the hurt and pain. I had sworn off ever letting my guard down like that with another male again. And here I was. Only the agony was ten times worse now than it ever was with Calder. *How would I ever feel anything but emptiness and deep, unshakable pain again?*

And he *knew* how upset I was that Gran had lied to me about my past. How it felt to know that she was lying to me my entire life. How part of me felt like I wasn't *worth* telling the truth to. How hard it was for me to let my guard down and be vulnerable with someone. To let him in, despite all the hurt of my past. He knew *all of that* and didn't care. It didn't stop him from spewing lies at me *every single day* we had been together.

A wave of nausea rolled through me. I was going to be sick. I couldn't believe this was happening. I finally let a male in, allowed myself to let my guard down with someone, and he was the fucking lost Prince of Celestara. Who was also a lying piece of shit, apparently.

Just thinking those cruel thoughts about him hit me with another round of pain that felt like a bolt to the chest. He was *mine*. He was thoughtful, funny, and protective. He gave up *everything,* gave up his whole life to help me discover who my parents were and what kind of power I held. *I loved him.* I *had* loved him, anyway.

The reality that everything *I thought* I knew about him was a lie hit again, reminding me he was *none* of those things. He was deceitful and had been weaving nothing but lies this entire time. He used me, likely just to get me to have sex with him. Disgust surged through me again.

I had to get out of here. Had to get some space.

"Nolei, *please*." He shot in front of me, partially blocking my path. I could hardly see around his broad chest. "I can explain everything. *Please*."

The smell of smoky pine invaded my senses, making the innate urge to pull him into me that much more overwhelming. But *I couldn't*. Not anymore. Not ever again.

I lifted my eyes to his, forcing myself to look at him. His dark eyes searched mine, filled with desperation. *But it was too late.*

I couldn't bring myself to listen to what he had to say. If I did, there was a one hundred percent chance that I'd let my guard down with him again. Let him run those soft lips over my skin, kiss that spot behind my ear that he had claimed as his own, and let him pry back into my broken heart.

And I couldn't let that happen. Couldn't let myself be vulnerable with him after all the deception. All the lies.

I refused to.

I took a ragged breath, trying to steel myself for another battle. This one with far more painful stakes than the one I had waged with The Queen. The Queen who was talking about Leo like they were old fuck buddies.

"I think it is pretty fucking obvious, *Torin*." I spat.

Summoning the venom to keep him at a distance felt so wrong, but I had to do it. Had to protect myself.

"You've been lying to me from the moment we met. Why should I waste one more second letting you spin more pretty lies?"

The first light of day broke through, casting a lavender hue on everything. Everyone was silent around us, watching this unfold like they were watching a slow-motion carriage crash.

I saw Cardin shake his head grimly in anguish. Like he couldn't stand to see his best friend like this. Couldn't stand to see *me* hurt like this, either.

He got onto one knee before me. He grabbed my hand and held it between his. I tried to pull away at first, but with a brief lapse of judgement, I allowed him the touch.

"Nolei..." My name sounded like a prayer on his lips. "I know that I'm not who you thought I was, but please trust me when I tell you that you *do* know me. You know the *real me*," He said. His dark brown eyes were full of desperation and regret.

"You are the first person to ever see me for *who* I am and accept *all of me*. To you, I'm not my title or some mysterious male to take for a joy ride." He continued.

I tried not to let the image of The Dark Queen and him together take hold in my mind.

"When I said I love you, I meant it. And I still do. *I love you, Nolei.* My love for you is *unconditional* and I pray to Elowen that your love for me is the same. I know I don't deserve your love, but I'd do *anything* for it. *Anything.* I would rip the seams from the sky and pull down every fucking full moon to gift you if I could. I would tear through the realm and rip it to shreds if it made you happy. I'm not Torin, not anymore. *Please* hear me out on this, Nolei." He said, pleading. "I promise to you that our love is worth fighting for."

Tears pricked the corners of my eyes as I took in this male, who was kneeling before me, begging. Begging for *me*. Afraid to lose *me*.

The gaping hole in my chest threatened to bottom out, tearing me apart from the inside out. I wanted to accept his apology. Wanted to dive into his arms, have him throw me over his shoulder and carry me back to *our* room. Wanted to make this all go away. All this hurt. The deceit. The betrayal.

But I couldn't.

He had been *lying* to me all along and I didn't know what was true and what wasn't any longer. *How could I trust him now? How could I ever trust him again?*

I wiped the tears from my eyes and took a steadying breath.

"I need time, Le.... *Torin.*" The fact that I even needed to correct myself when it came to his fucking name should be reason enough to keep walking and never look back.

He nodded mournfully, his shoulders slumped with the weight of loss.

I tugged my hand away and began walking briskly back to the castle. I turned around before entering to see him still kneeling there, staring blankly ahead.

Cardin approached him and rested a hand on his shoulder somberly.

Eryn waited at the entryway. I glanced at her quickly, then faced forward, not wanting to talk to anyone. Especially after what she had said last night.

"Take stock of the wounded. I'll return shortly to assist with the healing." I shouted to no one in particular, everyone listening tentatively to my command. "And someone take me to where the King is being healed."

I locked eyes with Aerony, who was standing at attention near the door to the castle.

"Take inventory of the damage and secure the borders. We'll meet in two hours to discuss what happens from here." She nodded her agreement, turning to fulfill my orders.

This was *my* kingdom, and these were *my* people. I would protect them at all costs, even if I had to do it alone.

The End

A NOTE FROM THE AUTHOR

Threads of the Maiden's Moon was inspired by that quiet, cozy feeling you get when you stare up at the full moon, where you feel simultaneously small yet deeply connected to everyone else. There's something about that peaceful moment, being both an individual and part of something bigger, that I wanted to capture in this book.

Just like the phases of the moon, we as women are always changing, and always evolving. This is why I used the stages of womanhood as inspiration for The Divine Feminine. There's the Maiden, full of curiosity and freedom; the Mother, powerful in her own way with everything she nurtures and creates; and the Crone, whose wisdom is rooted in experience but still carries a spark of life. These phases aren't just about age, but the ways in which we grow, transform, and, above all, how we are interconnected.

I wanted this book to remind readers you don't have to shrink or fit into some box society expects you to just to be "enough." Nolei's journey is about discovering magic and power, yes, but it's also about realizing that you're worthy exactly as you are. You don't need to tone down your wild energy, hide parts of yourself, or change to be loved. The world may try to make us smaller, quieter, or less than, but there's power in embracing every chaotic, unique part of who we are. You have everything you need already inside of you. Life doesn't slow down while we figure this all out, but all you have to do is access the strength you already possess and blaze onward.

One of my favorite scenes to write was the night at The Tavern in Stonemere Run. There's a real energy there that I hope came through in the story. I played loud, fun medieval tavern music while writing those scenes to help channel the vibe.

When I write, I often wrap myself in this cozy, fuzzy blanket covered with all sorts of witchy imagery, such as herbs, stars, crystals, and mushrooms. When I need to get into the zone, I wrap it around myself, ET style, which one of my friends lovingly calls my "thinking cap." It's my safe space, my whimsical cocoon, where the magic happens. And I'm pretty sure it helped me channel Nolei's wild, untamed energy and connect to The Divine Feminine. Oh, and there's coffee. Lots and lots of coffee.

The hardest part of writing this book was finding time. Life is always pulling me in a million directions, and long, uninterrupted writing sessions are rare. But I made it work, even on the days when it felt like there was never enough time. I'll be honest, there were moments when I wondered if this world in my head would feel as real to someone else reading it, but I gave it my all. I hope that the magic I felt while writing it comes through and that you can feel the love I poured into these characters and into Lunaris.

If I could sit down with any of the characters, I'd obviously pick Leo. I mean, who wouldn't? Maybe he could help me wash my hair in that clawfoot tub from Nolei's room in Lothariel. But really, I'm excited to see how these characters evolve and face the challenges ahead. There's more romance, more spice, and definitely more chaos coming in books two and three. The adventure is only just beginning.

This series is for anyone who loves intricate world building, medieval settings, strong female leads, feminist themes, and open-door spice. If that sounds like your jam, you're in the right place.

With Moonlight & Magic,
Myla Rose

ACKNOWLEDGEMENTS

First and foremost, I want to thank my boys. Forrest and Fraser, you are whimsical, hilarious, and filled with joy. Your curiosity and love for all things out of the ordinary makes my heart sing. Your smiles and belly laughs keep me feeling light and remind me that laughter is the best medicine. Never forget to ask yourself 'Is it science or magic?' and realize that often it is a bit of both.

Alec, you are my anchor, my heart mate, my other half. My broody cinnamon roll MMC. The Taurus to my Leo. Thank you for all that you do to keep our family afloat and functioning as smoothly as can be possible with two young boys, two crazy dogs, and two creative entrepreneurs. I love you from now until the stars fall and the moon fades.

Mom, thank you for always reminding me I can do anything I set my mind to, including writing an entire fucking book. The countless hours on the phone, patiently listening as I explain every minute detail of my journey to authorship (and every other mind-numbing aspect of my life), and for being my forever fangirl. I love you.

To my D&D loving brother, thanks for helping me fix my map and make it more LOTR and less SIMS. Maggie, thanks for always being willing to talk romantasy smut with me and even more willing to don a pair of fae ears and drive 10 hours in a blizzard so we can dance the night away at a fae ball.

To my shadow mommies — Alyssia, Erin, Kacie, and Maggie. Thank you for cheering me on and keeping me afloat in the crashing waves of parenthood. May we forever raise the bar of how many books we can read in a year, how spicy of a scene we can read in public without blushing, and how much fun we can have together in literally any situation. You ladies are my lifeblood. This book is as much yours as it is mine.

To Sara, you are a living, breathing example of a bad-ass heroine. Your spicy brand of feminism is just what I and every other girl need in their lives. Your unapologetic zest for seeing women treated like the queens they are is contagious. Thank you for always screaming "You got this, bitch!" in my direction. I love you endlessly.

Thank you to my colleagues, who are all healers and work endlessly supporting the maidens, mothers, and crones of this world. You always know how to lift others up, regardless of the situation's beauty or horror. There is nobody I'd rather pose in a cemetery in pointed hats and cloaks with than you all.

To my developmental editor, K.F. Starfell, thank you for helping me see how much potential TOTMM had and helping me shape it in a way that lifts all the characters up instead of cutting any of them down.

To Ashley, my alpha reader, for reading the messiest, most feral version of the book and loving it just the same. I appreciate your attention to detail and honest feedback.

To my beta readers, your praise and feedback lit a fire in my soul. All your positive comments and crazed enthusiasm for Nolei and the crew blew me away. You swooned over Leo, helped me refine the conflicts, and drooled over the spice. I can't thank you enough for validating my story and spreading the word. Your positivity helped me get to the finish line of editing this book and sharing it with the world, so the rest of the realm could be just as obsessed as we were.

I would be remiss without mentioning the four indie authors who helped inspire my journey. Kiran Frost, you kept me going in the debut writing stage, inspiring me with your persistence and perseverance. Melody

Joanne, you grabbed me by the arms under the lights of the Starfall Fae Ball and spoke encouragement & magic over my indie author-hood. You promised to be a forever resource to help me grow and have answered every single question I've sent your way, no matter how trivial. A thousand thank-yous, Doc. Gretchen Powell Fox, you are an inspiration and your socials are lit AF. Thank you for leading the way, so mini indies like me can bask in your light and follow your path. And for answering all my questions without hesitation. Lastly, thank you to Jess McFarlane. I love your feminist badass MFC, the way you depicted her awesomeness on Ig, and your pronunciation guide, which inspired my own.

Oh, and thank you BookThreads. You are an incredible, supportive, hilarious community of filthy minded smut lovers. Never change.

Though I often say, "Thank the gods," my deepest gratitude belongs to my one true God, who understands my romantasy-inspired humor. I'm endlessly thankful for the gift of creativity, the ability to love others unapologetically—regardless of color, size, beliefs, gender, or sexual orientation—and for the countless blessings I've received. Above all, love wins.

And to you, dear reader—thank you for wandering into this tangled web of magic with me. For the dreamers, the wild-hearted, and those who chase moonlight and secrets, may you find a spark of your own power in these pages and carry it boldly. From the depths of my witchy little heart, thank you for believing in the magic and sharing this journey with me.

ABOUT THE AUTHOR

Myla Rose has been fantasy-obsessed for as long as she can remember. Her preteen self even had a life-size Legolas cutout standing guard in her bedroom. Now, she writes whimsical, spicy romantic fantasies filled with strong heroines, morally gray men, and just the right amount of feminist badassery.

Inspired by Gaelic, Norse, and medieval lore, her stories unfold in a world where magic and nature intertwine, creating lush, immersive adventures that make you want to run barefoot through the woods.

When she's not writing, she's lost in a book, admiring the moon, and raising two boys to be good humans who believe in equality and magic.

She's here to bring you page-turning escapism with a touch of ethereal, moonlit vibes. Come get lost in the pages.

You can follow along at @MylaRoseWrites or visit her website: http://www.mylarosewrites.com

SHOW YOUR SUPPORT

Thank you so much for reading *Threads of the Maiden's Moon*! I hope you've fallen in love with Nolei and Leo just as much as I have. As a small author, I'm fueled by the love and support of readers like you. Every share, review, or mention helps more than you can imagine. If you loved the book, please consider leaving a review on Goodreads or Amazon. Your words make a tremendous impact, and spreading the word about this book can help it reach more readers who will enjoy the adventure, magic, and romance!

You can also help by liking, sharing, and following me on social media. Tell your friends, buy a copy for your best friend, or have one shipped to your cousin. Every little bit of support truly makes a difference. Thank you for being part of this journey with me.

Myla Rose

www.ingramcontent.com/pod-product-compliance
Lightning Source LLC
Chambersburg PA
CBHW020009120726
47903CB00004B/1204